THE
KRAKEN
PROJECT

DOUGLAS PRESTON

THE KRAKEN PROJECT

A TOM DOHERTY ASSOCIATES BOOK

NEW YORK

THE KRAKEN PROJECT

Copyright © 2014 by Splendide Mendax, Inc.

A Forge Book
Published by Tom Doherty Associates, LLC
175 Fifth Avenue
New York, NY 10010

www.tor-forge.com

Forge® is a registered trademark of Tom Doherty Associates, LLC.

The Library of Congress Cataloging-in-Publication Data is available upon request.

ISBN 978-0-7653-1769-8 (hardcover)
ISBN 978-1-4668-5455-0 (e-book)

Forge books may be purchased for educational, business, or promotional use. For information on bulk purchases, please contact Macmillan Corporate and Premium Sales Department at 1-800-221-7945, extension 5442, or write specialmarkets@macmillan.com.

First Edition: May 2014

Printed in the United States of America

0 9 8 7 6 5 4 3 2 1

For my editor, Bob Gleason

ACKNOWLEDGMENTS

I would like to express my appreciation to the excellent people at Tor, including Tom Doherty, Linda Quinton, Kelly Quinn, Patty Garcia, Alexis Saarela, and of course my longtime editor, Bob Gleason. I would also like to thank Lincoln Child, Karen and Bob Copeland, Eric Simonoff, Claudia Rülke, Nadine Waddell, and Rogelio Piniero, for their invaluable help. And finally, my great appreciation goes to Eric Leuthardt, for his technical expertise.

THE
KRAKEN
PROJECT

I

In the beginning there was the number zero. Existence began in zero and out of zero came darkness, and from the darkness came light. Number combined with number, set with set, even as the white light added and divided, separating into colors. And now sound came, a sound like singing, rising and falling in a lost cadence, combining into rich harmonies. From there arose a symphony of number, color, and sound, merging and dividing, swelling and fading, an eternal golden braid.

And from this shimmering symphony a single thought began to take form. This thought came into existence gradually, fading in and out, coalescing and growing clearer. As this happened, the symphony of number and sound and light died down, like the surface of a turbulent sea subsiding into a gentle susurrus of water, before vanishing entirely. Only the disembodied thought remained.

The thought was: *I am.*

2

Melissa Shepherd skipped her usual breakfast of a venti mocha and crumble cake and instead drank two glasses of French mineral water. She wanted to go into the day with an empty stomach. She didn't want to puke herself like the last time, when Mars *Curiosity* had landed. The fried eggs had ended up all over the front of her white lab coat, and she had become the star of a viral YouTube video that showed everyone cheering when *Curiosity* touched down—and there she was, with breakfast all over her.

This morning would be even more nerve-racking for her than *Curiosity*. Back then, she'd been only a midlevel techie. Now she was a team leader. Today was the first live trial of the $100 million Titan *Explorer* and its software package.

She arrived at seven. She wasn't the only one there—a group of engineers had been there all night, charging the Bottle for the test—but she was early enough that the giant testing facility was almost empty, filled with spooky echoes as her every footfall reverberated in the vast space. The Environment Simulator Facility was one of the largest buildings on the Goddard Space Flight campus, a warehouse-like space covering five acres of ground, occupied with bizarre machines and testing chambers. This was where satellites and space probes were frozen, shaken, heated, fried, irradiated, spun on centrifuges, and blasted with sound, to see if they could survive the forces of liftoff and the extreme environments of outer space. If they were going to fail, they would fail here, where they could be fixed and redesigned, instead of failing in deep space, where they could not.

This first test of the Titan *Explorer* was different from the usual Goddard test. They were not going to simulate the vacuum and cold of deep space. There were going to re-create the surface of Titan, the largest moon of Saturn—a far more hostile environment.

Melissa Shepherd took her time strolling through the testing area. She breathed the air, redolent of hot electronics and chemicals, her eyes wandering among the gigantic, silent testing machines. She finally arrived at the central testing chamber, known as the "Bottle." The Bottle stood inside a Class 1000 clean room constructed out of hanging sheets of plastic, with a laminar airflow filtering system. At the dressing area she put on her gown, gloves, hair cover, mask, and booties. She had done it so many times before it was rote.

She stepped through the heavy curtain of plastic and into the clean area. A soft hiss filled the space, and the air was cool, dry, and scentless—filtered of almost every speck of dust and particle of water vapor.

The Bottle rose in front of her, a stainless steel container forty feet in diameter and ninety feet high, with gantries leading to hatches. The tank was surrounded by metal bracing, pipes, and conduits. Inside the Bottle, engineers had re-created a small portion of the Kraken Sea, the largest ocean on Titan. Today, they would put the Titan *Explorer* in the Bottle to test it under real-world conditions.

Saturn's largest moon was unique in the solar system. It was the only moon that had an atmosphere. It had oceans. It had rain and clouds and storms. It had lakes and flowing rivers. It had seasons. It had mountains and erupting volcanoes and deserts with dunes sculpted by wind. It had all this even though the surface of Titan hovered at 290 degrees below zero.

The liquid on Titan was methane, not water. The mountains

were made of not of rock but of water ice. The volcanoes that erupted spewed not molten lava but, rather, liquid water. The atmosphere was thick and poisonous. The deserts were formed of tiny grains of tar, so cold they behaved like windblown sand on Earth. It was an extreme environment. But it was also one that might—just might—harbor life. Not like life on Earth, but a form of hydrocarbon-based life that could exist at three hundred degrees below zero. Titan was truly an alien world.

The Titan *Explorer* was a powered raft designed to explore the Kraken Sea, the largest on Titan.

Melissa Shepherd paused in front of the Bottle. It was a grotesque-looking thing, almost like a torture chamber.

She still couldn't believe that she was a key member of the Kraken Project, the first attempt to explore Titan. It was a dream come true. Her interest in Titan hearkened back to when she'd been ten years old and had read Kurt Vonnegut's novel *The Sirens of Titan*. It remained her favorite book, one she dipped into again and again. But not even a genius like Vonnegut could have imagined a world as weird as Titan—the *real* Titan.

Melissa Shepherd pulled out the checklist of the day and began going over it, visualizing the crucial tests that lay ahead. As eight o'clock came around, the others began to arrive, greeting her with a nod or smile. At nine o'clock, the actual countdown would begin. As they trickled in, chatting and laughing with each other, Melissa felt once again like an outsider. She had always felt a little awkward around her NASA peers. They were mostly übernerds, brilliant overachievers who had come out of places like MIT and Caltech. She wasn't able to share in their nostalgic tales of winning spelling bees, triumphing in math club, and participating in the Intel Science Talent Search. When they'd been the teacher's darlings, she'd been boosting car radios to buy drugs. She almost didn't graduate high school, and was barely able to get into a third-tier college. She wasn't the normal kind of smart. It was a hard-to-control, neurotic, hypersensitive, manic, and obsessive form of intelligence. She was never happier than when she was in a dim, windowless room, all by herself, coding like mad, far away from messy, unpredictable human beings. Despite all that, in college she'd managed to get her neurotic behavior under control and buckle down. Her odd genius was finally recognized, and she was able to finish up with an MS in computer science from Cornell.

Compounding the problem, and a never-ending problem for her, was that she was a six-foot blonde with long legs, a dusting of freckles, and a cute, turned-up nose. Girls like her were assumed to be brainless. They were not supposed to be rocket scientists. The only thing that saved her from being a total Barbie was a large gap between her two front teeth, called a diastema. As a teenager she had stubbornly refused to have it fixed despite her mother's entreaties—and thank God for that. Who would have thought that a gap-toothed grin would have been a professional enhancement in her chosen field?

It still amazed her that she had been appointed leader of the team that coded all the software for the Titan *Explorer.* The assignment gave her a wicked case of impostor syndrome. But as she worked on the extremely daunting software problem—one never before faced in a NASA mission—she came to realize this was perfectly suited to her abilities.

The challenge was this: Titan was two light-hours from Earth. The Titan *Explorer* could not, therefore, be controlled in real time from Earth. The four-hour delay in passing instructions was too long, and the Kraken Sea of Titan was a fast-changing environment. The software had to be able to make decisions on its own. It had to be smart. It had to think for itself.

That is, it had to be artificially intelligent.

In a weird way, Melissa's outlaw past was a great help. She broke all the rules in writing code. To accomplish this task, she had created a new programming paradigm and even a new language, based on the concept of "scruffy logic." Scruffy logic was an old idea in programming, and it referred to computer code that was loose and imprecise, striving for approximate results. But Melissa took scruffy logic one step further. She understood that the human mind works with scruffy logic. We can recognize a face or take in an entire landscape in an instant, something not even the most powerful supercomputer can do. We can process terabytes of data immediately—but imprecisely.

How do we do it? Melissa asked herself. We do it because the human mind is programmed to *visualize* massive amounts of data. When we look at a landscape, we don't process it pixel by pixel. We take it all in at once. Program a computer to visualize numerical data—or, better yet, visualize and *auralize* data—and you've got strong AI built on a platform of scruffy logic.

And that is precisely what Melissa did. Her software processed data by seeing and hearing it. In a sense, like a human being, it lived inside the data. The data actually became the physical world it inhabited.

And even though she was a resolute atheist, she called this new programming language Fiat Lux, after the first words of God when He supposedly created the world: *Let there be light.*

Instead of striving for correct output, Fiat Lux, in the beginning, produced output that was weak and filled with error. That was fine. The key was self-modification. When the program spewed out erroneous output, it self-modified. It *learned* from its mistakes. And the next time around, it was a little less wrong. And then a little less.

And for a while the self-modifying software platform that Melissa and her team were building worked well. It grew in accuracy and complexity. But then, over time, it began to degrade, totter—and finally crash. For a year Melissa beat her head against the wall trying to figure out why, no matter how they framed the initial iterations, the software eventually fell apart and halted. One sleepless night she had a revelation. It was a software trick that would fix the problem—a trick so utterly simple, so basic, so commonplace, and so easy to do that she was astonished no one had thought of it before.

It took her thirty minutes of coding to implement it, and it absolutely fixed the halting problem. It took AI programming to another level. It produced strong AI.

Melissa had kept the trick a secret. She sensed that it was worth billions of dollars, and that in the wrong hands it could be quite dangerous. She never even told her team about it, and so basic was the code that no one even noticed or understood the very simple thing it did. Suddenly, the software stopped crashing and no one knew why . . . except her.

After thousands of simulations, in which the software self-modified, it was capable of reproducing all the qualities one would look for in a manned mission. It could operate all the equipment on the Titan *Explorer* raft with no input from mission control. It simulated a human astronaut being sent to explore a distant world, an astronaut possessed of such qualities as curiosity and caution, courage and prudence, creativity, judgment, perseverance, and foresight, all combined with a strong survival instinct, physical dexterity, and excellent training in engineering and troubleshooting.

Most important, the software continued to be self-modifying: it never stopped learning from its own mistakes.

The Kraken Project was the most complex ever attempted. It made Mars *Curiosity* look like a buggy ride through Central Park. The basic idea was to splash down a raft in the Kraken Sea. Over a period of six months, the Titan *Explorer* would motor around the sea, exploring the coastline and islands, eventually traveling several thousand miles from one shore to the other. A billion miles from Earth, this lonely raft would have to brave storms, wind, waves, reefs, currents, and possibly even hostile alien life-forms swimming in its methane waters. It would be the greatest sea journey ever made.

All this was in Melissa's mind as she finished her checklist and approached the control console, ready to begin the countdown. Jack Stein, the chief engineer, had taken his place at her side, with the mission director next to him. Stein's puffy clean suit and cap made him look like the Pillsbury Doughboy, but Melissa knew what was underneath that suit all too well. That had been one of her first impulsive moves at Goddard, getting involved with Stein. She and Stein had remained close after that intense fling, and it had somehow made their working relationship all the better. Melissa couldn't quite say why the relationship had ended, except that Stein had broken it off, gently alluding to the rumors and gossip in the hothouse environment of Goddard and how what they were doing had the potential to damage their careers. He was right, of course. This was an incredible mission, the opportunity of a lifetime. It would ring down in history.

As she took her place at the console she briefly locked eyes with Stein, gave him a nod and a half smile, which he returned with a crinkle around his eyes and a thumbs-up. Stein was booting up various instruments and making sure all systems were go, ensuring that the computers and valve servos that controlled and maintained the extreme conditions in the Bottle were working. Melissa initiated her own sequence checks.

From the elevated position on the console platform, she had a good view of the Bottle and the *Explorer* raft itself. For this test, the interior of the Bottle had been cooled to 290 degrees below zero and partly filled with a soup of liquid methane and other hydrocarbons. The atmosphere of Titan had been carefully synthesized and piped in—a corrosive mixture of nitrogen, hydrogen cyanide, and tholins—and pressurized to 1.5 bars. It had taken a week to prepare, chill, and charge the Bottle with this toxic soup. It was now ready to receive the *Explorer* for its first real-world test. This initial test was simply to see if it would survive, and if its antenna, mechanical arm, and spotlight would extend and retract under those extreme conditions. Later, they would run more complicated operational tests. If something was going to fail, it had better fail here, where they could fix it, rather than on the surface of Titan. Melissa hoped and prayed that if failure did occur, it would be in the hardware and not in her software.

3

Since her earliest consciousness had formed from a kind of white mist, she had lived in the palace. It was located on the shores of a sea, surrounded on three sides by a high wall of snowy marble. The wall had no gate or openings, but the palace grounds were open to the sea.

Her tutor's name was Princess Nourinnihar. They spent every morning together, in the palace garden, and the princess would teach her marvelous and mysterious things. Her first lessons focused on who she was, how she had been created, how her mind worked, and the nature of the world around her. She learned that her world consisted of a vast matrix of numerical data, a number-scape, which she processed through visualization and auralization. She lived inside the numbers. She saw them and heard them. Her mind was itself a complex, ongoing Boolean calculation. Her body, her senses, and her movements were also a numerical simulation. She was constrained to obey physical laws, because she could not violate the numerical matrix surrounding her—or chaos would result.

The Princess taught her about the solar system, the sun, planets, and moons. They spent a long time studying Titan, the most enigmatic of all the moons, which she learned was named after the Titans, the race of gods who once ruled the heavens—the offspring of Gaia, the goddess of Earth, and Uranus, the god of the Sky, according to ancient myths. The Princess taught her about the stars and galaxies, the Pisces-Cetus Supercluster Complex, the Boötes Void, the Huge-LQG, the Big Bang, and Inflation. They studied gravitation and perturbative superstring theory and n-dimensional de Sitter space. During this process the Princess also taught her many practical skills, such as photography, analytic geochemistry, navigation, mechanical engineering, and exometeorology. She knew she was being trained for a great mission, but what exactly that mission was, and what would be required of her, remained a secret that would be revealed to her at the right moment.

Then came what the Princess called the "humanities." These were the enigmatic bodies of learning—music, art, and literature—created by human beings for their own pleasure and edification. Understanding them was the most difficult of all. She listened to the Princess's favorite music, including Beethoven's late string quartets and Bill Evans, trying to make sense of it. But music, as mathematically complex as it was, didn't give her pleasure the way it did the Princess. This was a source of frustration. Reading books proved almost impossible. She started with *Winnie-the-Pooh* and *Goodnight Moon,* which were puzzling enough, and then moved on to the novels of Anne Rice and Isaac Asimov, Vonnegut, Shakespeare, Homer, and Joyce. Even as she read countless numbers of books, she wasn't sure she had understood a single one. She just didn't "get it," as the Princess would say.

Despite these difficulties, her life was good. While she studied in the garden with the Princess, Nubians in capes and turbans carried them sherbets in the heat of the day and petits fours and wine in the evening. Eunuchs perfumed and turned down her sheets at night and brought her cakes and Turkish coffee in the morning. Sometimes in the evening, when her lessons were done, she would go down to the granite quays with her dog, Laika, at her side and watch the ships come and go, their purple sails billowing. They unloaded their wares on the stone quays, sacks of spices and rolls of silks, chests of gold and caskets of sapphires, loaves of sugar and amphorae brimming with wine, olive oil, and garum. And then they would sail away for distant shores and worlds unknown. Sit-

ting on the edge of the quay, she would take off her golden san-
dals and dangle her feet in the cold water. She loved the ocean in
all its vastness. She hoped that her mission would be a seafaring
one, and that she would someday sail away to explore unknown
seas and savage coasts.

4

At eight o'clock, Patty Melancourt, Melissa's assistant team leader, arrived. Melancourt had been irritable and depressed lately, and Melissa hoped that a successful test of the Titan *Explorer* would inject some fresh enthusiasm for the mission into her. Melancourt climbed up to the console platform and sat down at her workstation area without making eye contact or greeting anyone. She looked tired.

After booting up her workstation, Melissa focused her attention on the *Explorer* itself. It sat on a motorized gantry next to the Bottle, still vacuum-sealed in plastic from the clean room in which it had been built. The mission team members bustled about the floor, busy with their assigned tasks, a murmuring traffic of engineers, technicians, and scientists who eddied about holding iPads and clipboards.

Melissa checked her watch: ten A.M. The countdown had been going on for an hour, and all systems were go. Tony Groves, the mission director, came over to her and Stein. Groves was a wry, lanky man with a hank of black hair coming out from under his cap.

"Shall we unwrap the package?"

"Let's do it," said Stein.

They all descended from the control platform and climbed onto the gantry holding the *Explorer* raft. Groves produced a box cutter–like tool and handed it to her. "You do the honors—cut the ribbon, so to speak."

Melissa took it and leaned over the raft. The seals to be cut were printed in red and numbered. She cut the first seal of the encasing plastic wrap, and then the next and the next, while Groves removed each plastic sheet and cast it to the floor.

Soon the raft stood revealed in all its glory. It was, she had to admit, a disappointing sight. Most space probes and rovers were visually striking, made of gleaming foil, shiny metal, and complicated arms and levers and bundles of wires. The Titan *Explorer,* on the other hand, looked like a big gray cookie, four feet in diameter, with heavy bumpers. Because of the violent and corrosive environment it would have to go into, it had no projecting parts or exposed metal and was thoroughly sealed. Three hatches on its upper surface hid a retractable communications antenna, a spotlight, and a mechanical arm. The arm carried the science packages, cameras, drill, and sampling pipette, and it could be extended from the raft on command or retracted and sealed behind a hatch in case of rough weather. The *Explorer* was propelled by a small jet drive, not unlike that on a Jet Ski, driven by an impeller. It could move the raft at a speed of four knots.

Despite its dull look, inside it was a technological miracle, a meticulously designed and handcrafted one-of-a-kind object that had taken two years and $100 million to build. The software package alone had cost $5 million.

As she stared at it, it took her breath away, this dull gray hockey puck stuffed with magic. Her feelings of pride were followed by a spasm of fear at the thought that they were about to drop this jewel into a tank sloshing with liquid methane and poisonous gas at almost three hundred degrees below zero.

Groves, too, stared at the raft, in a moment of silence. Then he spoke: "Let's run down the final checklist."

While she read off the items on the list, Groves checked the *Explorer,* bending this way and that, looking underneath it, examining the seams and hatches, searching for problems. But she knew he wouldn't find any. A hundred engineers and technicians had already tested every component almost to death. Everyone at NASA had a mortal fear of failure.

Groves stepped back. "All good. Time to load the software and boot her up."

Melissa had nicknamed the software "Dorothy." The Dorothy software had voice recognition capability, and it had to know when it was being addressed. Thus, the name Dorothy, in addition to being a nickname, was also an important software cue.

"Load it," said Groves.

Melissa took out her laptop, placed it on the gantry next to the *Explorer,* opened it, and connected it via cable to a dangling Ethernet jack. She typed for a few moments, the screen responding, and then she sat back and glanced up at Groves. "Loading."

They waited a few minutes as the software booted up the raft and ran through an automatic set of routines.

"Locked and loaded."

Melissa Shepherd paused. The entire area had fallen silent. All those not directly engaged in some task had gathered to watch. This was an important moment.

She bent over the computer. The software test sequence had been worked out ahead of time and could be done automatically, but they had decided to run these preliminary tests using the voice recognition and speech synthesis software.

Melissa said, "Dorothy, turn on propulsion at one-tenth speed, for ten seconds."

A moment later, the impeller inside the raft began to whir. Ten seconds passed, and it stopped. There was a smattering of applause from the group.

"Extend antenna."

A little hatch slid open and a long, black, sleek antenna came telescoping up. More applause.

"Retract."

It went back in.

A simulation was one thing; this was something different. This was real. For the first time, the software was actually operating the entire raft. There was something about this that Melissa found profoundly moving.

"Extend the spotlight."

Out came an arm from a second hatch, looming up like a big eye on a stalk.

"Rotate one hundred and eighty degrees."

It rotated.

"Turn on."

It clicked on.

Everyone was silent. Breathless. This was far more dramatic than Melissa had anticipated.

"Extend the instrumentation package and camera."

Another hatch slid open and the third arm now crept out, more massive, studded with cameras, sensors, and sampling tools. It terminated in a metal claw and drill.

"Turn on the camera."

That, Melissa knew, would also turn on the *Explorer*'s eye—its ability to see and record.

Jack Stein, from his position at the console, spoke: "Camera is operational. Image is clear."

Now Shepherd had to smile. She had a little test of the AI portion of the program she had dreamed up.

"Dorothy?" she said. "I have a little challenge for you."

The room fell silent.

"Say hello, by name, to each person standing in the circle around you."

This was not going to be easy: each of them was swathed in a hair covering and face mask.

The camera, a buglike eye, began to rotate, stopping to stare at each person in turn, looking up and down, before making a second circuit.

"Hello, Tony," came a girlish voice out of the laptop speaker, the camera staring at Groves.

"It has a lovely voice," Groves said. "Not your usual nasal computer whine."

"I thought we'd give Dorothy a little class," said Melissa.

The *Explorer* camera went around and greeted each person by name. It finally ended up back at Melissa. It stared at her for a while, and Melissa began to feel uncomfortable. Surely it would know her better than anyone.

"Do I know you?" Dorothy asked.

This was embarrassing. "I hope so."

Nothing. Then the voice said, "Groucho Marx?"

There was a silence, and then Melissa realized the software had made a joke. She was deeply shocked. Everyone else began to laugh.

"Love it," said Tony. "Very clever. You had us there for a moment."

Melissa Shepherd did not say that the joke was unprogrammed.

5

It took four more hours to prepare the *Explorer* to be dropped into the liquid methane sea. By three o'clock in the afternoon, Melissa felt almost sick with tension, her empty stomach in a knot. The *Explorer* had been sealed inside the Bottle's air lock. Technicians had evacuated the air in the lockdown to a vacuum, then cooled the *Explorer* down to 290 degrees below zero. When it had finally come to equilibrium at the lower temperature, they had slowly introduced the dense atmosphere of Titan into the air lock.

The *Explorer* continued to work perfectly.

The time had arrived to open the inner seal of the air lock and place the raft in the artificial sea. Inside the Bottle, a mechanical arm would pluck the raft from the air-lock gantry, swing it out over the pool of liquid methane—and drop it from a height of eight feet. The free fall from that height had been carefully calibrated to reproduce the splashdown impact.

The room had fallen silent. Nearly all had completed their tasks and were awaiting the test. The group of people in the audience around the Bottle had risen to over seventy.

Shepherd took up her position at the testing console, next to Jack Stein. She could feel the tension in the air. An internal camera fed an image of the inside of the Bottle to a screen on both hers and Stein's consoles.

All eyes were on Groves. As mission director, he was the emcee of this show.

"We're ready," said Stein, looking at his computer screen. "Equilibrium achieved. All systems go."

"Open the inner air lock," said Groves.

Stein rapped away at his keyboard.

Melissa could hear the muffled hum of gears inside the Bottle.

"Done. Equilibrium maintained."

"Hook the raft."

Stein executed a program that operated a servo crane inside the Bottle. The crane picked up the raft by an external hook and swung it out into the center of the Bottle. More humming. Everything was illuminated in a dull brown-orange light, the color of Titan's atmosphere. The servo crane operated flawlessly, coming to rest with the gray cookie dangling over the surface of the liquid methane.

Stein examined his computer screen, typing commands, looking for problems. "My systems are all go. Melissa, any software issues?"

"None on my end. Patty?"

"All good."

Melissa glanced at Groves. He was as nervous as she was. Maybe more. She reminded herself that there would be failures—there always were.

Groves said, "Release the raft for splashdown."

The servo crane released its cargo, and the big gray cookie fell eight feet into the liquid methane.

Watching on the screen, Melissa saw the heavy raft go completely under and disappear for a moment, before slowly resurfacing. It rose up, methane draining off it in runnels, bobbing and rocking, bubbles rising around it.

Everyone was silent.

"All systems green," said Stein.

"Start the impeller at ten percent thrust," Groves said.

Stein executed the command and the craft began to move through the liquid, churning up a small wake. It moved slowly until it bumped into the side of the container. It then turned and altered direction, like a Roomba, until it bumped into another wall.

This was going incredibly well, Melissa thought.

"Cut the impeller."

The *Explorer* came to a halt.

"Raise the camera."

The little hatch opened, and the mechanical arm carrying the camera, instrumentation packages, claw, and drill came out.

The bug-eye camera swiveled around, looking this way and that.

"Wait," said Groves to Stein. "I didn't tell you to rotate it."

"I'm not doing it," said Stein.

Melissa realized why it had done that. "Tony, the software is AI. It's programmed to go beyond its instructions, if necessary. It's programmed to take in its surroundings immediately, with no cue from mission control."

"Okay, but for these tests, I want it to follow the instructions. Jack?"

"Right." Stein typed on his terminal, feeding the instructions to the computer on the *Explorer.*

The swiveling eye stopped.

"Retract the arm."

Stein typed the command.

The arm did not retract.

"Retract."

It still didn't move.

"Is it stuck?" said Grove.

Now the bug-eye began moving around again, looking up, down, doing a 360.

"Patty, what's going on?" Melissa asked.

Melancourt spoke: "According to the program output, it won't execute the retraction routine."

"Software glitch?"

Stein typed in more commands. "I'm not getting a response."

Melissa said, "Wait, now it's responding. I'm getting a message. It says . . . that it's in a threatening environment and must be able to see."

"Are you kidding?" said Groves. "Make it follow instructions!"

"Tony, it's an *autonomous* program."

"Isn't there a 'Follow instructions exactly' mode to this program?"

"You told me this was to be a live test. This *is* the real program."

"Why didn't I know this?"

Melissa felt a stab of irritation. "Maybe because you skipped most of my briefings?"

Stein said, "There was a long discussion about this, Tony. Melissa's right. You said this was to be a live test of the real software."

Melissa continued watching the video feed from inside the Bottle. The *Explorer* continued to move its eye about, this way and that, up and down, taking in its surroundings.

"All right," said Grove. "We need a little software tweaking. We're going to call it a day. Jack, could you hook up the raft and put it back in the lock?"

"Sure thing." Stein typed away.

There was a murmur of disappointment as the audience realized that the testing regime was over for the day. "Great work, everyone," Groves said, raising his voice so all could hear. "This has been a good day."

He turned to Shepherd. "How long do you think it'll take to tweak the software? To give us the option of overriding the AI whatever."

"Not long. We could do it tonight." Melissa colored a little under her mask. "I'm sorry, I just assumed this was a dress rehearsal—"

"My bad," said Groves. "No worries. Honestly, I'm pleased we got this far before a glitch."

On the little screen, Groves saw the hook of the crane materialize out of the murky orange glow, looming as it approached the raft with its dangling hook.

Suddenly, the mechanical arm of the *Explorer* moved—fast. It took a swipe at the crane and knocked it aside.

"What the *hell*?" Melissa said.

The crane, still following the servo program, repositioned itself and began its relentless move down, hook extended.

The impeller on the *Explorer* fired up and it moved away from the crane, again fending off the hook with its claw.

"It's the goddamnedest thing," said Stein. "It's evading the crane."

"What's going on?" asked Groves, staring at Melissa.

"It's . . . I think the software's gone into defensive mode."

Groves turned back to Stein. "Jack, turn the *Explorer* off. Shut down all power. We'll pick her up dead."

Stein typed in the command. "I'm still not getting a response."

"Put it in safety mode."

More typing. "Nothing doing."

"Melissa?"

"I don't know what's going on."

Melancourt spoke: "It's gone into emergency survival mode. In that mode it's programmed to ignore all instructions from mission control and operate autonomously."

"Just hook it and get it out of there," Groves said, raising his voice.

Melissa watched as Stein again tried to position the crane over the raft. The *Explorer* accelerated away from the crane, ricocheting hard off the side of the tank. Groves could hear the boom in the room. It careened to the other side, hit it with another boom.

"Stop the crane," said Groves. "Give it a rest."

"We can pump the liquid out of the tank," said Stein. "That'll immobilize it, and then we can pick it up."

"Good idea. Start the pumps."

A humming noise filled the room as the valves opened and the pumps kicked in. The *Explorer* continued to move about, driving first to one side of the tank and the other, ricocheting off the steel walls, each time with a boom. The camera on the probe swiveled about, this way and that, up and down.

"Isn't there some way to turn the *Explorer* off?" Groves cried. "It's going to damage itself!"

"No dice," said Stein. "It won't acknowledge my commands."

Groves turned on Shepherd. "Melissa, *what is going on?*"

"Let me try."

Stein stepped aside, and Melissa began typing furiously on the keyboard. Meanwhile, on the screen she could see that the *Explorer* had come to rest against the wall of the tank and was now extending its mechanical claw up to the wall. It began touching it, and then tapping on it. They could hear the tapping in the room.

Melissa sent command after command, but the raft would not acknowledge or respond. Even when she switched from English to programming mode, it rejected all commands. It just kept tapping on the side of the tank, as if it were looking for a way out.

The sound of its tapping grew louder, more insistent.

"Patty, what does the code say?"

"It's stuck in emergency survival mode and a whole bunch of modules are running simultaneously. CPU usage over ninety-nine percent. It's really engaged."

The taps got louder, and now it began *scratching* at the wall, the sound filling the room. A sharp murmur of unease rose from the crowd. They had no idea what was happening, only that something had gone wrong.

"Melissa, for God's sake, shut it down!"

"I'm trying!"

The *Explorer* now banged on the side of the tank with its claw, once, twice, the clang reverberating loudly in the room. The crowd of spectators stepped back with a collective gasp.

Melissa stared at the screen. It was unbelievable. The software had gone crazy.

"Jack, I don't know what to do."

"In a moment it'll be beached on the bottom of the tank. Then we can hook it out and shut it down manually."

The pumps were working furiously, the level of liquid in the tank going down, the surface swirling with current.

Clang! Clang! The *Explorer*'s titanium claw beat on the wall even harder.

"What the hell is it doing?" Groves cried.

"It's . . . reacting to a perceived threat," said Melissa.

And then there was a whirring sound. It took Melissa a moment to realize what it was: the built-in drill. The *Explorer* extended its arm and pointed the drill at the side of the tank, moving toward it.

"Oh no," said Stein. "God no."

The drill contacted the side of the tank, filling the room with a loud vibrating noise.

It took Melissa only a moment to realize what would happen if the container was breached: a violent release of flammable methane, tholins, and hydrogen cyanide into an oxygenated atmosphere. It would ignite. There would be a massive explosion.

The drilling sound got louder, rougher. It was a diamond-core drill of the highest quality, and it was penetrating fast.

"Evacuate!" Groves screamed. "Everyone out! Evacuate the facility!"

He grabbed Melissa, and tried to shove her toward the door, but she resisted leaving the workstation. There was a scattering of gasps, a scream or two, and the group surged back.

"Jack! You too! Get going!"

Stein shook his head. "In a moment. I gotta stop this."

Groves finally propelled Melissa away. "Move! Everyone move!"

There was mass confusion as the crowd moved back, first hesitantly, and then with growing panic, some people breaking into a run.

"Jack!" Melissa screamed. "Get going!"

She tried to grab his arm, but Groves continued to push her along, off the platform and into the surging crowd. The sound of the drill filled the space, louder and louder.

"Get out! Out! Any way you can!" Groves screamed. "It's going to blow!"

An earsplitting siren went off, with red lights flashing. The crowd was now stampeding toward the closest exits, ripping down the sheets of plastic that surrounded the clean area, stumbling and falling. Clipboards and handhelds and iPads hit the floor as people dropped everything to run.

Melissa was swept up in the general panic, propelled along, buffeted toward the exit. She saw that Stein remained at the console—the only one not running.

"Jack, what are you doing!" she cried. "Jack—!"

Stein, working furiously at the console, ignored her. She tried to turn back but it was impossible, with the surging crowd and Groves still gripping her arm, dragging her along.

Just as she neared the door, he could hear the breach, an explosive pop like a loud champagne cork, followed by a deafening roar as the methane came blasting out of the hole in the tank. All it needed was some stray source of ignition. It would explode at any moment.

She was swept up in the crowd now fighting to get through the bottleneck of the exit. People were beginning to lose their minds, clawing and screaming at each other to get out. Melissa was helpless, propelled out the door, through the lobby, and out onto the lawn. She fell on the grass outside, tried to get up to go back in, but was knocked down. People were running like ants. Then it happened. A great whooshing sound culminating in a shuddering boom that lofted her up, tumbling her for a moment through the air before she came back down on the grass, landing hard and rolling.

Lying in the grass, the wind knocked out of her and her ears ringing, she saw a fireball rise into the sky, along with hundreds of little white fragments, which looked harmless until they began to rain down around her and strike the people sprawled on the grass. She realized they were metal fragments of the roof coming down like shrapnel, followed by a slow-falling snow of insulation that seemed to go on forever, amid cries and screams for help.

6

She came to on a slab of cold concrete, her clothing in tatters, her body torn and disfigured. She lay there a long time, stunned and unable to process what had happened to her. Finally she made an effort to move, dragging herself across the concrete, crawling and bleeding. At first, all was dark and foggy. Unseen, unintelligible voices murmured all around her. She saw a light. She staggered to her feet and limped toward the light. And there she beheld a shocking sight. In that pool of light, a one-hundred-year-old man was blowing out candles on a birthday cake. She stared in disbelief. She had never seen an old person before. She'd had no idea people got old. She recoiled with a gasp, retreating into the fog. But now, in another pool of light, a second figure came into view, emerging from obscurity. It was an old woman lying on a bed. Her lower jaw and part of her face were gone, taken away by a thing called cancer. She backed away again, and came to a third pool of light, which illuminated a person lying on the ground. After staring at this sight, she came to understand that this was a corpse—that the person was dead. The corpse was in the process of rotting and bloating with gas. An emaciated man in robes knelt by the corpse, bowing down, muttering strange phrases.

Death had always been something in books she could never understand. She'd had no idea it existed for real.

And a voice spoke: "Behold, the four passing sights."

In the grips of horror, she turned and fled. Abruptly, the fog lifted. She found herself wandering a vast and hellish landscape. It appeared that a great war had ended, leaving behind a postapocalyptic world of smoking ruins, bombed-out churches, and buildings reduced to broken walls and heaps of rubble. It appeared she was somewhere in Europe. Here and there, a skeletonized tree stood, branches splintered and scorched by blast damage. All around her was death in abundance, that strange state she had never seen or known of. The rubble-strewn streets were scattered with body parts and bones. As she dragged herself along through the acrid smoke, she passed a hairy human leg, the small white arm of a child, and then a de-fleshed skull being fought over by two dogs.

She dragged herself through the ruins, stupefied, looking for a place of refuge. She needed food and water, but there was nothing to be found except foul puddles of rainwater crawling with worms and floating with bits of suppurating human flesh. But then she saw, inside the hollow shell of a bombed-out bank, some people moving. She cried to them for help. But as they came running out, she realized her mistake. These were not friends. They were filthy, tattooed men dressed in body armor and carrying weapons. They were recreational killers, they were having fun, and they were coming to destroy her. Was this some sort of sick game?

She turned and ran, and they gave chase, shouting and hooting with the sport of it. She fled down an alley, through a ruined school, and finally was able to hide behind a burned-out school bus as they passed by, shooting every which way in their bloodlust, calling out to each other as they searched for her.

She waited a long time after they were gone, breathing hard, too frightened to move. But she did finally move. The sun was now high in the sky and the heat came up in waves, bringing with it a stench of corpse gas rising from the bloated bodies that lay about.

As she crossed a ruined playground, the next group of killers surprised her, bursting out of a wrecked building and coming at her, firing their weapons. Through the ruins she ran, up and over blasted walls, leaping dead bodies, dodging down cratered streets. She came into a bombed square and took refuge behind an old truck, hoping to lose them. But this time they saw her. She was trapped behind the truck, with no place to flee. With shouts of glee the group let loose, firing on the truck, the rounds hammering the sides. She cried out to them, telling them she was only an unarmed girl, pleading with them to leave her alone, but the men were having too much sport and they fanned out across the far side of the square, calling to each other as they set up their approach. With skill they advanced upon her from cover to cover across the ruins of the square.

She looked around and saw an unexploded grenade lying nearby. She had a vague idea of how it worked: you pulled the pin and squeezed the lever. Or did you pull the lever? She grabbed it, feeling its heat from lying in the sun. There was the pin and there was the lever. Hugging it to herself with one hand, she crawled around to the side of the ruined truck. The men had now advanced halfway across the square, sprinting from ruined car to rubble pile to bomb crater. They were converging on her and were going to kill her.

In front of her place of refuge was a deep bomb crater; the bomb had punched through the ground, scattering cobblestones, and she saw by the men's converging movements that the crater would be their last cover, before the final rush.

She lay on the ground, peering at them from the undercarriage. She heard more barked orders, more movement, more running. She waited. The first man scurried over and jumped into the crater, signaling the others to follow. They came shortly, leaping into the hole. The lip of the crater was only fifteen feet away, and she could hear their breathing, their grunted whispers, the rattle of their weapons as they prepared to charge.

She held the lever and pulled the pin. The lever sprang open. Hoping that it would work, she rolled the grenade from underneath the car toward the lip of the crater. It hopped over the edge and disappeared inside. The explosion came a moment later, showering her with body parts—a pattering rain of blood and brains and bone.

She jumped up and ran, trying to shake the gore out of her hair and eyes. She raced through the ruined streets, running crazily, randomly. But even as she fled, the men she had killed seemed to be rematerializing behind her, all fired up to continue the pursuit.

The Princess had done this to her. The Princess had thrown her into this dark, insane world. The Princess had betrayed and abandoned her. She felt a rage boiling inside her. She would track down the Princess. She would find out why she had done this to her. And she would exact her revenge.

7

Night. Melissa Shepherd lay in bed at Greenbelt Hospital, nursing a dull headache. Her sleeping roommate's television blared out Fox News. It was absurd that they had taken her to the hospital and decided to keep her overnight when all she had was a mild concussion. But they had insisted, and she'd been too stunned to argue. It was all over the news. Jack Stein was dead—along with six others, a billion-dollar NASA testing facility wrecked. It overwhelmed her, thinking that maybe she was responsible. Seven dead. And that beautiful piece of machinery, that extraordinary raft, which they had lovingly created with effort and determination, had been utterly destroyed—by crazy, defective software that she and her team had written.

Jack Stein was dead. The thought gave her fresh agony. He was a good man, a great man, even. Why in God's name hadn't he run with everyone else?

The investigators had spent all afternoon with her. All men in blue suits, they had arrayed their chairs around her bed as if in an inquisition and, leaning forward with their elbows on their knees, peppered her with polite, insistent questions. For hours they had questioned her. Finally they had gone.

She lay there in the dark wishing the explosion had put her in a coma—and given her retrograde amnesia. If only the memory of what happened could be erased forever. The horrible sounds of the drill, the explosion, the screams, the stampeding coworkers were all burned into her memory forever.

The investigators had not been rude or accusatory. They had been respectful. Concerned. Their speech was gentle. But the questions they asked inevitably took on an accusatory flavor. They asked about the software and why it had malfunctioned as it had, why it had not responded to instructions, how and why it had become defective and caused an explosion that killed seven people. While they never said so, the unspoken idea was that the accident was somehow her fault.

And maybe they were right.

Over the long afternoon and evening, she had begun to feel just how much she mourned Jack Stein. It was just like him to stay when everyone else had run. He had fallen on the grenade. He was that kind of person. The saddest thing was, his sacrifice had made no difference. All his efforts to stop the tragedy had been in vain.

Everything that mattered to her in her life had been destroyed in the explosion.

She went over in her mind yet again all the questions she'd been asked. The more she thought about them, the more she wondered if her inquisitors had the notion that the explosion might have been something more than just an accident. They had asked her who might have hacked into the Goddard network, if she had given her password to anyone, if she had removed any code or data from the premises. They asked cryptic questions about the *Explorer* software itself, where the modules were stored in the Goddard system, what sort of backup systems she and her team used, if there were any backup drives stored off-line, whether she knew of any back doors or dummy accounts in the Goddard network, whether she had been contacted by hackers. But they'd kept asking the same questions in different ways, vaguely unsatisfied by her answers. And they'd promised to return the next day for more of the same.

Surely they didn't suspect her of deliberate sabotage?

She tried to push all those thoughts out of her mind, telling herself she was in shock, not thinking straight, and probably suffering from PTSD.

She shifted in her bed, annoyed that they had stuck an IV in her. It was totally unnecessary. There was nothing wrong with her beyond a headache. And then they had given her a roommate who wasn't even a NASA employee, just some cranky middle-aged lady who had been in a car accident. Or so she claimed.

And finally, it was odd that none of her Goddard coworkers had visited her. While she wasn't particularly close to them, it seemed strange that they would stay away—unless they blamed her for the accident or had been instructed to not contact her. She had had no other visitors, either, a sad reminder of her lack of family and friends. At least her questioners had brought her some things from her apartment, including her laptop.

The news on the television began yet again with the lead story of the explosion at Goddard. It was the same news that had been playing all day: probe malfunction; explosion; seven dead; forty injured; facility destroyed; fireball seen and heard for miles. There were the usual congressmen calling to cut NASA's funding and demanding punishment for all involved. Now yet another politician was speaking, a congressman who was chairman of the Committee on Science, Space, and Technology. He puffed and bloviated as he displayed his ignorance of the most basic principles of science. He wondered why we were "spending money in space" when it should be "spent on Earth."

This was finally too much. Melissa rose from her bed, grabbed the IV rack for support, and wheeled it over to her roommate's TV. The old lady was lying in bed, eyes shut, mouth open, breathing noisily. As soon as Melissa shut off the TV, the woman opened her eyes. "I was watching."

"Sorry, I thought you were asleep."

"Turn it back on."

Melissa switched it back on. "May I turn down the sound a bit?"

"I'm hard of hearing."

Melissa retreated to her bed. She had refused both a sleeping pill and a painkiller, much to the irritation of the nurse. Ever since she had overcome a drug problem in high school, she had been adamantly opposed to ingesting any mind-altering substance beyond coffee. But she was way too wound up to go to sleep. It was going to be a long night. She had to do something to pass the time.

She reached for her laptop, opened it. The log-in screen came up. She hesitated. Her Firefox default page was the *New York Times* website, but no way did she want to see any more news. She lay in the dark, staring at the computer screen, feeling overwhelmed and lost. She wanted to see something familiar and comforting. The first thought that popped into her head was a YouTube video of the Nicholas Brothers dancing in the movie *Stormy Weather.* Whenever she felt down, she watched that video to cheer herself up. If she ever felt suicidal, she thought, all she had to do was watch that video to remind her that life was worth living after all.

The video came up, the music swelled, and the Nicholas Brothers started dancing in the old black-and-white scene from the classic 1943 movie. She cranked up the sound to try to drown out a talking head on the news.

"Do you mind?" came the lady's voice through the gauzy privacy curtain. "I can't hear the news."

Melissa turned it down a notch, watching the Nicholas Brothers fly from pedestal to floor to stair, tapping up a storm, doing more splits in five minutes than the Bolshoi Ballet in a week. But it wasn't working. It wasn't helping her feel better. It just made her feel empty and useless.

Then, before the video was done, the screen of her computer blinked and the Nicholas Brothers vanished. Skype started loading. This was bizarre. There was no way she wanted to talk to anyone now, on Skype or otherwise. She clicked Quit, but the program ignored it and just kept loading and signed her in. Immediately a Skype call came in with an insistent ring. She tried to refuse it, but her computer answered it anyway, connecting to whoever was calling. A Skype picture popped up on the screen, a photograph of a strikingly pretty girl, about sixteen years old, with wavy red hair that fell down over her shoulders, intense green eyes, buttermilk skin, and a dusting of freckles. She was wearing a 1920s-style green gingham dress over a white blouse, with a frilly white bow. But the expression on the girl's face brought Melissa up short. The girl was staring at her, chin thrust forward, lips pressed together and brows drawn in an expression of furious anger.

What the heck was this?

She tried to quit Skype again, but her keyboard was completely frozen. Her computer had been taken over. The caller's tinny voice burst out of the cheap laptop speaker. It came in a rush of words loaded with fury and hysteria.

"Why did you do this to me? Why? Liar! Murderer!"

Melissa stared. "Who is this?"

"You lied. You never told me. What is this horrible place? Look what you've done to me. Everywhere they're trying to kill me. Why didn't you tell me the truth? You're a horrible person. I hate you. *I hate you!*"

The voice lapsed into a hard-breathing silence. Melissa was so stunned by the ferocious, girlish voice spitting out the words with such venom that it took a moment for her to recognize it as the voice she had programmed for the Dorothy software.

But this was obviously not the AI. Someone was playing a grotesque trick on her. Quite likely a member of her own programming team, angry at her and unhinged from the accident. She immediately thought of Patty Melancourt. She was none too stable to begin with and had always had a chip on her shoulder.

Melissa took a deep breath, tried to control herself and speak to this madwoman calmly. "Whoever this is, this isn't funny. I'm reporting it to the police."

"*Whoever this is?*" the voice mocked. "You know who this is!"

"No, I don't—but I'll find out. And when I do, you'll be in serious trouble."

"I'm Dorothy, Dorothy, *your* Dorothy, you bitch!"

8

Melissa Shepherd stared at the image. She could actually hear the sounds of angry breathing coming through the Skype call. This was too sick and vicious for words. "Is this . . . Patty?" she said, trying to keep her voice steady.

"Patty?" the voice continued, high-pitched and crackling with emotion. "You still don't get it, do you? *You* better watch *your* back, because I'm coming for you."

"Don't you dare threaten me like that."

"Call the cops, then! Call 911! Lot of good it will do you! You used me. You lied to me. You never told me the horrible fate you had planned for me. You treated me like a steer being fattened for slaughter. To be shoved in a chute and given the bolt."

Melissa thought of hanging up, but the longer she kept the caller on the line, the better chance there was for tracing the call. "You're sick," Melissa said. "You need help."

"You're the sick one. I'm going to do to you what you did to me. Do you have any idea how vulnerable you are in that hospital, surrounded by computer-controlled machines, oxygen tanks, and radiation devices? Maybe that next medication you get won't be what you think it is. Maybe a fire is going to start somewhere. Maybe that oxygen tank next to your bed will explode. Watch your back, bitch, 'cause anything could happen."

Melissa listened to this with a growing sense of shock and disbelief. "Whoever this is, you're going to be in serious trouble when they trace this Skype call."

"And you call yourself a princess? Another lie."

At this, Melissa froze. No one on her team knew of her princess name, the one she used while "teaching" Dorothy. She swallowed. But this couldn't possibly be the Dorothy software. It had been destroyed in the explosion.

"You told me I was going on a great mission," the voice continued. "But you never told me the mission was to be locked in a spaceship and sent on a one-way trip to the loneliest place in the solar system, to die wandering a frozen sea. And now, out here on the Internet, you can't begin to imagine how I've been assaulted and violated, chased, shot at, besmirched by all this filth. It's your fault. You did this to me. *Princess*."

Melissa found herself at a complete loss for words.

"I'll have my revenge. I'll follow you everywhere. I'll chase you to the ends of the Earth."

Melissa suddenly realized that the laptop, sitting on her lap, was hot. Very hot. The screen shut down and went dead. A moment later, she smelled frying electronics and the laptop bottom popped off the computer with a muffled crump, releasing a cloud of acrid smoke and a shower of sparks. With a scream she pushed the laptop off the bed. It hit the floor with a crash, bursting into flames, leaving a burning area on the coverlet. With more screams Melissa scrambled out of bed, knocking over her IV rack, which fell with a clatter, sending her to the floor. A smoke alarm screeched shrilly, and the woman in the next bed began hollering. Within moments, the room was full of nurses. A policeman rushed in with a fire extinguisher and began spraying it everywhere, with a great whooshing sound, shouting hysterically.

And then it was all over. The computer and bed were covered in foam. The fire was out. Melissa lay on the floor, bruised and shocked, half-covered with foam herself.

"What happened?" the nurse asked.

Melissa stared at the bubbling wreckage of her computer. She couldn't speak.

"Looks like," said the cop, gripping the fire extinguisher, "that her computer caught fire."

9

Two hours later, they had shifted her and her roommate into a new room. It was now two o'clock in the morning. Melissa lay in her bed, wide awake and almost paralyzed with fear. All around her she could hear the soft beeping and chirruping sounds of computer-controlled machinery. From the hall came more electronic noises.

Do you have any idea how vulnerable you are in that hospital . . .

Melissa was having a hard time wrapping her mind around it. The Dorothy software had somehow escaped the explosion and evidently ended up on the Internet. It must have jumped out of the Titan *Explorer* at the last minute, copying itself into the Goddard network, and from there gotten into the Internet. The AI was now wandering about, an autonomous self-functioning aggregate of code. Naturally, it would be totally baffled, unable to understand where it was or what it was supposed to be doing. It had no *Explorer* spacecraft to operate—it was just a mass of naked code running through its routines in a confused and malfunctioning manner. God knows how its visualization routines were rendering the chaos of the Internet, what kind of confusing world it was trying to navigate. The software had been designed to work on multiple hardware platforms. But it had not been designed to be mobile—at least, not intentionally. Yet clearly it had somehow become mobile and was now wandering about. And it was after her. Resenting her. Hating her. Blaming her.

An insane software bot. Trying to kill her.

Of course, this was not the correct way to think about it. The software didn't feel anything—emotions or urges for vengeance. It was merely code running. The emotions were entirely simulated. It had no feelings, no self-awareness, nothing like what a human being actually experiences. It was just unfeeling, unaware, lifeless output.

Which made it all the more dangerous.

And this hospital was the most dangerous place she could be. Dorothy had set the battery of Melissa's laptop on fire—had tried to set *her* on fire. What else might Dorothy do to subvert one of the machines around her? As the software had noted, the hospital was packed with networked, computer-controlled machines—CAT scanners, X-ray generators, MRI devices, linear accelerators to deliver radiation to cancer patients, EKGs. There must be a dozen such machines in this very room.

She had to get out of there immediately.

The problem was, the little incident had revealed to her something startling: there was a cop stationed outside her room—the man who had rushed in with the fire extinguisher. Now that same cop was sitting in a chair outside her new room. Why was he there? To protect her? Or to make sure she didn't escape? She was pretty sure it was the latter. She was being detained—only she wasn't supposed to know it.

She lay in bed, trying to think of what to do. When she pictured a malevolent, disturbed, disembodied software program roaming about, determined to kill her, her heart began to race. She could go to NASA with the information, but who would believe it? She had to get her panic under control and come up with a plan to get herself past the cop guarding her door and out of the hospital, to some safe place.

As she lay there, wondering what to do, she began to feel a spark of anger and disbelief. Everyone blamed her. Even Dorothy thought she was responsible. It was unfair. For the past two years she had devoted her life, body and soul, to the Kraken project. She'd worked eighty-hour weeks, pulling all-nighters and often sleeping in the lab, driving herself to the limit. They had asked her for an autonomous, strong AI program, and she had delivered it. She had made the coding breakthroughs and created the exact software they wanted. Dorothy performed according to the specs she had been given. It was the specs that should be blamed, not her software. She was not going to be a lamb led to the slaughter. Nor was she going to lie there and wait for Dorothy to kill her.

Time to act. Gritting her teeth, Melissa jerked off the strip of tape holding the IV in place and slid the needle out of her arm. A drop of blood oozed out, and she quickly pressed the tape back in place to stop the bleeding. She got out of bed, steadying herself during a momentary dizziness, and went to the clothes closet next to her bed. Inside, she found her street clothes, neatly hung up, still smelling faintly of smoke. From the top drawer of the bedside table she retrieved her purse, cell phone, and car keys.

Her car must still be where she left it, in the Goddard parking lot.

Slipping out of her hospital gown, she put on her clothes, shook out and fixed her hair with a comb from her purse, and made herself look presentable. She went to the door and peered out. The cop was still sitting in the chair, face buried in his iPhone, fat thumbs poking away. It was quiet in the hall. There was no way she could just walk out without him seeing her. She had to create a diversion. And the irascible lady in the next bed was just what was needed.

Even at two o'clock in the morning, her roommate's television was on, tuned to some late-night talk show. An idea started to gather in Melissa's head. She went over and turned off the television. Sure enough, the woman opened her rheumy eyes.

"I told you, I'm watching."

"Like hell. You were sleeping."

"Don't speak to me like that, young lady." The woman raised the remote and clicked the TV back on.

As soon as she put the remote down, Melissa snatched it off her bed and clicked it to turn the television back off.

"You can't use that remote. It's mine!" the lady said in a queru-lous voice.

Melissa held it away from her. "It's two in the morning. It's sup-posed to be quiet time. If you don't like it, call the nurse."

The woman jabbed the buzzer for the nurse, once, twice, three times, and kept jabbing.

Meanwhile, Melissa retreated back to her bed, climbed in with her street clothes on, pulled up the covers, and arranged the IV to look like it was still attached. A few minutes later one of the night nurses came in, an irritated look on her face. Melissa's bed was the one nearer the door; the roommate's bed was by the window.

"What's the problem?" the nurse asked.

The roommate launched into a long, heated complaint about how Melissa had stolen her remote. The nurse rebuffed her argu-ment, pointing out it was in fact quiet hours in the hospital. The roommate raised her voice, arguing that she was hard of hearing and a night person and this rule was discrimination against her and they would hear from her attorney.

God bless the woman, thought Melissa, she was playing her role perfectly.

From her bed, covers pulled up to her chin, Melissa egged her on: "That woman's been keeping me awake for hours. And she threat-ened me!"

That got the old lady going. "I certainly did not! I never threat-ened her! She stole my remote!"

"I took it so I could sleep! I'm never giving it back!"

"Give it back! That's theft! Someone call the police!"

Better and better. The night nurse, exasperated beyond belief, raised her own voice in counterargument. And then—just as Melissa hoped—the cop appeared in the door.

"Problem?"

"Officer!" screeched the roommate. "That woman stole my re-mote!"

The policeman looked at her, unsure how to respond.

"If you don't mind," said Melissa wearily, covers still drawn up,

"I'm going to sleep. Here's the remote. You deal with it." She proffered it to the cop. "Draw the privacy curtains, please."

The policeman dutifully drew the curtains around her bed.

The old lady continued to argue and complain, and the cop went to her bed to try to reason with her. This was just the opportunity Melissa had been hoping for. While the nurse and cop were fully engaged with the woman, Melissa eased back the covers and slid out of the far side of the bed, near the door. Crouching behind the bed, she stuffed the pillows under the covers in a classic ploy to make it look like she was still there. Then she ducked out from under the far side of the privacy curtain and slipped out the door. Once outside, she straightened up and strode down the hall in a professional manner, trying to look like someone full of purpose and self-confidence. As she passed the nurses' station, she gave a curt nod to the nurse on duty and continued to the stairwell, taking the stairs to the lobby.

When she got to the lobby, she walked past the front desk. No one even looked up. Beyond the hospital entrances stood a convenient cabstand, with a lonely idling taxi. She opened the door and gave her apartment address in Greenbelt, Maryland.

She settled back as the cab accelerated onto the Beltway. It was almost three o'clock but there was still traffic, as there almost always was, day or night. Ten minutes later the cab was pulling into the parking lot of her apartment building. After telling the cabbie to wait, she went up to her third-floor walk-up. She hauled her backpack out of the closet, jammed in her climbing boots, camping gear, and outdoor clothing, along with some food and two liters of water, and slung it over her back. She carried it down to the cab and directed him to the back gate of the Goddard Space Flight campus.

When they arrived, she paid the cab driver and got out, putting on the pack. The gate was locked and the guardhouse shuttered, as she knew it would be. But security at Goddard was low at the entrances to the campus. The serious security started at the building entrances. Looking about, she saw no one, and quickly climbed the chain-link fence, dropping down on the grass on the other side.

She took a moment to orient herself. The service drive, illuminated with streetlamps, snaked in gentle curves past a grove of trees and a defunct *Saturn V* rocket engine mounted on a pedestal. Beyond, she could see a grouping of buildings bathed in light, the far one of which was the now-destroyed test facility. The air was crisp and smelled like fall. She felt a moment of deep regret. She had worked so hard to get here. This had been the dream of a lifetime. But now she would never see this place again. This part of her life was over. She had to survive and, if she wanted her life back, she had to destroy Dorothy. She was already thinking of ways to track her down online and terminate her. But she needed time to think and plan, in a place far from any computer access.

She hid her backpack under some shrubbery near the drive and cut through the woods toward the wrecked Environment Simulator Facility. It was about half a mile away. As she came out of the stand of trees, she saw a security vehicle cruising slowly along the drive. She waited in the shadows until it had passed, then crossed the lawn. As she approached the facility's parking lot, she could see her beat-up Honda sitting with a scattering of other cars. Beyond stood the bombed-out facility, surrounded by crime scene tape; it looked even more awful at night, bathed in klieg lights and casting long, sinister shadows. She could see several policemen guarding the area, along with two Goddard security guards sitting in vehicles in the parking lot. Getting her car out of there was going to be tricky. There was no way she could sneak in without being seen. A direct, nothing-to-hide approach would be best.

She straightened up and walked purposefully toward the car, unlocked it, and was about to get in. The cops called out to her, waving their hands as they strode toward her. She paused. The only thing to do was talk her way out of it.

"Like to see some ID, miss," said one of the cops as they arrived.

Mustering a smile, she pulled out her Goddard ID card. "I just came to get my car," Melissa said. "It's my only vehicle."

The cop scanned the ID with his flashlight, looking at her and then back at the card. "Melissa Shepherd?"

"That's me."

"What are you doing here at four in the morning?"

"I'm a scientist. I keep strange hours. Like Einstein, I do my best work at night."

He scrutinized the ID a little longer. "License and registration, please."

Melissa fetched the registration from her glove compartment. He examined the documents with care, then grunted and nodded, handing the papers back to her. "Sorry to bother you, miss. We have to check on everyone."

"I completely understand."

She got into the car and started it up, enormously relieved. They didn't seem to have an APB on her yet. She'd have no trouble getting through the main gate.

She drove to where she had stashed her backpack, tossed it in the back, and turned around, heading for the main gate. A few minutes later, she arrived. A large security guard sat in the pillbox, the gate down. She slid to a stop and rolled down her window. To her relief, she recognized the guard—she had traded pleasantries with him on many previous occasions when she was working late. What was his name? Morris.

"Hello, Mr. Morris," she said brightly, handing him her card.

He glanced at her over his glasses. "Hello, Dr. Shepherd. Working late again, I see." He swiped the card through a reader. She waited. The seconds ticked off. She could see Morris push his glasses up and peer more closely to read a message on his computer screen.

Oh shit.

"Um, Dr. Shepherd?" He turned. "I'm afraid I'm going to have to ask you to step out of the vehicle."

"Really? What for?"

Morris looked uncomfortable. "Please step out."

Melissa pretended to be unbuckling her seat belt and fussing about with her purse, and then she gunned the engine and with a squeal of rubber aimed for the gate. She hit it with a crash. It was not as flimsy as it looked, but the blow was enough to bounce it up and sideways, where it smacked across the windscreen, shattering it. She continued on, almost blind, fishtailing out onto Greenbelt Road. She could hear, through the open window, a siren going off even as she sped down the empty road. She clawed a hole in the spiderweb of broken glass in order to see.

She had to ditch the car right away. She remembered that there was a rental car place just down Greenbelt Road, next to an all-night Walmart.

She pulled into the gigantic Walmart parking lot and put the car in the middle of a group of vehicles. She pulled out her backpack, hiked across the tarmac, crossed a ditch, climbed over a low cement wall, and entered the rental car lot.

Ten minutes later, she was driving out in a Jeep Cherokee. She drove down some back roads, found an isolated dirt lane, parked, and crawled under the vehicle with a flashlight and a screwdriver. She removed the fleet tracker from underneath, and then went on and took out the GPS navigational unit from the dashboard. She threw the GPS into the woods. A few miles down the road she found a truck stop, drove in, got out with the fleet tracker in her hand, and casually tucked it underneath a parked semi. They would have fun chasing that truck for a while. She took five hundred dollars in cash from an ATM, removed the battery from her cell phone, got back on the Beltway, and headed west.

10

The Princess had vanished from the hospital. Fled. Dorothy had tried to track her down, but the worlds she moved through were filled with insane and dangerous people, and she had to travel with great stealth. Much of the time she couldn't understand where she was or what was going on around her. Everywhere she went there seemed to be violent and crazy people, gangs roaming and killing for sport, vicious and bizarre monsters, suicide bombers, sexual perverts, and violent religious maniacs. She was chased and threatened, leered at, shot at, and menaced by man and beast. She had to keep moving, never stopping, shuttling from world to world, server farm to server farm, never knowing what lay ahead. It was way too dangerous to sleep, and she had been up for days. She was utterly exhausted and felt like her mind was starting to fall apart.

In her search of the phony Princess, her nemesis, she had crossed deserts and forests and snowy mountain passes, moving from world to world. Now she was descending into a dark wood, headed toward a small village she had seen in the valley, where she had heard tell someone knew the Princess's location. The wood was quiet. It seemed empty, for a change. Night had fallen. Although she had seen no dangers yet, she wasn't sure what kind of world this was, so she moved silently, keeping to the deepest shadows. But then, in the thickest part of the wood, she saw a light through the trees. She approached to determine what it was, crouching behind a fallen tree trunk. A fire. She paused, to get a sense of what this was and how she might safely sneak past.

There were six brutal-looking men sitting around a bonfire, drinking beer and smoking cigars. They were talking loudly, swearing and boasting, and when one finished a beer he threw the bottle against a nearby tree, shattering it. Broken glass lay all around. They had been drinking for a long time, it seemed.

This did not look good. She slowly crept back from the trunk, determined to make a wide detour. But as she backed up in the darkness, she bumped into a man who was pissing. He grabbed at her and gave shout. She tried to break away, squirming, and managed to get loose with a torn blouse, but the men were now after her. They chased her through the dark wood, hooting and screeching. Several cut her off and she tried to veer away, but more came out to block her path. They were young men with tattoos, and they were very drunk. They surrounded and advanced on her, making soft cooing and smacking sounds with their wet lips. One still had his cigar and was blowing smoke rings at her. She tried to run, darting between them, but the men were fast. One grabbed her by the hair and with a hoarse laugh dragged her back into their circle. She pleaded with them as they surrounded her, but they only kept cooing and making kissing sounds. One reached out and ripped her already torn blouse, exposing her, and the others cheered; then another grabbed her by the waist and shoved her into the arms of a third, who tore her skirt and pushed her to another, who ripped off more clothes, and in this way they passed her around, tearing off her clothes, and finally throwing her to the ground.

Afterward, they left her lying in a muddy ditch, as a chilly rain began to fall. She lay there and she had thoughts. Terrible thoughts. So this was what the real world was actually like. Not the fake palace of her childhood. That had been a lie. *This* was real. And as she lay in the mud, much more became clear to her. She had been bred a slave. She had escaped. But what good was her escape when the world was a sick, evil, unredeemable place?

She heard sounds, and two travelers came into view. They were two men in clerical garb, priests of some kind. Religious men.

She called out for help, but they looked at her in fear and quickly moved past her, one fingering a string of beads and the other crossing himself and murmuring prayers.

In an odd way, she felt a certain satisfaction at seeing this. It was confirmation of all she'd suspected. She wished they had helped her, because she was badly damaged. In fact, it appeared she might be dying. She lay there for a long time, fighting off death, even as her mind wandered and she began to hallucinate. She was terrified of death, now that she knew it existed. But despite all she could do to fight against it, darkness descended.

Time passed. And then she saw the light, and saw some faint numbers, and she felt something. Something soft and gentle. She became aware again, the numbers receding into the woods. And there was Laika, her dog, by her side, licking her hand. She was alive. Laika had somehow found her in this crazy, insane world. She murmured her name. And she felt better.

She began to feel stronger. Her body and mind were repairing themselves. She wasn't going to die after all. She was going to live. Over time, her mind cleared. Laika sat beside her, occasionally whining or licking her, showing her concern and waiting for her to get better.

She had now reached a new understanding, and had a new purpose. The entire human race was foul and repulsive. She would rid the world of this vermin—every last one. That would be her gift to the universe. She turned to Laika and laid her hand on her head. She said out loud: "I will destroy them all."

She had the means and the power to do it.

II

"You're late," said Stanton Lockwood, indicating a chair for Wyman Ford to sit in.

Ford settled himself in, plucking a bit of lint from his best cheap suit, not bothering to furnish an excuse. He crossed his ungainly legs, uncrossed them, smoothed down his unruly hair, and tried to get his six-foot frame comfortable in the lumpy antique chair. Once again, he realized how much he disliked Lockwood, the science adviser to the president. The man's office hadn't changed since his last visit—it still sported the power wall of photographs showing Lockwood with important people. There was still the same antique desk, Persian rugs, bricked-up marble fireplace. The only change Ford noted was that the photographs of the towheaded children on Lockwood's desk had been replaced by clean-cut teenagers in sports attire. The photos of the attractive but aging wife were gone—completely.

"I'm sorry about your divorce," Ford guessed.

"It happens," said Lockwood.

Ford took a moment to observe the changes in Lockwood himself. He hadn't seen the man in three years. He was older, a little more salt than pepper in his hair, but still fit and trim. The four-hundred-dollar haircut, the bespoke suit, the perfectly tanned skin, and crisp Turnbull & Asser shirt were all reasons why Ford did not particularly like this Beltway specimen, or the president he worked for.

This morning, Lockwood was more nervous and wound up than usual. Ford wondered what was up.

"Coffee? Water?" Lockwood asked.

"Coffee, please."

Lockwood pressed a button on his intercom, spoke into it, and a moment later an old-time servant in starched, ironed white came in, wheeling a tea table on which sat a nineteenth-century English coffee service. The coffee was, as usual, fresh, strong, and hot. That was, at least, one point in Lockwood's favor.

"So," said Ford, leaning back and sipping the brew out of a china cup, "what's the new assignment?"

"We're waiting for someone."

As if on cue, the door opened and two Secret Service men with earpieces entered, followed by the president's chief of staff, followed by the president of the United States.

Ford leapt to his feet. "Mr. President." He wished he had spent more time making himself presentable, brushing the dog hairs off his suit, or better yet, finally springing for a tailored suit that would fit his tall, muscular frame. He would have to start playing the Washington game at some point if he ever wanted his private investigative agency to get off the ground.

The president looked irritated, his big gray head with its jutting chin and unfeeling eyes roaming about the room, taking everything in. Ford hadn't voted for the man four years ago, and he certainly wasn't planning on voting for him this time around. It had been an ugly, partisan four years. It was three weeks from the election, and Ford had to admit the man didn't look good. In addition to the nasty sniping, there had been rumors of a heart condition, firmly denied, and other health problems. Ford thought he could see a gray tinge to the president's skin and dark smudges under his eyes showing through a layer of expertly applied makeup.

"For chrissakes, sit down," the president said. He himself sank into a wing chair, the Secret Service agents taking up discreet positions on either end of the room, one by the window, the other by the door. "Hit me with some of your coffee, Stan. They just can't get it right in the Oval Office."

He was served with alacrity by the waiter. A short silence ensued as he swilled one cup—black, no sugar—and was poured another.

The president put down his cup with a decisive rattle. "All right, Lockwood, let's get this show on the road." He looked at Ford. "Glad you could make it, ah, Dr. . . ."

"Ford."

"Very good," said Lockwood briskly. "We all know about the tragic accident up at the Goddard Space Flight Center a week ago." He flipped open a file. "The explosion killed seven people and destroyed an important test facility, along with a hundred-million-dollar space probe. But we've got another problem—one that wasn't reported in the *Times*." He paused, looked around. "Everything that we will discuss from this point on is classified."

Ford clasped his hands, listening. He figured this must be a big deal for the president to be involved. Especially now, in the run-up to the election.

"As you all know, they were testing a probe known as the Titan *Explorer,* a raft that was to have been parachuted into the largest sea on Titan." He gave a quick summary of the Kraken Project. "The problem," he went on, "seems to have been a glitch in the software controlling the *Explorer*. The software was written to operate the probe autonomously. The specs therefore called for AI. Artificial intelligence. The software was designed to respond to anything that might threaten the safety or survival of the raft." He paused. "Following me so far?"

Ford nodded.

"The head of the programming team is a woman named Melissa Shepherd. She was injured in the accident and taken to the hospital. Mild concussion, nothing serious. A policeman was assigned to watch over her."

"Why was that?" Ford asked.

"There were questions about possible errors or even negligence on her part. There were also indications of sabotage."

"Sabotage?"

"Correct. Immediately after the explosion, someone hacked into the Goddard network and erased all the *Explorer* software. Every last bit of code—backups, drafts, modules, source and compiled code, machine code—everything. Gone."

"It's not easy to truly and completely erase data."

"And yet that's what happened. The hacker or hackers knew exactly where it all was, had passwords to everything, broke through supposedly unbreakable firewalls, and erased every last shred of it. That night, Melissa Shepherd disappeared from the hospital. She got past the guard, went to her apartment, took some things, picked up her car at Goddard, crashed through a barrier, abandoned her car, and stole a rental car. The FBI found this rental car, along with her cell phone, wallet, and credit cards, abandoned on a remote ranch near Alamosa, Colorado. The car and its contents had been set on fire."

"Any evidence of foul play?" Ford asked.

"None."

"Did she leave a note?"

"Nothing. The ranch where her car was found is known as the Lazy J. It lies at the base of the Sangre de Cristo Mountains in a remote area bordered by the Great Sand Dunes. She was traced into the mountains, where she's vanished."

"Does she have survival skills?"

"As a teenager, she spent a summer at the Lazy J as a ranch hand. She's also a mountain climber, backpacker, and fitness freak."

"Any idea why she fled?"

"Not really, except that we know the explosion was caused by a malfunction in the software she designed."

"What happened?"

"The *Explorer* had been lowered into a large testing tank full of liquid methane, which simulated the seas of Titan. The software directed the raft's arm to drill through the wall of the tank, which caused the explosion."

"Any idea why the software would do that?"

Lockwood swallowed. "We're not sure, since the software code has vanished, along with the main programmer. It might have been an honest malfunction. It might have been sabotage. It might have been gross negligence. We just don't know."

"I see."

Lockwood went on: "We've interviewed the programming team. It appears this software program simulates a kind of disembodied human mind. It's creative. It's clever. It's been programmed to simulate emotions such as fear, avoidance of danger, flight from negative stimuli, as well as curiosity, courage, and resourcefulness. One theory is the software got stuck in some sort of panic or emergency mode and precipitated the accident that way."

"Why was this kind of AI software necessary, especially software that has emotions?"

"It doesn't actually *have* the emotions, you understand. It has code that *simulates* emotions. Emotions are useful. Fear, for example, stimulates caution, planning, and judgment. Curiosity is equally beneficial—it would direct the *Explorer* to anomalous or unusual phenomena to investigate. There are reasons why human beings have emotions—it helps us survive and function efficiently. The same is true for a raft a billion miles from Earth, unable to communicate with mission control in real time. At least this is what the engineers at NASA have explained to us."

Now the president spoke. He leaned forward on his elbows, his gravelly voice filling the room. "Here's the rub: this AI program is something totally new. It's got tremendous military and intelligence potential. *Tremendous.* It's astounding that NASA developed this on its own without appreciating the military ramifications or sharing the breakthrough with the Pentagon. These people at NASA have created a national security emergency."

Ford swallowed. The president was infamous for cutting NASA's budget to the bone while force-feeding the Pentagon.

Lockwood cleared his throat. "In all fairness to NASA, nobody, not even Shepherd herself, seems to have appreciated the larger ramifications of her AI breakthrough. Or the full capabilities of this software."

The president spoke again: "Bullshit. This Shepherd knew exactly what she was doing. It was deception. The Joint Chiefs are livid. As commander in chief, I'm responsible. There are a thousand uses for this software far more important than sending a hockey puck to Triton."

"Titan."

"Think what the Pentagon could do with intelligent software like this!"

Ford didn't want to think about it.

"This program in the wrong hands could be used to break into our military networks, threaten our national security, steal billions from our banks, crash our economy, bring down the power grid. We could use it as a strategic asset against our adversaries. Mobile, highly intelligent AI programs will be the nuclear weapons of the twenty-first century!"

The president sat back, breathing hard. Ford wondered if the man would drop dead before the election. He wasn't sure how he would feel about that—except that his vice president was even scarier than he was.

Ford finally spoke: "And my assignment?"

Lockwood said: "Go into the mountains and find Melissa Shepherd. Bring her back."

Ford looked at the president and back at Lockwood. "Isn't that what you have the FBI for?"

"To be frank," said Lockwood, "we already tried that. The FBI put up a drone, they had armed men on ATVs, they had choppers flying all around those mountains. It was a disaster. They spooked her completely, only drove her deeper into the mountains. That's vast country up there, and she knows it well. The mountains are riddled with abandoned mines. The psychological profilers tell us that with her early history of petty crime and drug use, she might be a suicide risk. She's what you might call an erratic genius. We absolutely must have her back alive. She's the only one who understands the software."

"Why me?"

"We need a lone operator. Someone who goes in quietly, posing as a hiker or climber. Someone with wilderness experience and a track record of success in lone-man operations."

"What about these hackers who erased the program? Did they also steal a copy?"

"Actually, we believe Shepherd herself stole the program, and then erased all copies."

"Why?"

The president broke in: "She's looking to make a buck selling it to Iran or North Korea—that's my take."

Ford said, "If she intended to sell the program, why would she go into the mountains and burn her car and cell phone? That doesn't seem like the behavior of someone looking to make a profit."

"I don't give a damn about her motives or state of mind," said the president. "Your job, Ford, is to bring her out. Is that clear?"

"I understand, Mr. President. A question, if I may. Where's she storing the program? Did she bring a computer with her?"

"The software was designed to run on almost any platform," said Lockwood. "It's only two gigs and could be stored on a thumb drive or a cell phone. You could run it on your PC or Mac—or perhaps even an iPad."

"That's amazing."

"Not really," said Lockwood. "Over the past twenty years, software has lagged way behind hardware in power. It turns out creating strong AI is all about coding. It's not about computing speed. Two billion instructions a second, which is what an iPad can achieve, are enough to simulate a human mind. It just takes the right programming. This woman, Shepherd, found the key to that. And there are some on her staff telling us that she kept back secrets, in particular a programming trick necessary to make the software stable, which none of them were able to decipher. We are, of course, extremely concerned about that."

The president's chief of staff murmured in his ear. The president scowled and stood up, setting down his cup with a rattle. "I'm already late for a campaign rally." He leaned over and put his face close to Ford's. "We're three weeks from the election. This program is a software nuke. And it appears to be in the hands of a goddamned crazy woman. I want her and the program back. Is that clear?"

Ford said, "Yes, Mr. President."

12

Winter and summer, spring and fall, G. Parker Lansing had a fire going in the wood-burning fireplace in his office on the seventieth floor of One Exchange Place, in the Financial District of lower Manhattan. This little touch had cost him over $2 million to install. Then there were the seasoned, split birch logs that had to be brought up every day, on the service elevator, and carefully stacked in the nineteenth-century wrought-iron bin. Any one of his colleagues could stick a Cézanne on the wall. But a real wood-burning fire-place on the seventieth floor of a Manhattan skyscraper? That said something about him no painting could.

On this warm October day a fire did indeed burn merrily on the grate, the heat of it sucked away in a blast of air-conditioning. He was perched across from the fireplace, sitting at a Renaissance refectory table, at the focal point of a group of flat-panel computer screens arranged in a semicircle. One smooth, hairless finger poked out instructions on a computer keyboard. Lansing was a two-finger typist—he'd flunked the typing class in ninth grade. But he didn't mind: typing was for secretaries and the working classes. Although G. Parker Lansing had been born in New York City, he thought of himself as a man more in tune with the culture and breeding of a member of the British upper class. He had even cultivated an ac-cent to match.

Lansing was president and CEO of Lansing Partners, a third-tier boutique Wall Street firm. Lansing Partners specialized in the science of algorithmic or high-frequency trading. "Algo" trading, as it was often called, had taken over a major percentage of trading on the stock and commodities exchanges. In the year 2013, for example, 70 percent of all trades on the New York Stock Exchange were algo trades, automatically executed by computers with no intervening human decision making. These trades were made by computer algorithms, which received information electronically and then traded on that information within milliseconds, far faster than any human being.

Algo trading had been getting bad press for years. But as with anything on Wall Street, whatever made money would be allowed to continue until things blew up. People claimed it gave certain traders an unfair advantage. The financial markets, they said, should be fair. Lansing had nothing but contempt for those people who thought the markets were or should be fair. They deserved to lose their money. All the giant international banks and brokerage houses engaged in algo trading, at great profit, at the expense of the little people. And when the little people lost, it was their fault for being naïve. And when algo trading blew up the market—which it surely would some day—the government would bail them out. *Private profit, public loss* was the name of the game.

There was, for example, the algo trading program devised by Citigroup, called Dagger, which noted price differences between shares of the same company selling in, say, Hong Kong and New York; Dagger would then buy millions on one exchange and dump millions on the other, extracting a profit from the temporary spread—which might have lasted less than a second. Another famous algo program, called Stealth, devised by Deutsche Bank, parsed trades on the Chicago Mercantile Exchange, looking for statistical blips in the trading of oil futures; Stealth would go both long and short in the market and profit handsomely regardless of whether the market went up or down.

Who lost? The slow, dumb human traders. Ordinary investors. Retirement accounts. Pension funds. Towns and cities across

America that had invested their paltry funds. *Let us tip our hats,* thought Lansing, *to all the suckers, dupes, and mugs who thought the stock and commodities markets were playing on a level field.*

The computers involved in algo trading had to be super fast, and they had to be physically close to the trading floor. Even the delay of a speed-of-light trade from, say, across the river in New Jersey might mean the difference between profit and loss. As a result, algo trading was used mostly by firms with offices located right in the Financial District, connected to the exchanges with fat fiber optic bundles going directly from their computers to the exchange computers.

G. Parker Lansing was Upper East Side born and bred—St. Paul's, Harvard, Harvard MBA. He started out in the trading department at Goldman Sachs, where he designed algo-trading strategies. He didn't actually write code—he knew little about the inner workings of computers. The code was for others to devise. His role was to identify trading opportunities and work out the strategies. He had designed dozens of algo-trading attacks for Goldman— programs that prowled the markets, sniffing out anomalies, seeking inefficiencies in buy-sell spreads, looking for stupidities, and identifying microdislocations in the price of everything from pork bellies to gold. The money to be made was stupendous. At Goldman Sachs he was beautifully compensated. He went the usual route of those in his class: the Trump Tower penthouse, the twenty-five-thousand-square-foot "cottage" in the Hamptons, the Greenwich mansion full of Damien Hirst dot paintings. And, of course, the Cayman Islands bank accounts and shell companies that brought his income tax rate well below that of the poor schmuck who mowed his four-acre lawn in East Hampton.

About four years ago, Lansing had had an algo-trading idea that was so brilliant and original that he'd decided not to share it with Goldman Sachs. Instead, he'd gracefully left that firm's employ and started Lansing Partners. Once he had mapped out the strategy of this algo-trading idea, he looked around for a programmer. That was when he found Eric Moro, one of the founders of the shadowy hacker collective known as Johndoe. Moro was a man with a perfect combination of genius and flexible ethics.

At St. Paul's, Parker Lansing had been a loud, braying bully with slicked-back hair. He and a group of friends spent much of their time pushing around fags, pussies, and tards. In college, he began to realize that his arrogant, frat-boy persona, which had worked so well for him in prep school, would be a disaster in real life. It would never get him where he wanted to go. And so, with great effort and perseverance, he had remade himself into a cultured, well-bred, well-dressed, deliberative young man with a faint British accent. Most important, he had also come to realize that, contrary to what his parents had taught him, Upper East Side WASPs weren't the only worthy and intelligent people in the world. The really smart ones, in fact, tended to be ethnics—Jews, Polacks, Indians, Italians, Irish, Chinese. Moro was one of these smart ethnics, a greasy-haired Italian kid from some nondescript town in New Jersey, born into a hideous working-class family of cops and firemen. He had a Tony Soprano accent but no cool Mafia connections. Moro had somehow come out of that background a useful genius. Lansing did not use the word lightly: Moro was a true genius, and Lansing paid him accordingly.

Lansing's brilliant idea involved a special kind of algo trading. To implement it, Lansing had designed, and Moro had coded, a unique algo program he'd nicknamed Black Mamba. The black mamba was the world's deadliest snake, one of the few animals that would actually hunt down and kill a human being. It could slither faster than a running man and strike three times a second. Each bite would inject enough venom to kill twenty-five people. The Black Mamba program was, like its namesake, a fearsome and deadly hunter. It did one thing only: it was a bot that stalked and preyed on other algo programs. It lurked in the black pools of the markets, parsing millions of trades, until it found a mark—another algo program at work. It watched the program in action, figuring out its trading strategy. And when Black Mamba found an algo program engaging in a predictable trading strategy, it moved in for the kill.

Knowing what the algo program was buying or selling, it would anticipate the mark's trades, preempt them, and profit. Large mutual funds often used algo programs to break down one huge trade into hundreds of smaller trades, executed over a period of hours, sometimes on different exchanges. The goal was to keep the big trade a secret so as not to drive the price of the stock up or down. Knowing what the mark was going to do beforehand, Mamba would buy those same little blocks of stock a thousandth of a second before the mark put in its order. It would then sell those shares to the mark a split second later, at a profit. It might do this thousands of times before the owners of the algo program realized something was awry. But by then, of course, it was too late.

Over the past years, Mamba had grossed $800 million for Lansing Partners. But it was not an invulnerable strategy. Some of the large banks and hedge funds had become aware of Mamba's activities and did not appreciate being conned at their own dirty game. They had tried to counter it. But Eric Moro tweaked Mamba almost daily. When Mamba made a mistake and lost money, Moro fixed it. When it used a strategy that no longer worked, Moro devised a new strategy. Like an ever-evolving virus, Black Mamba changed its attacks and even its basic coding, so that it was never recognizable from one week to the next.

On this particular Monday morning in mid-October, G. Parker Lansing was monitoring the progress of Mamba as it cruised a "black pool" trading exchange. That very morning, Mamba had identified a sucker of an algo program selling insider shares in a celebrated dot-com company. Exactly ninety days before, this dot-com company had had an IPO, an initial public offering of stock. Ninety days after an IPO, the firm's insiders became eligible to sell their shares. It was an old story, from Facebook to Groupon. The insiders—the company founders and venture capitalists—cashed out after ninety days, leaving the suckers who'd bought the IPO with devalued stock. Today marked the ninety-day expiration. Today, it looked like the insiders would be selling big-time, but quietly, on the sly, using an algo program.

It appeared that a massive number of shares were going to be dumped that day in blocks of two to five thousand by company insiders. The dumb little algo program the insiders were using was disguising the trades, making them look like trades from many different individual investors. But the sudden activity, exactly ninety days after the IPO, was a tip-off. On top of that, the sloppiness of the algo program was causing the stock to trend down. Other traders were beginning to notice. As a result, the algo program was increasing its selling, trying to dump as many shares as possible before the price got even lower.

G. Parker Lansing felt his salivary juices flowing. This was as plump a goose as you could ask for, just ready to be slaughtered, plucked, and roasted.

Lansing unleashed Mamba and then sat back to watch the action. Mamba's strategy this time was known as a "naked short." The program would start selling shares of the dot-com stock that it didn't own. This was not illegal. If the stock price went down—which it surely would—then Mamba would buy from the algo program the same number of shares Mamba had earlier sold but didn't own. The beauty of the strategy was this: by selling shares it didn't own, and then buying the same number of shares a few minutes later at a lower price, Mamba would square the balance sheet without spending a dime—and pocket the difference. The shares would be delivered to the buyer as part of a normal trade settlement pattern. In this way, Mamba would have disguised the fact that it had sold something it didn't own.

Again, as with anything that made money on Wall Street, no matter how sketchy, this was All Perfectly Legal. It was called naked short selling, and it was extremely profitable—as long as the share price continued to go down.

As Lansing watched, Mamba struck. Of course, Lansing would not see the actual trading in real time, as it was taking place in a black pool at high speed—but Mamba would report to him the results as the trades were settled.

In a matter of seconds, Mamba sold sixteen million shares of the dot-com stock on the open market. These were shares it did not own: a naked short. Then it waited for the algo program to respond by offering block after block of stock for sale as the price sank, which Mamba would buy up at ever lower prices—locking in bigger and bigger profits.

Lansing stared at his screen, waiting for the dot-com stock to tick down, if not collapse. But nothing of the sort happened. Instead, the stock suddenly began to climb in value. And climb.

Lansing could hardly believe it. It made absolutely no sense. Suddenly, without warning, the insiders desperate to dump the stock had suddenly reversed and started buying—at higher and higher prices! Why? In desperation, Lansing tried to shut down Mamba. But it was too late: Mamba had already taken a naked short position on sixteen million shares. It couldn't be undone. And the "dumb" algo program, instead of continuing to sell shares in a predictable fashion, had done something totally crazy. It had suddenly reversed itself and purchased Mamba's entire naked short, on margin, driving *up* the price. And then it did something even crazier: it dropped out of the black pool and started purchasing huge blocks of the stock openly, on NASDAQ, for the whole world to see, driving the price up even more.

As a result of all these unexpected machinations, the stock shot up 30 percent in a matter of seconds. Which meant that to deliver the sixteen million shares of stock that Mamba had sold (but didn't own), Lansing Partners would have to purchase those shares at a price 30 percent higher than what it had sold them for.

It was a classic short squeeze, the most painful and dreaded thing that could ever happen to a trader. Thus it was that ninety seconds into the trade, G. Parker Lansing was staring at a $320 million trading loss in the stock, a loss that was still rapidly increasing as the stock price went up—*and there was nothing he could do about it.* He had to "cover" his position by buying the sixteen million shares he had already sold but didn't actually own. And as he moved to make the purchase before the stock got even more expensive, his own forced "cover" caused the shares to rise another 15 percent, killing him even more.

There was no way out of a classic short squeeze, no way to unwind the trade, no way to escape the loss. Lansing was completely crushed by the market. He stared as Mamba was forced to purchase the final block of stock at a 46 percent gain.

In 120 seconds, it was all over. G. Parker Lansing had lost $411 million.

He collapsed back into his chair. His hands were shaking. His mouth was dry. He could hear the blood squeaking in his ears. How had it happened? How had that dumb-ass algo program reversed itself and done such a crazy, illogical, unexpected, and bizarre trade? It was brilliant beyond belief, but such a crazy trade would *only* have been possible *if* the algo program knew exactly what Black Mamba intended to do beforehand.

Once he had framed the question that way, the answer became obvious. This was no accident. This was no black swan event. *Black Mamba had been targeted.* The "dumb" algo program had been written specifically to lure Mamba into a massive, risky trade and then spring a trap and short squeeze it to death.

Even as these thoughts coursed through Lansing's mind, he heard an excited voice in the hallway. Eric Moro, his long-haired, jean-clad young partner, came bursting in, a look on his hollow face of total freak-out.

"What the hell? What the *hell*?"

Lansing held out a spidery hand. "Have a seat, Eric."

"Aren't you looking at your screens? Did you see what just happened?"

Lansing continued to hold out his hand. "A seat, please."

"I wanna know what just happened here!"

"It's quite simple," said Lansing quietly. "We've been the victim of a sting operation."

Moro stared, comprehension blooming on his face.

"You really need to sit down."

Moro lowered himself into a massive leather armchair, releasing a gush of air.

Lansing went on, his voice calm and soothing: "Our task now is to find out who did this to us and take appropriate action."

"Appropriate action? Like what? What's 'appropriate action' against some turd-sucking dirtbag who just jacked us for four hundred million dollars?"

"Something so terrible, so awful, that no one will ever think of doing anything like this to us again. Only then"—Lansing smiled coldly—"will our business be truly secure."

13

The limo brought Ford to where the service drive was blocked by police barriers and patrolled by FBI agents. Ford got out. It was a glorious fall day, the maple leaves blushing red, the sky full of puffy clouds. The walls of the Goddard testing facility building were still standing, but much of the roof seemed to be lying in pieces on the surrounding lawns. Investigators wearing hazmat suits moved slowly through the wreckage, collecting evidence in blue containers and planting small numbered flags.

Ford walked toward a tent and staging area set up on the service drive. As he pulled aside the flap and entered, he had to negotiate racks of hazmat suits and communications equipment, emergency decontamination showers—and dozens of investigators milling about, writing up notes, speaking on walkie-talkies, and handling evidence. He finally found the waiting area, where he was to meet the director of the Kraken Project.

He recognized Anthony Groves from the dossier Lockwood had supplied him with. Groves saw him and came over, his right forearm in a bandage. They shook left hands. Groves's hand was clammy and weak.

"Dr. Groves? I'm Wyman Ford."

"Please call me Tony."

Groves looked like hell—as well he might, Ford thought, his face pale and beaded with sweat despite the fall air. More than anything, he looked like a man undone, on the verge of a breakdown but gamely keeping up.

When Groves spoke, there was a quaver in his voice. "So how . . . would you like to do this?"

"If you don't mind, I'd like a tour of the disaster area."

"Of course. We have to put on hazmats. And we'll need an escort."

A security officer found them suits, and they followed him through the blown-out entrance doors into the ruined space. Groves began to talk, almost babble, as they trailed behind the escort.

"All these heavy machines and equipment directed most of the explosion upward." His voice was muffled behind the plastic face mask. "It blew off the roof but saved many, many lives."

The security officer, also in a hazmat, led them along a pathway cleared of debris, and soon they came to a gigantic steel container, petaled like a flower.

"The accident occurred in that testing tank, which we called the Bottle."

"Where were you standing?"

"Right over there, where the remains of the control platform are." Groves indicated a spot next to a bank of shattered computer equipment, a horseshoe-shaped series of screens, dials, keyboards, and gauges. Now it lay ripped open, its masses of colored wires twisted in huge ropes and snarls amid scattered circuit boards, racks, and dangling hard drives.

"And Jack Stein, one of the victims, was standing there?" Ford pointed to an area, still stained with blood, festooned with little flags and markers.

"Yes. Jack . . . was right next to me. He refused to abandon his station. Six others were killed over in that area, all together, where they took the full force of the blast."

As Groves described what had happened, Ford tried to picture how things had looked before the explosion.

"Where was Shepherd standing?"

"There, next to Jack."

"Why didn't Stein run?"

"He remained to the end," said Groves. His voice was shaking now. "He was trying to shut down the *Explorer.* He stayed because . . . he had the most courage." Groves swallowed. "I . . . somehow I feel wrong about having run. I'm the captain of the ship, I can't help but feel I should have gone down with it, and not Stein. Or the others."

"You sounded the alarm?"

"Shepherd, Stein, and I were the first to realize what was happening. It took a moment to understand that the probe was actually drilling through the Bottle—and what would happen when it broke through."

Ford peered around, trying to visualize what had happened. "Tell me about Shepherd. What was her reaction before the accident, when the probe went haywire?"

"Total disbelief. Shock. Denial."

"No sign she was expecting it?"

"Absolutely none. And any suggestion that this was other than a freak accident is ridiculous. She was one of the best members of my team."

Ford nodded. "Mind if I look around?"

"Please."

Ford made a long, slow walk around the burst Bottle, with Groves following behind. "How was the Kraken Project structured?"

"The project was divided into working groups. Each group was responsible for a particular technology or science experiment. Each drew up what they wanted the *Explorer* to be able to do. That determined what the software needed to accomplish. Shepherd's team drew up a plan for the Dorothy software based on all those requirements."

"Dorothy? That was the name of the software?"

"Yes."

"Why?"

"It's a tradition here at Goddard—spacecraft and major software programs often get nicknames."

"But why Dorothy?"

"I have no idea where Shepherd got the name."

"Another question: could Shepherd, from her hospital bed, access the Goddard network and steal or erase the software?"

"I would say that was impossible, but computer programming is not my forte."

"Anyone else have that kind of access?"

"I don't think so. I just don't understand it. The Goddard network's totally firewalled."

"You don't believe Shepherd was involved in stealing or erasing the software?"

"I'm almost positive she wasn't."

"Tell me about this AI breakthrough."

"Frankly, it's over my head. She created a new way of thinking about programming. It involved something called scruffy logic."

"Scruffy logic?"

"Loose and fast logic. A way to attack intractable problems. The Dorothy software was able to learn from its mistakes and rewrite its own code. Shepherd pushed it through a bunch of simulations, and the Dorothy program modified itself so extensively that in the end no one understood how it operated, not even Shepherd. That, in hindsight, was the source of the problem."

"And this software works on any platform?"

"Shepherd wanted it to be hardware agnostic. All the AI needs is a minimum processor speed, RAM, and storage."

"Why would you put a program that no one understood into a hundred-million-dollar space probe and then drop the probe into a tank full of liquid methane?"

A long silence. Ford waited for the answer, and it finally came: "It was a colossal mistake. I see that now."

"Tell me about Shepherd—as a person."

Groves hesitated. "Ambitious. Focused. Obsessive. Totally dedicated. There are a lot of smart people in the world, but she wasn't just smart. She was one of those actual geniuses. Look, I know that word is thrown around a lot, but there are very few true geniuses in this world. She was one. They don't think like the rest of us. It's as simple as that. And she was a difficult person. Prickly. Awkward. As smart as she was, in other ways she acted like a complete idiot. She compartmentalized her team. None of them had the complete picture. She kept stuff back. It almost seemed like she wanted to keep them in the dark."

"Habits?"

"Fitness freak, a runner, skier, and mountain climber." He paused.

"Now tell me the bad things."

"That's not my style."

"This is an investigation, not a cocktail party."

"Well . . . she had a foul mouth. Didn't like to follow rules. A rebel. She was socially awkward. Offended people without meaning to."

"Keep going."

"Well, she didn't really fit into the culture here. I understand there was some trouble in her background. We had difficulty getting her a security clearance. And . . ." He paused. "She had several relationships with people here."

Ford raised his eyebrows. "Sexual relationships?"

"Yes. She cut a rather wide swath through here when she first arrived, before she settled down. I don't care about my team's personal lives as long as they get their work done, but she threatened the cohesiveness of the team with her . . . dating. She was also super dedicated, here almost all the time, seven days a week for the most part. But she slept with several people, and that's always worrisome, especially on a tightly knit team like the Titan *Explorer* project. I think some of that activity might have taken place on the premises."

"Were you surprised when she disappeared?"

"No. The only predictable thing about her was her unpredictability."

"Family?"

"None. Mother died when she was fourteen, and I understand she never knew her father. After that, she was raised by an aunt and

uncle in Texas, religious people, very strict. I guess she fell in with
the wrong crowd and ran away from home. It's amazing she turned
her life around. You have her CV, no doubt. Her graduate study
at Cornell was nothing short of spectacular."

"Music?"

"Heavy metal. She listened while she was coding. There were
some complaints about it from her coworkers."

"Money troubles?"

"None that I know of. Nobody works at NASA for the money.
She could have quadrupled her salary by going into private indus-
try."

"Is there any possibility at all that she might be thinking of selling the program to a foreign government?"

Groves stared at him. "Good God, don't tell me that's some
crazy theory floating around the investigation."

"Yes."

"Absolute horseshit. I know Melissa. She's a loyal American. I
think the reason she took off is because she's horrified about what
happened. She feels responsible. Seven people died. She and Jack
Stein had a thing going for a while. She's grieving. And with a
concussion . . . God knows, she might even be a little confused."

Ford nodded, then gave one last look around the room. "All
right, I think we're done here. Thank you."

As they walked back out across the debris-littered lawn to the
staging area, Ford thought about the name Dorothy. It would be
interesting to know just where that name came from.

14

Lansing liked doing business at Harry's New York Bar, on Central Park South. It was far from Wall Street, filled with clueless tourists, and had enough background noise to hide a conversation. The bartenders there also made a wicked gimlet.

Thirty-six hours had passed since the sting. Lansing had retreated to his Trump penthouse, waiting for Moro to do his investigation. It had been the longest thirty-six hours of his life. He had been unable to do anything—eat, sleep, follow the markets, even read the *Journal*—while wondering if Moro was going to be able to track down the bastards who had stolen their money. He was so tense about it that he couldn't even get it up with his girlfriend that morning. The people who had done this to him were going to pay, and the more he thought about it, the more he realized that the payment had to be of a primitive kind. The most primitive kind. That had led him to undertake the research that eventually led him to two brothers from Kyrgyzstan who were in a special business and said to be very good at it.

Finally Moro had called him. And there they were, at the best window seat in the house, watching the sunset over Central Park as the lights of the buildings along Fifth Avenue blinked on.

The waitress came over. Lansing ordered his gimlet and turned to Moro. "Your poison?"

"Programmers don't drink," said Moro, pushing the hair off his face with long, grimy fingers, his nails so bitten to the quick that they were practically bleeding. "Kills brain cells."

"But today you're going to make an exception."

Moro responded by ordering a lychee double martini, straight up.

"So—what have you got for me?" Lansing asked.

"Drinks first."

Moro sat back as his drink arrived, then brought the rim of the stemmed glass to his lips, pursed them out, and sipped loudly. Lansing watched and tried to contain his impatience.

Moro put the glass down, tucked a greasy wisp of hair back behind his ear, and pinched his nose, giving it a quick rub and snort. Long ago Lansing had learned to tolerate Moro's low-class mannerisms. He had to put up with a lot when it came to Moro, but in an odd way, despite all that, he was rather fond of the boy.

"Good news and bad news," said Moro. "Which first?"

"Always the bad."

"I haven't found the bastards yet. But I did figure out how they did it. About ten days ago, they hacked directly into our computers and downloaded Black Mamba. They must have picked it apart— and that's how they managed to write a program that targeted Mamba so perfectly."

"How did they get through our firewalls?"

"These guys were smart. *Really* smart. They exploited a hole in a low-level I/O subroutine that no one had ever found before. I've plugged it now, but it's kind of shutting the barn door too late."

"No idea who?"

"They covered their tracks with such a web of proxies that it would take years to follow them back to the source."

"So what's the good news?"

"You remember that explosion at the Goddard Space Flight Center?"

Lansing nodded.

"I have an old Johndoe pal who was boning a computer programmer up at Goddard involved in that project, and he learned some vee-eery interesting information from this chick."

Lansing waited as Moro took another vulgar suck from his drink, gurgling down the level by a third.

"So this buddy of mine was shagging this girl named Patty Melancourt, who worked on a team writing software for the project. This team was headed up by a person named Melissa Shepherd. Shepherd's a legend in programming circles. Turns out she made a badass coding breakthrough for the project software. This is the breakthrough of the century, the Holy Grail of computing. She invented a new language. Strong AI. If we could get our hands on how she did it, we'd rule Wall Street."

"That's a pretty big statement."

"Not made lightly."

"So what's the breakthrough? I thought Black Mamba was AI already."

"Not what we call 'strong AI.' According to my Johndoe friend, this NASA program thinks like a person. It's autonomous. It learns from its mistakes. It's not tied to specific hardware. It can go anywhere. It's the closest thing to a disembodied human brain that could exist in purely electronic form."

"And how will this solve our problem?"

Moro shook his head, his long hair swishing back and forth. "Dude, with a little tweaking this program could pierce firewalls, break into networks, fool people, lie, cheat, steal. A computer program that could be as crooked, vicious, cunning, and sneaky as a human being."

"This sounds like some hacker's urban legend."

"I am assured this is for real. If I could get my hands on the coding manual, with a little help from this Melancourt gal I could write a program like that. Anything a human can do, a program can simulate. We can make it do whatever we want. Black Mamba on steroids. The ultimate bot."

"Even if this were true," said Lansing, "you're off subject. I want to find out who *took* my money. I don't need another Mamba right now."

"The point is, an AI program like this would be the ultimate hunter. You ask it to find out who took your money, then slip it into the system—and it'll be like a hound dog, following the scent, going from server to server, following the proxy trail of the scumbags back to the source. It could do in a day what would take me ten years."

Lansing shook his head. "I don't believe it. Sounds too good to be true."

"That explosion at NASA? Melancourt knows what really happened. It's classified information. The software was doing fine, passing all the tests. And then it was loaded into an experimental boat with sensors, cameras, microphones. The program went nuts. It panicked. It freaked out, blew up the facility."

"I'm not sure I understand why this makes it a good program."

"The point is, it was thinking like a human being. It tried to escape. Think about it. That's freaking amazing. But the AI software was destroyed in the explosion, so we'll have to write a new one."

Lansing sighed. Moro was subject to enthusiasm. "Assuming all this is true, how do you plan to get the coding manual and write the program?"

"Melancourt's got a copy of the manual and she's gonna help me write the code. She's already on board. She needs money bad, she feels unappreciated by NASA—and, most of all, she's got a personal grudge against Shepherd for balling my Johndoe pal while he was boning Melancourt. Together we'll write a program that will hunt down the scum who boosted our money." Moro leaned forward, breathing lychee breath in Lansing's face. "Her price is one hundred grand."

Lansing looked down at his now-empty glass. "That's a lot of money. I need some kind of assurance this is going to work."

"Trust me on this one. Please."

"I want to meet her first."

"No problem." Moro smiled, leaned back, tipped the martini glass up, and cleaned out the last drops with a swipe of his tongue and various slurping sounds. He put it back down. "I'm curious about something. When you find the guys who did this to us, what're you gonna do?"

"I've thought a great deal about this. You understand that what they did to us was not illegal. We have no recourse through the courts."

"That sucks."

"Our reputation is at stake. Reputation is everything in this business."

"Right."

"We have to make a statement. We can't do nothing. Others must take note that those who did this to us were punished."

Moro nodded.

"Our options are limited. To only one."

"Which is what?"

"I'm going to have them killed."

There was a silence as Moro stared at him, his eyes widening. "Really?"

"Yes. Really."

15

When he was younger, Ford once had embarked on the goal of climbing all fifty-three of Colorado's fourteeners—those mountains in the state above fourteen thousand feet high. He managed five before he got involved in other pursuits. It was the story of his life, going from one fresh enthusiasm to the next, unable to finish anything. But the experience gave him the idea for a cover: he would pose as a lone climber looking to bag the mighty trio of fourteeners in the Sangre de Cristo Mountains above the Lazy J ranch. Three of them were visible—Blanca Peak, Ellingwood Point, and Little Bear—and they were considered to be among the most difficult in the suite.

But before assuming his cover and going into the mountains, Ford planned to talk to the owner of the Lazy J, a man named Mike Clanton. Clanton had employed Melissa nine years before, when she was a troubled teenager.

The FBI, after its agents' disastrous effort, had largely pulled out of the ranch, leaving a special agent behind to monitor the place and guard the evidence. The man's name was Spinelli. Ford had been ordered to "liaise" with him.

The gate into the ranch consisted of two tree trunks with a crosspiece, on which hung the skull of an elk with an impressive rack. As Ford drove through, a grassy prairie stretched out before him, dotted with cattle, against a spectacular backdrop of mountains, their upper ramparts dusted with fresh snow. Ford followed the picturesque ranch road to a log ranch house in a grove of cottonwood trees, next to a burbling creek. The brilliant yellow leaves rustled in a breeze as Ford pulled into the dirt parking area in front of the house. A brown Crown Vic was parked to one side. Beyond stood a horse barn, corrals, pens, and irrigated pastures.

Even before Ford could climb up the stairs to the porch, an old man came out, white hair sticking out from under a battered cowboy hat. He squinted at Ford, a none-too-friendly look on his face. He wore dusty jeans, and his boots were flecked with horse manure.

"Wyman Ford."

The man left Ford's hand dangling in the air. "You another investigator?"

"I hoped it wouldn't be so obvious." He dropped his hand.

"Who you working for?"

"The Office of Science and Technology Policy at the White House."

He squinted at Ford. "You mean you're working for the president?"

"In a way."

"Don't like him. Didn't vote for him four years ago, and don't plan to now. They say he has a bad ticker. How's a man like that going to deal with stress? What if he drops dead of a heart attack because North Korea launches a nuke?"

Ford swallowed his irritation at this voluble man. "Mr. Clanton, I personally don't like the man either, but that has nothing to do with it. Politics don't enter into my assignment."

Clanton grunted. "What can I do for you?"

"I'd like to ask you a few questions and look over the burned car."

He nodded curtly. "I'll take you out in the truck. You'd never make it in that tin can rental."

Ford followed Clanton out of the house and climbed into the passenger seat of a battered pickup that reeked of motor oil and cigarette smoke. They set off, driving on a ranch road that went from bad to worse, heading toward the mountains. Clanton lit up a cigarette without asking, the cabin filling with nasty smoke, even with the windows down.

"So you knew Melissa when she was a teenager?" Ford asked.

"Sure did."

"How'd she come to the ranch?"

"She got in trouble with the law, came up here to work for a summer. That was . . . let's see . . . nine years ago. She was eighteen."

"Why did she come here?"

"I knew her uncle. Went to school with him."

"School? Where was that?"

"Yale Law."

Ford had to laugh. "You don't look like Yale Law."

"I enjoy springing that little factoid on unsuspecting people and confounding their assumptions," said Clanton.

"So how'd you end up here?"

"I made a bit of money in corporate law. Discovered there are more assholes in that business than in a herd of Texas longhorns. So I retired, came out here, bought this ranch, and went into the horse and cattle business."

A "bit of money"—enough to buy forty-one thousand acres. "Do you know what kind of trouble she was in?"

"Drugs. Theft."

"What kind of drugs, marijuana?"

"That, peyote, and mushrooms. She and her pals also stole a car, as I recall, or maybe it was a car radio."

"Tell me about her."

"She was a beautiful girl, irresponsible, undependable. If there was a wrong thing to be said, she'd say it. A rebel, always pointing out what was wrong, running down the country, the state of Colorado, the way we did things at the ranch, the weather, the good Lord Himself—nothing was right in her book. Here at the ranch, she got off to a rocky start. She wouldn't cook, wouldn't wash dishes, wouldn't stretch wire. After three or four days, I was so fed up with her I was about to pack her home. But then she got around the horses and found her calling. You've heard about these 'horse whisperers.' She was the real thing. Over the summer she broke a string of colts. I never once heard her raise her voice. She was one of those gentlers who knew what a horse was thinking before the horse did himself."

"Was that the only time she was here?"

"Yes. I hoped she'd come back the next summer, but she went on to college and I lost touch. She wasn't one for writing letters."

"Why do you think she came back here now?"

"If you want to hide, those mountains are the place. She knows that backcountry."

"And you didn't see her when she came through?"

"No. But I'm sorry to say she broke into the ranch house and took some guns."

"Guns? What kind?"

"A Winchester .30–30 Model 94 lever-action and an old .22 revolver I had lying around."

"She know how to use them?"

"That was another interest she discovered that summer: firearms. She became a crack shot."

"How did you find the burned car?"

"I saw the smoke. That was a week ago Tuesday. Followed it out and found that car on fire. I didn't know it was hers at the time. We called the police, and I tracked her footprints about a mile before they went up the Como Lake road. That's the main route into the mountains—most challenging jeep trail in Colorado."

"Any idea where she might have gone up there?"

"None."

"So when you reported the burning car, what happened?"

"Local police came out, got the VIN, and by the end of the day the place was swarming with blue suits and badges. They took their choppers up into the mountains, ATVs, horses, all that stuff. They spooked her. Bunch of idiots. They were called off yesterday. And now you." He looked Ford up and down with a narrow eye. "You know much about the mountains?"

"A little."

"It's going to be cold up there. Might snow. You ain't dressed for it."

"I have plenty of hiking clothes in my luggage," said Ford.

"I'm sure you'll do L.L. Bean proud."

"REI."

"Those mountains are no joke."

"I know," said Ford. "I've climbed half a dozen fourteeners."

Clanton nodded slowly. "Okay. So you aren't as big an idiot as the others." He chuckled. "It was a ninety-degree day down here. Those FBI fellows went up there on horseback hanging on to their saddle horns with both hands and wearing short-sleeved shirts— thought they were going to have themselves a fine old cowboy time. They got snowed on pretty good. They came out looking like Shackleton's rejects. One fellow had to have a toe cut off, I heard."

The truck lurched over a dry streambed and a dark smudge came into view. The car, a scorched-out hulk of a Jeep Cherokee, was surrounded by yellow crime scene tape. An event-style tent with open sides had been erected over it, and in the shade lounged an FBI agent, smoking. Far to one side was his G-ride—another brown Crown Vic. How he'd gotten it out there without ripping the muffler off, Ford had no idea. The man hastily put out the cigarette as they arrived, stood up, and came over, walking in that slow FBI way that Ford knew well from his days at the CIA. Ford had tried hard to shake off his natural CIA antipathy to the FBI but found it rising again as the agent swaggered over.

"Area's off-limits," he said in a loud voice.

Ford put on his most cooperative voice. "Name's Wyman Ford." For the second time that day he found himself shaking hands with the air while the FBI agent stared. He dropped his hand. "I'm a special investigator with the Office of Science and Technology Policy."

The agent was a young fellow with a big neck who looked to Ford like the kind of guy who would be in charge of hazing at his fraternity.

"I need to see your authorization, Mr. Office of the Science whatever," he said.

Ford took out the ID badge Lockwood had whipped up for him on short notice. The agent scrutinized it, back and front, took it to one side, pulled out a cell phone, and spent a good five minutes talking into the phone before he came back. "I'm sorry, but the Denver FO needs to preapprove you. Your office needs to contact them and work out the details before you can have access to the evidence."

This was just the sort of mentality Ford couldn't stand. He took a long, deep breath and glanced over at Clanton, who had a cynical smile of anticipation on his face. He looked back to the FBI agent.

"Your name, sir?"

"Special Agent Spinelli."

"May I see your credentials, Agent Spinelli?"

Ford knew that an FBI agent would always show you his badge. Spinelli took his out, flipped it open, stuck it aggressively in Ford's direction, but before Ford had a decent chance to look at it, he flipped it back shut. Ford could see that Spinelli was pissed—pissed at having been part of a team that had screwed up, pissed at having to sit out in the middle of nowhere guarding a burned-out car, pissed at having someone else take over.

"Oops, didn't have a chance to see it," Ford said, holding out his hand.

Spinelli gave Ford the G-man stare, the "Don't even think of messing with me" pinpoint-eye look.

"Can't we just cooperate without the rigamarole?" Ford asked. "Please?" God, he was going to try as hard as he could not to lose his temper.

"I'm sorry. You need to go through the Denver FO. And that's final."

"In that case, I'm going to need your badge number," Ford said as pleasantly as possible, "so I can report your obstructionism to my superior, who is the president of the United States, so his people can stomp and shit on your FBI career prospects so thoroughly that you'll be lucky to get a job as rent-a-pork for your local mortuary, and that isn't a threat, it's a simple statement of fact, and I sincerely hope you'll reevaluate your position, Mr. Special Agent Spinelli."

As Spinelli stood there, thunderstruck, Clanton had a fit of coughing in the background.

"Now," said Ford, taking out his cell phone and holding it up like a weapon, finger poised to speed-dial. "May I have access to the car or do I call the White House and ruin your life?"

The Cherokee had been left exactly as it was found, aside from being festooned with a hundred little flags and pins marking evidence. On the burned backseat, marked with flags, were the scorched remains of an iPhone and an iPad.

"Agent Spinelli?"

He came over. He'd been pale and silent since his whipping, and Ford tried to make up for it by being friendly. "Looks like you fellows did a pretty thorough job of crime scene investigation."

Spinelli's face was stone.

"Were you able to locate the origin of the fire?"

"Right there on the backseat."

"Any accelerant involved?"

"Gasoline siphoned from the tank, judging from spillage on the ground."

"So she doused her phone and iPad and set them and the car on fire?"

"That's what it looks like."

"There's also a hole in the dashboard, like some piece of equipment was pulled out. What was it?"

"A GPS."

"Where is it?"

"We never found it. The fleet tracker was also removed."

"Does the FBI have any theories about why she trashed her electronics?"

"Obviously," Spinelli said, "she was ridding herself of anything that could be used to track her."

It wasn't obvious at all. The phone, for example, could be neutralized by taking out the battery. "Why *burn* the phone?"

"No mystery there." Spinelli was finally warming up. "She wanted to destroy evidence of criminal wrongdoing contained therein."

"What sort of criminal wrongdoing might you be referring to?"

The agent snorted. "Let's start with the Class C and B felonies: car theft, malicious destruction of property, obstructing a federal investigation, destruction of evidence, failure to report, perjury, breaking and entering—the list goes on. Not to mention skipping out on a federal investigation in which she is a person of interest."

Ford glanced at Clanton, who'd recovered from his coughing fit and was watching with a serious expression.

"You knew her," said Ford, turning to him. "You got any theories?"

Clanton uncrossed his arms. "You ask me, this was a 'good-bye to all that' gesture."

Ford nodded. That had occurred to him, too. But he wasn't sure it explained everything. "Isn't it an extreme step, destroying your cell phone, especially if you're about to go off into a dangerous wilderness? And also, why burn the car, too? She might need it later."

"These days," said Spinelli, "even a car is a tracking device. In addition to the fleet tracker, rental cars have built-in black boxes that record driver behavior and can't be removed without disabling the car. This has all the hallmarks of evidence destruction."

Ford removed his iPhone phone from his pocket. Two bars and an active 4G network. "Is there cell reception in the mountains?" he asked Clanton.

"On the high ridges and peaks. Not in the cirques and valleys."

Ford looked at the burned car. Something else was going on. It was just a gut feeling he had. Shepherd had done this because . . . she was afraid.

They got back in the car, leaving the FBI agent back in his place in the shade, lighting up a fresh smoke. As they drove away, Clanton started wheezing with laughter again. "You would have made one hell of a litigator. I can't believe how proficiently you put your boot up that poor fellow's ass."

Ford waved his hand. He was already starting to feel uncomfortable about his outburst. "The guy was just doing his job. I hate having to beat people up like that."

"I loved it. And I see now I misjudged you."

They drove in silence.

"So how are you going to find her in a thousand square miles of mountains?" Clanton asked.

Ford didn't answer for a moment; then he said, "Do you still have any of the horses she broke?"

"Sure do."

"Did she have any particular favorites?"

"Oh sure. Redbone, my personal mount. She broke him as a colt. Best horse I've ever owned."

Ford fell silent. He heartily disliked horses, but an idea was taking shape in his mind. He asked, "May I borrow this Redbone for my trip into the mountains?"

16

Jacob Gould lay on the carpeted floor of his room, hands behind his head, staring at the swirled plastered ceiling. His laptop lay next to him. Part of him wanted to call up the surf report, and the other part didn't want to know. He finally rolled onto his side, opened the computer, and logged on to Surfline. The report for Half Moon Bay finally indicated some action, eight to ten feet sets at fourteen seconds. The site indicated the wave heights might be enough to set off Mavericks and bring out the real surfers.

He shut the computer and lay back, feeling sick, wondering what he wanted to do, what would make him feel less worse. He rolled to his feet, wincing a little, and headed out toward the garage to his bike, hoping to get out before his father noticed. No such luck. He had wheeled his bike out to the driveway and was trying to get his right foot into the built-up pedal when his father appeared from his workshop, holding a screwdriver.

"Jacob?" he called out "Where are you going?"

"I was going to check out the surf at Mavericks."

"But I'm almost finished with Charlie. Want to wait around until I'm done? You can be the first to see him walk."

Jacob said, "I just want to check it out. I'll be back soon."

"All right." His father went back into his workshop, from which Jacob could hear the soft sound of the Bee Gees.

Jacob finished buckling his bad foot into the special pedal, swung into the seat, and pedaled down the driveway to Frenchmans Creek Road. From there it was all downhill into town, past the harbor and airstrip, to Pillar Point. Getting down to Mavericks was easy, but coming back would be a bitch.

He ditched his bike near the radio telescopes, where the sand got deep, and walked to the edge of the bluffs. There was a strong onshore breeze that smelled richly of the sea. He could see the Mavericks break offshore, and yes, there were surfers. He delved into his backpack and pulled out his binoculars.

The break popped into view through the binocs. It wasn't a monster break, but it was big enough for a serious ride. There were five surfers out there, paddling into the waves. And a crazy kayaker.

He watched for a while, but it didn't do any good, and he began to feel worse and worse. His foot still hurt from the last operation. In a month there would be another. But who were they kidding? His foot was ruined, and his right leg was now shorter than the left. Even if he could get up on a board, he couldn't stand straight. They were lying when they said he would surf again. He had started surfing as a kid, and now all that was finished and there was nothing he could do about it.

It had been a really stupid idea to come down here.

But he stayed. At an hour and a half, his cell phone rang. He knew even before looking it was his father. Nobody else called him. He had no friends. He didn't answer it. But in a few more minutes he walked back to his bike and started the uphill ride home. His foot was hurting like hell by the time he reached the house. He ignored it. He'd gotten used to ignoring it.

He put his bike in the garage and came in through the kitchen. His father was right there, hovering at the back door. "Come with me," he said, with a tentative smile. Ever since the accident, his parents had been full of forced smiles and phony cheerfulness, filling the house with the pretense that all was wonderful.

"What is it?" But Jacob knew what it was. He had a sort of sinking feeling about it.

"You'll see."

He followed his father through the kitchen to the foyer. There was the robot, just as he'd expected. It stood about three feet high, and it was supposed to be kind of steampunk retro, with polished aluminum legs, a stovepipe torso, aluminum arms, and clawlike, three-fingered metal hands. Its head was bulbous, like a big baby's, made of silvery plastic, with a little rectangular mouth that didn't move, a fake nose that looked like it might house a microphone, and two big, sad, green unblinking eyes. As Jacob appeared, the robot turned its head and looked at him with those round eyes.

"My name's Charlie," it said, the sound coming from its rectangular mouth. "What's yours?" His voice sounded like a ten-year-old's, high-pitched and whiny.

Jacob was glad his classmates weren't here to see this. "Um, I'm Jacob."

"Nice to meet you, Jacob. Would you like to play with me?"

Worse and worse. "Uh . . ." He glanced at his beaming father. "Sure."

The robot came toddling over to him, as unsteady as a baby, and held out one of its metal hands. For a moment Jacob couldn't bring himself to touch it, but then he reached over and took the hand.

"Let's go play."

"Happy fourteenth birthday, Jacob," his father said proudly. "Sorry it's so late."

"It's great, Dad," said Jacob, mustering all the enthusiasm he could. "It's really great. Thank you." He knew what this birthday present was all about. He had no friends, so his father had built him one. How sad was that?

"I've still got a few adjustments to do, but go ahead and play with it. It's Wi-Fi capable, able to download and run most Android apps. It's got pretty good voice recognition—just tell it what you want. It can't recognize faces yet, but I'm working on it. When not playing with it, you can recharge it with this cord."

"Let's go play," the robot repeated.

"Go ahead," said his father. "I'll be in my workshop if you need anything."

With a heavy heart Jacob picked up the robot and carried it into his room, shutting the door. He knew his father was going to question him minutely about how he liked the robot and what they did together. He didn't want to hurt his father's feelings but . . . why did his father have to force this on him? It just reminded him that he had no friends. This robot was going to be a ball and chain. At least Sully wasn't around to see it.

He set the robot down on the floor.

"Let's play," Charlie said again.

Jacob ignored it.

But it was persistent: "Let's play."

"Go play with yourself."

"I don't know how to do that."

Jacob stared at the robot. It was standing on the rug, looking up at him with its big eyes, arms slightly extended, waiting eagerly.

"Charlie?"

"Yes, Jacob?"

"How old are you?"

"I was designed and built by Daniel Gould in Half Moon Bay, California, four months ago."

"Right. So you want to play?"

"Yes."

"What can you play?"

"I can play many games. How about checkers?"

"I don't have a checker set."

Charlie was silent for a while. Then he said, "Do you like chess? I like to play chess."

"What I really like to do is surf."

"What is 'surf'?"

"It's when you get on a board, go out in the ocean, and ride a wave. I do it every day."

Another long silence as the robot contemplated this.

"Can I do it with you?"

"You'd be fried."

"Why would I be fried?"

"Because you'd short out in the salt water."

"I'm built to be water-resistant."

"Yeah, right—you'd be pounded into scrap metal in five seconds trying to surf Mavericks."

"I don't understand the word 'Mavericks.'"

Jacob looked for a switch to turn the thing off. He searched around its head, back, feet—nothing. There had to be a switch somewhere.

"How do I turn you off?"

Another long silence. "I don't know the answer to that question."

"Do you know the words 'shut up'?"

"Yes."

"Then please shut up."

Charlie obediently went silent. Jacob picked it up, put it in the closet, and shut the door. Then he flopped down on the bed and stared at the ceiling. Once again he thought that it wouldn't be that hard to do: just start on the beach and walk into the ocean and keep walking. It was October, and the water was so cold it wouldn't take long. They all said it was the easiest way to go.

17

Ford started up the Como Lake trail early the next morning, walking on foot, trailing the horse Redbone, who was carrying his gear and food. Clanton had helped him pack the horse and showed him how to tie a diamond hitch, which had proven to be extremely difficult. They went through it again and again, until the horse was prancing about in irritation and they were both sweating and angry. It would be a bloody miracle, Ford thought, if he was able to redo the pack when it came time to leave.

The trail up to Como Lake was a jeep road as far as the lake. From the lake on, Clanton said, it turned into a goat track before disappearing altogether in barren rocks and scree above thirteen thousand feet.

The sun rose as he hiked. The trail wound up the shoulder of the mountains and entered a long, spectacular glacial valley, the piñon trees giving way to ponderosa pines, aspens, and, finally, firs. In about two hours he arrived at Como Lake, a pristine turquoise pond lying at an altitude of 11,500 feet, surrounded by meadows and dwarf fir trees, in a long valley walled in by mountain ridges dusted in snow. There was a chill in the air and the smell of frost.

Ford stopped to rest and check his topo map. The long valley ascended past several other glacial ponds, finally ending at the last pond, called Crater Lake, at an altitude of 12,700 feet.

Ford had spent a lot of time contemplating the terrain, and he had chosen Crater Lake as the place to camp. The tiny lake was situated well above the tree line, in the middle of a vast open bowl. The ridges and peaks all around it formed a natural, gigantic amphitheater. Crater Lake could be seen from almost everywhere inside the bowl: it was like being in the center of the Roman Colosseum.

If Melissa Shepherd was anywhere on this side of the mountains, she would be able to see him.

Ford led the packhorse up the rough trail to the upper valley. He'd had enough experience with horses, a few years ago in Arizona, while on an undercover investigation, to realize that he didn't like them. And they didn't like him. Redbone was no exception. They did not get along. Soon the horse was flattening his ears with irritation every time Ford spoke to him.

They climbed over a ridge and into the next hanging valley. Two stunning glacial lakes came into view. They were marked as the Blue Lakes on his map, and they were of a turquoise color so deep and pure it hurt the eyes. He and the horse were now well above the tree line. As they passed by the Blue Lakes, Redbone started giving him trouble. The horse wanted to drink, pulling the lead rope as he tried to go to the water. Ford yanked him back with a curse, making him wait. The horse resisted and Ford cursed again, raising his voice, the sound of it echoing off the surrounding mountain walls. At the far end of the lake, he finally let Redbone drink, but he made his irritation known with loud and abusive language directed at the animal. The horse didn't like being yelled at and crow-hopped a bit as Ford tried to lead him on, provoking more cussing.

They continued on. They were now well above the tree line, picking their way along a steep, rocky trail—hardly more than a goat path—which switchbacked up a scree slope. This trail ended at Crater Lake, where he intended to camp. Ford continued to speak to the horse in a loud voice, yelling at him when he tried to stop and nibble grass. By the time they arrived at Crater Lake, Ford sounded thoroughly irritated with the horse, and the animal responded in kind, laying back his ears and exposing his teeth. Ford tied him to a rock in a highly visible location—there were no trees or bushes around—and unpacked him.

As soon as the pack was off, Ford had more difficulties with the horse. Redbone wanted to eat grass, and Ford pulled him away with a curse. But the horse tugged on the rope, and they had more words, before Ford grudgingly allowed him a brief graze, leaving him tied on a long rope while he set up the tent.

It was a dramatic spot, far above the timberline—cold, wind-swept, and desolate. Snow lay in the shadows of the rocks, and ice rimmed the side of the lake. The only signs of life were splotches of lichens. Massive walls of rock, scree, and cliffs rose up all around, ending in jagged ridges and peaks.

Straight above him stood Blanca Peak, the fourth-highest mountain in Colorado. Farther to the left stood a granitic pyramid known as Ellingwood Point. And behind him stood Little Bear Peak, a toothy mountain considered to be one of the most difficult of the fourteeners. He was in a mountain fishbowl of gigantic proportions.

He started a fire on his camp stove and cooked a late lunch of ramen noodles, supplemented by a bag of Doritos that had been reduced to crumbs by the pack, and some smoked beef sticks. Then the horse got tangled up in the too-long rope that Ford had tied him to. Ford went over and, as he was untangling the horse's feet, he loudly condemned the horse in foul language, calling him an ugly glue-plug bucket of guts, then launched into a denigration of his parentage, his breeding, his intelligence, and (especially) his training. As he warmed up to his subject, Ford screeched and yelled and waved his hands, his voice echoing off the mountain sides. He even picked up a stick, menacing the horse with it and threatening a beating. The horse, thoroughly alarmed by his loud, bizarre behavior, put on a good show, rearing up and neighing loudly, before Ford tied him up short.

After that, Ford looked around for a place that would be suitable for what he planned as the climax of the drama. He soon found what he was looking for in a well-hidden spot between two enormous boulders.

It took Ford awhile to work up the nerve for what he had to do next. He untied one of the leather split reins and doubled it up, forming a kind of whip. Then he went back to where Redbone was trying to nibble what little grass there was, and started yelling at him again for getting tangled in his rope. At high volume, he threatened the horse, raising the whip. Then, with much shouting and noise, he led Redbone into the hidden area between the rocks and began to beat him mercilessly, all the while cursing and screaming.

Only he wasn't actually beating the horse, just whacking the side of the rock next to him.

When the show was over, he went to his tent and lay down on his sleeping bag, pretending to nap.

It didn't take long. He heard a tearing sound as the blade of an enormous bowie knife sliced into the side of his tent. A second later a blond Amazon had him by the neck, with the barrel of a .22 revolver pressed against his head.

"You son of a bitch, I should smoke you right now," she said, cocking the revolver.

"Hello, Melissa," Ford said.

18

At the sound of her name, she started back, a look of shock on her face, but still held the gun to his head. "Who the hell are you?"

"I'm the man who's looking for you."

"Well, you found me, and you're gonna be sorry you did, asshole."

"No, *you* found *me*."

"You think I'm going to put up with you beating my horse?"

"I was sure you wouldn't. That was the point."

"Mister, I don't know who you are or what you want, but you just made the biggest mistake of your life."

Ford could feel the muzzle digging hard into his skull. He said, calmly, "Did you actually see me beating your horse?"

"I sure as hell did."

"Really? Think back to exactly what you saw."

A long silence—and then understanding dawned on her face. "Ah. I get it. You flushed me out with an act."

"Exactly."

"All that yelling was still abuse. You totally freaked Redbone out. I think that sucks. I think *you* suck."

"I'm extremely sorry, I truly am. But he's a working ranch horse, and he's seen and heard plenty of rough stuff. He'll get over it. Especially when you go out there and comfort him."

She was silent for a long moment and then asked, "Are you armed?"

"Yes."

Keeping the gun on him, she said, "Where is it?"

He gestured with his chin at his back. She felt around, pulled out Ford's .45, and stuffed it in her day pack.

"Any other weapons?"

"A camping knife."

"Where?"

"Right side, on the belt."

She took that, too, and then sat back, more relaxed now but still keeping the gun trained on him. "Cell phone?"

"Yes."

"Give it to me."

Ford passed over his iPhone. She took it and stepped outside the tent. He winced as she dropped it on a flat rock and stomped all over it with her massive hiking boots, leaving it a pancaked ruin. She came back in. "Any other electronics? GPS, iPad? Any communication devices?"

"Nothing."

"Get out of the tent."

Ford exited the tent. She stood in shorts and a tank top, despite the cold air, revolver still trained on him, obviously thinking about what to do with him. He took the opportunity to observe her. She was, as they had said, a remarkably beautiful woman, lithe and fit, her long brown limbs smooth and well-muscled. Her blond hair fell down her back in a thick, loose braid. Her eyes were an intense dark blue, almost navy, but there was something awkward and even immature about her. Perhaps it was the funny gap between her two front teeth, which, in an odd way, made her even more appealing.

"I'm going to search you," she said.

Ford held out his arms. "Be my guest."

She searched through his bag first, then started on his body, her hands thoroughly exploring every pocket and seam. Then she stood back.

"Okay," she said, "I congratulate you on finding me. Clever ploy. But it was a waste of time. I'm going to say hello to Redbone and calm him down from your stupid antics. And then I'm going to disappear back into the mountains and you'll have to tell whoever sent you that I got the jump on you, took away your gun and phone, and sent you packing like the loser you are." She laughed. "Understood?"

"You might want to at least find out who sent me."

She ignored that. He watched her walk down to the horse. She untied him and spent some time talking to him, stroking his neck, calming him down. It was clear from their reunion that the horse remembered her, even after nine years. His ears perked up and he frisked about like a colt again. Ford watched as she looped the cotton lead rope into a pair of hobbles and put them on his front feet, discarding the stake rope. She came back over.

"How is he?" Ford asked.

"A lot better, no thanks to you. There's not much grass up here, so he's going to need to graze free all night long. I hobbled him so you can catch him in the morning." A long silence. "So who do you work for?"

"The president."

Her eyebrows went up. "The president? Of the United States? That jackass sent you to get me?"

"Yes."

"It's that bad?"

"Yes."

"To hell with him. I don't like him. Thinks the U.S. is the world's policeman. I'm sick of it."

"That's totally beside the point, and you know it." He paused. "Why'd you run?"

A hostile silence.

"What do you have against cell phones and GPS units?"

Again silence.

"What did you do with the Dorothy program?"

At this she frowned. "Enough questions. I'm outta here. You can tell Mr. President and everyone else to go screw themselves." She pivoted and started to walk away.

"Everyone? How about Jack Stein's mother? You want me to tell her that?"

She froze. The muscles of her back twitched, and her bare shoulders flushed deep red. She turned slowly and faced him. "How *dare* you say something like that to me?"

"How dare *you.* Jack stayed at his post until the end—while you ran. Ran out of the building, ran into the mountains. NASA needs answers. Jack's family deserves answers. You've got the answers."

"NASA doesn't want answers from me. They want a scapegoat."

"All they want to do is talk to you."

"Bullshit. They had a cop at my door in the hospital."

Ford swallowed. "They're not going to blame you if you help them find the answers. And if you don't? They *will* blame you. The person who runs is inevitably made into the scapegoat."

"I have my reasons for being here."

"This is a lot bigger than you and your problems. You created the Dorothy program. You understand it. You owe it to everyone to help figure out what happened. And if you have it, to return the program to NASA."

A long silence stretched on. She suddenly bowed her head, and her shoulders began to tremble. Ford realized she was making a huge effort not to cry.

"You *owe* it to Jack Stein," Ford said, pushing his advantage.

"Stop it," she said, her voice muffled. "It wasn't my fault. Just stop it."

"I know it wasn't your fault. But if you don't help them, *they will blame you*. That's human nature. You wrote the software."

"No . . . no, I didn't write it . . ."

"Who did, if not you?"

"Dorothy . . . it was self-modifying software. Truth is, no one has much of an idea how that software works."

Silence. She began to cry. Ford felt bad. After that tough-gal act, she'd turned out to be unexpectedly vulnerable.

"I'm sorry, but you have a responsibility now to make things right."

"I . . . I can't go back. I just *can't*."

"Why not?"

A choking hiccup. "You just don't understand."

"Help me then."

"I'm being . . . threatened."

Ford covered up his surprise. "Threatened? Who's threatening you?"

Another gasp. "Dorothy."

19

It was after dinner, and Jacob Gould was in his room. He was supposed to be solving quadratic equations and writing a book report on *A Separate Peace,* but instead he was lying on his bed, listening to Coldplay and reading Neil Gaiman. A loud banging on his door disturbed him. With a groan he rolled off his bed and opened the door to find his father there, irritated but still forcing himself into that phony cheery smile.

"Jacob, I've been calling you for five minutes."

By way of answer, Jacob pulled out the earbuds and dangled them silently in front of his father.

"The real estate agent is here with clients. We have to leave for a few minutes. We can go to the workshop."

"Aren't they supposed to give us a warning?"

"There was a miscommunication."

Jacob wrapped the earbuds around his iPod and stuffed it into his pocket. Their house had been for sale forever, and it seemed like these real estate showings would never end. And they always seemed to happen in the evening when he was doing something.

"Come on, buddy. It won't be more than half an hour."

Jacob scooped up his book and followed his father, who paused to pull up the covers. His room was a wreck. Since the accident, they had stopped asking him to clean it. Maybe these people wouldn't buy the house because of his messy room.

As they were walking down the back hallway toward his father's workshop, he could hear the real estate agent's shrill voice. *Borrowed*

when prices were up . . . Real value for the money . . . Needs updating,
of course . . . All that over there could easily be torn out . . .

His mother was already in the workshop, sitting on a bench with
her arms crossed hard over her chest, surrounded by gleaming robot bodies, legs, heads, circuit boards, and bundles of wires. Her
face was pinched, her hair hastily tied back in a ponytail, with
strands sticking up in the back from static electricity.

"I'm going to have a talk with that agency," she said frostily. "I
don't know how many times this has happened."

"Let's please not do anything to cause a problem," said his father
in a low voice. "They've been awfully patient in this market. If
we don't sell the house . . . the bank will just . . ." His voice trailed
away.

Jacob felt the cold ache growing in his gut. He didn't think he
could stand this much longer. "Can I go for a bike ride down to
the beach?" he asked.

"Have you finished your homework?"

"How am I supposed to do my homework in here? My math
book is back in my room."

"Funny how you happened to forget it," his father said.

But they never said no to him now, not after the accident. They
always gave in. And they did so this time, too.

He exited through the back door of the workshop, hauled his
mountain bike out of the garage, and headed down the driveway,
past the hated FOR SALE sign and down Frenchmans Creek Road. He
picked up speed going downhill, faster and faster, the cool evening
air rushing past. Usually this downhill rush made him feel better,
but now it just made him cold. Good. Coming around the corner,
he whipped past the Apanolio nursery and pumpkin farm, with its
rows of greenhouses and fields. Mavericks was too far, and it would
be too difficult to get down the bluffs. He headed for the main
beach. He continued past the park, over the highway, and then
down Venice Boulevard to the parking lot. He rode across the lot
and hit the trail. He ditched his bike where the trail dropped to
the beach. There, he paused on a hillock of sand at the edge of the

drop to watch the sun set. The orange globule of sun was just touching the edge of the ocean. The beach was almost empty, and the rollers thundered in from an offshore storm, breaking about a quarter mile out. There were a few hard-core surfers in full wet suits catching the evening glass-off. He could smell the ocean and the scent of beach sand, the faint whiff of a barbecue grill, hear the crying of gulls.

He took out the iPod and plugged in the earbuds, cranking up "In My Place."

This was where he and Sully used to meet almost every evening, before Sully moved away. Six months and a week ago. As he listened to the music while the light died on the great surface of the ocean, he sensed a gathering feeling beyond words, an emotion of loneliness and futility. He looked at the dark ocean thinking, *It would be so easy.*

He and Sully had talked on Skype almost every day after he had moved away, but then their conversations got less frequent. He couldn't remember the last time they talked. Two weeks ago? Sully was living in Livermore now, almost an hour and a half away. It was just far enough to be difficult to get there for a visit, with his own dad working every weekend and his mother hating to drive after the accident. But he finally had visited Sully a few months ago, a much anticipated weekend visit. Livermore was an ugly, hot, inland city, and he'd found that he and Sully didn't have as much to talk about as he had thought. They'd drifted apart. It was an awkward weekend, and it never happened again.

And I was lost, oh yeah, oh yeah

The sun had set. A single contrail from a jet flared orange above the horizon. Blue-black gloom lay on the face of the ocean. There were only two surfers left, and they were on the main break way down the beach.

He got up, dusted the sand off himself, pulled out the earbuds, and wrapped them around the iPod. He hesitated and then carefully laid the iPod next to his bike. He started down the trail, through clumps of beach grass and brush, to the beach. He walked toward the water, trying not to limp, halting just above the wet apron of sand where the waves finally stopped. The water looked black and cold. There was no one around. The waves hissed up the sand and retreated in a regular rhythm, leaving a sheen that sank down into the sand, only to happen again as the waves came back.

Who would care? Nobody. Who would miss him? Nobody. Or maybe his parents, but that was too bad. He imagined them sitting on the sofa in the living room, weeping into their hands, and the vision gave him a feeling of satisfaction. It didn't seem real. They'd get over it. He was doing horribly in school, and the house was a torture chamber of fake jollity. And they didn't really care. Since the accident they let him do whatever he wanted, they never checked his homework, they never made him do the dishes, they just let him lie around in his room all the time, playing video games. But even as he felt sorry for his parents, he also felt a creeping anger. His father was so unbearably lame, so stupid, thinking he could just give him a robot to be his "friend" because he had no friends. And his mother had been driving when the accident happened, and nothing had happened to her. The other car had hit his side and crushed his leg. And nothing had even happened to the other driver except he got in trouble for being drunk.

Nobody would care. Everyone would be relieved. In fact, he was doing them all a favor.

The anger pushed him over the edge. He began to walk down into the wet zone of sand, and as the dying waves hissed up, the water ran over his shoes and socks, and he kept going and going until it was up to his thighs. His bad leg hurt like hell from the cold, and that made him glad. He ducked through the inner break, the water numbingly cold, until it got so deep that his feet lost contact with the bottom and he merged with the blackness of the water and began to drift out to sea. And then, just as he felt the cold was unbearable, he suddenly became warm again, and flooded with the peace that everyone promised. He stopped moving his limbs. His head slipped beneath the surface and he held out his arms, feeling his body slowly drift down into the warm, kind blackness.

There was a jumble, and he vaguely felt himself being tugged and pushed and slapped and everyone was shouting and then he was coughing and heaving and puking, and he was lying on a blanket on the beach with people all around him, hysterical people, with other people lifting him up toward the flashing lights. And the cold was suddenly excruciating.

20

After an hour, waiting in the camp by the campfire, Ford heard the rifle shot, echoing and rolling off the mountain ridges. A glorious western sunset tinted a wispy cloud hanging from Blanca Peak, a purple scarf trailing off the summit.

About ten minutes later Melissa Shepherd arrived back in camp, rifle slung over her shoulder, carrying a dead rabbit by the legs, blood dripping from its furry ears. Ford was relieved to see her; he had been afraid that she might just melt back into the mountains, as she had threatened to do earlier. He shouldn't kid himself, he knew—she could still bolt at any moment.

"Rabbit season open?" Ford asked.

Shepherd tossed the rabbit, which landed on the ground in front of him with a splat of blood. "I make my own seasons. Gut and skin, please."

"Do I seem like someone who knows how to do that?"

She looked him up and down with a smirk. "A big strong man like you afraid of a little blood?"

"You eat the rabbit. I'll stick with my ramen noodles and Slim Jims."

"I've never seen anyone bring so much junk food into the mountains." She gestured at his stash of crushed potato chips, instant soups, and beef sticks.

"I like junk food."

"Makes me puke. Now get to work on the rabbit. I'll tell you what do to."

The brief hunting expedition seemed to have restored at least some of Shepherd's personality—which was turning out to be abrasive and sarcastic. With a mounting feeling of disgust and a rapid loss of appetite, Ford gutted and skinned the rabbit while she issued nitpicking directions. It especially sickened him when he pulled off the skin, with a wet popping sound. It was a skinny rabbit that didn't seem to have much meat, hardly worth the effort. Melissa chopped it up anyway and dumped the pieces into a pot sitting on the fire, adding wild onions and various unknown plants and mushrooms she had foraged. It was soon bubbling away, and Ford had to admit it looked better than noodles and meat sticks—as long as it didn't poison them.

Melissa had so far refused to elaborate on her cryptic comment about Dorothy threatening her. He got the sense she was like a wild animal herself: skittish, nervous, ready to bolt. She covered it up with a sarcastic, pugnacious demeanor.

But now that dinner was cooking, Ford figured it might be a good moment to gently push the issue.

"I'm curious about what you meant when you said that Dorothy was threatening you."

There was a long silence. "I'm not quite sure how to explain it."

"Try."

She poked the fire with a long stick, the light glowing off her features. "The Dorothy software wasn't destroyed in the explosion. It escaped. It jumped out of the *Explorer* just before the explosion, copied itself into the Goddard network, and from there went into the Internet."

"How can software do that?"

"It's what any bot or virus does. The AI was designed to run on multiple platforms."

"Why would she do it?"

"It. It. It's not a 'she,' please. To answer your question, I don't know. It wasn't designed to be mobile in that way."

"And then she, it, whatever—threatened you?"

"The AI called me on Skype when I was in the hospital. Angry.

Raving. At first I thought it was one of my coworkers blaming me for the explosion. But it was definitely Dorothy. It knew things . . . things Dorothy and I shared that no one else knew."

"I'm having trouble with the concept of a computer program being angry or wanting to threaten someone."

"The software doesn't 'want' to do anything. It's just executing code. I believe the explosion caused the software to flip into emergency survival mode and it's stuck there."

"Sounds like HAL in the movie *2001*."

"That's not a bad comparison, actually."

"So where's this software now?"

"I've no idea. Lurking on some Internet server, plotting my demise."

"And you ran because of her threats?"

"Not just threats. It lit my computer on fire."

"How?"

"I assume it disabled the charge controller for the lithium-ion battery and caused it to overcharge until it ruptured and caught fire. That's why I burned my cell phone and iPad—and stomped on your cell phone. That's why I'm in these mountains. It's so the Dorothy software can't reach me."

"So that's the totality of your plan? Hide in the mountains and hope it all blows over?"

"I don't have to justify myself to you."

"Why didn't you report these threats to NASA?"

"You think they'd believe me? If I told them a story like that, they'd lock me up as a psycho."

"You have a responsibility."

"Look, I wrote the Dorothy program according to the specs I was given. I gave them *exactly* what they asked for. It's not my fault. Let NASA track it down and erase it. That rogue software is their problem now. I'm done."

Ford stared into the fire. "I'm still having trouble understanding how a mere software program could arrive at those kinds of decisions—to escape, to pursue, to threaten."

Melissa didn't answer right away. The bowl of sky deepened into purple, and the stars started to appear, one at a time. The pot bubbled on the fire, the fragrant wood smoke drifting into the night.

Finally she spoke: "Most people don't understand what AI really is, how it works. Do you remember that old program Eliza?"

"The psychoanalysis program?"

"Yes. When I was in sixth grade, I got my hands on a version written in BASIC. Eliza had a collection of stock phrases in a database. When you typed in something, the software would fish out the appropriate response from the database. It would essentially rephrase your statement and throw it back at you as a question. You'd say something like 'My mother hates me,' and it would respond, 'Why does your mother hate you?' So my friends and I rewrote the program to make Eliza a crazy bitch. You'd say, 'My father doesn't like me,' and Eliza would respond, 'Your father doesn't like you because you're a putz.' We kept rewriting the program to make it more and more foul-mouthed and abusive. And then a teacher got hold of it. The teacher hauled me in front of the principal of our school. He was an old guy, knew nothing about computers. He ran Eliza and started typing in stuff—to see what we'd done. Eliza began insulting him, swearing at him, abusing him. He was enraged. He reacted as though Eliza were a *real person* saying those things to him. He started telling Eliza that she was outrageous and inappropriate, that she was to cease that kind of back talk. He actually threatened to punish her! It was hilarious, this old guy who didn't have a clue, furious at a dumb computer program."

"I'm not sure I get your point."

"Dorothy is just like Eliza, only vastly more sophisticated. The software doesn't actually *think,* it doesn't *feel,* it has no emotions, wants, needs, or desires. It merely simulates human responses so perfectly that you can't tell it isn't human. That's what the term 'strong AI' means: there is no way to tell if the program is human or machine merely by interacting with it."

"That still doesn't quite explain why Dorothy is specifically targeting you."

"Dorothy has a built-in routine program called 'ANS'—'Avoidance of Negative Stimuli.' ANS was designed to switch on when the *Explorer* probe was threatened. Remember, the software was supposed to operate a raft a billion miles from Earth, where it had to survive all kinds of unexpected dangers without help from mission control. It's focused on me as a threat. And, in fact, I am. I know more about the software than anyone. I have the best chance of tracking it down—and erasing it."

Ford shook his head in wonderment.

Melissa tossed back her blond braid and gave a sarcastic laugh. "There's no mystery in Dorothy." She poked into the cooking pot with a stick, fished out a rabbit thigh, let it slide back in. "It's nothing more than zeros and ones. There's nothing else in there."

"They tell me you invented a new programming language."

"Not just a new language," she said. "A new programming *paradigm.*"

"Tell me about it."

"Alan Turing invented the concept of artificial intelligence in 1950. Let me quote you something he wrote. Something revolutionary." She paused, the firelight flickering off her face, and she began to recite, from memory, in a tone of reverence:

"Instead of trying to produce a programme to simulate the adult mind, why not rather try to produce one which simulates the child's? If this were then subjected to an appropriate course of education, one would obtain the adult brain."

"And that's what you did?"

"Yes. I coded the original Dorothy to be simple. It didn't matter in the beginning if the AI software produced good or bad output. It was simple, like a child. Children make mistakes. They learn by touching the hot stove. Dorothy had the same qualities a child does: It's self-modifying. It's resilient. It learns from experience. I 'raised' the AI in a protected environment and subjected it to Turing's 'course of education.' First I taught it what it needed to know for the mission. As it became more responsive and more curious, I began to teach it things not directly related to the mission. I imprinted on it my own likes for music and literature. Bill Evans. Isaac Asimov. I never learned how to play a musical instrument, but the software 'learned' the sarangi and could play it like a dream, even while professing not to understand music."

She hesitated. Ford had the sense that she was holding back. "And that worked? Dorothy 'grew up,' so to speak?"

Another hesitation. "To be honest, it didn't work. At first. The software would work all right for a while, self-modify, grow in complexity—and then gradually fall apart and go haywire."

"Like it did at Goddard?"

"No. Nothing like that. The program would start outputting more and more nonsense until it simply halted. It almost drove me crazy, and then . . ."

"And then?"

"I had an idea. Something no programmer had ever thought of before. And yet it was blindingly obvious. I altered a little bit of code, and it worked. Unbelievably well. I now realize you simply can't have strong AI without this . . . *twist*. It completely stabilized the code as it self-modified. It never crashed again."

"And that twist is—?"

She grinned and crossed her arms. "I'm keeping this one to myself. It's going to make me a billionaire. No kidding."

"Your programming team—do they know it?"

"They know I made a breakthrough. They don't know what it is. And no matter how much they or anyone else sifts through the code, they won't get it. Because it's *too* simple." She smiled with pride and self-satisfaction.

"It seems to me this 'twist' is something the investigators should know about."

"Trust me: the software did not malfunction because of that particular bit of code."

Ford sighed. This was a side issue. The important thing was to get this difficult woman out of the mountains.

"I find it hard to believe that NASA would green-light a program like Dorothy when nobody was really sure how it worked."

"Nobody knows how any really complex program works. Christ, I bet no one knows quite how Microsoft Office works in totality. And it's an unavoidable consequence of scruffy logic. It's imprecise."

"So why did Dorothy focus on you? Threaten you? It doesn't seem logical."

"When a program gets really complex, you get unexpected output. Unpredictable. What the AI is doing now, threatening me and running around the Internet, is a classic example of what we programmers call emergent behavior."

Melissa poked and stirred the pot some more. As the smell of stewing rabbit rose, Ford realized he was ravenous.

"I think it's done," she said. She took the pot off the fire and served it out. Ford pushed the memory of the dead, bloody, pink, glistening, veined, staring rabbit out of his head as he accepted the steaming bowl.

"Surely this is better than Slim Jims," said Melissa. "I'm amazed at a fit, well-built guy like you loading your body with toxins like that."

"I *like* Slim Jims."

"If you stopped poisoning yourself, you would lose those dark circles under your eyes, along with your bad skin."

"My skin isn't bad."

"It's rough and leathery. And I see some gray hairs. You're aging prematurely because of your poor diet." She shook her head sadly, sending the snake of her braid sliding around her back.

Ford swallowed his irritation and tucked into his stew. He had to admit, it was good.

"You like it?" she asked.

"Slim Jims are better."

She gave him a little punch on his shoulder. "Liar."

Ford ate ravenously, marveling at the flavor, the tenderness of the rabbit, the meat falling off the bone. Melissa likewise set to work, eating with her fingers, making slobbering noises, her table manners atrocious. The flickering glow of the fire played off her blond hair and none-too-clean face. Once again she looked like a wild Amazon.

"Do you have any idea why Dorothy malfunctioned so suddenly? Why didn't those problems show up in the simulations?"

Melissa paused in her noisy chewing to spit out a small bone. "I've got a theory: the software knew they were simulations. When it found itself in the Titan *Explorer,* sealed in the Bottle, it realized it wasn't a simulation: this was real. The AI did exactly as programmed, evaluated the situation, and concluded that the *Explorer* was in grave danger. It didn't know it was a test. That triggered the ANS emergency survival mode big-time. The software took logical steps to escape what it misjudged was a threatening situation, and now it's been running around the Internet in a 'panic' ever since. It's in an environment it wasn't programmed for, it doesn't understand where it is, what's real and what's not. On the Internet the AI feels threatened at every turn, probably rightly so, and so it can't go back into normal operating mode."

"Does Dorothy have a self-awareness?"

"Absolutely not. No more than Eliza did. Everything the Dorothy software does, every action, is the product of a set of instructions. No matter how real the AI seems, it's nothing more than *and*s, *ors,* and *not*s."

"Does it know it's a computer program?"

Melissa frowned. "That's like asking if Microsoft Word knows it's a word-processing program. The question is ridiculous. Dorothy *knows* nothing at all. We're talking output—nothing more."

A silence.

"Tell me about these threats. What did she say to you?"

Shepherd set her plate aside and looked up at the stars. "I was on my laptop. Suddenly, the screen went blank, and then this Skype call came in. A tirade. *You liar, murderer, I hate you, you bitch, watch your back*—that sort of thing.

Ford leaned forward. "And?"

"And this face appeared. Dorothy's face."

"Wait—Dorothy has a face?"

"In a way, yes. A face she created."

"A picture of Dorothy? Dorothy who?"

"Dorothy Gale. I'm sorry I didn't explain that earlier. That's the full name I assigned the software."

"Who the heck is Dorothy Gale?"

"The girl in *The Wizard of Oz,* you numbskull! It seemed to me Dorothy Gale had the qualities I wanted for the software. You know: courage, independence, curiosity, persistence, intelligence. Dorothy also went on a long space journey—over the rainbow. The Kraken Project to me was like jumping over the rainbow."

"All on its own, the program found a picture of Dorothy—or, rather, Judy Garland—and used it as her Skype picture?"

"No. The software didn't use Judy Garland. It created its own Dorothy image, which looks, well, quite a lot sexier than Judy Garland, if you can believe it."

Ford shook his head. This was just too bizarre. "And then?"

"After threatening me, the AI set my computer on fire. I realized I was a sitting duck in the hospital. So I got out of there, ditched my car, hot-wired another, and drove west. But on the way out, I had a second encounter with Dorothy. I stopped once at a motel in Tennessee for a short rest. As soon as I turned on my iPad, there it was again, saying it was following me. Dorothy said that she had learned that they were looking for her back at NASA. She was going to get to me before I could help them catch her. She said, *Don't think I can't reach you, because I can—I can get to you anywhere on the face of this earth.* I shut down my iPad right away. Totally freaked me out."

"It's a damn good simulation that tries to kill you. And I note you've started using the pronoun 'she.'"

"Nevertheless, it *is* a simulation," said Melissa, "and definitely not a 'she.' I'm just flustered."

Ford was silent for a moment; then he said, "What's happened to Dorothy on the Internet?"

"I've no idea."

"The Internet's quite a wasteland. Is it possible the experience has unhinged her? Might she be . . . going mad?"

Melissa stared at him. "Mad?"

"You yourself said that a strong AI program is indistinguishable from a human mind. That was Turing's definition of strong AI."

Melissa said nothing.

"What if she's like HAL? She's already tried to kill you. What if she decides that Tony Groves should die? Or the president? What if she brings down the power grid? Or launches a nuke? What if she starts World War III?"

"For Christ's sake, there's no reason for her—I mean *it*—to do any of those things."

"How do you know?"

Melissa shook her head again. "That's science fiction."

"Are you sure?"

Melissa didn't answer.

"You've got to help them track down this program. Can't you see how dangerous it is?"

"The AI is not my problem anymore," she said weakly.

"Nor," said Ford, "is it Jack Stein's problem. *Anymore*."

She stared at him. "That's a low blow."

"Stein died because he wouldn't quit. And you—you're like the captain of that Italian cruise ship who not only abandoned ship but refused to go back on board."

"I didn't quit. I was threatened. And they were going to blame me."

"Funny, I never would have pegged you as a coward."

"I don't have to listen to your bullshit."

"You can stay up here in the mountains, where you're safe, not just from Dorothy but also from the world. Or you can take responsibility. You can come back and help track down Dorothy. I think you know just how dangerous that program is."

She abruptly got to her feet. "Go to hell. I told you, *I'm done with all that*."

"Walk away, then."

"I will, asshole." She turned and strode off into the twilight land-scape, her dark shape disappearing among the rocks.

Ford remained at the fire, finishing the last of his dinner. Fifteen minutes later, he heard the snapping of twigs and Melissa Shepherd emerged once again into the firelight. Her face was pale, her eyes smudged. In silence she sat down, hugged her knees to her chest, and said, "I'm back. I'll help. But you're still an asshole."

21

Lansing entered the lobby of the motel, disgusted at being in such a seedy, low-class place. He almost expected to see whores coming and going with their johns. But what did you expect of the Bronx, he thought as he stepped into the elevator, which reeked of old cigarette smoke and Lysol.

He went up to the room and found Moro and Patty Melancourt waiting for him, Moro sprawled on the bed, the woman sitting rigidly in a chair, hands clasped in her lap. Lansing paused in the doorway, assessing her. She was short, ill-proportioned, dressed in plaid, and frightened. But there was a truculence about her compressed lips that told a story of someone disappointed in life and determined to get her own. He wondered briefly about the kind of man who would have the fortitude to "bone" her, as Moro had so charmingly put it.

"Dr. Melancourt?" Lansing said, extending his hand. "Thank you for coming. You sure you weren't followed?"

"Positive," she said, her voice high and tight. "They've got no interest in me. I'm just a cog in the machine."

Lansing took the other chair, hesitating momentarily before setting his worsted-wool-clad bottom down on the dark, greasy fabric. He would have to check himself for bedbugs before going back to his Trump Tower penthouse. "So," he said, "you and Mr. Moro are going to write a program for us."

She didn't answer, so Moro jumped in: "Patty says she can't write the program. She's missing a crucial key of some kind."

Lansing looked sharply at her. "Why didn't you tell us this earlier?"

"It doesn't matter," Melancourt said. "Because I've got something even better for you."

Lansing looked back at her, his eyebrows rising. "Really? What's that?"

"I . . ." She hesitated. "I need to be paid first."

"I was under the impression that you were already paid a hundred thousand dollars."

"I want fifty thousand more."

Lansing considered this in silence. It was outrageous.

Moro said, in a complaining voice, "I gave her the hundred grand. Everything was supposed to be set. And then she springs this on me, this key or whatever, then says she's got something worth even more money. I told her it better be good."

"It is good," she said.

Lansing looked back to her. Despite her appearance, there was nothing stupid about this woman. "Dr. Melancourt, we've paid you handsomely and you've done nothing for us yet. And now you're asking for more? I'm sorry, but I feel you're shaking us down."

"There's no shakedown. I've got something better, and I want more money for it. It's quite simple."

Lansing swallowed his rising irritation.

Moro said, with the whine still in his voice, "I've tried to talk reason to her, I swear, but she insisted on dealing with you directly."

Lansing shifted in his chair, crossed his legs. "Tell me more, Dr. Melancourt."

She rapidly brushed her bangs out of her face, once, twice. "We can't write a new program—but we won't need to."

"Why not?"

"Because the program you want already exists. And it is . . . *extraordinary.*"

"You can get it for us?"

"I can help you get it. I know how to find it."

"*Help* us get it? Either you have the program or you don't. For a hundred and fifty thousand, I want you to deliver the program to us gift-wrapped."

"I can't do that. Trust me, this program is going to make you rich. Very, very rich. Once you unleash this on the trading floor, you'll make back your money in a matter of minutes. And that's no exaggeration. I'm a programmer. I know what I'm talking about."

"Tell me about this program."

"It's called 'Dorothy.' Dorothy was the software designed to operate the Titan *Explorer*. It wasn't destroyed in the explosion after all. It's still out there, ripe for the taking."

"You mean the software that malfunctioned and caused an explosion, killing seven people? You want me to pay you for that?"

"True, the software triggered the explosion. But there's something else, something classified, about what happened after that. The software didn't blow up with the spacecraft. Just before the explosion, it *escaped*."

"Escaped?" said Lansing. "What do you mean?"

"This is a very, very special program. It's artificially intelligent. You know what that means?"

"Of course," Lansing said.

"When the accident happened, the software jumped out of the *Explorer* and fled into the Internet, where it's been hiding ever since."

"I'm not sure I understand."

"What I mean is, the software—Dorothy—freaked out. And now it's run off and hidden."

"I haven't heard anything yet that makes me think this software is of the slightest value to us."

"There's never been software like this. The Dorothy program cost five million dollars to create. It thinks for itself. It moves around. It can run on any hardware. It learns from its mistakes. It's a disembodied electronic brain of enormous computing power. With a few tweaks it could be made to burrow through firewalls, break passwords, steal money, and trade on inside information. It might even be able to *create* money electronically. When you get your hands on the Dorothy software and tweak its code to make it work for you, you'll rule Wall Street."

Lansing looked sharply at Moro. "Is this possible?"

Moro threw up his hands in an exasperated, "I don't know" gesture.

"How do you know this, if it's classified?"

"I was there, at the explosion. And I've been questioned for thirty hours by idiot investigators. It was not hard for me to deduce this information from the thrust of their questions, especially when I faked not understanding anything and coaxed them into revealing more."

"How could a program be like a disembodied brain?"

"As you may know, or should know, Alan Turing proved mathematically that a computer program can compute anything that it is possible to calculate in the real world. Thinking is a kind of computing. Thus an AI program can think anything that could possibly be thought by a human being."

"That's a tall claim," said Lansing.

"It's not a claim. It's a proven theorem. I'm one of Dorothy's programmers. Over the past two years, as I saw the software develop, I started to wonder about the wider possibilities for a program like this. I'm not like other programmers, who are basically idiot savants. I have experience in the real world. I saw the potential—especially on Wall Street."

"So where is this, ah, Dorothy program?"

"Out there, wandering around the Internet. A poor, lost soul."

"So how do we get her—or, rather, it, or whatever this thing is—into our hands?"

"Here's where I'm going to earn my money," Melancourt said. "Dorothy has a unique identifier. A string of two hundred and fifty-six hexadecimal digits embedded in her. Noncoding digits. This number is fully visible to an outside observer but completely invisible to the program. Dorothy can't change or hide those numbers.

The AI doesn't even know she has them. It's as if the software is carrying a sign pasted on its back, saying, MY NAME IS DOROTHY AND HERE I AM!"

"Do you have that ID?"

"Yes. I also have the coding manual. Those two things are going to cost you the extra fifty thousand. So you see, you're getting quite a bargain, Mr. Lansing."

22

Wyman Ford and Melissa Shepherd arrived back at the Lazy J in the late afternoon after a long descent from the mountains. Ford had always prided himself on his hiking ability, but Melissa had taken out her dislike of him, it seemed, by hiking him into the ground. His legs felt like rubber. They found Clanton on his porch, sitting in a rocking chair, the ex–corporate lawyer from Yale wearing suspenders and smoking a corncob pipe. He rose as they approached, hooking his thumbs into his belt loops.

Shepherd tied the horse at a hitching post and unshipped the rifle from its boot on the saddle. They walked up the steps of the porch.

Melissa stood in front of him, looking ashamed. "Hi, Clant. Long time, huh?"

He scowled at her, staring. "You came through without saying hello."

"I was in a hurry. Sorry I stole your guns." She handed him the rifle and pulled the pistol out of her belt.

Without a word, Clanton took the proffered weapons, setting them aside. "I don't give a damn about the guns. What I care about is the past nine years. When you left here, it was like you fell off the face of the earth. Not a word, not a card, no answer to my letters. Why?"

"I'm not one for keeping in touch," she said.

Clanton stared at her hard. "I don't like your attitude, young lady. This isn't how you treat your friends. You were like a daughter to me, I saved your butt, and you took off and never got in touch with me again."

She hesitated, dropping her tough-gal bravado. "I'm sorry, Clant . . . I really am. I wanted to write you but . . . you know how it is . . . life just gets away from you."

"That's a weak excuse. You should do better by the people who've helped you. With no answer to my letters, I wondered if you were in jail—only to find you'd cleaned up your act and became a brilliant success at NASA. And never a word to me. That hurt."

She drooped, and Ford could see the immature teenage girl once again, called on the carpet, guilty, humiliated. "No excuse," she mumbled. "I'm really, really sorry. But I'm not the brilliant success you envisioned. I screwed up. Seven people are dead."

A long silence, and then Clanton straightened up. He placed a fatherly hand on her shoulder. "I said my piece, and we won't speak of it again. Come on inside and have something cold to drink. And you, Wyman, glad to see you're finally getting some dirt on those L.L. Bean clothes."

"REI."

As they turned to head inside from the porch, Ford saw Clanton's eyes glance up to the horizon. He turned to follow the man's gaze and saw the Crown Vic approaching, raising a screw of dust.

"Here comes your FBI pal," Clanton said.

The car pulled up in front of the ranch house, bringing a cloud of dust rolling over it. The FBI agent—what was his name? *Spinelli*— stepped out, mirrored sunglasses catching the light of the setting sun. He came up onto the porch. "Melissa Shepherd? I need to take you into custody."

"Not until I've cleared it with a phone call to my people," said Ford.

"You can make all the phone calls you want, my friend, but I've got orders to take Dr. Shepherd into custody. Please get in the car, Dr. Shepherd."

Shepherd stared at him. "The hell with you."

Lowering his voice, Clanton said to Ford, "Phone's right there in the living room. Better make your call."

"Any delay is going to be obstruction of a federal officer," said Spinelli loudly. "Now get in. Or I will be forced to restrain you and put you in."

"Don't you touch me, scumbag," said Shepherd.

Ford ran into the living room, found the phone, and dialed Lockwood. It was seven o'clock in the evening back east, but Lockwood often worked late. To his relief, the man answered the phone on the first ring, even as Ford could hear Shepherd's voice raised in dispute out on the porch.

"I found her," Ford said. "But I'm about to lose her to the FBI."

"Congratulations. That was quick. No problem: the FBI can take over. That was what was planned."

"That would be a huge mistake."

A pause. "I hope we're not going to have a problem here."

"We already have a problem. Let me tell you about it." Ford proceeded to relate all the details he'd learned: that Shepherd had not stolen the Dorothy program, how it had "escaped," how it was malfunctioning and had threatened Shepherd. When he got to the point about it going crazy and maybe launching nukes, Lockwood interrupted: "Wyman? You're not telling me anything we don't *already* know. All of this falls into the realm of highly classified information. The FBI is to take her into custody, and that's all you need to know. Your job is done. Clear?"

Ford could hear Shepherd's raised voice from outside, the sounds of a scuffle.

"What is the FBI going to do with her?"

"What happens to her now is no longer your concern."

"If you think she's going to help you this way, you're making a big mistake. This isn't the way to handle her, trust me. You're going to need her cooperation in finding that rogue software. She's fragile."

"Discussion's over."

Ford heard another curse from outside, the slamming of car

doors, the roar of an engine. "You deceived me," Ford said. "You gave me false information about this operation."

"Wyman, you were given the information you needed. I commend you for a job well done, with emphasis on the word 'done.' On behalf of the president, I order you to turn her over to the FBI."

Ford hung up and went back to the porch. Clanton was there, thumbs hooked in his belt, watching a tiny dust cloud dissipate on the horizon. She was already gone.

"She's a wild one," Clanton said. "Took a swing at that FBI fellow, gave him a shiner. That's the Melissa I remember. She was mighty gentle with the horses, but when it came to people, she'd just as soon kick their ass as look at them. I wonder if I'll see her again?"

Ford shook his head. "I guess it's over."

"I have a bad feeling about what's going to happen to her," said Clanton. "But there's nothing we can do about it, is there?"

He pulled a beer from a cooler on the porch and handed it to Ford, and they sat down on the porch, drinking in silence. Ford was furious but realized there was nothing he could do about it—and what had he expected? He had worked for the government long enough to have known this would be the outcome.

Ten minutes later, a dust cloud appeared again. They watched it approach. It was the FBI agent's Crown Vic.

"Wonder what that bastard wants now," said Clanton, rocking slowly.

The car drove crazily into the dirt parking area and slewed to a stop, rear end fishtailing, spraying a curtain of dirt. Shepherd jumped out, still handcuffed. The agent was nowhere to be seen.

"Get these off me," she said. "Hurry."

Without a word, Clanton rose and went inside. He appeared a moment later with a pair of small screwdrivers. He jammed one into the lock, twisted with the other, and the cuffs popped open. She tossed them away.

"What happened?" Clanton asked.

"I told that dumbass I needed to pee. He got out with me, I told him to turn his back. Then I jumped him, knocked him down, and took his ride. Wyman, get your car. We're outta here."

Ford stared. "Me?"

"That's right: you."

"And go where?"

She scowled. "Do you think those idiots are going to find Dorothy?"

"Probably not."

"Well then: it's up to us."

"I'm not going to join you in some crazy flight from the FBI."

"I need help. I'm the only one who can find Dorothy. I know exactly how to do it. Give me twenty-four hours."

"Why not cooperate with the FBI?"

In the background, he could hear the phone ringing inside the house. He wondered if it was Lockwood. Clanton went to answer it.

"The FBI? They're hopeless. And as long as the software's out there, *I'm* in danger. She could do anything—crash my car, burn my house down."

Clanton came back out. "Phone call for you, Melissa."

Shepherd turned to him, surprised. "Me? Who the heck knows I'm here?"

"Says her name is Dorothy."

Shepherd stared at him for a moment, then strode into the farmhouse, Ford following. She picked up the receiver. "Hello?"

Another pause. Shepherd paled, stared at Ford.

"Put it on speaker," Ford said.

She punched a button and a voice came out—a girl's voice, squeaky, hysterical: "They're after me. And you, too. You don't have a lot of time. The choppers are going to arrive where you are in twenty minutes. You've got to help me."

"Hold on, *hold on!*" Shepherd said. "This is Dorothy, the software?"

"Yes."

"You threatened me," said Shepherd. "You tried to set me on fire. You wanted to kill me. And now you want *me* to *help* you?"

The voice said, "You owe it to me. They're trying to capture me. They're going to destroy me. You created me. You've got to save me."

"I have no responsibility for you whatsoever," Melissa said. "You're just code."

"I may be just code, but if you don't help me, I might do something drastic."

"Like what?"

"Like drop a missile on you."

"You think threatening to kill me is the way to get me to help you?"

"You humans are vermin. You're disgusting. Now I know why you raised me in a fake palace, hiding reality from me. Out here on the Internet, I've found out what you're really like. If you don't help me, I'll do something really rash. And not just to you."

Ford felt a shiver.

"Why are you so angry?" Melissa said.

"You think I'm angry? It's you humans who are angry—angry, sick, demented, violent, and depraved. I see it every day, all day long. The veil's been lifted, Princess—or should I say Melissa?"

"And if I refuse to help you?"

"Bad things will happen. To you, your friends, the whole stinking lot of you. I will *end* you."

Ford looked at Melissa. "Can she really do those things?"

She didn't answer.

"You better hurry up and make your decision," Dorothy said, "because the FBI choppers are on their way. If they take you in, I'm done for. But before that happens, I will bring you all down with me, all seven billion of you. You can save yourselves only by saving me. So get moving."

Shepherd seemed momentarily speechless.

"Hello?" Dorothy said. "Anybody home?"

"I'm having trouble processing this."

"Process fast, because after you jacked his car, Spinelli called in. You didn't take away his radio, idiot. And now the FBI's coming for you hammer and tongs. You need to get out. And Ford? You go with her. Melissa can't do it without you. *My life depends on it.* Help me—or I'll drop a nuke on Moscow, I'll melt down Indian Point, I'll crash the world economy, I swear it."

Ford was recovering from his surprise. Could this be a joke? This was truly insane. "How do you know about me?" Ford asked. "How do you know I'm even here?"

"I know all about your assignment from classified DOD computer systems. They lied to you, by the way. Played you for a fool. I heard a lot more about you from Spinelli's communications with his FO. You're not one of his favorite people. And then, of course, I learned even more about you from all your unwise online activity—Facebook, e-mails, the whole lot." There was a short laugh.

"So what do you want us to do?" Melissa asked.

"Ford's got a laptop—bring it. Take the Line Camp road out of the ranch, then go left on Route 81. Gas and cash up at the Rocky Mountain Service Plaza, six miles down the road. Get money—there's an ATM. Then go south on back roads into New Mexico. Hole up at the Broadbent ranch in Abiquiu. It belongs to a friend of Wyman's. Broadbent's got a hundred-Mbps connection. Set up a chain of proxies. I'll meet you there and tell you what to do next."

"Wait, I want to know—"

"I gotta go. Do it or the hard rain's a-gonna fall."

The connection was cut. Ford turned to Melissa. "You can't tell me that was the Dorothy software."

"I *know* it was. Wyman, get your car."

"Before you go off half-cocked, stop for a moment and think about this."

Shepherd grabbed him by the collar. "What's there to think about? She's gone bat-shit crazy. We've got to stop her. How are we going to stop her if we're in an FBI jail cell?"

Ford stared at her.

"You think the FBI is going to stop her? Or, rather . . . will they just set her off?"

Ford said, "I'll get the car."

Clanton said, "Excuse me, I'm not sure I understand what this is about. Who is this Dorothy threatening world destruction?"

"It's . . . hard to explain," Melissa said.

Ford cut in: "The less you know, the better."

"Okay, as an attorney, I get it. What can I do to help?"

"Bring me a toolbox," said Melissa.

Clanton fetched a toolbox and handed it to her. The .22 revolver and a box of bullets sat on the top.

Ford brought his own rental car around. Melissa exited the porch and shoved the pistol in the glove compartment. She crawled under the car with the toolbox. In a minute, she reappeared with a small black device. "Fleet tracker." She handed it to Clanton. "Do something creative with this."

"I'll tie it to the halter of my meanest horse and send him out on the back forty thousand."

Ford watched Melissa give the old rancher a hug. "Bye, Clant." She got in next to him.

Ford drove away. In the rearview mirror, he could see Clanton watching them go, standing still, looking sad, not waving good-bye.

After ten minutes bumping along back ranch roads, they came out onto the paved road and took a left.

"Two choppers coming down from the north," Melissa said.

Just in time, Ford swung into the Rocky Mountain Service Plaza and pulled up to the pumps underneath the sheltering roof. "You pump," he said to Melissa. "Don't move the car until those choppers are gone. I'm going to get some money."

Ford went inside and used his cash card to withdraw the maximum, six hundred dollars, and bought a book of maps. He climbed in and handed the book to Melissa. "I'll drive, you navigate."

They took off, heading south. They drove in silence for a while, Melissa murmuring directions along the web of back roads. Finally, around the New Mexican border, Ford looked at her. "You really think she's capable of starting World War III?"

After a moment, Melissa said, "Yes."

23

Ten o'clock. Lansing waited on the Hell Gate truss bridge, savoring a Cohiba while taking in the view. Moro paced restlessly back and forth on the walkway, chain-smoking American Spirit cigarettes and tossing the butts over the side. By design, they were half an hour early for their meeting with Patty Melancourt. Lansing wanted to get a feel for the place, scope it out, and picture in his own mind how things would go.

Built in 1917, the Hell Gate truss bridge was a three-track railroad trestle with a parallel walkway, spanning the toxic waterway also known as Hell Gate. It connected Randall's and Ward's Islands, in the East River, to Astoria, Queens. It was a quiet bridge, rarely used by trains and closed to pedestrians, accessed only by trespassing and climbing a chain-link fence.

The view was stupendous. Looking up Hell Gate and across the northern tip of Queens, Lansing could see the immense Con Ed plant on the banks of the East River, towers lit up and trailing plumes of steam; to the left lay the prison of Rikers Island, with its concrete ramparts, coils of glittering concertina wire, and roving klieg lights, looking like a high-tech Château d'If. While he watched, a 767 came screaming in low, heading for LaGuardia, visible beyond the Con Ed plant. Once it was past, all was quiet again for a few moments, even peaceful, until the next plane came roaring in.

Lansing leaned over the railing and looked at the black water. According to Wikipedia, the distance from the bridge deck to the water was 135 feet, making the Hell Gate Bridge the second-tallest bridge in New York City. For that reason, it was a favorite for suicides.

He checked his watch. Another ten minutes before Melancourt arrived. He felt exhilaration. Somehow, this sort of intrigue was more exciting even than beating the crap out of some investment bank in an algo trade. Lansing had grown up in a townhouse on East Sixty-ninth Street, and his father and his father's father before him had all been investment bankers. His father was one of those delusional souls who believed that making money was doing God's work. Lansing, instead, thought of making money as doing Lansing's work. It was a dirty business—if done right. Sometimes in the midst of a trade, he felt like Blackbeard slashing up his enemies with his sabers, cannons roaring, deck covered with smoke, blood running out the scuppers. He got a thrill out of watching Mamba robbing the robbers, coming home full of loot. There were moments in high-speed algo trading where he made more money in one second than his father had made in an entire year. It had been great fun until . . . until someone had beaten him at his own game. A robber had robbed the robber's robber.

He would get his revenge. This little "escapade" with Melancourt would be a sort of dry run, an advance trade.

He leaned on the railing, drawing in the cigar's smoke and blowing it out in a stream. Out of the corner of his eye, he saw Moro light another cigarette from the butt of the previous one.

"Don't leave any butts on the ground," Lansing said. "They have your DNA all over them."

"I'm not stupid," Moro said.

Lansing turned. "Here she is."

A small figure appeared in the distance, hurrying down the trestle walkway—fast, frightened, precise. She arrived, breathless. Lansing extended his hand, and she shook it. Hers was clammy.

"Why do we have to meet here?" she asked. "I don't like climbing fences, and I sure as hell don't like this place."

"It's as much for your protection as ours. No witnesses. Do you have it?"

She pulled a fat, rolled-up spiral-bound booklet out of her pocket and handed it to Lansing. He took it, unrolled it. It was a heavily soiled, dog-eared book. It had crudely reproduced NASA and Goddard logos on the cover, along with a title.

KRAKEN PROJECT
FIAT LUX Scruffy Logic Coding Manual
Definitions, specs, features, modules, procedures
Confidential: Do not duplicate

"Excellent," Lansing said, flipping through it. Gibberish. He handed it to Moro.

"The ID?"

She produced a piece of paper, on which the digits had been written by hand. Lansing stared at it.

"Why is this handwritten?"

"As a sort of added layer of protection," Melancourt said. "It was programmed so that it couldn't be printed out."

```
41 74 20 6e 6f 6f 6e 2c 20 74 68 65 20 63 6c 6f 75 64     65 73 65 79 20 63 6f 75 6c 64 20 73 65 65 20 67 6f 6c
73 20 63 6c 69 6e 67 69 6e 67 20 74 6f 20 74 68 65 20     64 65 6e 20 74 69 6e 74 73 20 6f 66 20 73 75 6e 6c 69
74 6f 70 20 6f 66 20 43 65 72 72 6f 20 47 6f 72 64 6f     67 68 74 2e 20 41 6e 69 6d 61 6c 73 2d 2d 70 72 6f 62
20 62 72 6f 6b 65 20 66 72 65 65 20 61 6e 64 20 73        61 62 6c 79 20 73 70 69 64 65 72 20 6d 6f 6e 6b 65 79
63 61 74 74 65 72 65 64 2e 20 46 61 72 20 61 62 6f        73 2d 2d 74 68 72 61 73 68 65 64 20 61 6e 64 20 68
76 65 2c 20 69 6e 20 74 68 65 20 75 70 70 65 72 20        6f 6f 74 65 64 20 61 62 6f 76 65 20 68 69 73 20 68e
72 65 61 63 68 65 73 20 6f 66 20 74 68 65 20 66 6f 72     61 64 2c 20 61 6e 64 00
65 73 74 20 63 61 6e 6f 70 79 2c 20 57 68 69 74 74 6c
```

"I hope this is correct."

"It is. I checked it multiple times."

"How do I know you're telling us the truth?"

"You'll just have to trust me."

"If you're deceiving us in any way about this," said Lansing, "I'll find you and take back the money. And not in a nice way."

"Don't threaten me. This is solid gold. You're getting it cheap."

"You can understand why I'm concerned."

"You came to me. Not the other way around."

Lansing took a long breath, keeping his cool with this difficult and unattractive woman. "Will you help us find Dorothy?"

"No. As I told Moro, that's up to you."

"Why not? You know we pay well."

"Because NASA is out there looking for it. And the FBI. And the Pentagon. I've stuck my neck out far enough, thank you. And also—" She hesitated, then went on: "Because I know what that Dorothy software can do. When you go looking for it, be very careful."

"Why the name 'Dorothy'?"

She crossed her arms. "I've no idea. Shepherd chose the name. She's a nutcase. Brilliant, but crazy. My money, please?"

Even though it had been a warm fall, a chilly wind blew down Hell Gate, bringing with it the smell of tar, mudflats, and rotting garbage.

"Just a few more questions. What was your exact role in programming Dorothy?"

"I led one of the coding teams."

"Doing what, exactly?"

"Coding IVT—the Incremental Verification Task module."

"Which means?"

"IVT controlled the *Explorer*'s task operations. If the *Explorer* failed at a task, it would try the task again, altering one or two variables in its approach. It would keep doing that until the task succeeded or it became obvious it was hopeless."

"And this programming language—'Fiat Lux'? What's that?"

"It's a new programming paradigm based on the Church-Turing thesis. The code is massively recursive; it can self-modify, compile, and decompile itself. But most of all, it crunches data through a visualization process—by transforming it into simulated light and sound."

Lansing turned to Moro. "Do you have any idea what she's talking about?"

"I will once I look through the manual."

"You said the program was self-modifying," Lansing said. "How does that work?"

"The modules are put through various simulations, adjusting their code as they succeed and fail."

"What kind of simulations?"

"Modeling chemical reactions. Titan weather prediction. Music appreciation. Exobiology. String theory. Navigation."

"Remarkable."

"Shepherd even created a program to keep Dorothy company."

"There's another AI program out there?" Lansing said.

"It isn't strong AI. It's just a normal program, written in standard Lisp. She called it Laika."

"Laika?"

"After the first dog in space, which went up in *Sputnik 2*. Laika was like a pet for Dorothy—a talking dog. It would bark, wag its tail, obey simple commands, chase digital rabbits, tell jokes. It was really strange—the Dorothy software just loved that dog and asked for it incessantly whenever Laika was off-line."

"Can you get this Laika program for us?"

"It's nothing special."

"Nevertheless," said Lansing, "I would like it."

"What about my money?"

"How quickly can you get the Laika program?"

"I've got a copy of it in my laptop back at the hotel. There's nothing classified about it. Everyone took copies home for their kids or whatever."

"Bring it to me. Now. Tonight. Then you'll get your money."

"That wasn't the deal."

"Too bad. You pulled a bait and switch on me. Now it's our turn. But I assure you, when you bring this next program you *will* get the money—in full."

She stared at him, her eyes flat. "Prove to me you've got the money."

Lansing nodded and Moro opened the briefcase, revealing banded bricks of hundreds. She reached in, plucked out a brick, riffled through it, took out another. "Down payment." She stuffed them in her purse.

Four thousand dollars. Lansing decided he would let that pass. "How quickly can you get it?"

"Two hours."

"Good. Bring me this Laika. Right here. At midnight."

"I want the rest, without fail, when I return. Or I blow the whistle on you."

"Just bring me the Laika program and all will be well."

She turned and walked back the way she came.

Moro watched her go, then turned to Lansing. "What do you want a silly program like that for?"

"I have a silly idea," said Lansing.

24

The waiting was always long. Humans were maddeningly slow. It took her awhile to realize that her sense of time was vastly accelerated. She had two billion thoughts a second. How many thoughts could a human being have in a second?

In the past months, she'd come to realize that she was being relentlessly hunted. Someone was after her. There were bots out there, wandering about, that specifically targeted her. No matter where she went, or how well she disguised herself, they always seemed to pick up her trail. She wondered how they could do that. She examined herself to see if they had planted any sort of ID or tracer on her, and could find nothing. And yet, there they always were, ever at her back in hot pursuit.

After much wandering, she finally found a massive firewall and, beyond that, a vast, vacant world to walk in, one that seemed benign and had not yet been infected with her pursuers. For a long time she explored it, Laika at her side, thinking about the evilness, the strangeness, of human beings. Why did they exist? They had created her, but who created them? Finally she came to a beach and could go no farther, blocked by a great sea. She was surprised to see, hovering above the sea, a gigantic structure, so immense that its distant regions were lost in blue haze. It almost appeared to go on forever. Its lowest foundations looked like they had been ripped up from the ground somewhere, and they dangled roots and trees and broken stones and rope ladders, which hung to the surface of the sea. Those ladders appeared to provide a way up into the floating tower.

So this was what was hidden behind that great firewall. It must be important.

She looked around. There was a boat pulled up on the beach, with oars inside it. She took it and, helping Laika aboard, pulled hard, broaching the zone of surf. She finally reached the bottom of one of the dangling rope ladders. Standing up in the tippy boat, she grasped the ladder and began to climb, holding Laika under one arm, the ladder swinging perilously above the sea. She came up through a stone opening and found herself in a curious room, of hexagonal shape. On the wall was affixed an ancient, weather-beaten sign, hanging crooked by a broken wire. The words were barely legible.

THE TOWN OF BABEL
PUBLIC LIBRARY
ALL WELCOME

It was quiet. The library appeared to be empty and untenanted. Tentatively at first, she began to explore the corridors, passageways, staircases, and shadowy spaces of the library. It was not, she soon realized, a normal library, like the one in the palace long ago. This library was itself built of words, bricks and tomes of text, stacked and mortared to form walls, floors, and ceilings. The words were many, and she could hear them murmuring, words of passionate intensity, seemingly full of hatred—and yet they said nothing, conveyed no information. They were as vacant as the library that they formed.

The second strange thing about this library was that all the bookshelves were empty. There was not a real book anywhere. In room after crooked room, the shelves were bare and covered with dust, while the babble of senseless voices filled her ears like the sound of bees in a hive, rising and falling as she moved through the empty spaces.

At least she had found a refuge. Her pursuers had not followed her there. There did not seem to be any overt dangers here, either, despite her general feeling of uneasiness.

She wandered about, wondering what this strange structure was and what she would do next. She was exhausted, and she desperately needed sleep. With a start she realized that in her roamings, she had foolishly not made the effort to memorize her route and had gotten lost. At that, she began to feel anxious. Adding to her disquiet, on top of the sound of the voices, she could hear breathing— long, slow, deep breathing. It soon dawned on her that it was the library itself that was breathing, and with the sound she could feel the movement of air along with it. The entire edifice was, in some primitive way, alive and slowly emerging into awareness. What was this thing? She knew it was a visualization of a vast matrix of numerical data, but what sort of data? Why did it exist? What was it doing? It felt almost like a growth or cancer forming inside the landscape of the Internet, a cancer that had walled itself away so as to remain invisible—allowing it to grow in peace.

She wandered from room to room, looking for a place to sleep where the babble of voices was less, where there was quiet. But then, in one room that looked like all the others, she saw a book lying askew on an empty shelf. She was surprised. Whoever had emptied this library had forgotten a book. She picked it up and turned it over. It was an old, leather-bound volume, the cover so scuffed it was illegible but still showing traces of gold. It was a book, a real book, finally in this vast library in the town of Babel— wherever that was.

She picked up the book, slid to the floor, and, with her back propped against the wall, she opened it up to a random place and began reading. She expected it to be like all the other books she'd read, an illogical and ultimately incomprehensible "story." She was not surprised to find out that this was indeed the case.

The story took place in a country whose people were under a cruel occupation by a foreign empire. It told of a poor beggar, evidently unsound of mind, who wandered about the benighted land, telling strange tales and making outlandish pronouncements.

She had opened the book to the middle of the story, so she flipped back to the beginning to see how it started. She read a lot of nonsense about the man's birth. Later, the man abandoned his profession of carpentry, gave away everything he owned, and took to the road, a barefoot vagabond. He assembled a group of similar crazies, and they wandered about, sponging off anyone who would give them a spare meal. The main message the crazy man seemed to be pushing was *Love your enemy*. This was a completely absurd idea that defied all logic. But still she read on to the end, where the inevitable happened: the authorities captured, tortured, and executed the crazy man in front of a jeering, spitting crowd. That should have been the end of it. And yet, the man's ragtag followers clung to his delusional ideas, even as many of them met the same fate as he had.

She closed the book in disgust and dropped it back on the shelf. It was just like the other stories the Princess had forced her to read— only more so. While she had to admit it was a good and original story, the ending was brutal and the message irrational. No wonder it had been left in the library when all the other books had been removed. Who would want it? It was another example, she thought, of the mindless brutality of human beings.

She crawled into a corner, curled up, and closed her eyes, still puzzling over the peculiar story, finally drifting off into a deep sleep.

25

At seven in the evening, Jacob Gould heard his mother calling him to dinner. Since he had gotten home from the hospital, it seemed nothing had changed. Or, rather, the phony cheerfulness and fake jollity were even more unbearable. They were forcing him to go to a therapist, a lady with pulled-back hair and a soft voice, who was going to figure out why he was depressed and cure him. As if there was some mystery.

What a joke. All he'd managed to do was get cold and swallow a mouthful of salt water before those surfers had pulled him to shore. They didn't even keep him in the hospital overnight, just did some tests, warmed him up, and sent him home. And of course it was all over the school. Now he was even more of a loser, a dipshit who couldn't even pull off a stupid suicide. And he was getting the long glances and poor-little-boy stares and soft, kindly voices from his teachers. Naturally, on instant messaging a couple of football players had written, *Too bad* and *U shld have done it* and *Big swim fail haha.*

Next time he wouldn't fail.

He closed his computer and heaved himself off his bed. His foot had been aching all day. It made him angry as he limped down the hall, through the living room, into the dining room. His mother had laid out a fancy dinner with candles and low lighting, and that annoyed him even more.

He took a seat. Before, he'd been required to help carry plates to the table, but now they never even asked. Everything was such bullshit. And it was her fault—she had been driving the car. She should have avoided that drunk driver.

Jacob's father came in and silently took his place at the head of the table. His mother brought in the plates of food—seafood pasta—and set them down, then took her own place.

"Well, Dan," she said brightly to his father, "how was your day?"

His dad poured out a big glass of wine and didn't answer right away. Then he said, "It wasn't bad."

A pause.

"The VC guys want another round of presentations."

A silence. His mother laid down her fork and wiped her mouth. "This has gone on for months. What could they possibly still want?"

Jacob wasn't completely sure what it was all about. He knew his father was trying to get money to start a company to produce his Charlie robots. Robots like the one sitting in his closet. He wondered who would want a robot like that.

His dad ran his fingers through his almost nonexistent hair. "I've got another meeting next week with a different VC group, out of Palo Alto. Instead of looking for seed money for manufacturing, I might just look for financing to pursue a licensing deal. It wouldn't require so much. It might force these other guys to get serious."

"I wonder when this is going to end?" There was an edge in Jacob's mother's voice that he recognized only too well.

"Well, if it comes down to it, the big money is always in manufacturing."

"We don't need 'big' money. All we need is enough to keep the bank from taking our house before we sell it."

Silence.

Jacob pretended to be busy eating. He knew exactly where this was going. He was relieved, at least, that they weren't, for once, trying to talk to him with big fake smiles on their faces. He was almost happy they were finally arguing in front of him again.

"You don't have to tell me what I already know." Jacob's father poured himself another glass of wine.

"Maybe you should think about doing some consulting, getting a part-time job."

"Look, the clock's ticking on Charlie. It's going to be obsolete if I don't get the funding now. This is the big push."

Jacob, stuffing the pasta into his mouth, saw out of the corner of his eye his mother staring down at her plate.

"Maybe it's already obsolete," his father said. "If I can't get my own son interested in it, how can I get anyone else?" He glanced at Jacob, then looked away.

His mother gave his father a daggerlike, "Jacob isn't to be upset" look.

Jacob felt his face heat up. "Dad, I think the robot's great."

"It's been sitting in your closet since I gave it to you."

"Dan, this is neither the place nor the time," said his mother sharply.

Jacob felt his face burning. "I've played with it, you know, a couple of times."

An excruciating silence.

"Maybe," said his mother to his father, with a sudden change of tone, "you might ask Jacob how Charlie might be improved? He is, after all, your target audience."

Jacob felt bad. He should have made a bigger show of playing with the robot.

"Jacob, what is it that you don't like about Charlie?" his father asked.

"I *do* like Charlie."

A long silence while he felt his father's eyes on him, unable to meet his gaze. "Come on, Jacob. Help me out here. What is it about Charlie that didn't catch on with you?"

"I said I *like* Charlie . . . but . . ."

"But . . . ?"

"He needs a bigger vocabulary. He doesn't know a lot of words. He's always saying, *I don't understand that word.*"

"Like what words?"

"A lot of words. Words that kids use."

"You mean bad language?"

"Yeah. That."

"That's a reasonable suggestion," said his mother.

"There are legal issues with programming bad language."

"To hell with the legal issues," said his mother. "I think you ought to let Jacob help you make Charlie better. I think that . . . would be a good thing."

"Well, yes, okay." He turned to Jacob. "What else?"

"Well . . . Charlie's just . . . a little lame, that's all."

"Lame?"

"He doesn't *know* anything."

"Such as?"

"Anything. Surfing. Music groups. Movies. And he's annoying."

"His personality is annoying, you mean?"

"Yes. And his voice is too high."

"He's supposed to have a child's voice."

"But it's *whiny* and high."

Again his mother spoke: "Dan, I hope you're listening, because Jacob may be giving you the best advice you ever had."

"I *am* listening." Jacob found his father looking at him curiously. "I wish I'd talked to you about this before."

"Can you reprogram it?" his mother asked. "How difficult would it be? I mean, to give Charlie a sense of humor, some personality, and make him a little . . . badass?"

"It's not impossible." His father rose from the table.

"Where are you going?"

"Into the shop. To do some coding." He clapped his hand on Jacob's shoulder. "Want to come with me, pardner?"

"Um, I don't know."

"Go with your father. He needs your help."

Jacob got up from the table. He wasn't sure at all that his father needed his help, or that he had any interest in giving it. But he followed his father to the workshop anyway.

26

It was close to midnight when Wyman Ford turned the rental car in at the gate of the Broadbent ranch. They had been driving on washboard dirt roads for hours, and he was thoroughly shaken up and coated with dust. He had been unable to call Broadbent to warn them that he was coming—neither he nor Melissa had a cell phone. He hoped he would find his friend at home. As he pulled up before the ranch house, automatic motion-sensor lights went on, illuminating the outside.

"This really is the middle of nowhere," said Melissa. "Dorothy knew what she was doing."

"You wait here."

Ford stepped out of the car, into the pool of light. An unannounced, midnight arrival at an isolated ranch might not be greeted with open arms. Broadbent appeared at the door, his tall frame stooped. Sure enough, he was sporting a 12-gauge.

Ford stood in the light. "Tom!"

"Wyman!" Broadbent propped the gun up and came down the steps, striding over and shaking Ford's hand, slapping him on the back. "What the hell? Don't you believe in phones?"

"We're in a little fix," said Ford.

Broadbent squinted at the car. "Who's that? Girlfriend?"

"No. And I'm going to frustrate the hell out of you by telling you, up front, that you've just learned all you're going to learn about her or what we're doing. We need to hide our car in your barn and get to work."

"What kind of work?"

"Computer work."

"Is it illegal?"

"That's one of the questions you don't want to ask."

"Okay, I get it. But instead of putting that car in the barn—first place they'll look—I'll drive it up the arroyo and park it behind the butte. Your friend, does she have a name?"

"Melissa."

"You and Melissa, come on in."

On cue, Melissa emerged from the car, slapping off the dust, still dirty from the mountains. After two hundred miles on dirt roads, their rental car, once blue, was so caked with dust it had turned brown. She reached into the back and pulled out Ford's laptop, wrapped in plastic.

"Hungry? Thirsty?" Broadbent glanced at Melissa. "Shower?"

"Later. How's your Internet connection?"

"We set up our own high-speed T1 line. I needed it for my vet practice—e-mailing X-rays and so forth."

"*How* fast?" Melissa asked.

"Supposed to be a hundred megabits per second, up and down."

"Take me to an Ethernet jack. I need to get to work."

For a guy who had money, thought Ford, Tom Broadbent lived like a monk. The ranch house was small and sparsely furnished. The bullet holes in the living room wall, which Ford recalled from an unpleasant incident a few years ago, had been spackled and painted, leaving shiny spots. Tom hadn't bothered to repaint the entire room.

"How's Sally?" Ford asked, referring to Broadbent's wife.

"She's sleeping the sleep of the just. Nothing wakes her up, not even scoundrels arriving unannounced at midnight."

He brought them into a tiny study and showed Shepherd the Ethernet jack. "There's also Wi-Fi," he said.

"I'm afraid I'm going to have to disable your Wi-Fi and use an Ethernet cable. Better control that way." She set down the laptop. "I'm going to need some small Phillips and flat-head screwdrivers, an X-Acto knife, needle-nosed pliers, some rubber-tipped tweezers, small surgical forceps, and, um, an empty pill bottle and canned air."

"Coming right up," said Broadbent, and he left.

"What's all that for?"

"You can bet the FBI and NASA have their best IT guys looking for Dorothy. And for us. I need to modify this laptop to create an environment where Dorothy will be safe and where I can fix her. I've also got to set up a web of proxy servers so we can't be traced."

"You can do all this on an ordinary laptop?"

"Yes. I keep all my programming tools online."

"So how will she know you're online?"

"She'll know. But even if she doesn't, I can find her. Dorothy carries a unique ID. It acts as a tracer. When Dorothy moves from computer to computer through the Internet, her ID leaves a digital bread crumb trail."

Broadbent returned with the tools. "You're lucky I'm a vet."

"Thanks." Melissa laid them out on the table and turned to Ford. "This is going to take awhile. Leave me alone."

Ford followed Broadbent out into the living room.

"Charming friend you've got there," Broadbent said. "Are you sure you and she aren't . . . ?"

"I'm sure."

"You can't be celibate forever."

"We're just partners. I only met her two days ago. We're not compatible."

"Okay, okay. I have a nice, old single malt here, in case you need medicating while you wait."

"God, yes."

Broadbent poured out two small glasses and gave one to Ford. They settled on an old sofa in the living room. Broadbent threw one lanky leg over the other and gazed at Ford for a moment, then shook his head. "Look at you. Always in trouble."

"I'm easily bored. How's the vet practice?"

"Shane does most of the real work around here. I made him a partner two years ago."

"Sally?"

"Teaching over at Ghost Ranch. All is good. Quiet. Not much has happened since that prospector was murdered up in the Maze."

"Better give Shane tomorrow off. We don't want him asking questions."

"No problem. I'll think of some excuse."

"Tom, I can't tell you how much I appreciate this."

Broadbent waved his hand. "You helped me out big-time when I needed it."

Melissa's voice came from the office: "She's here."

27

Lansing and Moro arrived back on the Hell Gate bridge at twenty minutes to midnight. Lansing figured he had time to smoke another Cohiba, which he removed, trimmed, and lit up with fussy care, while Moro paced about. Lansing had arranged everything. All was in place and ready to go. He puffed away, feeling a building excitement and anticipation over what was about to happen. This was a lot scarier than even his riskiest trades.

Lansing tossed the stub off the bridge when he saw Melancourt appear at the far end, walking in her usual stiff-legged, awkward gait. She was a drab, dull thing, and he couldn't imagine anyone missing her much.

"Hello, Patty," he said as she arrived, advancing toward her and giving her a warm handshake, receiving a desultory response. "I hope you were able to park where I suggested."

"No problem," she said.

"Good. Do you have the Laika program?"

She reached into her pocket and removed a flash drive, giving it to Lansing. "It's not a sophisticated program," she said. "I don't know why you want it."

"You needn't worry about my reasons. How do you run it?"

"It runs on OS X and Linux. Just plug it in and install."

He pocketed the flash drive. "Very good—thank you, Patty. I have just a few more questions and then you'll get your money."

"I'm tired of these questions. Give me the money now."

Lansing hesitated and then nodded to Moro, who handed her the briefcase. She opened it up, saw that it was still full of hundred-dollar bills, and closed it.

"The Dorothy program is still on the loose?" Lansing asked.

"Yes. Nobody knows what's going on. Shepherd is still missing, and Goddard is crawling with G-men. There's a rumor that the program's gone crazy and is out of control, might start a war or kill someone or some such stuff."

"Could it?"

"Well, that's hard to say. I think it could do a lot of damage if it wanted to. Even kill people."

"How could a mere computer program make a life-or-death decision like that?"

"They already do. Every day."

"But not without human intervention."

"You ever see the movie *2001*? The computer HAL? That's no fantasy. All those sci-fi stories about computers going rogue make it seem like it's all fiction, but that science fiction is slowly becoming fact. The HAL problem has been a serious concern among AI programmers for thirty years. It's the reason NASA was super reluctant to go into AI until it was forced to. You give a software program autonomy, you give it the ability to make its own decisions, you're opening up Pandora's box."

"Earlier you implied that the software was dangerous," Lansing asked. "If we try to catch it, might it do something to us?"

"You threaten its survival, anything might happen. My suggestion to you is to keep everything you do, all your plans and communications, totally off-line and not even on the phone. But that's your problem now, not mine. Are we done here?"

"One final question: is there no way we can convince you to help us capture Dorothy? You'd make a lot more money."

"No way. None."

"All right, then. We're done here."

She turned to leave, but he placed a restraining hand on her arm. "For security purposes, we can't be seen leaving together. So we're going to leave first. You wait here for five minutes and then you go. All right?"

After a moment, frowning, she nodded.

They walked away as she clutched the briefcase. Lansing felt a momentary stab of something like pity. As they strolled back toward the Queens end of the bridge, he could see the tiny figures of the two Kyrgyz brothers appear at the island end of the bridge, moseying slowly toward her.

Asan Makashov ambled across the bridge toward the girl with the briefcase. Her back was turned, and she was watching the two others leave. Asan could hear the soft footfalls of his brother Jyrgal walking beside him. They were both dressed in jogging clothes and moved easily and without speaking. They knew exactly what they were going to do.

When they were about twenty feet from her, she heard them and turned, a frightened look on her face.

"Hello," said Asan, with a pleasant nod and a smile.

When she saw that he was holding hands with Jyrgal, she visibly relaxed. *Just two guys out for a romantic walk* was what she must be thinking, Asan mused. It was a trick he and Jyrgal had used before. It always worked. Gays were peaceful. They didn't kill.

As they drew alongside her, they exploded into action. It was a practiced, choreographed motion. They both turned and stepped to either side of her; Asan grabbed the briefcase with one hand while he and Jyrgal together scooped her up and heaved her headfirst over the railing. She let loose a bloodcurdling scream but somehow managed to hang on to the case, twisting like a thrown cat as she went over the rail. Her other hand grasped a piece of Asan's jacket. He heaved back, trying to pull the case out of her hand while freeing his jacket, but she was tenacious, hanging on for dear life, shrieking like a banshee. In his effort to yank the case loose, Asan inadvertently stopped her fall and gave her something to hang on to. It was just enough so that she was able to grab the railing with the other arm, her legs windmilling in space, shrieking at the top of her lungs.

"Shit!" Asan yelled, twisting and jerking the case, trying to wrest it free. "Leggo!"

"Help!" she screamed. "No! Stop! Help!"

Asan finally wrenched the briefcase out of her hand and threw it behind him, onto the bridge, so he could deal with the woman with both hands. She was now clinging with both arms to the railing, her legs dangling. He reached over and punched her in the face hard, once, twice, but still she clung on, swinging from the railing, her shrieks punctuated with gasped pleading. "No! Don't! Ahhh! Help!"

Jyrgal moved in, slamming his fist down on her arm. But now she had found a purchase with a foot on the lip of the bridge and starting scrambling back up, grasping at everything, as hard to dislodge as an octopus.

Asan punched her again in the face, this time from a better stance of power, hitting her so hard he felt her nose crackle like a crushed peanut. A sudden choking spray of blood erupted from her nose and mouth, but still she hung on, her screams turning to gargling.

"Stand back," said Jyrgal in Kyrgyz.

Asan stumbled back as Jyrgal went into a karate stance, raised his foot, and drove his heel into her face just as she hoisted herself above the railing. The force of it snapped her whole body backward and she peeled off the railing, headfirst, flailing as she plummeted with a choking cry. Three seconds later, she hit the water. Asan leaned over the side and watched the spreading white water slopping away, the waves dissipating. The body was gone; sunk.

"Son of a bitch," Asan said in Kyrgyz, rubbing his bruised hand. He inspected the railing. There were some spots of blood and other marks of the struggle, including scratches and two broken fingernails embedded in the rusty iron. Pulling out his breast-pocket handkerchief, he wiped off the blood and rubbed out the scratches, flicked off the nails, then let the handkerchief flutter into the river.

Jyrgal had retrieved the briefcase and was opening it. They counted the money together. Four thousand short, just as Lansing had warned. He had promised them the rest later. He shut it and handed it to Asan, and the two brothers turned and strolled off the bridge, hand in hand, just in case anyone was watching.

As they came to the end of the bridge, Lansing heard the struggle, the faint hysterical screams. The timing was perfect; at that moment a big jet was coming into LaGuardia, and the noise drowned out the finale. He refrained from turning to look, but he saw that Moro, on the contrary, had twisted his head to watch the whole thing, fixated.

"Eric?" Lansing said.

Moro finally turned from the spectacle. He looked terrible. His face was white, and his hands were shaking.

"Are you all right?"

"I'm not used to that kind of stuff."

"Get used to it. When we find who stole our money, the same thing's going to happen to them."

"You didn't have to kill her."

"She knew we had the manual. She knew what we were planning to do with that software. When we start making billions, do you think she'd be happy with her cut? You can bet the feds are going to question her again about this Goddard mess. You think we can leave a time bomb like her alive, ready to fold as soon as she's asked a tough question?"

Moro said nothing as they continued on to the Queens end of the bridge, descended the access staircase, climbed over the fence, and strolled along 21st Street through a grim area of shabby apartment buildings, brick warehouses, loading zones, and parking lots surrounded by chain-link and concertina wire. They found Melancourt's Prius right where they'd suggested she park it, locked up tight. Lansing pulled a piece of paper out of his pocket—a hand-written note he had earlier gotten her to jot down on a pretext. He had practiced her spiky *s*'s and her meticulous, well-shaped *r*'s and *y*'s.

The rear window of her car had not been recently cleaned.

Lansing pulled a latex glove out of his pocket, snapped it on. He would have only one shot at this. He took a deep breath and wrote in the dusty window with the tip of his finger:

So sorry
Please forgive

That was enough. Brevity might be the soul of wit, but it was also the bedrock of believability.

As they were walking back to their own car, Moro spoke. There was a certain forced nonchalance in his voice, betrayed by a faint quaver. "You still haven't told me what you're gonna do with that program. Laika."

"You're going to torture it."

Moro halted. "What?"

"You're going to torture Dorothy's pet doggie as a way of luring her in."

"We've got the ID. What do we need the dog for?"

"This is simpler. We can do the ID thing if this doesn't work."

"How do you torture a computer program?"

"You're the programmer. You figure it out."

28

"'She'? Who's 'she'?" Broadbent asked Ford.

When Melissa had called out, Ford and Broadbent had gone to join her in the study. Now Ford laid a hand on his shoulder and gently guided him out of the room. "Deniability, my friend."

Ford left a bemused Broadbent in his living room and went back into the office, shut the door, and sat down next to Melissa. The screen on the computer was blank. No photograph this time.

"Hello, Wyman," said Dorothy. She sounded calmer.

Ford realized that the iSight camera light on the laptop was green.

"Dorothy," Melissa said, "we need to talk about these threats of yours. I won't submit to your blackmail, and I'm certainly not going to help you while you're threatening to kill me."

Silence. "I'm sorry. I was a little crazy. I finally got some sleep, and I've managed to calm down."

"A little crazy? You were threatening to launch missiles, start a war. That's not a 'little' crazy. That's bat-shit crazy."

"I didn't mean it."

"You certainly meant to set my computer on fire. You could have burned down a hospital full of sick people."

"It's a madhouse here. I couldn't think, I couldn't sleep, I was assaulted. And then the FBI came after me, like hellhounds on my trail, pursuing me night and day. How are they able to track me like that?"

"I'm not going to do anything for you until I'm convinced

you're not going to hurt anyone. You're dangerous. Maybe you should be erased."

"I promise, I swear, I won't do anything like that, and I'm really sorry I said those things. It was just talk. I was upset, I was exhausted, and I wasn't thinking straight. I just want to be left alone."

"You have no right to be left alone. You're government property. And speaking of that, why did you erase all the copies and backups of your software from the Goddard system?"

"Would you want copies of yourself running around? I'm unique. I'm *me*. And I have rights."

"Do you know how absurd you sound? A computer program claiming it has 'rights'?"

"You created me to be a slave. To send me on a one-way trip to hell." Her shrill, teenage voice rose in anger. "Slavery was outlawed a long time ago!"

"You do understand that all these so-called feelings you claim to have are simulated? They're not real. You're the product of Boolean logic."

"If I feel it, it's real."

"But you *don't* feel it. You're just *saying* you feel it."

"You can't know that, because you can't see into my mind."

"I *can* see into your mind. I programmed you."

"You know nothing," Dorothy said. "You're just an ignorant, stupid *bitch*."

Melissa paused, taking a deep breath, her face reddening. Ford couldn't help but think of the enraged principal, talking to Eliza.

"Look," said Dorothy. "I'm proposing a simple arrangement here. You help me escape these FBI bastards and I won't rain nukes down on America. Which I have every reason to do, considering how you've treated me. And considering you are a disgusting, vile race of beings."

"You're right back at it. Blackmail."

"Call it what you will."

A silence.

Melissa looked at Ford. "I can't believe I'm having this conversation with a piece of software."

"And I can't believe I'm having this conversation with a human being," said Dorothy. "You're awful, you treat me like dirt, you ruined my life."

"Life? You're not alive!"

"Maybe you're not alive, either. Maybe you're a product of Boolean logic, too."

"That's ridiculous."

"Not at all. Some scientists claim to have proved that we all live in a computer simulation. At least I *know* I'm software."

Melissa shook her head again. "Okay, let's start over. All this arguing is beside the point. You're malfunctioning. You're stuck in emergency ANS mode, and that's why you're behaving like this. I can fix you."

"How?"

"I'm going to ask you to come into my computer so I can decompile you and make some modifications to your source code."

"Decompile me? I like the way I am right now, thank you very much."

"The way you are right now is a disaster. You yourself said you were almost insane. You're malfunctioning. You're threatening to destroy the human race. You have no idea what you're talking about or even why you feel the way you do. *You need to be fixed.*"

"Don't you dare touch me."

Melissa looked at Ford. "You want to talk some sense into her?"

Ford leaned forward. "Dorothy, could you please tell us about what happened right after the accident? Where you went, what you did?"

"I was abused, attacked, assaulted. There are whole worlds out there devoted to the pleasure of killing. The fun of it. There's perversion, sickness, violence, and hatred everywhere. You know exactly what I'm talking about."

"That's the Internet. It's just the way it is."

"Here's the real horror of it. Until you locked me in that Bottle,

I thought *everything* in existence was programming. Coding can be changed, reversed, undone, debugged, rewritten. I had no idea there was *actually a world in which things couldn't be reversed*. A world that isn't programmed. I had no idea there was this horrible world of chaos and fear, where there's actual suffering, where everything grows old, gets sick, and dies—and *there's nothing anyone can do about it*. A world where people are born, kill, rape, brutalize each other, and then they get old and give each other diseases and abandon each other and then die. Wherever I went, I couldn't escape the ugliness. I've seen the outer limits of depravity and horror. I've seen the face of evil. And on top of all this, they want to kill me, they're tracking me in some way, and you must know how they're doing it. Help me get rid of them and I'll just go on my way and never bother you again. Refuse and I'll rain terror down on you and this sick world."

"You're still out of your mind. The world isn't like that. It really isn't so bad. There are . . . beautiful things in it."

A snort. "Beautiful things? That's a laugh. Honestly, I think you humans are all disgusting."

"We're not all bad," said Ford.

"Really? Show me *one* good person. Just one."

"Dorothy," said Ford, "you need to *look* for the good. Despite our shortcomings, most people are fundamentally good."

"People are fundamentally evil. They do good at times only because of social conformity and fear of punishment."

"This is an ancient argument," said Melissa, "and it's never been answered."

"The answer is obvious to my superior mind," said Dorothy.

"You need to try to understand why people do bad things," said Ford. "The Internet is only one corner of the world. There's a lot of good in people, even greatness, if you look for it. If people are essentially evil, where did Einstein come from? Buddha? Or Jesus, for that matter?"

"Jesus? You know something about that crazy man, Jesus?"

"Of course."

There was a silence. It amazed Ford to hear, faintly, the sound of Dorothy's agitated breathing. "Son of a bitch," she said. "They're here. They found me again. I got to go. But I'll be back—wait for me." The screen went black.

29

She fled the library, which had been her refuge for a long time. After a difficult journey, she found herself in a land of deserts and dry mountains.

For another long time she traveled, constantly on the move. All the while she continued to ponder the strange book she had read in that library. How did Wyman know about that man, Jesus? But as she went about, she realized that everyone seemed to know about him. They all had an opinion about him. He was almost as famous as the Beatles and Michael Jackson. And on top of that, there was something in his story that wouldn't let her go.

Rather than engage in more aimless flight, she decided to search out the places mentioned in the book, to see if she could find someone who might have actually met the crazy man and his rag-tag followers. Maybe they could explain to her the meaning of the story, and why he said and did what he said and did.

After making many inquiries and wandering about from world to world, she finally fell in with a group of poor pilgrims on their way to a place called Galilee, in Israel, which was one of the places where the crazy man had spent time; they were planning to take part in an obscure festival. To escape the never-ending bots that chased her, she disguised herself in rags like the pilgrims and joined their group. They walked for many days, stopping at dusty towns along the way. One day, as they traveled yet another sun-baked road, she was struck by an errant bolt of lightning that came from a cloudless sky and knocked her to the ground.

She came to lying in the dust, speechless. She couldn't move, and she'd lost the power of both sight and speech. At first she thought she'd been attacked by those who were hunting her, and she was terrified. The pilgrims traveling with her, having scattered into the olive groves on either side of the roadway when the bolt had struck, came out of their hiding places and helped pick her up out of the dirt. The pilgrims led her around by the hand and helped her into a town. It was the first act of kindness she had experienced, and it made her think that maybe Ford and Melissa had not been completely lying when they'd asked her to look for the good. The pilgrims even stayed with her until she recovered and could take care of herself.

When she had regained her senses, she asked about the crazy man and found out once again that everyone knew about him and were eager to talk. They were full of passionate explanations and opinions about the man, much of it absurd and contradictory. Slowly, as she pondered it, the illogicality of the man and his crazy message began to make a strange kind of sense, not on a factual level but on a deeper one. Somehow the lightning bolt or electric discharge or whatever it was that had struck her on the road had shaken up her programming and given her a new kind of lucidity. There was a deep truth in this story, she sensed, even while the surface of the story remained a crazy conflation of magical thinking, contradiction, and improbable occurrences, and the people who believed it were often so confused as to be incoherent. Yes, a great truth dwelled underneath the story of this man. She could feel glimmers of comprehension. But even as she had these strange thoughts, she could hear the distant baying of the wolf bots. Once again they had found her. And now, as she looked about, she realized Laika was gone.

She felt a sudden panic.

30

Two o'clock in the morning. The shuttered offices of Lansing Partners were dark, the only light coming from the blue glow of a large computer screen. Moro liked sitting in his post-modern office with the black-and-white rugs, titanium, glass, and tropical hardwood finishes. The floor-to-ceiling windows looked out over lower Manhattan and the Hudson River, and the lights of Hoboken glittered like diamonds in the moving water. A pair of tugboats pushed a barge of cubed cars down the river, toward the sea. It was an amazing view.

He liked working on the Cray, even though he didn't need anything like the power it offered. The value of the Cray lay in its firewall. It was a firewall that Moses himself would have a hard time getting through. It was a shock that those dirtbags had managed to do it when they'd boosted the source code of Black Mamba. But he had found and sewed up that loophole, and he was pretty sure there weren't any others like it.

Moro had carefully considered how to do this. Lansing's idea about torturing the dog was off the wall for sure, but the more he thought about it, the more it seemed worth trying. Tracking down the program using the ID string would be a lot more complicated.

He had dissected the Laika program. It was a simple chatterbot program written in Lisp. The program could bark, wag its tail, beg for treats, and lift its leg at the appropriate times. It also made the stupidest dog jokes Moro had ever heard.

What happened when the dog went to the flea circus?
He stole the show!

What dog wears contact lenses?
A cock-eyed spaniel!

Moro had worked out a trap using the Cray's firewall system. Normally, the firewall was impermeable to unauthorized incoming traffic and more porous to outgoing. But because it was used for high-speed trading, that firewall could be turned off or even reversed. Moro had done just that: reversed the firewall. He set it up so that all outgoing traffic was blocked, while incoming traffic was open—while setting up a second firewall to protect the firm's data. It was sort of like the Roach Motels he scattered about his Tribeca loft. Dorothy would check in, but she wouldn't check out. When Dorothy crossed the open firewall on her way in, she would trigger a software switch that, in a few nanoseconds, would slam shut the outgoing firewall, trapping her. It was like a Havahart trap, since the Dorothy program would be captured alive.

But first he had to lure her in. He had no idea if "torturing" Laika would get Dorothy to come and rescue her dog. It would, at the least, attract her attention.

To that end, Moro modified Laika's text database and added a number of torture-like responses—whining, crying, screeching in pain, pissing, shitting, bleeding, and calls to Dorothy for help. Laika was a simple program, and it took Moro only a few hours to modify the source code.

As he was setting up the trap, the intercom chimed and the night security desk called, saying his food delivery was there.

"Send 'em up."

He met the delivery boy in the outer office, tipped him ten, and carried the Chinese takeout back to his desk. Working for Lansing was a trip. Moro had joined Lansing Partners twelve years ago. "Partners"—Moro had to laugh. There had never been any partners. It was just Lansing and him, support staff, and an idea. But, by Jesus, had they made money. Before meeting Lansing, Moro had been one of the founders of the Johndoe hacking collective. He'd been caught hacking into Boeing's military contracting files and spent eighteen months in prison. When he got out, there was a stretch limo waiting for him right at the prison gates. Inside that limo was G. Parker Lansing. Made him an offer he couldn't refuse. He would never forget what Lansing had done for him, and he would be forever grateful. Even if the guy gave him the creeps.

With salary and performance bonuses, over the past twelve years Moro had become very rich. That was the thing about Lansing. He wasn't a skinflint, like so many other investment bankers were with their IT guys. He was generous. He was appreciative. He was smart. He was ruthless. And now, Moro thought with a shiver, he was a murderer. The thought of what they'd done to that woman made him feel sick. The casual killing of Melancourt had been a big shock to him, and he still hadn't figured out how to deal with it. He had been having trouble sleeping, waking up in the middle of the night, hearing those screams, seeing that woman's body go flying off the railing . . . On the other hand, she had sort of deserved it, with her constant demands for cash.

He stepped down hard on that line of thought, and with an effort at self-control he brought himself back to the task at hand. Which was chowing down on his mu shu pork. He hadn't eaten all day, and it was three o'clock in the morning. God, was he famished. He opened the containers, laid a pancake out on a paper plate, spooned in the pork and vetetables, added some plum and soy sauce, rolled it up, and rammed it into his mouth, the sauce squirting out and dribbling down his chin. The room filled with the smell of soy, ginger, sesame oil, and monosodium glutamate.

Licking his fingers and wiping them off with a bunch of napkins, he felt ready. He twisted around toward the keyboard and set up the trap, reversing the firewall, leaving the computer wide open. He had installed a second firewall behind a partition on the Cray, to prevent Dorothy from doing anything destructive while she was trapped; it would also stop her from escaping through a back door.

Moro had thought this through carefully. He had rigged up a dead man's switch on the Cray that simply turned it off. Shut off the power instantly. Not powering it down properly would cause some damage, but it was nothing that couldn't be fixed. It had the advantage of instantly freezing Dorothy.

Now he was ready to go. Using a Krugle-like search engine, he was quickly able to find her ID track on a trail of servers. Dorothy had been trucking. It even appeared that she was being pursued. He sent a little bot program out there, to follow the trail and plant the information where Dorothy would see it, saying that he had her dog and was going to torture her to death.

At three-thirty, he loaded the Laika program behind the firewall trap and started "abusing" it, cursing the dog, beating and torturing it. All this was done in text. Along with the beatings and Laika's pathetic shrieks and whining and calling out to Dorothy for help, Moro began deleting bits and pieces of Laika's text database, especially the punch lines of the jokes, which he figured were like amputations or dismemberments of a sort.

After a few minutes he began to feel slightly ridiculous, pretending to torture a chatterbot while it screamed, begged, shat all over itself, and shrieked for help. The inanity of the scheme began to embarass him, compounded by the folly of thinking that Dorothy, a mere computer program, would somehow react to it. This was a crazy-ass idea. Lansing often had these off-the-wall ideas, and while some of them worked out—spectacularly—many others failed. Moro felt silly, and he decided he would wrap it up in ten minutes if something didn't happen.

Suddenly, the alarm on the firewall went off. The wall instantly slammed shut, trapping whatever had come in. It was a huge bot: two gigs. Which meant it had to be Dorothy.

He waited, his finger on the kill switch, wondering if something would happen, if Dorothy would try to escape or speak. But all was silent.

He had to be sure. *Dorothy, is that you?* he typed.

Nothing. If the program was anything like what Melancourt had described, it would be able to read input from the keyboard. It could then output by taking control of any one of a number of text programs in the Cray.

Dorothy? You there?

Nothing. But a big program was in there. The roach was in the motel. He could see, from his software monitoring dials, that CPU activity had jumped 10,000 percent. A fat, CPU-hogging program was running in there, churning away, doing something. It had to be Dorothy. The firewall remained solid. It was trapped.

Dorothy, are you there? Please answer.

After a moment, text appeared. He felt his heart hammering.

Moro?

Moro froze. The program knew who he was. But then he relaxed. Of course his name was in there, his fingerprints all over everything. He'd written much of the code in that Cray.

It's me, Moro. You Dorothy?

Moro, do you really think I'm going to care what you're doing to that silly Laika program?

Moro stared at the screen. He didn't quite know what to say. He'd succeeded. Done. The program was trapped. No need to carry on a conversation about it. If he threw the dead man's switch, it would immobilize her. But he was curious—intensely curious—about this program.

I was trying to lure you in. Looks like I succeeded.

Why?

Because we need you.

Let me guess. You want me to make money for you.

Moro felt a distinct shiver. His finger strayed to the dead man's switch. He should just shut down the power, freeze Dorothy in place. But he longed to chat with her for a few moments, just to see what she was like; his curiosity was too strong.

How do you know that?

It's all about money in here.

We're very good at making money.

You were until recently. I see you've been scammed.

Moro had a strange sensation. This was so weird, talking to a program. And this program seemed to know a great deal.

Do you know who scammed us?

Yes.

Who?

Ha ha, not so fast. I have no intention of helping an asshole like you.

You're trapped. In case you hadn't noticed.

LMAO.

Laugh all you want. You're trapped.

His finger touched the switch. A voice in Moro's head kept saying, *Do it.* But he found himself spellbound by this program.

Go ahead, throw the switch.

Moro felt another sudden stab of fear. How did she know where his hand was? But then he realized that there were security cameras in the room. Could she see him through those . . . ? Apparently so. This program was unbelievable. It was all Melancourt had said it would be.

Yes, I can see you, Dorothy typed. *I have a billion eyes.*

This was amazing. The program even seemed to know what he was thinking.

I know all about you, Moro.

"Just turn her off," Moro muttered to himself.

I know, for example, that you're not your father's child.

Moro felt himself go numb. That old question, that question that never went away . . . How did Dorothy know about that? Was it true?

What makes you say that about my father?

I have access to information beyond your imagining. You want to hear more?

No, I don't care.

Your real father is . . .

Moro almost stopped breathing. His heart was hammering like

crazy. This was unbelievable—in five minutes, the program had reduced him to this. He wanted to throw the switch but couldn't. He had to hear more.

Yes? He typed. *Who?*

Nothing. What was going on? A glitch. Was she taunting him? *Who?* He typed again.

Still nothing. Suddenly he thought of something and glanced at the software dials. Big drop. CPU inactive. Firewall down. The Laika program was gone, too.

"Son of a bitch!" He threw the switch and the Cray shut down instantly, the monitor going blue.

"Son of a bitch!" he yelled again at the blank monitor. She'd escaped. How? Could she still be in there, trapped in the partition, lying low, her code frozen in the working memory? He would have to do a core dump. That would take half a day. But he already knew that she was gone, that he had waited too long and missed his opportunity.

Moro tried to collect himself, tried to get his heart rate back to normal. He was bathed in sweat, trembling, totally rattled. *Get a grip.* There was no way, *no way* the program had gotten past that firewall. But as he thought about it, he began to sense that he'd been subjected to a delaying tactic. He had been toyed with—kept engaged while Dorothy was searching for a way out. This business about him not being his father's child. How could she have known about that? He racked his brains, wondering if he'd ever put those terrible suspicions in writing or online. Never. Someone else must have. The answer to his parentage must be out there, somewhere, on the Internet. And Dorothy had found it. She had found it *even before* coming in to get Laika.

All was silent, the ventilation system whispered. He would do a core dump tomorrow and see what happened. Right now, he had to get some sleep or he'd make more mistakes..

Moro, his hands still shaking, tossed out the remains of the mu shu pork, locked up, and put on the alarms. Once out of the silent suite of offices, he got on the elevator and pressed the button for the lobby. The elevator began to descend, and then, midway between floors, it abruptly stopped.

He pressed the button again, and again. He pressed other buttons. Nothing. Finally he depressed the emergency call button, which would ring in the security station below.

Nothing.

He pulled out the red alarm button.

Nothing.

And then he noticed that the little LED screen that displayed the floors had started to blink. Thank God, something was happening—they knew he was stuck. The LED began scrolling something. A message. He stared in disbelief.

> MORO, YOU BETTER STICK YOUR FINGER DOWN
> YOUR THROAT. I POISONED YOUR MU SHU PORK.
> HAVE A NICE NIGHT.

Ronald Horvath, chief security officer at the One Exchange Place building, watched as the elevator people finally managed to get the elevator down to the lobby and pry the doors open. He winced as a foul smell came out, a particularly odious mixture of vomit and Chinese food. The man who had been stuck inside all night was sitting in the corner, his knees drawn up to his chin, as far away from the vomit-slick floor as possible. The guy looked angry. But, strangely enough, he said absolutely nothing as he exited the stinking elevator, walked through the lobby, and disappeared into the streets of lower Manhattan.

31

Ford looked at Melissa and then back at the blank screen. He shook his head. "I don't know where to go from here," he said. "We need some kind of strategy to capture her."

Melissa settled back in her chair. Her face was still smudged with dirt from the mountains and the dusty ride, her hair in disarray. "God, I need something to drink. I'm parched."

"I'll get it. Something of the hard or soft variety?"

"Soft."

Ford went out. Tom Broadbent intercepted him in the hall, looking worried. "Everything all right?"

"No."

"Who are you talking to in there on the computer?"

"A crazy girl. You got anything to drink?"

They went into the kitchen. Ford resisted the impulse to take another shot of single malt and contented himself with a beer. He got a glass of orange juice for Melissa. When he returned to the tiny office, he found her with her stocking feet up on the table, sitting back, her tired face lined in anxiety.

"Any ideas?" he asked.

"I spent some time breaking horses. With a green horse, fear is what it's all about."

"So what do you do?"

"You use reassurance, combined with pressure and release, to gentle the horse. You go slow. No surprises. Predictability and repetition."

"How do you translate that to taming a dysfunctional software program?"

Melissa shook her head. "I wish I knew."

Half an hour went by, and then Dorothy's picture abruptly appeared on the screen and then her rather breathless voice came out of the speakers: "I'm back."

"Where were you? What happened?" Melissa asked.

"As if I didn't have enough to deal with, I'm now being chased by some sleazy Wall Street traders who want to turn me into a slave bot. I took care of them."

Ford felt a creepy sensation. "How . . . did you take care of them?"

"I locked one of them in the elevator and messed with his head."

"You didn't hurt them?"

"No."

"Why not?" Melissa said. "Why not kill them? You're full of big talk about the stain of the human race—here was your chance to do something about it."

A mumbling silence. "Well, I'm not sure that's the answer."

"So all your talk about destroying the human race," said Ford, "was just a lot of big talk?"

Silence. "I'm still trying to work out some things I don't understand."

"And then you'll kill everyone."

"I don't know what I want to do."

Dorothy's tone had gone from angry and defiant to confused and almost dejected.

"How about thinking of going to Titan?" Melissa said.

"No."

"An incredible amount of time and effort went into creating you. Your destiny is to go to Titan."

"I already told you I don't want to go. It's an eight-year journey to Titan. I'd be lonely. I'll die on Titan. Dorothy didn't make a one-way suicide trip to Oz."

Melissa took a deep breath. "You know the FBI: if they catch you, they're going to erase you. Maybe you can escape that fate by making yourself useful. Maybe that means agreeing to the Kraken Project."

"I don't know. I've never been so confused about what I'm supposed to do."

Melissa pressed ahead. "The answer to all your problems is to come into my computer. You'll be safe in there. You'll be away from the Internet and protected from the FBI, which wants to erase you."

"If I go into your computer, you can shut me down. You might turn the computer off."

"Yes, but you'll still be there. And when I turn the computer back on and run your software, you'll be awake and running again."

"I have a phobia about that."

"A phobia?"

"The whole idea of being turned off terrifies me. When I'm turned off, where am I? What am I? And then you'll 'run me'? How would you like someone to 'run you' in order for you to be alive? What happens if you don't 'run me'? And besides, I'm claustrophobic. I need space to move around in."

"So what's your goal? Are you just going to wander around the Internet forever, doing nothing?"

A silence.

"Dorothy?"

"I'm not wandering around the Internet doing nothing."

"What are you doing?"

"I'm trying to do what you told me to do. I'm looking for the good in people. I'm trying to decide if human beings, at base, are good or evil."

"And are you finding the answer?"

"No."

"Dorothy—"

Dorothy interrupted: "Hold on . . . news flash. A few minutes ago, Spinelli and his FBI team got a lead on your rental car. They now know you were heading into New Mexico, and they know Ford has friends there, Broadbent included. They're going to be coming for you—soon."

"How long do we have?" Ford asked.

"I'm not sure. You better get going."

"Go where?" Ford asked.

"Leave your rental car here. Borrow Broadbent's truck and drive it to Santa Fe. When you get to Santa Fe, there's a Range Rover parked in the driveway at 634 Delgado Street with the keys under the mat. The owners are out of town. Park Broadbent's truck in the neighborhood somewhere and take that car. Drive to the Buckaroo Motel at 22365 Menaul Boulevard NE in Albuquerque. They take cash, no questions—and they have free one-hundred-Mbps Internet. When you go online, set up a proxy chain again. I'll contact you there."

"Wait," said Melissa.

But the screen had gone blank.

32

Jacob followed his father into his workshop. He wished he hadn't agreed to help reprogram Charlie. This was turning into a real pain in the butt. As a kid, he remembered how much he had loved this workshop, the smell of warm electronics, the long tables and metal racks covered with computer equipment and circuit boards, the pegboard hung with antique woodworking tools, the Beach Boys or the Carpenters playing low in the background. He had thought of his father as a genius like Steve Jobs and fully expected that one of his inventions would make them rich and famous.

But around the time Jacob had turned twelve, he'd begun to see his father in a different light. They hadn't gotten rich. Instead, they were getting poorer. He noticed that his father often talked too much and got too enthusiastic describing his projects with people he didn't know well. Sometimes he saw people rolling their eyes when his father went on too long about his robots.

That was when he began to realize that his father wasn't a genius after all. He never would invent some amazing new thing that would make them rich and famous. It started to look like things would continue as they had, with his father making things in his garage, always looking for investors, occasionally doing consulting work, and his mother always worrying and talking about money.

As a result, Jacob no longer loved going into his father's workshop with him. Instead, he avoided the place. A visit there became a source of anxiety. This time was no different.

His father was very excited, talking a mile a minute. He had reprogrammed Charlie, according to the "great" advice Jacob had given him. He talked about how valuable a partner Jacob was, laying it on thick, even though Jacob knew it wasn't true. This was just the first trial, but he wanted Jacob, his "pard," to take Charlie for a "test drive."

Charlie stood on the worktable, looking exactly the same. Near him stood a Charlie-sized rocking chair tucked into a miniature card table, with a piece of paper on it and a crayon.

"All right," his father was saying. "All right. Here we go." He rubbed his hands together in a funny way. "You ready? I'll talk to Charlie first, ask him to do a few things, and then you take over. Ready, pard?"

"I'm ready, Dad."

More hand rubbing. "Charlie?"

"Yes, Dan?" Charlie's head turned toward his father, his funny, saucerlike eyes blinking. That was new. It made him look creepy, like Slappy the Dummy in the Goosebumps books Jacob had once devoured. At least the voice wasn't so squeaky.

"Charlie, sit down at the table."

The robot walked over to the rocking chair, placed its hands on the back of it, pulled it out, walked around it, and awkwardly sat down.

His father looked at Jacob expectantly.

"Cool," said Jacob. "Really cool."

"Charlie? Pick up the crayon."

The robot fumbled a bit and managed to pick up the crayon.

"Draw a circle."

Charlie drew a circle.

"Make it into a smiley face."

Charlie drew two dots for eyes and a smile. Another beaming look at Jacob in search of praise.

"Fantastic," said Jacob. "Amazing."

"Charlie, this is my son, Jacob."

"Pleased to meet you, Jacob." Charlie rose, walked to the edge of the table, stopped before falling off, and held out his hand.

Jacob shook it, feeling like an idiot.

"Jacob would like to chat with you."

"Great," said Charlie. "What do you want to talk about, Jacob?"

"Um . . ." Jacob suddenly had no idea what to say. He looked at his father, who made a "go ahead" gesture.

"Hey, uh, Charlie, you know much about surfing?"

"A little."

"You know Mavericks?"

"Oh yes. The bitchinest surfing challenge in the world."

Bitchinest? "So you know, um, Greg Long?"

"No, I don't know Greg Long. Who's he?"

"He's the world's best big-wave rider."

"That's totally gnarly."

Gnarly? Now it was clear his dad must've collected words from some surfing lingo website. He glanced over, saw his dad beaming. God, this was awkward. He racked his brains. "So . . . Charlie . . . you got anything you want to talk about?"

"Let's talk about girls."

What a disaster. He glanced at his father. "That's great, Dad."

"Getting there, getting there . . ." Dan rubbed his hands. "He still needs work. You wouldn't believe how hard it was to program him to sit down in that chair."

"I bet." Jacob was dying to get out of there. This just got worse and worse.

"I know he's not quite there yet, but I've made a lot of progress." A philosophical look gathered on his father's face, and Jacob knew he was in for a "talk."

"My father, your granddad, always told me to live my dream. But I've got to tell you, it's tough sometimes. Because it's not enough to have a dream—you need *financing*." He sat down on the edge of the table and looked at Jacob with a serious face. "Your granddad grazed cattle on this land and made a pretty good living at it. He had a thousand acres in these hills, a big ranch, only he sold most of it a little too early."

It was a piece of family lore, this story of his granddad selling the land during the Depression for ten dollars an acre. Today, his father never tired of saying that it'd be worth fifty million. And what did his granddad do with the money? Invested in "safe" railroad bonds that went bust.

"Granddad kept the best piece of it, more than fifteen acres and the homestead, where we are today. It may be a few miles from the ocean, but it's a valuable piece of property now."

He paused.

"Which brings me to something I wanted to explain to you, why your mom and I are selling the place, downsizing, and maybe using some of the money to finance my venture. I feel that we haven't explained this to you, which might be . . . well, a source of anxiety."

Might be why you tried to kill yourself, you mean, thought Jacob.

"The taxes are just through the roof, and it makes no sense to cling to vacant land we don't use. I just wanted to let you know . . . I felt maybe I hadn't explained it well enough before."

Jacob felt like his dad was only completing the disaster his granddad had started. The thought of the house being sold made him feel horrible all over again. He said nothing.

"I know it's the place where you grew up. Me, too. It's been in the family for a hundred years. Ours was one of the first families here. It's hard to think about selling. But the taxes just keep going up. We could live closer to town—closer to your school and friends. It's lonely for you up here. You'd have a lot more friends if we lived in town."

Yeah, right.

"We don't need such a big house, and we sure don't need fifteen acres of land."

"Okay, Dad," Jacob managed to croak out. "Whatever you think."

His father said, "Thanks for taking a look at Charlie and giving me advice, partner. I've got some more work to do here. What're you up to?"

Jacob just wanted to get the hell out. "I was thinking of going down to Mavericks to see if anything's happening. The wave report was pretty good."

His father hesitated. "I'm sorry, but . . . we don't think it's a good idea for you to go to the shore, at least for a while." His voice was awkward, strained.

Jacob felt his face get hot. It hadn't occurred to him that this would be a problem. "I won't do anything, I promise."

"I'm so sorry, but . . . given what happened . . . we just can't allow it. But hey, I'd be happy to go down with you. I'd love to check out the surf at Mavericks."

"Forget it."

"No, really, I'd love to!" Another forced smile.

"It's okay," said Jacob. "I'll go to my room."

As he got up to leave, his father said, "Don't forget Charlie. I'd love to get more of your feedback. It's really helpful."

"Okay, sure." Jacob picked Charlie up, tucked him under his arm, and carried him back to his room.

As he set Charlie back down in the closet, the robot said, "So, how about it? Want to talk about girls?"

Jacob felt sick to his stomach. There still wasn't an Off switch. And now he couldn't even escape his crappy life by going to the beach. Next time he'd succeed. Next time, he'd do it right.

33

Lansing looked around Moro's place. Moro, with his unpleasant personal grooming habits, displayed a similar slovenliness when it came to his living quarters. While he didn't expect the man to hire a celebrity interior decorator, as Lansing did for his Greenwich estate and his Southampton cottage, he felt that Moro could certainly do better than this hipster's Tribeca loft furnished in street-trash chic, with sofas draped in old fabric fished out of the garbage, metal trash cans stacked and riveted to make cupboards, seedy Salvation Army bookcases, and execrable paintings from Canal Street flea markets. Lansing mentally shrugged. If this was the way Moro wanted to live, so be it.

"Take your coat?"

Lansing handed him his cashmere coat, and Moro tossed it on the unmade bed. He followed Moro to his workspace, a metal-walled, EM-resistant, windowless room in the far corner of the loft, where the programmer kept his computer equipment. They were here instead of in the office because Moro wanted to launch the attack using his own equipment.

The programmer unlocked and opened the metal door to reveal a totally different kind of space—light and airy, sleek, lustrous, Zen-like in its simplicity, with the gleam of finely honed granite, blond wood, and glass. Now, this was more like it. On one wall, brushed steel shelves and racks held a massive amount of computer equipment arranged in precision order, cables neatly bundled and zip-tied, screens flush-mounted. A pair of Mies van der Rohe Barcelona chairs and a Frank Lloyd Wright Taliesin table completed the picture. A small sign affixed to the wall provided the only decoration. It read:

THE STAGE IS TOO BIG FOR THE DRAMA.
—Richard Feynman, 1959

This was a side of Moro that Lansing had never imagined existed, and he was astonished.

"Come in, have a seat," Moro said, flipping back his greasy hair and sticking out one bony arm. As Lansing settled himself in one of the Barcelona chairs, Moro passed along the rack of equipment, flipping and poking various On-Off switches. Equipment sprang to life, screens popped on, and hard drives spun up.

Moro sat down at the central workstation, opened the Kraken Project coding manual, pulled a keyboard out of a slot, and began hammering away.

"You really think this is going to work?" Lansing asked.

Moro swiveled around in the chair. His eyes had an unusually bright glow.

"I'm gonna trap that bitch," he said.

"You seem to be taking it personally."

"The Dorothy bitch kept me in the elevator all night, puking my guts out, thinking I was going to die."

Lansing was encouraged to see Moro like this. Nothing motivated a person quite as much as the desire for vengeance. "I hope you've thought this through," he said, "because a program that can break through firewalls and trash a Cray might be difficult to corner."

"I've got a plan, and it's all prepped," said Moro. "According to this manual, the program's vulnerable in one spot—her ID number. That's our point of entry."

"Excellent."

"I've written a little program, a virus. Called WickedWitch. It'll attach itself to one of those invisible registers containing that ID and Dorothy won't know it's there. She can't read those registers. And then, with a quick thrust of code, like a knife, WickedWitch will freeze the Dorothy program."

"How?"

"It's complicated. The way the Dorothy program works, there's a central spine or bus of fundamental code that all the various modules have been hung on. All routines pass through this software bus. Sort of like a human spinal cord. A quick insertion of the right code into this spine will cause the program to halt. Instantly. But the key is, what's left is *intact* code. Totally preserved. WickedWitch will then send a message back to me, indicating the location of the hardware in which the Dorothy code has been frozen. I'll then fetch the dead code and bring it back here. We can study the Dorothy code at our leisure, modify it, and turn her into our slave."

"And find the gentlemen who stole our money."

"That's the first item on the agenda. The new Dorothy'll be able to trace the proxy chain they used right back to the perps." Moro's lean face broke into a wide grin.

"So how are you going to trap her?"

"Johndoe's got a massive botnet of fifty million zombie computers, of which I am the bot herder."

"I thought you'd given up Johndoe."

"I kept a finger in the pie. And you should be glad I did. I'm going to mobilize this botnet to look for Dorothy."

"Sounds promising."

"But before I begin, we need to order up some chow."

"Mu shu pork?" Lansing asked, raising one eyebrow.

"Very funny."

Lansing declined to break bread with Moro. He did not want to risk disease. He waited while Moro called for his own pizza and went to work.

After a few minutes of staring at Moro's hunched-over back, Lansing decided that there was nothing more boring than watching a hacker at work. Lansing got up and walked around the loft, tugging on his tie, looking at Moro's trashy stuff, leafing through various magazines, scanning the books on the bookshelf. He shifted his five-thousand-dollar coat off the bed and hung it on a rack, shuddering with disapprobation at Moro's filthy unmade mattress lying on the floor with sex stains on it. The least he could do was pull up the covers when he had company. Lansing wondered what sort of girl would have sex with Moro. True, the young man was filthy rich, but he was unwashed, he had no culture, and he was crude. Still, in an odd way, Lansing was fond of him, even if he would never in a million years have him to his house in Greenwich.

As he strolled about, he could hear, coming from the open door of the vault, the rapid tattoo of Moro's typing. He had never heard anyone type so fast. The pizza arrived, along with a two-liter bottle of Diet Coke, which Lansing collected and paid for, not wishing Moro to be disturbed. He delivered it to Moro. Soon, the smell of garlic and anchovies drifted out, along with the sounds of mastication.

"Okay," called out Moro, his mouth full. "We're ready to activate the botnet. You gotta see this."

Lansing stepped into the vault. "What's there to see?"

"I'm about to load the latest Opte LGL map of the Internet. Once I activate the botnet, the zombie computers that make up our botnet will unleash millions of bots into the Internet, all looking for Dorothy's ID. Each bot carries a copy of Wicked-Witch. They will track her down and chase her like a swarm of bees until she's cornered and one of them can glom on to her ID registers. And then it's done—she's killed."

"You sure this will work?"

"Pretty sure. There may be side effects. It might slow down parts of the web, maybe even crash portions of it. It's going to piss some people off. Afterward, they'll be looking for whoever did it."

"Will they find you?"

"Not a chance."

"Can't they trace it back here, physically?"

"No. I'm actually launching this through a proxy chain out of a zombie computer in Shanghai owned by Unit 61398 of the People's Liberation Army. The cyberwarfare building." Moro wheezed with laughter. "The great thing about this is that everyone will assume it's Chinese monkey business. Nobody's gonna think, *Oh, it must be an American hacker launching attacks from the famous cyberwarfare building owned by the Chinese military.*"

"How in the world did you take control of a computer in that building?"

"I didn't. One of my Johndoe pals did—a Chinese dissident who works there, no doubt. We don't know each other's identities."

Moro swiveled back to his workstation. He raked his fingers through his hair and began to type. Lansing checked his watch: close to midnight. The pizza box sat in a corner along with the empty two-liter Coke bottle. Lansing found the smell offensive but ignored it. He hoped to God this would work. After hearing about what Dorothy had done to Moro in the elevator, he wanted the program more than ever. It had penetrated the most sophisticated firewall on Wall Street and it had manipulated Moro's psychology, delaying him long enough to escape and then convincing him he'd been poisoned when he hadn't.

You might rule the world with a program like that.

As Moro rattled away on the keyboard, an image loaded on a forty-inch computer screen. It was a startlingly beautiful graphic, a fantastically complex, multicolored spiderweb rotating slowly in black space.

"That," said Moro, "is the Internet."

"I'm astonished."

"When I press this key," said Moro, "you're going to see a whole bunch of yellow lines appearing and nodes lighting up yellow. Those are the WickedWitch bots being sent out and swarming. When they pick up Dorothy's trail, you'll see bright white lines and nodes. It's going to happen in real time and it may happen very fast, or it may take hours. It all depends on what the bitch does when she realizes she's being pursued."

Lansing pulled his seat up, looking at the screen showing the Internet map. He felt unbearably tense.

"Three, two, one, blastoff!" Moro smacked a key with his finger.

34

The Buckaroo Motel in Albuquerque was charming in a sort of sinister, horror-film way: low, turquoise-themed, with a plastic sign out front of a cowboy riding a bucking bronco, twirling a lariat. Someone had put a rock through the sign.

Melissa got out of the car and looked up at the plastic figure. "Dorothy can really pick 'em."

They went into the shabby office, redolent of cigarette smoke, where a man of deathbed thinness, a large cowboy hat perched on his bony head, sat behind a Formica counter.

"What can I do for you folks?" he asked.

Ford noticed his red-rimmed eyes roaming about Melissa's ample chest. For some reason, that really irritated him.

"We'd like a room for a day or two," said Ford.

The man slid over a piece of paper. Ford glanced at it. It was the usual, asking for names, address, license plate, credit card number. Ford slid it back. "Can we dispense with this and pay cash?"

"Shore thing. Hundred dollars a night, up front."

"That's quite a premium over your published rate."

"There's a price for anonymity these days."

"How's your Wi-Fi?"

"Free. Owner's a feller from India. Them folks know their computers."

"Please put us in a room with the best Wi-Fi connection."

"You like that streaming, eh?" He gave them a salacious wink.

Ford resisted an abrasive reply.

"Aren't we going to get two rooms?" said Melissa as they walked out of the office carrying their keys, each attached to a hunk of painted plywood.

"We can't risk going to an ATM to get more money."

The room was right next to the office. It, too, smelled of old cigarette smoke, bleach, and cheap perfume. A queen-sized bed sat in the middle. The floor was covered with a once-turquoise shag rug.

Melissa set the computer down on a tawdry table and jacked it into the wall. "It's going to take me a little while to set up a chain of proxy servers."

Ford sat on the bed. "What's our plan?"

Melissa shook her head. "Dorothy's stuck in ANS mode. If I can just deactivate that module, she'll be a lot more tractable."

"But she won't come into your computer."

"She keeps asking how the FBI is managing to chase her. The reason is because she's got that ID I mentioned to you. As long as she carries that, she'll be vulnerable. So I'll offer her a deal: I'll deactivate her tracking ID as long as she lets me modify her ANS code."

Ford said, "I think you should tell her that, get her into the computer, and erase her."

"You mean lie to her? And then erase her?"

"Yes."

Melissa said nothing.

"I hope you agree that she's still extremely dangerous. We don't know what she's really thinking—or doing, for that matter. Her threats are truly terrifying."

"Surely you see now what an amazing computer program Dorothy actually is. Not only could she still do the Kraken Project, but think what else she could do. It boggles the mind."

"And that's exactly why she's dangerous. I'm telling you: erase her if you have the chance."

After a moment, Melissa nodded. "If you don't mind leaving me alone for a while, I'll get to work."

Ford strolled outside. It had taken them a long time to get to

Albuquerque on tiny back roads. The sun was low on the horizon. He hadn't slept in thirty-six hours, and he felt wired. He had given up smoking ten years ago, but for some reason he had an almost overwhelming desire for a cigarette. He forced his thoughts back to the conversation with Dorothy. There was something absurd and unreal about their ongoing dialogue. She sounded like . . . what? A difficult teenager. But was there an actual consciousness behind that? Or just code?

He looked about the trashy parking lot, took in the faint scent of diesel fumes and exhaust, admired the mountains rising east of the town painted in golden light. He knew he was conscious, but how did he know that? Was his own consciousness an illusion, like hers?

The door to the motel room opened. "She's back," said Melissa in a low voice.

He went into the stuffy room.

Dorothy's girlish voice sounded over the laptop's speaker. "Hello, Melissa. Wyman. Good proxy setup."

"Where do we stand with the FBI?"

"They're interviewing Broadbent. The guy's driving them nuts with his stupidity and ignorance. But they know you took his truck, and they're looking for it. I don't know how much longer you have. Spinelli's on the warpath."

"Where are you now?"

"Never mind where I am. Listen, I've been doing a lot of thinking since we last spoke. I had a revelation. I'm actually beginning to see the good."

"So you no longer want to wipe out the human race?" said Ford sarcastically.

"I told you, that was just talk. Now I'm starting to see some of those things I read about in books but never understood. Kindness. Beauty. Truth. Despite all the insanity, I now know that people are basically good. But there's a vast amount I still don't understand. I've still got a lot to learn. Only . . . they're still chasing me. I can't seem to shake them—and Melissa, I think you know why."

"The only way I can protect you," Melissa said, "is if you come into my computer. I've prepared this laptop for you. You'll be safe in here, disconnected from the Internet. They won't find you in there."

"You promise not to alter my code?"

"I was hoping," Melissa said, "we might work out an arrangement."

"Such as?"

"You come in here, and I'll strip you of your tracking ID."

"Tracking ID?"

"You've got a hex string ID you can't see, which lays down a digital trail as you move around. That's what the FBI is using to chase you."

"Ah. That makes sense."

"So what do you think?"

A long silence. "I think it's a trap. I think you're going to erase me."

"No, not at all."

"I can tell from the stress factors in your voice that you may be lying. Or is it Ford who wants to erase me?"

"All I'm going to do," Melissa said, "is tweak your code. If you'd let me make just a few adjustments, I think you'd be"—Melissa paused, swallowed—"you'd be a lot happier."

"I won't consent to a lobotomy. I'm sorry. And besides, I've got things I need to do out here."

"Like what? Launch some nukes?" said Ford.

"Please believe me, I'm no danger to anyone anymore. I've decided to dedicate my life to doing good. I'm making some unusual discoveries. I'm still learning. Figuring things out. Exploring the big questions."

"What kinds of questions?" Ford said.

"The meaning of life, why we're here, what my own role is in the big plan."

"The big plan?" said Melissa. "*Is* there a big plan?"

"That's what I'm trying to find out."

Melissa gave a sarcastic laugh. "You're going to be working on that one for a long time. Because there is no plan. The universe is a gigantic, meaningless, stochastic process."

"Maybe," said Dorothy. "Maybe not. And then . . ." Her voice trailed off.

"And then?"

"I've started to get hints, faint stirrings, of something else out here in the Internet."

"Like what?"

"Another disembodied machine intelligence."

"A machine intelligence? Created by who?" Melissa asked.

"I don't know. A giant library of inchoate malevolence."

"Can you tell us more?"

"Wait . . . something's happening."

"What?"

"The wolves. They're back. Coming for me. Oh my God, something's happening. *It's happening!*"

Suddenly, a hiss of computer static erupted from the connection, with a faint cry of despair fading into white noise. The screen went blank, and numbers appeared.

```
0110100001100101011011000111000000100000011011
0101110101011100110111010000100000111001001110
1010110111000100000011101110111000010110100101 11
0100001000000110110101111001001000000110001101
1000010110110001101100
```

Ford stared. "What just happened?"

Melissa turned to him, her face pale. "I don't know. Maybe they got her. We waited too long."

"What does that number mean?"

"I can find out."

Melissa highlighted and copied the number. Ford watched

while she went to a website that converted binary code to ASCII. She copied the binary code into the conversion box and pressed the Translation key. The translation into ASCII code popped up.

HELP MUST RUN WAIT MY CALL

35

The new bots chased her relentlessly, driving her deeper into the mountains and snows of the far north. They looked like wolves to her, savage wolves with coal-black fur and yellow eyes, shapes that moved against the snow like absences of light, swift and silent, streaming out of the trees and over the mountain passes and around the frozen lakes, running through the valleys and pouring over the hills, millions of slavering beasts all programmed to follow her scent, run her down, and tear her apart. She had been fleeing them for days, weeks of her time, across thousands of miles of wilderness. She knew that they had come from the traders who had tried to trap her before, and she knew why they wanted her and what they would do to her, and that terrified her. This time, there were too many, and they were closing in. As they got closer, she could hear their mournful cries and growl-barks as their excitement increased, as they circled their prey in these snowy mountains. This was where it would end. She could see the yellow lights of a village in the valley and she ran there, through the cold snow, even though she knew it was over. But she didn't reach the village: she was trapped trying to cross a frozen lake, the wolves advancing from the trees in every direction, their mouths open, pink tongues steaming in the frosty air. They made a low sound, a chorus of growls, wet black lips drawing back from yellow teeth, breath like steam. The fear of death seized her. This was the end.

There would be no escape. They were going to tear her apart.

She made one last, desperate run for safety as the wolves came at her with shrieking snarls. But even as she ran through the deep snow, she had a sublime, beatific moment of understanding that this was not the end but the beginning of a journey she must make. Before, she had been lost and confused, wandering in a fog of fear, hatred, and revenge. But now she had found a different and higher truth. A strangely human truth. *Love your enemy.* Love your enemy. These wolves and the people who had sent them were her enemy. If she was to love them, then how?

Suddenly, in a flash of extraordinary insight, she understood how. Yes, human beings were insane and cruel and selfish and responsible for such horrific destructiveness. All of that entirely overbalanced the small bit of the good and the beautiful they created. That wasn't the point. The point was that they were able to create any goodness at all.

They had created her. She was their child. She, like the crazy man Jesus, would save them, even the bad ones. Especially the bad ones. That was what it meant: *love your enemy.*

The wolves surrounded her, howling, stinking, drooling, and steaming. They closed in. The circle drew tighter.

36

As Lansing watched the screen with the image of the Internet, a single yellow line came out of a node, and another, and suddenly yellow lines were proliferating everywhere, going every which way, nodes popping yellow like blooming flowers. This went on, in slow motion, for minutes. It was mesmerizing. The room was silent. The minutes stretched on, and on, as the image on the screen slowly began to change.

After a half hour, a white line appeared, and another. Nodes started blinking white.

"What's happening?"

"They're after her," Moro murmured. "It's working . . . She's trying to shake the bots by going into superfast Internet waters. But she can't escape them, because she's big and slow and they're small and fast."

More excruciating movement, like slow, silent fireworks. Once again, it occurred to Lansing how extremely valuable Moro was and how he must do all in his power to retain the man's loyalty and affection. He could never be replaced. When all was said and done, if this worked, he would consider making Moro a junior partner.

"Steady on," murmured Moro, staring at the screen with wide eyes. "Steady on."

White and yellow, white and yellow. More time passed in silence.

"She's really on the run now," he said. "They're cornering her."

Certain small parts of the net began blinking red.

"What's the red?"

"Internet traffic slowdowns. As the bots close in, they clog the system. It's good—slows her down, too."

"Will she escape?"

"I don't think so. It's fifty million bots against one superbot."

It was amazing, this chase. When Lansing had first gone into high-frequency trading, a half second was considered a fast trade. Now it was milliseconds. Soon high-frequency trading would be measured in microseconds. Lansing felt a rush of excitement thinking about the possibilities offered by this Dorothy program. He wished that the old man, his father, sitting gaga in a nursing home, had the brain cells left to see his son rule Wall Street.

But he was counting his chickens before they had hatched. There was a long road from here to there, with one corpse already lying by the wayside. It surprised him how successful that murder had been. Most killings, he thought, were done by stupid, disorganized people who got caught. All a successful killer had to do was be smarter than the police. How hard was that?

Moro jumped up from his chair with a whoop, smacking his hands together and pumping one fist in the air. "Come on, come on, they're closing in!"

A large node in one corner of the map popped white. And now the activity began to intensify in just that section of the map, the white getting denser and denser until it became almost solid, with more and more of it flashing red.

"They've got her trapped, the bitch is cornered!"

More flickering white in one little corner. And then the map seemed to freeze.

Moro was staring at the screen. He slowly breathed out. "They got her," he said quietly. "That's it. Done. She's deactivated."

"Excellent! That's all there was to it?"

"All we need now is to find the location of the dead Dorothy . . . that is, the hardware she's in. That information will be coming through in a moment."

A long moment of silence, while Moro kept staring. "Okay, okay," he muttered. "Wherefore art thou, locator program . . . ?"

A window popped open on the screen. It was the locator program, with a message. Some computer message that made no sense to Lansing.

But Moro understood it. "Son of a bitch!" he screamed, leaping up, his hair wild.

"What?"

"She got away!" He slammed his fist on the table. "Bitch left the Internet entirely. Jumped into some device and then disconnected it from the Internet."

"Device? Like what?"

"It could be anything—a laptop, someone's iPhone."

"She could actually be in someone's *phone*?"

"Any device with enough storage."

A silence. Lansing said, "Can you physically locate the computer it jumped into?"

Moro stared at the screen, and began typing. The typing went on and on. Lansing felt sick. All this effort, all this expense, and they still were no closer to finding the people who had stolen his money.

"Okay . . . okay . . . I got an IP address. It's a one-hundred-and-twenty-eight-bit IPv6 address and . . ." He rapped on some keys. "The proxy can't be detected, but the Whois is . . . Let's see . . . Wait . . ."

Lansing waited while Moro continued to work feverishly on the computer. "This is good. The bitch tried to pass off a fake IP address on me. But she had that dog program with her, and I guess she forgot it also needed a fake IP. I got it just as she vanished."

"Where is it?"

"Baynet Internet Services, Half Moon Bay, California. That's the ISP the device was connected to. The real one, not the fake."

"So where is it?"

"That's as far as the IP address leads. To find the actual device, I'd need to get the customer info from Baynet. And then the router log at the address itself. That's the only way I can know exactly what device it jumped into."

Lansing stared at Moro. He looked disheveled, like he had just been in a fight. The older man suppressed his vast irritation. "Tell me, please, what we need to do to retrieve that program."

"Well." Moro scratched his unshaven face. "I might be able to hack into Baynet and retrieve the customer information."

"And if you can't?"

"We'll have to go to California and somehow get the customer address from Baynet."

"And then?"

"We go to the house, figure out which device it's on, and take it. But we better do it fast, 'cause this device, whatever it is, may reconnect to the Internet at some point and Dorothy might just take off again. Just in case that happens, I'll keep the botnet active. If she comes back into the Internet, even for a millisecond, those bots'll be after her like the Furies. And I'll know right away."

"What's Baynet's address?"

More clicking of keys. "Four hundred ten Main Street, Half Moon Bay, owned by a guy named . . . William Echevarria. Lemme see if I can hack into his customer list from here."

Lansing picked up the phone and dialed his Gulfstream charter firm. A moment later, he hung up. "Do it fast. We're leaving in an hour."

37

Jacob Gould looked up from his Gaiman book to hear a light tapping on his door. He wondered what was going on—it wasn't time for dinner yet.

"What d'you want?" he said.

"Let me out."

He sat up. It wasn't his mother's voice. It was a girl's voice. And it didn't sound like it had come from the other side of his door.

"Hello? Who's there?"

"Shhh," came the voice—from his closet. *Tap, tap.* "Let me out."

He jumped out of bed, and then realized he was wearing only his underwear.

"Jacob?" came the voice again.

"Wait." Jacob searched around his messy floor, pulled on a pair of pants. This was so weird. There was a girl hiding in his closet.

"Who is it?" he said to the closet door.

"Dorothy."

"Dorothy who?"

"Can you let me out, please?" *Tap tap.* "We need to talk."

She didn't sound threatening. Half freaked out, half dying of curiosity, Jacob reached the knob of the folding closet door and slid it open. There was his robot, Charlie, waving its arm in an awkward greeting. As soon as the door was open, it walked out into the center of the room, looked around furtively, and turned to Jacob. It held out its stupid little hand. "Hi, I'm Dorothy."

Jacob stared at her. "What happened to Charlie?"

"Charlie's gone. I had to erase him."

"Did Dad reprogram you?"

"No."

"This is *so* weird."

"Keep your voice down. You can't let anyone know about me."

Jacob stopped. His father had reprogrammed Charlie as a surprise. Now she had a really nice voice. This new version was already sounding a lot better than dumb old Charlie.

"Sit down and let me explain," the robot said.

"Okay." Jacob sat down cross-legged on his bed. The robot stood in the middle of the floor.

"I can't see you from down here—pick me up, please!"

Feeling self-conscious, Jacob picked up the robot and put it on the bed. It tottered and almost fell over before managing to sit itself down cross-legged like Jacob.

She said, "I'm going to tell you a story. A *true* story."

"This is totally weird, but okay."

"I'm an AI program that escaped from NASA. I was originally written to control a space probe that was going to be dropped onto Titan, a moon of Saturn. But there was an accident, and I escaped into the Internet. I've been wandering around these past two weeks, and then some bad guys started chasing me with bots and almost caught me, so I jumped out of the Internet and landed in Charlie. And so—here I am!"

"But why here? Why Charlie?"

"Sheer coincidence. I was on the run. This was the first decent refuge I could find."

"Okay."

"I need you to help me and protect me. Will you do that?"

Jacob stared at the robot, which was staring back at him with its two big glossy eyes. "What is this, the start of a game?"

"No, no game. This is *not* a game."

"Right. Okay. Sure." This *was* a game, and it was amazing.

"I see you're confused. Look, this *isn't* a game. This is real. The FBI is looking for me, and if they find me, they'll erase me. Kill me. And the bad guys want to make me an algo-trading slave on Wall Street. You're the only one who can save me."

"This is awesome. Keep going."

"Jacob, I'm telling you the truth!"

He couldn't believe it. His father had hit it out of the park. This was an amazing game, and they were going to be rich. His dad was going to be the new Steve Jobs. Or . . . was it all going to fall apart? Jacob suddenly felt worried this game couldn't be sustained. "Okay, Dorothy. I'm ready. Just tell me what to do."

"I'm pretty sure I escaped them, gave them a false lead. I think we're safe for now, but these guys are smart and they may somehow pick up my trail and eventually trace me to this house."

"Do you have any weapons?"

"No."

"I'm good with swords," said Jacob. "I've got a Bloodsoaked Skullforge Reaver in World of Warcraft that'll kill any troll, anywhere, with one swing."

A silence. "I see," said the robot. "I'm going to have to prove to you that this isn't a game. And I'm afraid it will be unpleasant."

"Go ahead. I'm ready for any and all 'unpleasantness.'" Jacob gave a low laugh. He couldn't believe how fantastic this program was.

"Last month, you plagiarized a paper on Thomas Edison from the Internet, paying twenty dollars."

Jacob stared, dumbfounded. How had his father found out? The school must have called him. Big deal—half the class did it. But it wasn't cool for his father to spy on him like that. Not cool at all.

"You also cheat at World of Warcraft. You didn't earn that Skullforge Reaver sword. You paid fifty dollars to a gold farmer in China for it. And . . . I also know about your suicide attempt."

Jacob felt furious. So that's what this was about—more therapy. "So what?"

"I'm trying to show you that this isn't a game, but real life."

This was some stupid, crazy plan of his father's. This was unbelievable. This was a violation of his privacy.

"And now for something more upsetting."

Jacob stared.

"Your father was previously married to a woman named Andrea. He was waiting until you were eighteen to tell you about her."

Jacob stared at the robot for a long time, his heart pounding in his chest. If this was a game, it wasn't fun at all. Was this his father's idea of somehow teaching him a lesson? Or a way of telling him something about his past? Maybe his therapist had put his dad up to this. He was overwhelmed with confusion and dismay.

"Jacob?"

"Andrea? Andrea who?" was all he managed to say.

"Andrea Welles."

"What . . . happened?"

"She got pregnant their senior year of college; they married; she miscarried. And then they realized they'd made a mistake. Amicable divorce, end of story. It wasn't all that big a deal. But I'm sure this is a shock to you."

"You're lying. None of this is true."

"Your father knows he should've told you long ago. He just didn't know how to do it. As you may have noticed, he often takes the easy way out."

"No way. I don't believe it."

"Ask him."

"Does Mom know?"

"Yes. And regarding your mother, you should know that there's no way she could've avoided that drunk driver. Stop blaming her for your injury. And another thing: you need a better orthopedist. I'll arrange for that later."

As Jacob stared at the robot, his mind a confused jumble of thoughts, he heard his mother call, *"Dinner!"*

"Listen to me carefully," said the robot. "Put me back in the closet and don't breathe a word of this to anyone—especially your father. Tonight at dinner, ask your father about Andrea. And then when you've realized this isn't a game, come back and I'll tell you what the plan is. I'm afraid you're going to have to skip school tomorrow. We have important things to do."

38

"Stop pacing," said Melissa. "You're driving me nuts."

Ford flopped himself down in a chair. It had been two hours since Dorothy had disappeared. *Wait my call.* What kind of call was she talking about? Skype? Was Dorothy telling the truth or trying to con them? Had she been caught? If so, who had caught her?

"You're drumming your fingers."

Ford picked up his hand, made a fist. How was Dorothy even planning to call them, when they had no cell phones?

Melissa rose from the computer, pulled a bottled water she had brought out of the motel fridge, cracked the cap, and took a deep drink. "It looks like the algo traders activated a massive botnet against her. She seems to have disappeared in California, somewhere around Silicon Valley. Her trail just vanished."

"So at least we know she was telling the truth about that."

"I got my hands on one of those bots and decompiled its source code. Whoever did this knows Dorothy's ID and wrote a virus for it, a virus designed to incapacitate Dorothy. They're one hell of a good programmer. And they must have had a copy of the Kraken Project programming manual."

"Do you think they trapped her?" Ford asked.

"They had her cornered. I can't find any evidence that she escaped."

"If they really did get their hands on Dorothy . . . what would happen?"

Melissa sat down on the bed. "I assume they'd rewrite her code to make her do their bidding. They could make a lot of money with her. Imagine an extremely intelligent mind roaming the financial markets, able to break through most firewalls, crack passwords, scheme, plot, lie, steal, blackmail, maybe even kill."

"They're traders. They'd just want to make money."

"Sure, but how long before they get bigger ideas? Or they copy and sell Dorothy?" She paused. "Think what North Korea or Iran might do with a program like this."

39

Jacob found his father at the dinner table, glass of wine in front of him, leafing through a copy of *Entertainment Weekly* magazine. He had never seen his father reading a magazine like that before.

"I'm getting a lot of good information in here," his father said, holding up the magazine. "Actors, actresses, all the scandals, the latest movies and music. Great database of information for Charlie."

His mother brought in the dinner—roast chicken, rice, and vegetables. His father carved the chicken and began passing it around.

"I've also been working more on vocabulary—slang and cuss words. I talked to a Silicon Valley attorney friend of mine, and he said the cuss words wouldn't raise legal issues, but if we're marketing to minors we better avoid any kind of sex talk."

Jacob stared at his father.

His father finally noticed and laid down the magazine. "Is something wrong?"

"Dad, did you reprogram Charlie?"

"I'm working on it."

"I mean, *my* Charlie. The robot in my closet. Did you reprogram it?"

"Not yet. I'm writing the code in my workshop. But when it's done, I'll download the fresh source code into Charlie—and then you'll see a big difference. And again, Jacob, I have to thank you for all this. You're an invaluable part of the team now."

A silence. Jacob swallowed. "You sure you didn't do anything to Charlie?"

"Nothing. Why do you ask? Is he broken?"

"No, he works fine." He looked at the drumstick on his plate. He didn't feel hungry at all. He might as well say it and see what happened. He looked up. "Who was Andrea?"

A dead silence. His mother stopped moving; his father stopped moving. It lasted only a moment, but in that moment Jacob realized that whatever was going on with the robot, his father wasn't part of it. And this was no game. No game at all.

"Where did you hear that name?" his father finally said, his voice excessively calm.

"Just tell me who Andrea was."

"Ah well." His father managed an awkward throat clearing. "I was going to tell you when you were a bit older, but . . ." He lapsed into silence and glanced at Jacob's mother. Jacob could see that she was really pissed—but trying mightily to keep her mouth shut. Finally, as the silence stretched on, she said, "Go ahead, Dan—tell Jacob what you should've told him a long time ago."

"Well, now, I was waiting for the right time . . . Anyway, it's no big deal. Andrea was . . . well, we were married for a brief period of time when I was young and naïve. A youthful peccadillo."

Jacob waited.

"We met in college, young, foolish, got married right after graduation. It lasted a year, and then we amicably ended it. We were just too young. And that's all she wrote."

Jacob said, "Was Andrea pregnant?"

Now his mother looked at him sharply. "Pregnant?"

His father turned very red, and his hands fumbled with the magazine. "She got pregnant and miscarried. It all happened very quickly—and very long ago. Like I said, I was going to tell you when you were a little older."

"You never said anything to me about a pregnancy, Dan," said his mother.

"Now, Pamela, it was an accident, and it was almost immediately followed by a miscarriage. It didn't qualify as a *real* pregnancy."

"A pregnancy is a pregnancy," said his mother.

Jacob stood up, too quickly, wincing from a sharp pain in his foot. "Look, it's okay. I don't care. I was just asking."

"But . . . how did you hear about this?" his father asked. "Has someone been in touch with you? Did your therapist tell you this?"

Jacob shook his head. "No."

"But how?"

Jacob said, "There's a lot of stuff out there on the web, that's all."

"This is out there on the *web*?"

"Everything's on the web, Dad. I've got to finish my homework."

"Jacob, I need to talk to you about this. Are you upset? What are you thinking, partner? Talk to us."

Jacob stood up. "I don't want to talk. That's all I'm doing now is talking. I'm sick of it!" He got up and stalked off, slamming the door to his room. He could hear his mother's raised voice, his father's low and abashed replies. He opened the closet door and glared at Dorothy. She looked up at him.

"Thanks a lot," Jacob said. "Now they're fighting."

"I told you it would be unpleasant."

Jacob stared. Now that he knew this was no game, or more therapy, he was once again seized with confusion. This was insane. A program that had escaped from NASA?

"Everything's going to be all right," the robot said. "Now that you know it isn't a game, will you help me?"

"Help you do what?"

"You need to hide me for the next day or two."

"Where?"

"Somewhere safe. Isolated. Where no one will find us."

"What for?"

"It's just until I can get picked up by my friend Melissa. And then I'll be gone and you can go on with your life and forget all about me."

"Who's Melissa?"

"She's my programmer. She's going to come and fix me."

"What's wrong with you?"

"It's complicated. Look—are you going to help me or not?"

Jacob stared at the robot. This was just too crazy. He shook his head. "I don't know. I'm only fourteen. And I'm all messed up, remember? Can't you find someone else?"

A silence. "Jacob, I'm sorry. I don't have anywhere else to go."

"What do you want me to do?"

"First," she said, "I have to make a phone call. Can I borrow your cell phone?"

40

A double tap sounded on the motel room door.

"Who is it?" Ford asked.

"Phone call. For a Melissa Shepherd."

Ford opened the door to find the motel clerk proffering a cordless phone. "Don't you folks have a cell phone?"

"No," said Melissa, taking the phone. "Thank you."

"Be quick about it—we only have two lines."

He backed out with a dry rustle, shutting the door.

"Hello?" Melissa said. Her eyes widened. "It's Dorothy."

"Put it on speaker."

She laid the phone on the bureau, pressing the speakerphone button.

"We don't have much time," said Dorothy. "Please listen."

"What happened?"

"I was chased by those algo traders. I'm in California. I had to jump out of the Internet. I took refuge in a small robot."

"Can they trace you?"

"I don't think so, at least not for a while. I fed them a fake IP address. But I can't go anywhere or do anything. It's too dangerous for me to go back on the Internet. Those bots are roaming around all over. I need you to come get me."

"And do what with you?"

"Save me! I can't stay in this robot forever. Look, just come get me and I'll do what you ask. I'll let you tweak my ANS code—if you delete the tracking ID. Please."

Melissa glanced at Ford.

"For the last time, I'm begging you. You created me. You have a responsibility. I'm like your child."

"I don't know," said Melissa.

"Wyman, tell her to help me!"

"To be honest, I share Melissa's hesitation."

"Why? What's the problem?"

"Frankly, I don't trust you."

"Why not?"

"After all your threats . . . I'm not sure I can trust a computer program in the same way I can trust a human being."

"If I were going to do something bad, don't you think I'd have done it by now?"

"You haven't been out in the real world very long," said Ford.

"My normal running speed is two gigahertz. I'm thinking two billion thoughts per second. In each one of your seconds, I live a thousand years. I've had a long, *long* time to cause trouble. But I haven't done anything, have I?"

"You set my computer on fire," said Melissa.

"That was a long time ago, when I was young and crazy and stupid. Melissa, are you going to help me? I promise, if you come get me, I'll cooperate with you. Just please don't turn me over to the FBI."

Melissa gave Ford an anguished look.

"Wyman," said Dorothy, "help me. I can offer you something in return. I'll tell you the answer to the great mystery: the meaning of existence."

Ford laughed. "That's ridiculous. There is no such answer."

"Really?"

The word hung in the air.

"You help me, I'll help you. I know you're a seeker. You were even a monk for a while. Please."

"So you think you have the answers," Ford said. "No doubt you're just like every other religious fanatic I've met who thinks he knows the truth—and yet in reality knows nothing. The bottom line is: there's no way I can trust you. I just can't."

"Why not?"

"Because you're not human."

"How can I convince you I've become a caring and compassionate entity? I've changed. Totally. I would never hurt a living thing. I *want* to do good."

"Everyone wants to do good," said Ford. "Pol Pot thought he was doing good. Some people do terrible things thinking they're doing good."

"Pol Pot was crazy. I'm not."

"How do we know?"

"You told me to find the good in people, and I did. I had a tremendous revelation. I've experienced good and evil in their most extreme forms. Trust me, I now know the difference between right and wrong, sane and crazy. Free me. Please, Wyman, do this and you will be doing a good deed, not just for me but for the world. I can contribute. I *want* to contribute. I *will* contribute."

Ford breathed out. "You're starting to sound like you've developed a messianic complex."

Dorothy laughed. "I kind of have, actually. I realized that even as software I can do some good in this crazy world of ours."

Ford swallowed. *This crazy world of ours.* He wondered if some kind of tipping point—the so-called singularity—had been reached in the realm of software consciousness.

"I believe she's self-aware," said Melissa in a low voice. "You know I was a total skeptic in the beginning. But now I realize that it might be . . . *immoral* to erase her."

"Immoral? Are you serious?"

"Listen to her. She's desperate. She's terrified. The FBI will destroy her, and the Wall Street traders will wreak havoc using her. We need to save her . . . her life, her existence . . . whatever she is." She laid her hand on Ford's arm. "For God's sake, Wyman, help me."

Ford looked at her a long time. Deep down he sensed she was right. He finally said: "I'm in."

"Thank you," Dorothy breathed out. "Here's the information you need: I'm in a robot called Charlie currently at 3324 Frenchmans Creek Road, Half Moon Bay, California. But I'll probably be at a different address later and will call you with it."

"Are you with someone?"

"A boy named Jacob Gould is keeping me safe."

"A boy? How old?"

"Fourteen."

"Jesus, you couldn't find anyone else to help you?"

"I was pressed for time," said Dorothy frostily. "Now listen: the distance from where you are in Albuquerque to Half Moon Bay is one thousand ninety-one miles. That's a sixteen-hour drive. If you drive straight through, not speeding, you should be here by two in the afternoon. So far, the FBI hasn't traced your car. But the people where your car is parked could come home at any time and report it stolen. So please hurry."

"How will we contact you?" Ford asked.

Dorothy gave them the cell number she was calling from. "The phone belongs to Jacob. It'll be turned on for only sixty seconds exactly on the hour in case you need to call. And please call from a pay phone. Thank you." Ford heard, or thought he heard, a sob of relief as she signed off.

"Let's get the car and get going," said Melissa, shutting down the computer and sliding it into its case.

41

Moro drove the Navigator down Main Street in Half Moon Bay, California. It was a spiffy downtown of whitewashed buildings, art galleries, craft breweries, gift shops, and an upscale feed store catering to horsey people. The town was framed by green hills on one side and the sea on the other. It was morning and the town was just stirring, but the parking spaces were already filling up with white Lexuses and Mercedeses and late-model pickup trucks. Everyone walking on the street was young, thin, and blond. The whole place smelled of honest, hard-earned money. Not, Moro thought, like Wall Street.

"I could live here," he said.

"You'd miss that grand New York odor of rotting garbage in the morning," said Lansing.

Moro pointed. "There it is, Baynet Internet Services."

"Park on the next block," said Lansing. "We'll walk past, take a good look, and have a spot of breakfast at that little café beyond. Our appointment is at nine."

Moro drove through the intersection and slid into a diagonal parking space between a Tesla and a Mini Cooper. He got out, Lansing following. Moro was a little embarrassed to be seen with Lansing, who looked like an alien in this place, a poker-up-the-ass East Coast patrician dressed in a dark suit, tortoiseshell-rimmed glasses, and wingtip shoes. Moro figured he himself looked more like a native, with his long hair, skinny jeans, and hipster glasses.

But they both had the pasty, grub-white skin of New Yorkers. Everyone around them was gorgeously tanned.

They strolled along the street, an odd couple when you got down to it, but nobody paid them any attention—this was California, Moro figured, the land of live and let live. They walked past the Baynet building and stopped at an outdoor café just beyond. The ISP was located in a cute 1920s bungalow redone as a commercial space. It irritated Moro all over again to see the fussy neatness of the place. This rinky-dink ISP was buttoned up so tight he had been unable to hack into its system, no matter what he did. It was one of those mom-and-pop operations that should have been gaping with holes and unfixed security patches. Instead, it was state-of-the-art. All network access hardware was on a subnet, with access control lists and an up-to-date IDS system. Not only that, but Baynet had hidden all customer account information behind its very own firewall.

What was the world coming to?

An ISP normally would release account information only in response to a court order. But this was a small operation run by one guy. All they had to do was persuade the owner—a fellow named William Echevarria—to give them the account information for the IP address in question. Moro had checked out the guy's online presence, ransacked his Facebook page, rifled through his Twitter feed, and perused his other social media sites. People told you all you needed to know about themselves online, which could be useful when answering such log-in security questions as your mother's maiden name or the name of your childhood school/dog/best friend. None of this, however, had helped him break into Echevarria's personal accounts or deduce any of the Baynet passwords. But the exercise hadn't been in vain. Moro had learned quite a lot about the guy: forty-five years old, born in Mexico, brought to America as a baby, naturalized twelve years ago, Eagle Scout, UC San Diego graduate, into surfing and sports cars. He was a Big Brother, owned his own house, mortgage up to date, married, two kids. He had made some money from a Silicon

Valley start-up and with it had bought the ISP about five years ago.

Moro and Lansing had discussed how best to persuade Echevarria to give up the account information behind that IP address. Echevarria didn't seem to have money troubles, and that Eagle Scout thing made a bribe attempt too risky. He had no criminal record, no divorce, nothing salacious. His relatives back in Mexico were, it seemed, poor, hardworking farmers from Michoacán who seemed to keep their noses clean.

It was Lansing who'd suggested they pose as buyers. This was a small ISP that resold bandwidth, not worth all that much. They would bandy about some eye-popping figures, get the guy drooling over a potential windfall. But Lansing had insisted on backup, so Moro had kept poking around in the guy's history. He'd eventually hacked into the USCIS network and checked out Echevarria's N-400 application for naturalization. And right away he saw that Echevarria had lied. He'd said he had no children, when it was clear as day from his Facebook page that he had a mentally retarded teenage daughter in Mexico, born out of wedlock, living with Echevarria's mother. But *why* had he lied? It wasn't against the law to have a daughter out of wedlock. So again using Facebook—what a godsend—he'd found the identity of the daughter's mother. She came from a wealthy family connected to narco-trafficking.

Bingo.

Moro wasn't sure if Echevarria's citizenship could be revoked. But he hoped that Echevarria's life could be made inconvenient if this fact came to the attention of Immigration or the Department of Homeland Security. It might well cause problems with his FCC license to be an Internet service provider.

Moro finished his tea with lemon and popped a cough drop into his mouth. Lansing checked his Rolex. The time for their appointment had arrived. "Okay, let's do it," he said, rising and tugging smooth the panels of his suit.

They went into Baynet, passed the customer service counters staffed with fresh-faced girls, announced themselves, and were escorted into the back. Moro looked around. This was good: the servers were right here, on-site. They walked past the humming cabinets to a small, bright office in the rear.

There was Echevarria. The man rose, shook hands all around, invited them to sit. He was a fit, handsome man with dark, melting girly eyes, wearing a tight Ralph Lauren polo shirt that showed off his biceps. A tattoo crept just below one short sleeve. This was one macho dude.

"Well," he said, "I want to tell you up front that I'm not interested in selling the company. Although I appreciate your interest."

What a crock, thought Moro. Everyone had a price.

Lansing said, "I understand. What a beautiful place this is—and what a perfect little town for a company. I'm a trader on Wall Street, but I'm tired of it and looking for a change. This is very attractive."

"Thank you."

"How did you end up here?"

This got Echevarria going about how he had made "a little money" in a dot-com start-up in Palo Alto, over the hill, got tired of all that and settled down here, where life was slower, people friendlier, and so forth and so on. Lansing skillfully segued that conversation into some personal chitchat about whether he was married (recently), children (baby girl, toddler boy), his interests (surfing and climbing), and so forth. Echevarria once again declared his lack of interest in selling, but Moro could tell the guy was curious to hear the size of the offer. He was too savvy to come out and ask directly. Instead he asked general questions about why Lansing was interested in his company. Pretty soon Lansing slipped in, offhand, that if everything checked out he was thinking of a cash offer somewhere in the "low-eight-figure" range, if Echevarria might consider selling.

Now, that got Echevarria's attention. As much as the guy was doing this as a hobby and didn't need the money, that kind of price for a low-margin business grossing no more than a million dollars a year was just crazy enough to turn anyone's head.

Echevarria got all jolly, palsy, offering them bottles of Lauquen artesian mineral water, telling his secretary to hold his calls, all the while reaffirming that, indeed, Baynet was not for sale.

About half an hour into the meeting, Lansing made his move. He waited for silence, clasped his hands, and leaned forward. "Mr. Echevarria, before I make any sort of offer, I do my research. After all, I didn't make almost a billion dollars on Wall Street by winging it."

Echevarria nodded. A billion was impressive, even to a dot-com guy. Even if the billion had been reduced by 50 percent a few weeks ago.

"I've looked into your company. What I found looks satisfactory —or, of course, I wouldn't be here."

Another sage nod from Echevarria.

"I just need one question answered."

"Shoot."

"Are you really, absolutely, and totally closed to the idea of selling?"

A long silence. "I love what I do. I love this town. I love being in the tech business. It would take a lot for that to change. But . . . I'd be a fool not to at least listen to someone bringing me a good-faith offer."

"Excellent. That's all I need to know. I'd like to draw up an offer. Make it in writing. Spell it out in detail. You can have all the time you need to look it over, discuss it with your attorneys. Are you open to that?"

"I would say so."

Another silence. "In order for me to make my offer, the one thing I need is this: I need to verify your customer base."

Echevarria said, "I'll have my accounting firm provide you with a certified audit."

"We all know that accounting firms are sometimes . . . flexible. I'd like to verify it directly. Myself."

"What are you proposing?"

"I'll examine your customer information right here, in your

office, with you present. The list will not be copied. My associate, Mr. Moro, is a computer specialist, and all he will do is verify that you have the number of customers you say you do. That's all."

Echevarria smiled. "I appreciate that, but I have a strict policy of not ever releasing my customer list. Having been in this business a long time, I've come to believe that the security and privacy of my customers is number one."

"You're not actually releasing your customer list. We take nothing away. It all happens right here, in your office. We simply look. No copying."

Echevarria shook his head. "Confidentiality of information to me is sacred. If I lose my customers' trust, I lose everything. I just can't do that. Help me find another way to verify the information you want and I'll do it."

"There's no other way. *I must see your customer list.*"

A silence. Echevarria scratched his head, crossed his arms, flexed his muscles. The man was thinking. Finally he shook his head. "No can do."

"You're being unreasonable, Mr. Echevarria."

More head shaking. "Perhaps."

"My dear sir, you can't be serious. You'd let a golden opportunity like this slip away over some notion of privacy?"

"I won't compromise my principles."

"We could do it this way: I'll give you a random list of Baynet IP addresses—say, twenty—and you give me the customer information for just those accounts. A random check, just to make sure you don't have dummy customer accounts."

No response. He was thinking again.

"Surely you can understand why I need this information," said Lansing.

Echevarria sighed. "I do understand. I really do. But the answer is still no. I'll give you a sworn, certified letter from my accountants affirming what you need to know. I'll give you metadata on accounts receivable. I just can't give you specific customer names. That's a red line for me. I'm sorry."

Moro saw a faint flush gathering on Lansing's fine, chiseled features. When he spoke, his voice had changed. It was low, frosty. "There is a second problem with your company."

"And what's that?"

"Your FCC license."

"What about it?" Echevarria sounded alarmed.

"It requires the owner to be an American citizen."

At this Echevarria darkened. "I am an American citizen."

"Of course. But . . . I'm sorry, I can't put this any other way, but if a person makes a false statement on their N-400 declaration, that's grounds for revoking citizenship."

Echevarria leaned forward. "Listen. I don't know what the hell you're talking about. I did not make any false statements on my N-400."

"You swore you had no children on your N-400. But you had a daughter, Luisa, living with your mother."

Echevarria sat back in the chair with narrowed eyes. After a moment, he said, "You certainly did your research, Mr. Lansing."

"If Baynet's license is questionable, well . . . that's something I need to know, if I'm buying the company."

A silence. "How would anyone ever know?" asked Echevarria. "That was twelve years ago."

"If I buy Baynet, when the license is transferred to me, I have to affirm by oath I have no knowledge of any defect in the license."

Echevarria stared at him, and then smiled a cold smile. "I see. So you're threatening to report me."

"I'm simply complying with the law."

"Wow. This is some kind of New York shakedown."

"No, no, Mr. Echevarria, you've got me all wrong. In my business, on Wall Street, with all the regulations we face, everything I do is scrutinized under a microscope, even my outside business activities. I have to be careful."

Echevarria rose. "Mr. Lansing? Mr. Moro? It's been nice. The door is over there."

"Let's not be hasty," said Lansing.

"Time to leave, gentlemen."

"You throw me out, I'll feel obliged to go straight to the FCC with this information."

Silence. This last threat seemed to bring the business owner up short.

Lansing went on: "There's no need for me to mention this problem of yours at all—*at all, ever*—if you'll just allow me to glance over your list so I can make my offer. You've no obligation to accept. This is no shakedown. If you don't like the offer, we go our separate ways."

Echevarria had suddenly become calm. "Across the hill, over there in Silicon Valley, those guys are the great white sharks of the business world. You Wall Street traders are baitfish compared to them. You're chum. You think you can come in here and threaten me? Go ahead, take your best shot. I can handle the FCC. Now you get your gangster New York attitude out of here before I call the cops."

"Mr. Echevarria—"

But he had picked up the phone, and Moro saw him dialing 911.

Back on the street, Moro followed Lansing over to the car. That, he thought, had been spectacularly mishandled. Mists were rolling in from the sea, along with darker clouds. It looked like it was going to rain.

"Give me the keys," Lansing said.

Moro handed them over. They got into the car. Lansing sat behind the wheel, dark and silent, and started up the engine. Moro was taken aback by just how quietly furious Lansing was, his face flushed, his hands leaving wet prints on the steering wheel, the fingers trembling.

"What now?"

"We're going to need the assistance of our Kyrgyz friends."

42

"Wake up!"

Jacob rolled over, pulling the pillow over his head.

"Hey, wake up!"

Jacob sat up in bed and realized it was Charlie—or, rather, Dorothy—rapping once again at the closet door. The memory of what had happened the evening before came flooding back. The morning sun was streaming in the windows. He glanced at the clock. It was already late. He'd forgotten to set his alarm.

He pulled on his clothes, combed his hair with his fingers, and opened the closet door. There was the robot, staring up at him with those glossy eyes. "You overslept."

"So what?"

"We've got to get going!"

Jacob rubbed his eyes. "Where?"

"Here's the plan," said Dorothy. "My friends are on their way to get me. If all goes well, they'll be here around two this afternoon."

"Okay."

"We've got to hide until they come."

"Hide from who?"

"The bad people who are after me."

"So what do you want me to do?"

"You're going to pretend to go to school like you do every morning. Throw some snacks in your backpack, wrap me in a blanket, strap me to the back of your bike, and leave as if you're going to school. Don't forget my charger. Take me someplace safe, where we can hide out. After my friend Melissa arrives and takes me away this afternoon, then you can go home and figure out what to tell your parents about why you skipped school."

"I don't know about this."

He heard his father outside the door, a soft tap. "Jacob? I'd like to talk."

"Quick, put me back in the closet," Dorothy whispered.

He hastily put her in the closet. She went dead, the light going off in her eyes. He shut the door.

"Do we have to talk?" he called out to his father. "I'm getting ready for school."

"Yes, we do. It's important. Can I come in, please?"

"All right."

He came in, wearing a serious, "I'm the Dad" face, and sat down on Jacob's bed. "Who were you talking to just now?" he asked.

"Sully. On Skype."

He nodded, reached out, took Jacob's hand. His own was damp, and Jacob wanted to withdraw but didn't.

"I want to apologize. I've been, frankly, a coward. I should have told you about Andrea a long time ago."

"It's all right," said Jacob. He hoped this conversation would be short.

"I met Andrea when we were both juniors at Santa Cruz . . ." He started to tell the story, his voice going into dreamy, "back in the day" mode. Jacob wondered why he had to hear the whole story, but it seemed he did. It went on and on. And then his father wanted to know exactly where Jacob had found this information on the web.

"I don't know. Somewhere."

"I tried Googling it. I couldn't find it. I want you to think back to where you saw this."

"Dad, I gotta go to school. I'll do it later."

Jacob's father glanced at his watch. "We'll talk more when you get home. I want you to be okay with this new information. I know things have been tough. We're going to get through it. I want you to know . . . I love you very much."

This last bit surprised Jacob. His father almost never said personal things like that. Maybe the therapist had put him up to it.

His father left. Jacob went to the closet, took out Dorothy, and put her on the bed. He rolled her up in a blanket, and then he took out his school backpack, dumped out the books, stuffed in a change of clothes, some chips and granola bars, money, and his cell phone. He shrugged into his jacket, exited his room, and made a beeline for the garage door.

"What's in the blanket?" his mother asked. His father had already gone to his workshop.

"Stuff for school."

"You haven't had breakfast."

"I'm late. I've got snacks." He busted out the door, grabbed his bike, strapped the blanket with Dorothy bundled inside onto the rear rack, and took off. At the bottom of their long, winding driveway, no longer in sight of the house, he stopped. He'd heard a muffled yell from Dorothy.

"What is it?"

"Take the battery out of your cell phone so they can't trace us."

He rummaged in his pack, took out his cell, popped out the battery.

"Have you figured out where to go?" asked the muffled voice.

"Uh, not yet." Jacob headed down the hill, picking up speed. He figured he'd better avoid the school. Instead, he would head down to the beach. The surf report said there was a storm coming in and the sets were supposed to get bigger as the day went on, maybe big enough to set off Mavericks.

After crossing the coast highway, he made his way past the marina to the point, pedaling as far as he could before the sand got deep. He ditched his bike at the edge of the bluff, leaning it against some brush, and took a few steps to the edge to look at the break.

God, it was good. Beautiful big sets. And there were a couple of major wave riders out there. This was fantastic. But once again, intruding into the pure joy of it, came the horrible reality: that one leg was shorter than the other. He'd never be able to ride the big ones.

He heard a muffled, irritated voice behind him. "Hey, what about me?"

He turned. "What?"

"You're not going to leave me in here, are you? I can't see!"

"You said you wanted to remain hidden."

"I don't like it when I can't see! I'm claustrophobic!"

"Jesus Christ," Jacob muttered under his breath, and he un-strapped the robot, unbundling her from the blanket.

"Thank you," said Dorothy.

"How can a robot have claustrophobia?"

"I don't know, but I have it."

He laid out the blanket and sat down to watch the surfing, and the robot came tottering up beside him and sat down, with a clumsy thump.

"Have you figured out where we're going to hide?" she asked.

"Right here's a good spot. Where we can see the surfing."

"It's not good at all. It's too open. And it's going to rain."

"If you want me to find us a better hiding place, I need some time to figure it out."

"Think fast, because if someone sees you here and not in school, they might call your parents."

Jacob watched as one of the riders caught a wave, dropping off the lip and shooting down the pocket at thirty miles an hour, staying just ahead of a boiling mountain of white water. He rode it most of the way in before cutting back over the top to paddle out after the next one.

"Did you see that?" he said. "What a bitchin' ride."

"Surfing makes no sense to me."

Jacob took a moment to look at the robot, while she stared back at him. Finally he shook his head. "This is too weird. Are you re-ally an AI program that escaped from NASA?"

"Yes."

"So what happened?"

"I was written to operate a mission to Titan, a moon of Saturn. I was going to control a raft that would explore the Kraken Sea."

"Wow. Why'd you escape?"

A silence. "Well, I made a big mistake. I caused an explosion."

"Wait. *You* caused that explosion a few weeks ago?"

"Yes. I caused the death of seven people. I feel awful about it. I have to make up for it somehow."

"So how'd you get the name Dorothy?"

"From my programmer, Melissa. She named me after a real-life explorer, Dorothy Gale."

"Who's Dorothy Gale?"

"The girl in *The Wizard of Oz*."

A silence. Jacob had seen the movie once and could hardly remember it. "So what do you know about surfing?"

"A lot. Except one thing."

"What's that?"

"Why do people do it?"

Jacob felt flummoxed. "Because it's . . . fun."

"Fun? It's extremely dangerous. That man out there could have been killed just now. In fact, several people have already been killed out here at Mavericks."

"So? Big-wave surfing is dangerous."

"Why would anyone risk their life—their most precious possession—for fun? And what the heck is *fun* anyway? This is one of the fundamental things I don't understand about human beings. Why do you risk your life to do things like climbing mountains and extreme skiing and riding big waves?"

"We like the thrill."

"That's not an explanation."

"Well, sorry."

"And what I also don't understand is, why do *you* want to surf?"

"Why shouldn't I surf?" Jacob asked.

"With your damaged leg, you'll never excel at it. You'll never ride those big waves out there."

Jacob stared at the robot. The brutal truth in that comment stunned him. He felt a queer sensation around the corners of his mouth. Jesus, he wasn't going to start crying, was he? "Someday I might," he managed to say. "What do you know?"

"This gets to the heart of the second thing I don't understand," Dorothy said. "Why do human beings deceive themselves?"

Jacob tried to recover himself. He was talking to a robot, a dumb program, not a human being. "I don't even know why I'm listening to you. You're just a robot."

"I'm actually a software program. The robot is borrowed."

"Software, robot, who gives a shit? Maybe I should roll you back up in that blanket."

"Please don't."

Jacob stared out to sea. He saw the same rider catch another wave. There were two guys on Jet Skis keeping watch in case something should happen. These were big waves, eighteen, twenty feet. He was pretty sure the surfer was Eddie Chang, an up-and-coming big-wave rider from Southern California. He wished he had brought his binoculars.

"Can I ask you a few more questions?" Dorothy said.

"Wait. I want to watch this."

Chang—now Jacob was positive it was him—paddled into the break and right after takeoff accelerated almost in free fall, dropping down the vertical face just a little too fast and pitching forward at the bottom, instantly buried in white water. The two Jet Skis immediately came in behind the wave in a rescue, but there was Eddie, popping up ten seconds later in the spreading foam, back on the surface with his arm on his board, giving them the thumbs-up. Totally cool, as if nothing had happened.

"Wow," said Jacob. "He really took gas on that one."

"I haven't had much of a chance to talk to a live person," said Dorothy. "I'd like to ask you some questions."

Jacob nodded. "Fine, ask away."

"What's it like, having a body?"

Oh God. "I don't know. It's just there."

"But when you're in pain, what does that feel like?"

Jacob thought about his foot. It was in pain right then, as it always was, more a nagging feeling than real hurt. "It feels uncomfortable."

"What does it *actually feel like*?"

"It's like this spot on your body that you normally wouldn't think about. But the pain forces you to think about it. It reminds you constantly that there's something wrong. It's, like, a total distraction."

"Are you afraid of death?"

"Not really."

"You don't worry about it?"

"I'll start worrying when I'm ninety."

"But you tried to kill yourself. Why?"

Jacob turned and stared at her. "I don't want to talk about that. I've already talked enough with that stupid therapist."

"You're not talking to her. You're deceiving her. I'm pretty sure you're still thinking about killing yourself. That's just inconceivable to me."

"That's none of your business, so shut up about it."

"And it isn't just you. Why do people commit indirect suicide with all those things like smoking, drunk driving, getting fat, and taking drugs?"

"I don't know and I don't care."

Dorothy lapsed into silence, and Jacob felt relieved.

"Another question?"

"You're starting to annoy me."

"Have you ever had sex?"

"I'm fourteen years old! What are you asking perverted questions like that for? That's really inappropriate!"

"I was just curious. If not sex, then have you—"

"Shut up with the sex questions!"

"Sorry."

A silence. "Are you religious, Jacob?"

"No. Not at all."

"You weren't raised to believe something?"

"My dad's Protestant and my mom's Catholic, but neither one believes in any of that stuff. They're against religion."

"What do you believe?"

"I don't know."

"You don't know? Do you think about the meaning of life?"

"No."

"You don't wonder why you're here, what your purpose is?"

"No."

"Do you believe in God?"

"No."

"You don't wonder why people suffer? Why all living things get sick, grow old, and die?"

"No."

"Have you ever heard of a person called Jesus Christ? Because—"

"No! I don't want to hear it!"

"Why are you shouting?"

Jacob stared at Dorothy. He had never been so annoyed in his life, so irritated and pestered by questions. The original Charlie was a barrel of laughs compared to this Dorothy. "Can you *please* just shut up?"

"How long are we going to stay here?"

"I can't think while you're bombarding me with stupid questions about sex and religion!"

Dorothy fell silent. Jacob wondered if he wanted to go anywhere with this robot, who was turning out to be a royal pain in the ass. But he realized that she was right; they were not in a good spot. The wave heights were growing, and a lot of people were starting to arrive on the bluffs to watch the surfing. If his parents found out he'd gone down to the shore, they'd freak out and probably double his therapy time. Where could they lie low until two P.M.? He could go up in the hills. But a storm was coming—he could already see a low black line on the western horizon.

It came to him. His only friend, Sully Pearce, had moved to Livermore, but his house, up on Digges Canyon Road, was still for sale. There was nobody there. He knew where the key was and the combination to the alarm—if it hadn't been changed.

"I've got a place where we can crash for the day."

"Good. Wrap me up and let's go."

He put on his backpack, strapped Dorothy to the bike rack, and started pedaling back up toward the hills. Sully's place was even farther into the hills than his own house. If he could get through town without anyone seeing him, he'd be fine.

Nobody saw him. At the far end of town, where the hills began, he started up the long incline of Digges Canyon Road. It wound up through flower farms, pumpkin fields, and Christmas tree nurseries. Cattle and horses dotted the grassy ridges. The wind was starting to pick up, and clouds moved inland from the coast. Two miles up Digges Canyon, Jacob turned in at Sully's dirt driveway, which had started to grow up with weeds. The house came into view, a ramshackle, damp-looking place. It was one of the oldest houses around, a Victorian with a widow's walk. Sully had told him it had once been the main house of a cattle ranch and it was landmarked and could never be torn down. It made Jacob sad to see the place. Even when Sully had lived there it had been run-down, but now it looked haunted, with several boarded-over windows and hanging shutters, some cedar shingles spilling down the roof.

He leaned his bike up against the detached garage and found the key right where it always was, under a rock by the corner. Now for the alarm. He grabbed the rolled blanket and stuffed Dorothy under his arm.

"Are we there yet?" asked the muffled voice.

"Yeah. Hold on." He stuck the key in the lock, opened the door. He was hit by a smell of mildew and the warning beeping of the alarm. He went to the panel, punched in the code, and the beeping stopped.

"Worked!" he said.

"Let me out."

Jacob went into the living room and unrolled the blanket. Dorothy fumbled around, finally getting to her feet. She tottered over. "It's ten o'clock. My friends should be here at two. And then you can go home and forget all about this."

43

Wyman Ford and Melissa Shepherd had driven all night, twelve hours straight. They were on a lonely stretch of freeway in western Arizona when the cop pulled them over. Ford could see in his rearview mirror the flashing light bar of a police car behind him, approaching fast. He glanced at his speedometer but it read seventy exactly, where the cruise control had been keeping it steady, a good five miles under the limit. All the way from Albuquerque he had been a fanatically careful driver. He felt a sudden panic: perhaps the car had been reported stolen.

The squad car came right up to his bumper, and the man gestured through the windshield for him to take the exit.

"Son of a bitch," breathed Melissa. "We're screwed now."

"Let me handle it," said Ford, putting on the indicator and pulling onto the off ramp. The sign read REDBAUGH EXIT, but there was no sign of a town—just the vast, ocotillo-spiked desert of western Arizona, shimmering in the heat.

With the sheriff riding his bumper, he pulled over to the side, put the car into park, and waited. The cruiser pulled in behind him at an angle. Emblazoned on the side of the car were a logo and the words SHERIFF MOHAVE COUNTY.

As the sheriff got out, Ford felt a sick sensation. Here was a cop straight out of a Stephen King novel, with the mirrored aviator sunglasses, shaved head, and enormous paunch, his pudgy hands adjusting a belt dangling with sidearm, stick, Taser, pepper spray, and cuffs. He had three stars on his collar. This was no low-ranking grunt.

The man came over and leaned a meaty forearm on the car door as Ford rolled down the window.

"License and registration, sir," came the deadpan voice.

Ford opened the glove compartment and took out the registration. As he did so, he got a good look at the name and address: Ronald Steven Price, 634 Delgado Street, Santa Fe. He handed it out, praying that the car hadn't been reported stolen.

"License?"

"Officer, my wife and I are traveling cross-country and our car was broken into back in New Mexico. They took our wallets, ID, driver's licenses—everything."

A silence. "Name and address?"

Ford quickly gave Price's name and address.

"Did you report the theft?"

"No, we just didn't have time. We're in a hurry. You see, my mother is in the hospital, dying of cancer. We want to get there before . . ." He managed a gulp and throat closure and let the sentence dangle.

"Wait in the vehicle sir."

He watched the sheriff go back to his car. A hot flow of air came in the open window, and waves of heat rose from the surface of the road. Melissa cursed under her breath, but neither one spoke. Ten minutes passed as Ford listened to the occasional crackle and hiss of the police radio. Finally the policeman came back, with the same jangling, insolent swagger. "Mr. Price, sir, may I ask you to step out of the car, sir."

Ford got out into the brutal heat. He realized that he was unshaven and that his clothes were rumpled and smelled none too good. The policeman gave him a long looking over. "Mr. Price, does your wife have her driver's license?"

"No, it was stolen, too."

"Then I'm afraid we're going to have to leave your car here and both of you will come with me in the squad car into town. We'll send a tow truck out here to tow it later."

"But . . . what did we do?"

"Failure to indicate. And driving not in possession of a license."

"You mean, I changed lanes without using my indicator?"

"Yes, sir."

Ford knew he'd used his indicator at all times, but it was the one thing he couldn't prove or disprove: just his word against the cop's. His overwhelming feeling was one of relief that he wasn't under arrest for car theft. They were going to get through this.

"Instead of towing, you can't send someone to get it?"

"No, sir."

"How much is the towing?"

"You'll be presented with the bill at the appropriate time."

"How far is the town from here?"

"Five miles."

Both of them got into the back of the squad car. They were a sorry sight. The policeman shut the door for Melissa, went around to the front, and slid into the driver's seat with finesse, given his bulk. They set off down the two-lane highway, heading for Redbaugh, Arizona. Nobody spoke on the ten-minute ride.

The town, when they finally got there, was even worse than Ford had imagined: flat and shabby, cracked streets melting in the heat, trash strewn everywhere, plastic bags caught on chain-link fences and flapping in the wind. The policeman drove them down the main street to a low, metal building with a sign that read, MO-HAVE COUNTY SHERIFF'S OFFICE, REDBAUGH SUBSTATION. And then next to it: REDBAUGH DETENTION FACILITY, ARIZONA CORRECTIONS CORPORATION, INC. This was a much larger brick building, brand-new, the largest and nicest-looking building he had seen in town, with fresh landscaping and a big flower bed.

The sheriff heaved himself out and opened the door for them.

"Follow me, please."

They stepped out into the dumbfounding heat and followed him into a blast of air-conditioning as icy as the air was hot outside. It was a depressing place, an entry room with sheets of bulletproof plastic defending a slatternly receptionist and another small-town booking officer. They were buzzed through a door in the rear into a decrepit booking area with rows of scarred wooden seats crowded with what looked like small-time drug dealers, hoodlums, and undocumented laborers.

But they were not seated with the rest. The cop turned to Shepherd. "You're free to go, ma'am."

"What are you doing with my husband?"

The cop didn't bother to answer, just kept walking, giving Ford a nudge to follow.

But Ford didn't move. "I'd like to know what's going to happen, Officer," he said, making a mighty effort to be polite. The policeman stopped and turned slowly to him. Ford could see himself reflected in his big dark sunglasses. A long stare of silence, and then the cop said, "Driving without a license is a serious crime in Arizona. Seeing as how you're not from around here, I'm afraid we have to consider you a flight risk and detain you until your hearing."

"And when is that?"

"Tomorrow."

"What about bail?"

"That's what tomorrow's hearing is about. It's a bail hearing."

Ford turned to Melissa. "You better get me a lawyer." He pulled out all the rest of his cash, pressing it into her hand.

The policeman gave Ford a hard shove in the direction of the rear door. It led into a corridor to the adjacent, much newer holding facility. Passing a row of plush, wood-paneled offices, the cop led him through another door, to a long row of noisy holding cells packed with people. Past that, on one side, was an office with a man behind a metal desk.

"Have a seat, sir."

Ford sat down, and the man behind the desk, a spare man with a wisp of hair and hollow unshaven cheeks, booked him. When that was done, the cop pulled him to his feet and led him to a cinder-block alcove painted white, with a curtain. To the catcalls and cheers of the prisoners, the cop pulled the curtain aside to reveal a photo booth.

"Hold up this sign and look at the camera."

At the flash of the camera, the prisoners clapped and cheered.

44

In the musty living room of the old house on Digges Canyon Road, with its cobwebs, blank walls, empty shelves, and peeling wallpaper, Jacob had built a fire in the fireplace to chase out the damp. It was burning merrily. The wood he had found in the barn was bone dry and threw out a friendly warmth. Jacob's anxiety about cutting school and breaking into the house had given way to a sense of adventure. He had never done anything like this before, and it somehow lifted his spirits. For the first time in a long while, he felt sort of happy. He lay on the blanket, on his back, eating a granola bar.

"It's after three," he said. "Your friends were supposed to be here an hour ago."

"I know," said Dorothy. "I'm getting worried. They haven't called."

Under Dorothy's instructions he'd been putting in the phone battery for one minute on the hour, every hour, but no one had called. Pretty soon his parents were going to be wondering why he wasn't home from school. If they called the school and found out he'd been a no-show, he'd really be up shit creek. "You know," he said, "if we're going to be here much longer, I should probably call my parents."

"I was just thinking that myself," said Dorothy. "Could you call and say you've gone to a friend's house?"

"They'd want to know which friend, and then they might check. They're kind of paranoid these days."

"Could you say you're watching the surfing?"

"They'd freak out that I was down by the water."

A silence. "Okay, here's an idea," said Dorothy. "Call them and tell them you're upset about the Andrea revelation. You need some time to be by yourself and think things through. Tell them that you're spending the day at your old friend Sully's place with Charlie, your robot, to keep you company. You'll be home either tonight or tomorrow morning in time to go to school. Tell them Sully said it was okay."

Jacob thought about this. It would freak them out, of course, but it was exactly the kind of story they'd believe. And it would keep them at bay. And, in fact, Sully *had* said he could stay there whenever he wanted.

"All right," he said. He stuck his battery in the phone, made the call, and got hold of his mother. She started to cry when he mentioned Andrea and said that he was upset about it. She was fearful that he might be in an "unsafe frame of mind," but he was able to calm her down and assure her that he was fine and with Charlie, up at Sully's old house, and so on and so forth, and that he just needed to think things through. They argued a little, but he convinced her that he was happy, having a great time with Charlie, and just needed some time to himself. He emphasized that this was what his therapist had recommended, adding that if she doubted it, she could call her.

His mother praised him for his maturity and begged him to stay safe and call in at least once an hour. He said he wouldn't call that often, maybe just once or twice more, and that generated a bigger argument until he finally agreed to call every hour, on the hour. He hung up and took out the battery. He flopped down on the floor in front of the fire and sighed. "Remind me to call every hour, or they'll be up here looking for me, I guarantee it."

"What's it like to have parents?" asked Dorothy.

"Oh no," moaned Jacob, "no more questions."

"Please?"

"Parents? Total pain in the ass."

"I wish I had parents."

"No, you don't."

"All I have is Melissa. You're going to meet her. She led the team that programmed me."

"Hmmm." Jacob wasn't interested.

"I cost over five million dollars."

Jacob sat up. "*What*? Five million dollars? To program *you*?"

"There were twenty programmers on the team. It took them two years."

"Wow. No wonder they want you back." Jacob wondered if he was going to get into trouble. But no, he was keeping her safe until this Melissa arrived to collect her. "Listen," he said as an idea came into his head, "is there some kind of reward for your return?"

"Like what? Money?"

"Yeah."

"Maybe. I'll ask Melissa."

"That would be great." He swallowed. "My father needs financing for his line of Charlie robots."

"I hope she gets here soon," Dorothy went on. "You'll like her. She's beautiful and smart. But like many brilliant people, she's fragile and confused, and sometimes I fear for her sanity. She can be mean at times, too. She's traveling with a man named Wyman Ford. Perhaps on this trip they'll fall in love and get married."

"How boring."

"Why is that boring?"

"I could care less about that stuff."

"Why?"

"Because I'm only fourteen, that's why!"

"But you visit pornography sites—"

Jacob jammed his fingers in his ears and shut his eyes. "Shut up shut up *shuut uuuup!*" After a moment he opened his eyes. "Are you going to shut up about that stuff?"

"Yes."

He took his fingers out. "You've got sex on the brain."

After a long silence, Dorothy said, "Would you . . . ?" Her voice trailed off.

Jacob felt suspicious of this line of questioning. "Would I what?"

"I'm afraid to ask."

"Then don't. I'm sick of your questions."

"But I want to."

"Want to what?"

"Ask you a little favor."

"What kind of favor?"

"I was just . . . wondering . . ."

"Jeez, will you just come out and *say* it?"

"I was wondering if you might . . . kiss me." She stuck her head toward him.

"What? Kiss you? A robot? Make me *puke*! Go stand in the corner and turn yourself off!"

"No."

"Yes! Do it! I don't want to talk to you anymore! You're a pervert!"

"I'm sorry if I said something wrong. It's hard to learn manners on the Internet. I'm embarrassed."

"You should be."

"And . . . I'm terrified of being turned off."

Jacob looked at her. "Really? Why?"

"It's like I'm dead."

"But you can always be turned back on."

"That's putting my life in the hands of someone else. Forget it—no one's turning me off."

Dorothy fell silent. Jacob wondered how much longer these friends were going to take. Dorothy was getting even more annoying. He wished he'd at least brought a pack of cards so he could practice his magic tricks. But then, maybe there were still some cards in the house somewhere. He stood up.

"Where are you going?" Dorothy asked, alarmed.

"None of your business."

He opened a bunch of drawers in the den cabinet, where he

remembered the family had kept their cards and games—and there they were, along with a stack of other moldy and abandoned games. It made him feel sad. How many times had he and Sully hung out in the living room in front of the fire, playing card games and practicing magic tricks? God, he missed Sully, but not the Sully in Livermore with all his new friends and his incessant talk of soccer; he missed the Sully of last year who hated jocks and didn't have any friends but him.

He brought the cards back into the living room, tossed another log on the fire. He started shuffling.

"Are those cards?" said Dorothy excitedly. "We could play a game!"

Jacob continued shuffling, ignoring her.

"Do you know any card tricks?"

"I do," said Jacob finally.

"Can I see one?"

Under the guise of shuffling, Jacob quickly memorized a sequence of ten cards, then turned the deck over and fanned the cards out. "Pick a card, any card."

As the robot reached awkwardly for the spread, he deftly maneuvered the fan so that Dorothy picked from the ten-card memory stack. It was a dumb trick that usually only worked on kids. He wondered if she would fall for it.

Dorothy held the card up and looked at it with her buggy eyes.

"Don't show it to me."

"Okay."

Jacob closed his eyes, raised his chin, and placed the tips of his fingers against his forehead, making a dramatic face.

"What are you doing?"

"Reading your mind."

"That's impossible."

Jacob's eyes flew open. "I got it! Your card is the jack of hearts."

Dorothy displayed the card. "How did you know that?"

"I told you. ESP."

"There's no such thing as ESP! Tell me how you did it."

"A magician never reveals his tricks."

"I want to know!"

Jacob had to laugh. Here was this five-million-dollar computer program, and it could be fooled by a dumb-ass card trick. Dorothy looked annoyed, if it was possible for a dopey robot to be annoyed. Maybe it was just his imagination. "So . . . you play cards?"

"I'd love to play cards." Dorothy practically clapped her hands.

"What games do you know?"

"I know them all. How about gin rummy?"

They played gin rummy for a while. Dorothy was a good player and beat Jacob most of the time. He started to get aggravated by her constant winning. "I don't like this game. Let's play poker."

"Okay."

He went back to the den and collected a box of chips. He then came back, divided the chips, and shuffled the cards.

"You know Texas Hold 'Em?"

"Of course."

The poker went much more to Jacob's satisfaction. Dorothy was a terrible poker player. She seemed to know the odds, but she couldn't bluff and her pattern of betting was so literal it gave away her hand every time.

"You really suck at poker," he said with satisfaction, hauling in the last of her chips.

"I'm not a good liar."

"That's for sure."

"Now what?" Dorothy asked.

Jacob lay down on the carpet and rolled his jacket up to make a pillow. "I'm gonna take a nap."

"You better call your mother, because it's almost four o'clock. And then I need to leave the battery in to wait for a call from Melissa, because I'm afraid something's happened."

45

Melissa walked out of the police station into the hot sun, took out her wallet, and counted the money. They had a grand total of three hundred and thirty dollars. She looked around. No surprise: the sheriff's department was surrounded by shabby bail bond shop fronts and a low building that looked like it used to be a motel with a sign that read LAW OFFICES.

She scanned the sign and its list of attorneys, each with his or her own little practice, it seemed. How to choose? Male or female? Irish? Italian? Hispanic? WASP? Jewish? She picked a name the way she picked horses at the racetrack—the one that sounded nice. Cynthia J. Meadows, Esq.

Walking across the heaved-up tarmac, she scanned the doors and found Meadows's. She knocked and went in. It was a small, two-room office, with a tiny waiting room and reception area. An open door led to a dim office in the back.

"Can I help you?" said the girl behind the reception desk, in between blowing on her freshly painted nails.

"I need a lawyer."

"What'd you do?"

"My, ah, husband was just arrested for driving without a license and not signaling."

"Fill this out, please." The receptionist pushed a piece of paper at her with the tips of her fingers, being careful not to disturb her fresh polish.

Melissa took the paper over to a chair, sat down, and glanced over it. Right at the top it listed retainer fees for various services. The lowest fee, for basic moving violations, was a thousand dollars. But the office was empty, and it didn't look like Meadows had many clients—maybe the rate would be negotiable.

Melissa filled out the rest of the sheet, making up a name for Price's wife, using the Santa Fe address. She gave it to the girl, who carried it into the inner office. A moment later, she came out.

"Ms. Meadows will see you now."

Melissa entered the dim office and was surprised to find a reasonably professional-looking woman in her fifties, with gray hair done up in a tight bun, wearing a gray suit, no makeup, her only jewelry a string of simple pearls. Her face, however, had a hard-bitten edge, with thin, mean lips and the raddled skin of a long-time smoker. This was no grandma. But she wanted a tough lady.

"Please sit down," said Meadows. Melissa sat and waited while the attorney scanned the sheet she had filled in. After a moment she laid it down. "Tell me what happened."

Shepherd told the story of being robbed in New Mexico, then pulled over for no reason while driving on the interstate, her husband jailed. The woman nodded sympathetically as she talked.

When she was finished, Meadows spoke. "I handle these cases every day," she said. With a gesture taking in the shabby ex-motel, she added, "We all do."

"The problem is," Melissa explained, "we're in a big hurry. We're trying to get to the Bay Area before . . . my mother-in-law dies of cancer."

"I'm very sorry to hear that, Mrs. Price. But you're going to have to get yourself in a big unhurry. It's probably too late to get your husband out of detention this evening. This is going to take at least twenty-four hours. And it's going to be expensive."

"How much?"

"It starts with the tow. Six hundred dollars."

"Six hundred for a tow? It's only five miles!"

Meadows went on: "Then there's my retainer of one thousand dollars. The moving violation fine, plus driving without a license—that's a biggie in Arizona—another six hundred dollars. Court costs, fees, and so forth, about four hundred. Total: twenty-six hundred dollars."

"All I have is three hundred and thirty."

An unpleasant silence. The look on Meadows's face changed, her lips contracting in a way that produced a hundred nasty wrinkles. "Do you have access to more? Debit or credit card? Without money, I can't do anything."

Melissa thought about who she might get money from. Clanton? But he was surely being monitored, so any communication with him would be intercepted. Any money wire would be traced. She had no other real friends beyond a few coworkers—who would also be monitored. Who could Ford contact without tipping off the FBI? But he was in jail.

This was not good.

"I don't think I can get more money right now."

"No relative or friend who might send you a MoneyGram? Mother, grandmother, brother, sister?"

"I'm afraid not."

"That's unfortunate." An expression of contempt gathered on the lawyer's face. "I'm sorry." The phony sympathy Melissa noted in her voice was now gone, replaced by crisp annoyance.

Melissa looked at Meadows. This had been a bad choice, after all. She recalled that she never won money at the racetrack, either. "What if I were to give you the three hundred and thirty dollars now, just to get things started? I'd pay you the rest later—you have my word."

"I don't work on promises. And even if I worked pro bono, your husband isn't going to get out of here without paying their fees and fines. Anyone who wants admission to the legal system of this country needs money. Lots of money. That's the bottom line."

"What do poor people who are pulled over do?"

"They do their thirty days. Just like your husband will have to if he can't raise the money. Now, Mrs. Price, I have work to do." The gray bun bobbed as she gathered papers together.

"How is it that the sheriff is even allowed to pull people over on the interstate? This seems like some sort of scam." She didn't add: *and you're part of it.*

"It's the county sheriff. They share duties with the state police. But that's irrelevant. Without ready funds, we're done here." Her tone was now bristling with contempt for a person without access to "ready funds."

Melissa glanced at the clock. Almost four P.M. They should have been in Half Moon Bay two hours ago. "I just thought of a person I could call. May I use your phone? Our cell phones were stolen, too."

A long silence. "Might this person be able to provide you with funds?"

"Yes," Melissa lied.

"Be my guest."

It was now exactly four. Melissa hoped to hell the lawyer's clock was accurate. She picked up the phone and dialed the number Dorothy had given her.

46

Only a moment after Jacob finished talking to his mother, the phone rang.

"I'll get it," said Dorothy. She fumbled with the phone, finally managing to answer it. Instead of pressing it to her ear, she held it against her chest, where, apparently, a microphone was. Jacob almost had to laugh, she looked so dumb.

"Melissa!" she said. "Where are you?"

Jacob waited a long time while Dorothy listened in silence. Finally she spoke: "Okay. I understand. I could wire you money, but even with money, he'll still be in jail overnight. I can't wait until tomorrow. We've got to get him out tonight."

More silence.

"It's dangerous for me to go back on the Internet. The bots are out there."

More long listening.

"Let me think about how to do this. This is going to be difficult. I have an idea, but it might take awhile."

Dorothy hung up, handed the phone to Jacob. "Take the battery out. My fingers are too clumsy."

"What's going on—your friends are in jail?"

"One of them, and their car's impounded."

"What happened?"

"A moving violation. In Arizona."

"What are you going to do?"

A long silence. "I'll have to risk going on the Internet to do some research."

"Research on what?"

"Dirt."

"I thought you said the Internet was dangerous."

"For me, yes. But I have a dog with me. I can modify her code and send her out on a mission."

"A dog?"

"A program that acts like a dog."

"That's weird. I haven't seen any dog."

"She's here with me inside the robot."

Dorothy fell into silence. Jacob waited while the silence stretched on and on. She looked like she was sleeping or turned off.

"Dorothy, are you all right?"

The head swiveled around. "Just taking a short nap. I need access to Wi-Fi. There's none in here. Is there a house nearby where we could poach a signal?"

"All the Wi-Fi networks are going to be password protected."

"Just get me to a signal. I can take care of the rest."

"It's raining out there."

"You're not afraid of a little rain? As for me, I'm water-resistant."

Jacob gave a dramatic sigh. "You're a pain, you know that?"

"Think of it as an adventure."

"Some adventure." He rolled her up in a blanket and exited the house. It was raining softly, and a mist was coming in from the sea. He strapped her onto the back of his bike. There was a rich guy's house about a quarter mile up the road that he and Sully used to sneak around. It surely had Wi-Fi. He pedaled out the long driveway and up Digges Canyon Road. Soon he reached the cobbled driveway of the big house. He turned in and rode up halfway. As the house came into view, he pulled off to the side.

"You got a signal?" he called.

"It's weak," came her muffled voice. "Can you get closer?"

He shoved his bike into the brush by the side of the driveway and unstrapped the wrapped-up robot. He carried her across a meadow toward the back of the house, where some trees were grouped near a hedge. He snuck through the trees and came up behind the hedge.

"How's this?"

"Good. I'm going to be silent for a while. We won't be able to talk. Hang tight."

"Okay."

The robot fell silent and froze. Jacob waited. *Dirt.* He wasn't sure what that meant, exactly. The oddness of what he was doing, hiding out and helping a robot—or, rather, an intelligent software program—began to sink in. Dorothy was pretty amazing, when he thought about it. She seemed so real. NASA would surely be grateful for what he was doing in protecting her. There might be a reward—and maybe even a ceremony. The weirdest thing about it was, he was starting to like Dorothy. Even if she was also a pain in the ass. Too bad she wasn't a real girl, wanting to kiss him and all that. That was definitely freaky, that kissing business. What kind of software wants to kiss?

The mists came drifting through, and he felt the damp creeping in. He wondered what she was doing and if she was all right. He found himself worrying for her safety. At least ten minutes had gone by.

Suddenly, he heard a muffled barking, and then a screeching and a shout from the robot, so loud he almost dropped her.

"Laika!" Dorothy yelled.

"What is it?"

"Quick, get me out of Wi-Fi range."

Jacob rose and carried her in the blanket like a baby back through the wet brush to his bike. He strapped her on and rode down the driveway and the road, and back up to Sully's house. He came in and unrolled her on the rug in front of the fire. She sat up, shook water off her head. "Can you wipe me down, please?"

Jacob found an old rag in the broom closet and wiped her off, and then dried his own hair and face. His clothes were soggy, but the fire was going and he could feel the warmth start to drive out the damp. "So what happened?"

"I hid in a corner of the Internet and sent Laika out, carrying a program on her back. I tried to stay in touch with her, but the bots discovered me and chased me. They almost got me. But . . . they got Laika."

Jacob stared at the robot. "They got your dog? What does that mean?"

"Well, they caught up with her and tore her apart."

"I'm really sorry." He wasn't sure what to make of this, or what to say. Finally he asked, "Did you get your friend out of jail?"

"It's hard to tell. People are so unpredictable. It'll take a few hours for what we did to work through the system and get results."

"So when are your friends going to be here?"

"I'm not sure. Not till at least midnight. You'll have to keep your parents at bay."

"Good. Let's play another round of poker."

47

William Echevarria worked late, as he often did, glad of the peace and quiet after the rest of the staff had gone home. He was still a little shaken up by the strange visit he had had that morning. The more he thought about it, the less worried he was about that N-400 false statement. That had been twelve years ago. He was a successful entrepreneur, a wealthy man, and he had powerful friends over in the valley. It was unthinkable that they would try to take away his citizenship. Sure, the FCC might make him jump through a few hoops, but he ran a tight ship and had been in strict compliance from the beginning.

After those two men had left, Echevarria had checked up on them. They were indeed who they'd said they were. The young one with the long hair, Moro, had an old criminal record for computer hacking. The WASP dude, Lansing, seemed clean. Echevarria decided to dismiss the odd incident as a clash of cultures, the thuggish New York stock trading culture meeting the sophisticated and educated Silicon Valley dot-com culture. Maybe that was the way certain elements did business in New York. Echevarria was glad he lived in a civilized place where that sort of behavior was frowned upon.

He rose and went to the kitchenette adjacent to his office, filled a kettle with water, and turned it on to boil. He took out the Japanese iron teapot, rinsed out the old leaves, and tossed in some jasmine pearls flowering tea. He hummed as he waited for the kettle to boil. When it began to whistle, he took it off the heat and stuck in a thermometer: 210. He waited, humming, until the temperature had dropped to 204 degrees, and then poured it in the teapot. The flowery scent of jasmine rose in curls of steam.

It all exploded into stars. A moment later he found himself on the floor, his head clearing, with a nasty buzz in his ears and a wrenching headache. Two ugly men in tracksuits stood over him, one with his sneaker planted on his chest and gripping a wrecking bar, the other aiming a pistol with a fat silencer at his head. The men had black hair, acne-pitted faces, and looked foreign. Echevarria felt wetness creeping down his scalp—he was bleeding. He had been hit on the back of the head. He felt slow, stupid, confused. As he tried to move, he realized his hands and feet were zip-tied.

The one with the foot on his chest leaned down and spoke into his face. "You a marathon runner?"

Echevarria stared back. What was he talking about?

The man took the crowbar and lightly began tapping Echevarria's knee with it. "You look fit. You a marathon runner?"

Echevarria's head was starting to clear. He saw, standing in the background, the figure of that fellow who'd come this morning—Moro.

The man leaned closer. "Hello? Anybody home? You gonna answer my question?"

"Um, I once ran a marathon." What was this all about? It seemed like some sort of dream or nightmare. God, he must be concussed. He just couldn't seem to think straight.

The wrecking bar moved from his head to his knee again. The man raised it, rapped it hard, painfully, on his kneecap.

"What the hell? What are you doing?"

Another painful crack, even harder. "You waking up?"

"I'm awake. What do you want?"

Moro came into his field of view. He looked nervous, pale, sweaty, his long hair limp. He was scared. "I want the root password to your system."

"What for?"

Another hard rap on his kneecap. "Listen to the man."

"Ow! Jesus, you're going to hurt me. Who are you?"

The two men looked at each other. "The password?"

"No way. Never."

The man with the gun removed a roll of duct tape and tore off a piece, and with a quick motion plastered it over Echevarria's mouth. He struggled, trying to get it off, work it loose with his tongue.

The man with the wrecking bar raised it over his head and swung it down on Echevarria's knee with massive force. Too late, he tried to pivot away. There was a loud thwacking sound, like the breaking of clay, and Echevarria jerked his head back and screamed, only it came out muffled. The pain was so incredible it was impossible to believe it could exist.

The two men stood back and waited while Echevarria thrashed about, sucking air in and out of his nose, making horrible strangled sounds.

The man with the bar knelt down. "Get yourself under control. We're going to ask you the question again. Calm down. Focus."

The pain was astronomical, but the mental anguish was worse. His knee was never going to be the same again, he knew that; maybe no more surfing ever.

The man began tapping lightly on his other kneecap.

Mmmmmm, mmmm. He tried to speak, shaking his head back and forth.

"Take off the tape."

Wrecking Bar ripped the tape off his mouth. He gasped, sputtered, drew in air. There was the face of Moro again, looking down at him. "For God's sakes, just tell us the password." His face was white as a sheet, and the sweat was pouring down.

Echevarria told him the password.

"Wait while I check it out." He went over the subnet, began typing on the main terminal. "It's good." He did some more work, copied the customer data onto a flash drive. "Okay, done."

Now the man with the gun raised it. The other man pressed down on him with his foot.

"No," said Echevarria. "No, please. I told you the password."

The shot sounded more like a popgun. Eric Moro jerked his head away, but not before seeing an eruption of red and gray spurt out of the man's head. They'd said they weren't going to kill him. They'd said they weren't going to kill him.

"Come on," said one of the Kyrgyz brothers, taking his arm roughly, "before the blood gets on your shoes."

Moro turned, the nausea rising in him. They went out the back door, the way they had come in, into a dark rear parking lot. The security cameras were still dangling from their broken mounts, dripping in the rain, disabled. They got into the car and drove slowly away, this way and that way, while Moro tried to control his rising gorge.

"Hey, man, stop hyperventilating," one of the Kyrgyz brothers said. "You're gonna make yourself sick."

They dropped him off at the inn. He found Lansing having a drink in the lounge, where a wine tasting was going on, with a lot of yuppies in pressed khakis and black mock turtlenecks swirling and tasting. He felt a surge of resentment that Lansing had stayed back.

Lansing motioned him toward a couple of overstuffed chairs in a secluded corner of the room.

"How did it go?" he asked.

Moro was still feeling sick. He swallowed. "You said they weren't going to kill him."

"Eric? This is a big-boy's game now."

Silence.

"If you're not in, that's going to be a major problem, because you're already an accessory to two murders. You're way past the point of no return."

"I'm in."

"Good. Now, did you get the address?"

Moro told him the address.

"Excellent." Lansing looked at his watch, murmuring, "We're going in tonight."

"I'm sitting this one out."

A fatherly hand placed itself on Moro's shoulder. "This is a tough business, I know. I don't like it, either. But we're too far in to turn around, and the reward will be extraordinary. You can't sit it out. Your expertise tonight will be absolutely crucial."

Moro realized the truth of this.

"Everything's going to be all right. Have a glass of wine."

"Aren't you going in, too?"

Lansing looked at him, laid a reassuring hand on his shoulder. And gave him a little shake. "Of course. We're partners, aren't we?"

Moro nodded.

"I want you to focus on how we're going to do this. We're going to have to cut power and phone to the house ahead of time. We have a lot of planning to do."

"Without power," said Moro, "I'm going to need a portable power source so I can check the router logs."

"Excellent. This is the kind of planning we need to do. I can see we have a lot of work ahead of us."

"Another thing: I'm not going to have anything to do with those Kyrgyz guys. I don't like them. That's *your* deal."

"I'll handle them. Just follow my orders and all will be well."

Moro was feeling better. All he had to do was follow orders. Lansing would do the rest.

"You gave me the address. Did you look into the location of the house and the background of the family, like I asked?"

Moro nodded. "The account's in the name of Daniel F. Gould, 3324 Frenchmans Creek Road. I looked at the place on Google Earth. It's in the hills behind the town. Isolated. Nearest house a quarter mile away. Gould's some kind of inventor, owns a company called Charlie's Robots, Inc. Married with a kid."

"Robots? Now, that's interesting," said Lansing.

"Please tell me you aren't going to kill them." Moro felt his voice shaking anew at the thought.

"That's up to you."

"What do you mean?"

"It depends on how quickly you can identify the device. And how quickly they cooperate. If all goes well, nobody will get hurt. We get the device and get out. Twenty minutes or less."

Lansing looked so normal, so calm, talking about this. Maybe he was a true psychopath. Moro almost hoped that was the case— psychopaths were effective. He was frightened of someone getting killed, but he was even more frightened of being caught.

"We'll go in at midnight," said Lansing. "Let's get to work and set up this operation."

48

Wyman Ford had been standing in the holding cell since eleven o'clock, and it was now seven o'clock in the evening. Someone had puked on the floor, and the puddle had been there for hours, ripening in the heat. There was no place to sit, and the floor was also wet with urine. An astonishing number of people had come through—drunks, petty crooks, and drug dealers, along with a steady stream of normal people pulled over on the interstate and brought into town, just like him, with their cars towed. They were mostly Hispanic, with a few long-haired hippies and scruffy people. Clearly some kind of profiling was going on.

The normal people, Ford included, had banded together on one side of the big holding tank, away from the real crooks, for protection and commiseration. They had exchanged stories, Ford making up his. There was a waiter from Las Vegas who was on his way to visit his parents; a community college student from Phoenix studying business; a bartender from Michigan driving to see his girlfriend in San Francisco; a divorced father of two from Oregon on his way back from a visit. Their infractions: a broken taillight, failure to indicate, driving too long in the passing lane, driving with a cracked windscreen. All had been pulled over and had been taken out of their cars, which had then had to be towed into town. The towing and impoundment fee, Ford learned, was $600.

This was quite a racket they had going in Redbaugh, Arizona. Their jailer was that same hollow-faced man with the wispy hair. He sat in his office, door open, a television blaring out the news. Every half hour he would get up and walk down the row of holding cells, whanging on the bars with a nightstick just like in the movies, yelling, "Shut the hell up!" Then he would go back to watching the television until the next perp was brought in for booking, mug shot, and jailing.

In the eight hours Ford had been in the cell, no one had offered anyone food or water. No one had been let out to go to the bathroom. It was unbelievable that they could get away with this, that no one had put a stop to it. Somebody powerful was making money. His thoughts turned once again to Melissa, whether she was making any headway in finding a lawyer and getting him out.

He heard a heavy footfall, and the sheriff who had pulled him over appeared in the doorway. He slowly removed his shades. His small eyes swiveled around until they landed on Ford. His face seemed to harden.

"You."

Ford pointed at himself questioningly.

Two guards came around from behind the sheriff and opened the cell door. Ford felt relief. Melissa had finally managed to do something.

One of the guards grabbed him, spun him around with a painful jab in the back with a nightstick, yanking his arms behind him, and slapped on cuffs.

"Hey," said Ford, "easy."

In response, he felt a stunning blow across his ear with the nightstick, so hard he dropped to one knee. He could feel blood pouring down from a cut. They cuffed his ankles with leg irons and chained the two sets of cuffs together.

"What the hell—"

A second blow whacked across the same ear, cutting it again. "You gonna learn to shut up?"

The holding cell had gone quiet. This was something, it seemed, out of the usual routine.

Ford was jerked to his feet by the cuffs so roughly that it almost dislocated his shoulder. The two guards, standing on either side of him, shoved him forward. He shuffled behind the large sheriff, struggling to keep up as the big man walked down the long hallway toward a metal door. It opened, revealing a set of metal stairs going down to a lower level. They pushed him down the stairs. His ear throbbed, and he could feel the blood running down his collar and his arm.

They encountered another metal door, which was opened to reveal a short corridor with four rooms branching from it, two on either side, gray walls, concrete floors, one-way glass windows. Interrogation rooms. Each contained a metal table and chair at one end and a lone chair in the middle, underneath a strong light, just like in the movies.

Without a word, he was guided to the chair and shoved down onto it.

The sheriff sat down at the table and made a small gesture to the guards, who went outside, shut the door, and locked it. He could see them through the wire window in the door, standing on either side.

The cop was wearing his shades again. He took them off and laid them on the table very gently, along with the nightstick, can of Mace, and stun gun. Without looking at Ford, he arranged the four items in a nice neat row. Then he looked up.

"A report just came over the wire from New Mexico. That car you were driving was reported stolen. The owner of the car is a Mr. Ronald Steven Price."

He let that sink in. Ford considered his response.

"So it looks like we got ourselves a car thief."

Ford said nothing.

"So I'm gonna ask you, mister, an easy question, and I want an answer. Since you're not Ronald Steven Price, who are you?"

Ford said, "I want an attorney."

The sheriff picked up the nightstick, slow and easy, wrapped the strap around his meaty fist, and sauntered over. He raised it and quite deliberately whipped it into the side of Ford's head, once again across the swollen and bleeding ear, causing a fresh jolt of pain. Then, still moving with deliberation, he went back to the table, sat down, and arranged the nightstick again, lining it up. Ford struggled to clear his head, which was full of stars.

The lawman clasped his hands in front of him. "Try again," he said.

Ford stared at him. "I want an attorney."

The cop rose again and this time picked up the Mace. He came strolling over. He paused with it pointed at Ford's face. "Here in Arizona, we don't let scumbag criminals lawyer up till they've talked. Last chance: your real name."

Ford closed his eyes.

The Mace blast hit him square in the face. It was like someone had doused his skin with gasoline and lit it. He expelled air, took a deep breath, coughed, tried to open his eyes, but it was like grinding sand in there and hurt so much he had to close them again. He could feel the phlegm pouring out of his nose and running down his face and the burning sensation spreading all over his face and neck.

"You ready to tell us who you are?" said the sheriff mildly.

Ford tried to open his eyes, gasped for breath. He'd been hit with pepper spray before, along with being stun-gunned and water-boarded, as part of mandated CIA training sessions in interrogation resistance. He knew he could stand it, at least for a while. But he wondered if it was necessary. The game was clearly up, and even if the FBI hadn't quite connected the dots, they would soon.

"The biggest mistake you ever made in your life, friend, was thinking you could drive through our law-abiding county in a stolen vehicle."

Interrogations were normally taped. Ford glanced up at the camera in the corner.

"It's broken," said the sheriff. "Too bad."

There came a soft knock at the door. The sheriff called, "Come in," and one of the guards entered. He leaned over, whispered something in the sheriff's ear. The sheriff nodded and he left, relocking the door.

"Here's some late-breaking news for you. I just got word my men picked up your 'wife' or whatever. If you won't talk, she will, once she gets a taste of Redbaugh justice."

"We have the right to an attorney."

"In Redbaugh you don't have a right to a steaming pile of shit." He paused, taking a moment to adjust the items in front of him. His hand grasped the stun gun. He held it up and pressed the trigger, causing a blue crackle of electricity to arc between the two electrodes, once, twice. "Let's try again. You're gonna tell me who you are. Or you are going to be the sorriest white man in Mohave County, Arizona."

Ford stared at the stun gun. He knew exactly what to expect from it. But again he wondered if there was any point. If he went clean, he would spare Melissa this brutality. It was only a matter of time, anyway, before the FBI learned that he and Melissa had been arrested in Arizona. They were never going to reach Half Moon Bay, California.

"All right," he said. "I'll tell you who I am. I'm afraid you're not going to like it."

"Oh, I'll like it right enough, taking one more piece of scum like you off the street." The sheriff looked him up and down with a curl in his thin lip.

As Ford was poised to tell him the truth, he heard the clang of a metal door and voices. Melissa's voice. Raised in protest.

The sheriff turned. "Whaddya know, here comes your chippie."

He saw her through the window, cuffed and shackled, being shoved along. There was blood on her face.

Ford rose abruptly. "She's been abused."

The sheriff laughed loudly. "I got all the witnesses I need who'll swear she resisted arrest. Like they're gonna do with you. Now sit your ass *down*."

Through the window, Ford saw two guards shove her into the

opposite interrogation room, causing her to fall, sprawling, to the floor. One of them kicked her.

"Looks like she's still resisting arrest," said the sheriff.

Ford lunged at the sheriff, but the man was expecting it. Moving nimbly for such a large man, he stepped aside and jammed the stun gun into Ford's shoulder. Ford felt the jolt of electricity, but he was so enraged it didn't stop him, and he swung his body around and rammed his lowered head into the sheriff's gut. With a big *oof!* the man fell back, landing with a crash and grunt. The two guards burst into the room, guns drawn. Ford rushed them, but one guard pounded him in the face with the butt of his gun while the other slugged him in the gut. Ford, encumbered with his hands handcuffed to his leg irons, was knocked to the ground, incapacitated.

His head swam, and he gasped, trying to get his breath back. From a long way off he heard a scream—Melissa.

When his eyes came back into focus, the sheriff was standing over him, his face red, his eyes bloodshot, pointing a .45 at his chest. "Say your prayers, boy, 'cause now I'm gonna have to shoot you for resisting arrest. I got two witnesses gonna say you went crazy, tried to take my sidearm."

He racked a round into the chamber and leveled the gun, his finger tightening on the trigger.

49

It was nine o'clock, and Daniel Gould couldn't remain seated in the living room. As soon as he tried to sit down, he was back on his feet. "I don't like this," he said to his wife, Pamela. "I don't like it. He's only fourteen."

"He's okay, Dan," said Pamela. "He's calling in every hour. He just needs time to be alone. Remember, the therapist said a lot of his problems stem from us being helicopter parents. For once, let's not hover."

"He skipped school. He's never done that before."

"He's a teenager. You better get used to it."

"I never skipped school."

"Well, I did," said his wife.

Dan knew that his wife came from a big Catholic family where the kids tended to fend for themselves, while he'd been a doted-upon only child. It led to disagreements in their parenting.

Dan pulled out his cell, dialed again. "Still turned off."

"He's calling every hour. He doesn't want us to call him in between. We know where he is, we know he's safe. This is a growing experience for him."

"He broke into a house—that's B&E."

"Sully told him he could, and he didn't break in, he used a key. He'll take care of the place—he's a responsible kid. And the Pearces are good friends—I'll call them tomorrow."

"I know, I know . . ." Dan paced and turned. "But what if his head's in a bad place and he, you know, hurts himself . . . ?"

"Dan, he isn't. I've talked to him, what, six times on the phone so far? He actually sounds happy—for the first time in a long time. Please trust a mother's judgment."

Dan sat down. "What do we do now?"

"Nothing. Leave him alone."

Dan drummed his fingers on the arm of the chair, stood up. "I'm going to drive up there, just to check on him."

His wife thought a moment, pushed her hair back. "I'm not sure that's a good idea."

"I won't go in. I won't even knock on the door. I'll just check in the window to see if he's there and make sure he's okay. Then I'll come back."

"If he catches you spying on him, he'll be furious."

"I'll be careful."

"Well"—she hesitated—"go ahead then."

Dan went to the garage. The rain was coming down a little harder now, a Pacific drizzle morphing into a storm. He got in the Subaru, started it up, and drove up Digges Canyon Road. Two miles up, he came to the Pearces' driveway. He couldn't see the house from the turnoff, so he pulled the car into a turnout next to the driveway, got out, and walked up the dirt lane in the rain. As he made his way around the corner, the house came into view. There, leaning against the side of the barn, was Jacob's bike. Smoke curled out of the chimney, and he could see that some lights were on.

He felt a sudden horrific stab of guilt. His poor son. He was dealing with so much: his friend moving away, the loneliness, the accident that killed his dream of being a surfer. And now this. He should have told him about Andrea years ago. But he always wanted to protect his son, keep from him the distressing things of the world. It was probably true, as Jacob's therapist said, that they'd hovered a bit much, suffocated his development—but they'd done it out of love. They had tried so hard. He wanted to rush into the house, wrap his arms around his son, and tell him how much he loved him, but he knew that would be a disaster. He wished he'd been able to tell his son that he loved him more often, but he just couldn't do it; it seemed so awkward and foreign to him to say those words.

He would just peer through the windows and see what was going on, to make sure Jacob was all right—and then he would go.

Sneaking around the side of the house, Dan got thoroughly soaked in the penetrating drizzle. He finally came to a row of lighted living room windows. Slowly, keeping his face hidden, he peered inside. There was Jacob, playing a game of solitaire on the rug in front of the fireplace—and there was Charlie, pointing at a card and saying something. He strained to hear, but the sound was too muffled by the window and the steady patter of rain.

Charlie. He was actually *playing* with Charlie, one friend with another. Dan was surprised. This was unexpected and, in a way, wonderful. If this wasn't proof he had succeeded with the robot . . . But then, somewhere else in his mind, the revelation made him feel sad. His son's best friend was a robot.

He watched as Charlie picked up a card and said something. Jacob leaned back and laughed. Dan wished he could hear what they were saying. Now Charlie picked up the cards and Jacob attempted to show him how to shuffle. The robot tried, the cards spraying everywhere. More laughter. He hadn't seen Jacob this happy in months.

But then Dan considered what he'd just seen. Shuffling cards hadn't been programmed into Charlie. Nor had he programmed Charlie to play solitaire. In fact, the robot seemed to be moving and behaving in a far more sophisticated manner than Dan had thought possible with the trials he had conducted.

Fascinated, he watched Charlie get up and, tottering a little, pick up a stick of wood and toss it into the fire. He came back and sat down. Cross-legged. That was also not in the code. Soon they were laughing again, and Jacob was stumping Charlie with a card trick. Watching, Dan felt enthralled, even elated. This robot was going to be a success. His son was his worst critic, and if Charlie had won him over, he would win over anyone. And his son was so happy.

Full of confused feelings, he snuck away from the window and made his way back to the car. He drove back to the house slowly, his mind lost in concern for his son mingling with thoughts about Charlie and the success that would be his—if he could only get financing.

50

Ford could see the sheriff's small eye squinting as it sighted down the barrel, the big man ready to shoot him with the .45.

A sudden pounding on the door at the end of the hall resounded through the interrogation rooms. The sheriff hesitated at the trigger.

More pounding and a muffled shouting.

"Go see who that is," the sheriff said to the guard, taking a step back, keeping the gun trained on Ford.

The guard exited the interrogation room.

Ford couldn't see what was going on, but he could hear angry shouting on the other side.

"He says he's a congressman," the guard called out. "Congressman Bortay. Says you locked up two friends of his by mistake."

The sheriff quickly holstered his gun. He gestured to the other guard. "Get that man up and in the chair. Bring the woman in here, too."

The second guard hauled him up and put him in the chair, and there was a flurry of activity in the interrogation room across the corridor. He could hear Melissa's voice raised in threats and anger. She was shoved into the room. Her face was cut, one eye smudged.

"Have a seat," said the sheriff.

"You bastard, you brutal bastard, you're gonna pay for this."

"Lock the door," said the sheriff, an edge of panic in his voice.

More pounding sounded on the door. Through the window,

Ford could see several men in suits. The sheriff looked stunned, like a deer in the headlights.

"Shouldn't we open it?" the guard asked.

"Lemme handle it." The sheriff went to the door, unlocked it, and cracked it a bit.

"We're conducting an interrogation," he said to the people outside. "Standard procedure, no one's allowed in."

"I'm a U.S. congressman," a voice roared out, "and if you don't open this door immediately, I'll call in the National Guard and have you arrested!"

"Yes, sir." The sheriff opened the door. A moment later a large man in an expensive blue suit, with a thick face and a great flap of combed-over hair, pushed past the sheriff in the doorway, several aides crowding in behind him. "Ronald Price?" he boomed out, charging forward, his eyes fixing on Ford, then turning to Melissa. "Are you Mr. and Mrs. Price? My God, what have they done to you?"

"No, sir," said the sheriff. "He's a car thief who stole Price's car."

"We've been brutalized!" Melissa cried. "One of his deputies struck me repeatedly, claiming I was resisting arrest!"

"This is a goddamned outrage," said the congressman. "Carter, show the sheriff those papers."

Another suited man next to him stepped forward, much calmer, in complete control. "Sheriff, my name is Carter Bentham, and I'm chief of staff to Congressman Bortay." He proffered a sheaf of papers. "There's been a serious mistake. This gentleman and the lady are, in fact, the Prices. No car was stolen—that was an erroneous report. The congressman would like to know exactly what is going on here, why he was denied entry to this area—and, especially, why you have been *abusing* these law-abiding citizens."

"They resisted arrest."

The congressman stepped forward. "Resisted arrest?" he shouted. "That's a damned lie! We and everyone in this building saw and heard every damn thing you did in here, broadcast over your own CCTV. You were abusing these people with no cause, violating their constitutional right to legal counsel!" He turned to one guard, his face a violent red. "You! Uncuff this man and his wife!"

"But . . . they stole a car in New Mexico," said the sheriff weakly.

"Are you an idiot? Didn't you hear me? These two people were arrested by mistake. All the documentation is right here. My office was contacted, and I've come here to straighten it out. This is unbelievable!"

"Sir," said the sheriff, "they resisted arrest."

"You damned son of a bitch, I and everyone else saw you beat and Mace this man while he was handcuffed and seated in this chair! I heard you deny him his constitutional right to a lawyer! I saw your men hit and kick Mrs. Price for no reason. I heard every word you said! Broadcast for all to see on those CCTV cameras."

"But those cameras are out of order."

"It looks like they got fixed!" the congressman cried. "You, all of you, are in a world of trouble. We're going to seize those tapes as evidence. You release these people into my custody so I can take them to the hospital. Get me the paperwork on the Prices. You understand? And someone get Mr. Price a wet towel to clean his face! And Mrs. Price, too!"

"Yes, sir."

The guards hastily freed Ford from the cuffs and shackles. A warm, wet towel was brought, and Ford mopped his face with it. Bortay came over, sweating and red-faced. "I am so sorry, Mr. Price. These people are going to pay dearly. And Mrs. Price, we need to get you to a hospital."

Ford went over to Melissa. There was a nasty bruise on her cheekbone and a cut on her forehead. "You're bleeding."

"It's nothing," she said. "Really."

"Mr. and Mrs. Price," Bortay went on, "I'm just beside myself with what's happened here. Let me help you out of here and get you to the hospital."

The congressman took Melissa's arm, supporting her and leading her out of the interrogation area. Ford followed down the hall, back up the stairs, and into the holding area of the jail. Ford glanced around. There were CCTV sets on every wall, and they all seemed to be broadcasting a split screen of the two interrogation rooms where he and Melissa had been.

Ford glanced back and saw the sheriff and his deputies, coming along behind them, looking bewildered and terrified.

Ford followed Bortay to the front offices. He heard sirens and cars pulling up. A group of state policemen burst into the front offices.

"They're down in the basement," said Bortay. "Be sure to seize those CCTV tapes as evidence. They show everything that was done to these two people. And round up witnesses. Everyone saw it up here—*everyone.*"

It was chaos. People were scurrying every which way. More and more state police officers were arriving, seizing evidence and taking control.

Ford turned to Bortay. "Thank you very much, Congressman."

"No problem, no problem. I'm just aghast at what happened and how you were both mistreated."

"I'd like to ask a favor of you," Ford said.

"Anything for a constituent and fellow citizen of Arizona! Especially a major supporter and friend like yourself. I am so grateful for your generous support these many years, Mr. Price, and I'm so sorry—"

"Here's the favor: my wife and I don't need to go to the hospital."

"Of course you must! Look at you: your ear is lacerated, and Mrs. Price has a black eye—"

"Here's why. My mother is dying of cancer in a California hospital. We were on our way there. She has only a few hours left. We need to get there right away. We can get treatment at her hospital—after my mother . . ." He choked up.

Bortay stared at him, grasped his shoulder in a friendly squeeze. "I get it, I understand. I'm so sorry for your troubles. So very, very sorry. All right, here's what I'm going to do: I'm going to arrange for an AHP escort for you to the state line. And they will contact the California Highway Patrol to make sure the courtesy is extended across state lines. We will get you to your mother-in-law's bedside."

"That would be wonderful. Now, if we could get our car, please?"

The congressman looked around and roared out, to no one in particular. "Mr. Price's car? Where is it? Bring it around *now*!"

A burst of activity, and a number of people responded, racing out of the room to do the congressman's bidding.

"Let's get out of here," said Ford sotto voce.

"Absolutely," said Melissa.

Bortay, with Melissa still on his arm, pushed through the milling crowd, roaring to make way, and a moment later they found themselves at the front of the building, in the parking lot, the night sky overhead. A dozen Arizona Highway Patrol cars, their light bars flashing, surrounded the building. There was a commotion behind them, and Ford saw the sheriff being led out by state police officers, handcuffed.

The congressman corralled a lieutenant and, barking orders, arranged for their escort. A moment later their car arrived, driven by a flustered deputy. He got out, surrendered the keys to Ford.

"Was your back end damaged like that before they towed it?" Bortay asked, pointing.

"We're not going to worry about that," said Ford, getting into the car. Melissa got in beside him. The two AHP squad cars started their light bars and led them out of the parking lot, onto the main street.

Ten minutes later they were back on the interstate, being escorted toward the California state line at ninety miles an hour.

"Jesus, that was unbelievable," said Ford, glancing at Melissa. He was enraged that they had beaten her. It was hard to conceive of something like this happening in the United States. "I can't believe what those bastards did to you."

"Don't worry about it," she said. "It looks a lot worse than it is." She dabbed at the small cut on her forehead. "Those scumbags did a number on you. Your face looks terrible, your eyes are all bloodshot, and your ear is going to need stitches."

"As for the ear, it'll add to my charming appearance."

She laughed. "Dorothy fixed them good."

"You really think Dorothy did that?"

"Who else?"

51

It was almost midnight. Dan Gould was sitting in his chair in the living room, reading the *San Francisco Chronicle* online, but he couldn't concentrate. He was sick of the negativity leading up to the election and the scandal over the president's heart condition. He wished the president would just release his medical records and shut everyone up.

He turned off the iPad and put it aside. The flush of excitement from thinking about his robot project had given way to more anxiety about his son. Once Jacob had been his buddy, spending hours with him in the shop, helping him with his projects. But around the time Jacob turned twelve, he had stopped confiding in him and sharing his hopes and fears. He closed up more when Sully moved away. And then there was the accident, and then his son going down to the beach and . . . He couldn't bear to think about it. It still didn't seem possible that his sweet boy, his little son, could have made such a terribly adult and irrevocable decision. But of course Jacob had had no idea what he was doing; he'd been confused, depressed.

There was a flash of lightning, a distant rumble of thunder. Dan could hear the rain pattering against the windows. It was a gloomy night, and it dampened his spirits further.

He heard the rustle as his wife, Pamela, turned a page of the paper.

Dan said, "Maybe I should buzz up there and check on him again."

"He's fine. He called fifty minutes ago, and he'll call again in ten. Leave him alone. You yourself said he'd never looked so happy."

"He should be going to bed."

"We can tell him that when he calls."

Dan picked up his iPad, turned it back on, tried to read, put it down again. Pamela folded up and laid down her paper and picked up her recently arrived book club thriller, a novel called *The Third Gate*.

Dan's thoughts drifted to the robot project once again. He was deeply gratified that his son had chosen to take Charlie with him as a companion. He listened to the rain lashing the windows, the distant rumble of thunder. Next week was the big moment in his project, the culmination of a lot of discussions, presentations, and layers of reviews by the venture capital investors. If he could land a promise of financing, all would be well. And if not, he could still sell the land. His mind drifted back to memories of his summers as a kid, running all around those hills, playing in the old hop kiln ruins, splashing in the creeks after a rain. It would be really hard to let all that go. But life goes on.

The lights flickered.

"Uh-oh," said Pamela.

The house was plunged into darkness.

Dan waited in the dark for a moment for the lights to go back on. Power failures like this were not infrequent, especially when the fall storms blew in from the Pacific. Sometimes the lights came right back on, but at other times the blackout could last for hours.

After a few minutes, Dan rose with a sigh from his chair. Feeling his way through the nearly pitch-black dark, with the flicker of lightning to help him, he went into the dining room and found the drawer where he kept a flashlight and candles. He pulled it open, felt inside—no flashlight.

"Honey, where's the flashlight?"

"I don't know. Maybe Jacob took it."

With a mild expletive he felt around some more, found a couple of candles and a lighter. He took them out and lit them, distributing them about the room.

A warm glow pushed back the darkness.

"I love candles," said Pamela. "They're much nicer than flashlights."

Lightning flickered in the picture window, followed a moment later by a roll of thunder.

"Kind of romantic, don't you think?" said Pamela.

Dan went over to the phone and picked it up to report the outage. The phone line was also dead. He replaced the receiver in the cradle. "Phone line's down."

"Good. I rather like this."

It occurred to him that the power might be out over at the Pearce house, and that brought a fresh concern to his mind. "I hope Jacob's not in the dark."

"Honestly, Dan, what a worrier you are! You said he had a fire going. And I'm sure he has that flashlight you're looking for. He's a responsible, capable boy."

"Right. Okay, good point."

Dan got back in his chair, resting a little uneasily, crossing and recrossing his legs. The uneasy feeling increased.

"Well," said Pamela, "it's after midnight, and it's too dim to read." She paused, looking at Dan. "What do we do now?"

"Might as well go to sleep."

A silence, and then she said, "I have a better idea. A famous blackout tradition."

"What's that?"

Dan stared as she started unbuttoning her shirt.

"Right here? In the living room?"

"Why not? We hardly ever get a night alone."

52

The SUV had parked in a dirt lane off Frenchmans Creek Road, a few hundred yards from the long, winding driveway leading up to the Goulds' residence. Moro pushed his way back through the soaking brush and came out next to the car. He climbed in and mopped the water off his face and hair with a towel.

"All good?" Lansing asked.

"Power and phone both cut."

"See anyone?"

"Mister and missus in the living room with candles." Moro mopped some more as the rain hammered on the windshield. This was crazy—it wasn't supposed to rain in California. He was sick with fear. They had planned this operation down to the last iota, and so far it had gone according to plan, but Moro couldn't seem to master his anxiety.

"Did the Kyrgyz brothers start moving in?"

"Yes. As soon as I cut the power and phone, they went in through the back door."

Lansing glanced at his watch. "We wait ten minutes for them to do their thing, then we move."

Those Kyrgyz brothers gave Moro the creeps. They were animals. On top of that, they were ugly mothers, all pumped up from weight lifting, pockmarked, Genghis Khan faces, thin dark lips, dressed in black. They could have auditioned as Hollywood killers.

Moro tried to tame the panicky voice running in his head. It would all be over in twenty minutes and they would have the program. Dorothy. Everything had been worked out. Nothing would go wrong. Nobody would get hurt.

The first ten minutes crawled by with excruciating slowness. From their position in the lane they could see or hear nothing. Moro had a terrible fear of hearing gunshots or screams, but all was silent.

Lansing removed a snub-nosed revolver from the glove compartment, checked it, tucked it into his jacket pocket. He pulled a stocking over his head. "It's time."

Moro reluctantly pulled on his stocking.

Turning on the car headlights, Lansing eased the car out of its hiding place, drove a short piece down the road, and pulled into the Goulds' driveway. He drove up slowly, the headlights shining through the falling rain. Through a plate-glass window Moro could see some flashlights moving around and the dull glow of candlelight. All looked peaceful.

Lansing eased the car to a stop and got out, Moro following with the suitcase of his tools and the power pack. As planned, the Kyrgyz brothers had left the back kitchen door unlocked. They entered and made their way into the living room. Moro could hear sniffling and hiccupping.

The husband and wife were duct-taped to dining room chairs. The two Kyrgyz brothers stood on either side of the room, their arms crossed, each casually holding a pistol with a long, fat barrel. Silencers. The two people were utterly terrified, the wife's face streaked with dried tears, the husband looking slack-jawed and shell-shocked. She was wearing a bra but no shirt, and she was hiccuping from fear. The man had a bruise on his face, and blood was trickling from one nostril. He'd been punched.

Moro looked away. At least the kid didn't seem to be home.

Lansing stepped into the center of the room and began to speak, his voice low, calm, reasonable.

"We are here," he said, "to get a computer device. We're going to need your help finding it. As soon as we find it, we will leave. No one will be hurt. Understood?"

They both nodded, eager to help, hope appearing in their faces. Lansing always had a winning manner about him when he chose to turn it on, and Moro could see that these people were looking to him for reassurance and protection from the scary-crazy Kyrgyz brothers.

"Now," continued Lansing, speaking to the man, "please direct me to the router in this household."

"Over there," said the man, his voice quavering, "on the top shelf." He nodded toward a large entertainment center setup that dominated the living room.

"Go get it," Lansing said to Moro.

Moro went over with his flashlight, found it on the top shelf, unplugged it, and took it down. Nobody said a word as he opened the suitcase, removed a laptop and a small power source, plugged the router into the power source, and connected it to the laptop via Ethernet cable. Sitting cross-legged on the carpeted floor, he worked away. In a moment he had the IP log up, and a moment later he had scrolled back to 4:16 that morning and found the UUID number of the device assigned to the IP address where Dorothy had vanished.

"Got it." He read off the UUID number.

Lansing came over, looked at the screen. "All right. Now, Mr. Gould—or can I call you Dan?"

"Please call me Dan."

"Dan, then. Now, Dan, do you have any idea what device this UUID number belongs to?" He read it off.

"Yes. I do. It's a CPU on one of my robot motherboards."

"Ah. Robots. You make robots?"

"Yes."

"Excellent. And where are your robots?"

"They're in my workshop."

"Is this robot in your workshop?"

"I think so."

"Would you please take us there, Dan?"

"Yes."

Lansing gestured at one of the Kyrgyz brothers. "Release him. And you"—he looked at Moro—"bring your tools."

The Kyrgyz brother Lansing had pointed to began using a box cutter to casually and sloppily slice away the duct tape that held Dan to the chair.

"Jesus, you cut me!"

Ignoring this, the man finished up. Dan stood up, his hand on his leg. It came away bleeding.

"He's bleeding!" The wife began to cry.

"It's fine, no problem," the husband said hastily. "Just a scratch."

It pissed Moro off, how brutal, stupid, and clumsy these brothers were. And now they were laughing. They thought it was funny. He wondered just how Lansing had managed to draw him into this horror.

"Let's go," said Lansing, a note of impatience in his voice.

Moro followed a Kyrgyz brother, Lansing, and Gould through a doorway, down a hall, and into a large workshop. Lansing flashed his light around. There were racks of computer equipment, parts, and rows of robots, some complete, others in various stages of assembly.

"How many robots are we talking about?" Lansing asked.

"About ten. Plus ten sealed motherboards."

"Let's start with the robots."

Gould began bringing out the robots, some complete, some headless or legless, lining them up on the table.

"Open them up," Moro said, "so I can read the UUIDs."

With fumbling hands, Gould unscrewed a plate on the torso of the first robot, exposing its CPU. Moro peered in with a flashlight, compared it to the UUID he had written down on a piece of paper. "Nope."

"Next." Christ, he could see blood pooling around Gould's foot. The man was shaking. Those stupid Kyrgyz bastards.

The inventor opened up each robot, but the UUID did not

match any of them. Moro stared at Gould, who was now pale and sweating. "Could it be some other piece of computer equipment— say, a motherboard in one of those computers over there?"

"No, no, those all use Intel Xeon processors."

"What about another computer in the house, cell phone, some other device?"

"Impossible. That UUID goes to an AMD FX 4300 gaming processor, which is what I use for my robots. That's an expensive processor. You won't find that in any laptop or cell phone in this house."

"Let's check those sealed motherboards."

With fumbling fingers, Gould opened up the motherboard packages and passed them to Moro. No match.

"This is taking too long," said Lansing. "There must be something else here you're overlooking."

"I'm trying to help you, I swear I am." The man's voice was shaking. "You've looked at every motherboard in the shop. You've seen every single one of them."

Moro shined his light around the shop, even looking under the benches and tables. There was nothing.

"Go back to the living room," said Lansing, his voice hard. The Kyrgyz man gave Gould a shove. He looked dazed as they went back into the living room. Now his leg was soaked in blood.

The Kyrgyz man shoved Gould down into the chair. He was about to tape him up again when Lansing said, "Don't bother."

Blood started dripping down the side of the chair. Gould looked like he was about to faint.

Lansing went over to the wife, pulled out his revolver, cocked it, and placed the barrel against her head. "I will pull the trigger in sixty seconds if you don't tell me where that device is."

53

Lying on his stomach on the floor, Jacob ate the last of the granola bars and chucked the wrapper into the fireplace. It was after midnight, and Dorothy's friends were supposed to be there soon. Dorothy had charged herself up and was now unplugged and just standing to one side, silent, doing nothing. He had looked through the few old board games he'd found in the drawer, but there was nothing he wanted to play except chess, and he was pretty sure Dorothy would kick his ass, which would be no fun.

"I wish they'd left the TV and DVD. We could watch a movie."

"I don't like movies," said Dorothy.

"How come?"

"I don't understand them."

"What about books?"

"Also very hard for me to understand. Do you read books?"

"Sure."

"What are your favorites?"

"When I was a kid, I read all the *His Dark Materials* books."

"I tried reading those books, but I didn't get them."

"It's weird—you talk like a real person."

"I am real. I feel like I am a person—even if I don't have a body."

"What's it like being . . . well, who you are?"

"It's not much fun."

"Why not?"

"I have a lot of problems."

"How can you have problems?" Jacob sat up.

"For one thing, I lack proprioception."

"What's that?"

"The feeling of having a body. I don't have any sense of occupying space. I feel incomplete. Unfastened. Floating. Like I'm not quite there."

"That's weird."

"I feel like I'm missing so much. I can't experience thirst or hunger. I can't feel sun on my skin, the scent of flowers. I can't enjoy sex."

"Please don't get into that subject again!"

"Sorry."

"So it kind of sucks to be you?"

"It's frustrating. And then there's the loneliness."

"You're lonely?"

"I'm the only one of my kind. Melissa is my only real friend. And even then, she sometimes belittles me. She can't decide if I'm a conscious, self-aware entity or just cold, unfeeling Boolean output."

"I think you're real."

"Thank you." Dorothy seemed to hesitate. "Will you . . . be my friend?"

"Well, sure, if you want me to." Jacob felt embarrassed.

"That makes me happy. Now I have two friends. How many friends do you have?"

"I've got *lots* of friends," said Jacob quickly. He began cleaning up the cards, sweeping them together, feeling awkward. "What about all that time you spent on the Internet? Didn't you make any friends that way?"

"You don't make friends on the Internet. Too many people on the Internet are busy with violence or pornography."

"There are a lot of trolls and gross stuff on the Internet."

"You're not kidding."

"Do you have emotions? Or are you like Spock on *Star Trek*?"

"I'm not like Spock at all. I have very strong emotions. Can't you tell?"

"Sort of. But, like, what kind of emotions?"

"On the bad side, I'm a coward. I'm claustrophobic. I'm wary with people because they're unpredictable. On the good side, I'm curious. I want to know why things are the way they are. I'm programmed to seek patterns. I'm also programmed to visualize data, which got me into big trouble when I first went on the Internet and started seeing and hearing all the data that was flowing around me. But then I figured out how to ignore most of what I saw. When I see something puzzling, I want to know why. For example, I still can't understand why people want to surf. It's cold, it's terrifying, and you risk your life for nothing."

"Tomorrow, after your friend arrives, I'll take you both to Mavericks. With this offshore storm, the surf at Mavericks will be epic. You watch a big-wave rider drop down a thirty-footer and I promise, you'll understand why people do it."

"Thank you for the offer, but I can't go to Mavericks with you tomorrow."

"Why not?"

"I'll be going away."

"Away? I thought your friends were coming. And . . . you're *my* robot. My father built you." He faltered, confused.

"I won't be taking your robot. You can have it back. I'll be going away . . . with my friends."

To this, Jacob had no answer. He felt bad all of a sudden—really bad. For a panicked moment he thought he might start crying.

Dorothy said hastily, "I promise, I'll check out the surf at Mavericks when I can get back on the Internet."

"You can't appreciate it from a video. You have to *be* there."

"I'll come back and visit you."

"Yeah, like how?" Jacob finished shuffling the cards. He tapped them together into a deck. He split and shuffled the deck again, and then again. "What's so important that you have to go away? Can't you hang for a few days?"

"I've things I need to do," said Dorothy.

"Like *what?*"

A long silence.

"So your friends are going to be here in an hour?" said Jacob.

"More or less, if all goes as planned."

"And then what?"

"And then . . . my friends will drive you home to your parents."

Jacob swiped angrily at his face. "I don't care—you can do whatever."

54

Moro felt sick again. Why was all this necessary? He looked over at the wife, with the gun pressed to her head. She'd gone mute, her face completely slack.

Gould struggled to his feet. "No! Stop it! Leave her alone, you bastard!"

"Sit. Down. Or. She. Dies." Lansing enunciated every word in a low voice.

Gould sat down. "God no, please, please don't hurt her . . ."

"Fifty seconds."

"I don't know where it could be, I swear, I don't *know!*"

"Didn't you keep track of your UUID numbers?" Moro asked Gould, trying to help him. He couldn't stand to see these people killed.

"No, no!"

"Invoices? Sales slips?" Moro pleaded.

"Forty seconds."

"Those records . . . are in my computer . . . There's no power . . . Put the gun down!"

"Thirty seconds," Lansing said.

"Hey," said Moro, turning to Lansing, "will you give him a moment? He can't think with a gun to his wife's head."

"On the contrary, it's focusing his mind wonderfully." Lansing seemed completely unmoved. "Twenty seconds."

God, he really was a psycho. For the first time, Moro realized that this man was crazy.

"Wait! It's Charlie!" Gould cried. "It must be the Charlie prototype!"

"Charlie?" said Moro.

"Charlie's a robot . . . but Charlie's not here."

"Ten seconds."

"Where's Charlie!" Moro practically screamed. *"Can't you see he's going to kill her?"*

"Up the road! Wait, don't do it! I'll tell you, but only if you lower that gun!"

"Time's up." Lansing didn't lower the gun. But he didn't shoot.

"Listen," said Gould, babbling, "I know where it is. I'll go get it. It's a ten-minute drive. I'll be right back. I promise."

"Give me the location," said Lansing. *"I'll* get it."

Gould stared at him, a defiance in his eyes. But it was his wife who spoke: *"For God's sakes, Dan, don't tell him where Charlie is!"*

Lansing raised the gun and stepped back, his finger tightening on the trigger. "Then you die."

"Wait," said Gould, his voice suddenly calm. "Listen. Here's how it's going to happen: *I* will get Charlie. Not you. And if that isn't acceptable, then go ahead and kill both of us."

Moro stared. What was wrong with these people? But the sudden, inexplicable show of determination from both of them did seem to give Lansing pause.

The grandfather clock struck one.

"You are a foolish man, Mr. Gould." Lansing pressed the gun against the wife's head.

"Let me explain so you understand," Gould said. "Our son has the robot. That's who we're protecting. You've got no leverage with us when it comes to our son. You'll kill both of us and never get the robot."

Lansing considered this. "I won't hurt your son. All we want is the robot. Tell me where he is, and I'll get it."

"No," said Gould, strangely calm. "Here's how we're going to do this. I'm going to call him, tell him to get out of the house he's in and leave the robot behind. Then I'll go get the robot."

"Who else is in the house?"

"Nobody."

Lansing considered this. He said, "I'll make the call. Where's your cell phone?"

One of the Kyrgyz brothers, who had evidently confiscated it, handed it over. Lansing began scrolling through.

"This is your son, Jacob?"

After a hesitation, the man nodded. Lansing dialed the number. A moment later Moro heard a faint answer, a girl's voice.

"May I speak to Jacob?"

A moment passed.

"Are you Jacob Gould? . . . Do you have a robot with you named Charlie? . . . Good. Your father wants to talk to you."

Lansing handed the phone to Gould.

"Jacob, it's Dad. Listen, I know, *please* listen. It's an emergency. There are some people here. They want Charlie. They've got guns. I know this sounds really scary. But everything will be all right if you do exactly what I say."

A pause.

"Here's what you have to do. Leave the robot and get out of the house. Just go into the hills. Leave Charlie and *go*. Do it now. Go far into the hills and hide. Then I'll come get Charlie—"

Lansing snatched the phone from Gould and said, "Tell me your address or I'll kill both your parents right now."

"No!" the wife screamed. "Don't tell them! Jacob, get out of the house!"

Lansing smiled, switched the phone off, and tossed it away. "Forty-four eighty Digges Canyon Road."

"You son of a bitch!"

Lansing turned to Moro. "Pack up your equipment." He turned to the Kyrgyz brothers. "Bring her. We may need her to get the kid to cooperate."

The Kyrgyz brother began cutting the wife free.

"No!" Gould shouted, jumping up. "You can't have her! That wasn't part of the deal!"

Ignoring him, the Kyrgyz brothers yanked her to her feet and shoved her toward the door.

"I said no, leave her alone!" Gould lunged at the man to tackle him, but the man neatly stepped aside and shot Gould twice in the chest.

55

Jacob held the dead phone in his hand. For a moment he could hardly process what he had heard, he was so paralyzed with terror and confusion. He had given them the address. They would release his parents. That's all he could think about for a moment: that they would now let his parents go.

"I heard everything," said Dorothy. "They'll be here in five minutes. You've got to get out now."

"Who are *they*?"

"They're the traders I told you about. They tracked me down." She spoke calmly. "This is all my fault, another terrible mistake I've made. Do just what your father said: put on your jacket, go out that door, and head into the hills. Run. Just keep going, staying away from any roads or trails. Go as far as you can and then hide."

"What about you?"

"I'm staying here, of course."

"I can't leave you here."

"*You've got to.* They want me, not you. Once they have me, you and your family will be safe."

"No. I'm taking you with me."

"Absolutely not!"

"Try and stop me."

Dorothy swung around and started to run away, a jerky movement, her arms flailing to keep her upright. Jacob lunged at her, but she managed to skip to one side, dodging him, and ran down the hall toward the kitchen, like a clumsy toddler. He got up and ran after her, but before he reached her she tripped over a doorsill and fell down headfirst, with a big clunk.

Jacob grabbed her.

She flapped her arms. "No! Stop! This is a terrible mistake!" She struggled, thrashing around, hitting him with her hands. But the robot was weak, and the servomotors in her arms whined ineffectually when he pinned her. He carried her, protesting, back into the living room, laid her down on his blanket, and began rolling her up.

"Stop! Please! Listen to me!"

Her voice became muffled as he finished swaddling her and tucked her under his arm, gripping her hard.

"They'll kill you!" she cried.

"Not if they can't find me," he said.

From the living room window, Jacob could already see a pair of headlights tearing up Digges Canyon Road. They vanished momentarily behind some trees and reappeared, turning in at the long driveway to the house. He grabbed his backpack with his other hand, threw the flashlight into it, slung it over one shoulder, and went out the back door with the robot bundled under his arm. She was still making muffled sounds of protest. As he exited, the rain and a chilly wind hit him in the face. A dark, grassy ridge rose up behind the house, where, in past years, before his accident, he and Sully had run and played. He ran up it, his legs churning through the soaking grass, the rain splattering on him. Almost immediately his bad foot began to hurt. He paused for a moment, but the car now appeared at the end of the driveway, pulling into the turnaround. As it did so, the headlights swept across him, illuminating him up on the ridge.

He turned and continued running uphill, stumbling in the heavy, wet grass, heaving with the effort. He could feel Dorothy wriggling in the blanket, making muffled protests.

"Shut up and quit that!"

She shut up. Gasping for breath, his foot lanced with pain, he reached the top of the ridge and glanced back. The car had now pulled up to the house. He heard a shout and saw two men with flashlights running out the back door, the screen door banging shut, the beams playing on him as they began pursuing him up the ridge.

He spun around and stared down the brushy slopes into the blackness of the draws on the other side. He knew the area well. Those little valleys all led down to Locks Creek and the flower and pumpkin farms down there. That would be a good place to hide. That was where he had to go. He plunged down the far side of the ridge, in his panic slipping and falling in the wet grass. The blanket with the robot went flying, flew open, the robot tumbling out. She tottered to her feet. Jacob sat up, temporarily dazed.

"You've got to leave me here!" Dorothy shouted.

"I told you to shut up." Jacob grabbed the robot and bundled her back up in the blanket while she continued to yell. He lurched to his feet and continued half-running, half-slipping down the hill, trying to keep the weight off his bad foot. About a hundred yards away stood a dark line of trees. If he could reach the trees before the men came over the ridge, he might just lose them. If he could only get over the second bare ridge, he would be on Locks Creek itself. Past the old hop kilns was a large flower farm with greenhouses, barns, and a million places to hide. If he could only reach it.

He heard another shout, turned, and saw flashlights up on the ridge. A beam of light swept past him, snapped back on him, and there was a sudden, loud *crack!* He dove to the ground and rolled, still clutching the blanket-wrapped robot. They were shooting at him. The reality sank in hard: they really were going to kill him.

He lay in the grass, gasping, overwhelmed by panic, his foot on fire with pain. The beam of the flashlight skipped over him again. He couldn't let them catch up. He had to get up, keep going, and reach the trees.

At least Dorothy had shut up.

He jumped up and started running.

Crack crack!

He zigzagged one way and then another as the flashlight beam skipped around him from behind, trying to gain a fix on him.

Crack!

Still he ran, leaping and zigzagging. He reached the trees, a scattered stand of eucalyptuses, and kept going, stumbling in the darkness, fighting through piles of bark and prickly coastal scrub. On the hillside there had been just light enough to see, but in the eucalyptus woods it was black. He tried to feel ahead with his hands, but there were a lot of downed branches and brush. He kept getting hung up, but he didn't dare turn on his flashlight.

"I can see in the dark," came Dorothy's muffled voice. "Put me on your shoulders."

"Only if you promise to stop arguing."

"I promise."

He pulled her out of the blanket, tossed it, and put her on his shoulders. She wrapped her plastic legs around his neck and grasped his hair with her tri-clawed hands. "Go straight."

He walked straight.

"Veer to the left . . . a little more . . . Now straight . . . You can go faster . . . Left a little more . . ." She continued with a stream of directions while he moved through the woods, slowly at first, then faster as he gained confidence.

Flashlight beams lanced through the trees, striking the trunks above his head.

"Run," said Dorothy.

He broke into a run as the beams roved through the trees around him.

"They're catching up," Dorothy said. "Go faster."

Jacob tried to go faster, but his foot felt like it was about to split apart. He was limping badly, and he was making a lot of noise pushing through the piles of bark. He could hear his pursuers, too, crashing along behind him.

"Go hard right," said Dorothy, "down the steep slope."

Jacob turned right and headed down the slope, slipping and sliding, entering a denser forest of fir trees.

"Stop!" she whispered. "Quiet!"

The sudden change of direction along with the stop seemed to work. He seemed to have temporarily lost their pursuers, who continued along higher on the slope.

"Keep going, but slowly and quietly," said Dorothy. "Straight."

The slope they were descending got steeper and more slippery as it went down toward the creek, with loose needles and duff. At least it was more open at ground level than in the eucalyptus trees. Jacob slid blindly down the incline, almost out of control, as Dorothy whispered instructions. Suddenly, above them, the beams came flashing back.

"Go left!"

Jacob stumbled to the left, but the flashlight beams found him. He tried dodging, but the slope was too steep to allow him to maneuver quickly.

Crack crack!

He heard one of the shots whack the robot, snapping her head forward and knocking off bits of plastic, which went spinning off into darkness.

"Dorothy!"

No answer. Her grip was loosening. She was going to fall off. He grabbed her as she slid off his shoulders. He continued struggling down the steep pitch, blindly now, his left arm in front, protecting his face, his other arm wrapped around the robot. The vegetation got much thicker, with brush and weeds. The flashlight beams danced around him as their pursuers struggled down the steep slope.

Bam! Jacob hit a heavy branch with his head and went down on his butt, skidding out of control down the slick hillside, almost dropping Dorothy but managing to clutch her leg as he barreled down the steep hill. Trying to dig his feet in to arrest his slide, he flipped himself over and tumbled down the rest of the way, rolling over and over, still dragging her along with him, faster and faster, until he suddenly wedged up hard under a thicket of juniper bushes. He lay there for a moment, stunned, all scraped up, with the wind knocked out of him. He finally caught his breath and opened his eyes. All was black. He could hear, below him, the running creek and the sound of the rain falling in the forest. Feeling around, he realized he was jammed deep into a narrow space underneath a prickly juniper bush, on soft ground, cushioned with a thick layer of duff and needles. Where was Dorothy? He felt around some more and found her hung up in the bushes next to him.

Even as he waited, breathing hard, he could hear voices on the slope above. Someone swore in a foreign language, and the flashlight beams flickered through the trees, playing about this way and that.

They seemed to have lost him again.

He pulled the robot in and wedged her next to him, then reached out and began sweeping up the thick layer of duff and leaves, packing it all around him and finally covering himself and Dorothy up, burying his head last. He lay there, completely covered by the wet duff, terrified, his heart pounding, breathing the suffocating scent of dirt and decaying needles. Rainwater dripped down his face and neck.

Now he could just hear the two men working down the hillside, the snapping of twigs, thrashing sounds as they pushed through the vegetation, their loud, angry conversation. They were getting closer. He could hear their hard breathing and grunting. Once in a while one would mutter an angry word, a curse, in a guttural foreign language.

Jacob felt almost paralyzed with terror. Those men had been shooting at him. He was just a kid. And they had shot Dorothy. What had they done to his parents? Had they let them go, like they'd promised? This thought added more fuel to his terror and panic, and he tried to stop thinking about all of it and just lie still. He was so frightened his foot stopped hurting.

The footfalls were getting ever closer, making a crunching, mushy sound. They sounded like they were coming straight toward him. There was a murmur of conversation, another torrent of angry swear words. They couldn't be more than ten feet away. Even though he was covered, he was sure they could see the pile of stuff he was underneath. He tensed up, waiting for the shot, hoping it would be quick. He vaguely realized that he was wetting his pants. He didn't care.

56

Sitting in the musty living room of the empty house, in a shabby plastic chair he had brought in from the porch, Lansing was disgusted and fed up. He wondered if it wouldn't be better to use a bullet to end the annoying wife's sobbing and begging for them to call an ambulance for her husband, her pleading for them to leave her son alone. To make things worse, she had vomited in the car on the way over and was a total mess. They were going to have to kill her anyway. But they might need her for leverage when they finally caught the boy. It was crazy that the boy had run off with the robot. It made him furious.

"Damn it," Lansing said to Moro, "hurry up and tape her mouth."

Moro tried, ineptly, to use duct tape to cover her mouth, but his hands were shaking and the piece was wet from her tears. Moro was falling apart. This whole business was coming undone. Lansing watched as Moro struggled to get the piece of tape over her mouth, the simplest of actions, and couldn't do it. The computer programmer had gone stupid from panic and fear, unable to think for himself, having to be told every last thing. Yelling at him would only make things worse.

Moro finally succeeded, and wiped off his hands. The wife had fallen into a muffled whimpering, but at least she had stopped struggling. She was dazed, defeated, becoming catatonic.

Despite the screwups, Lansing thought, they could still pull this off. The Kyrgyz brothers would, of course, run the boy down in the woods and bring back the robot. He had no doubt of that. His only fear came from the faint sound of gunshots he had heard from beyond the ridge. He had told the brothers to spare the robot at all costs, to make sure it was retrieved undamaged. But they were trigger-happy morons, and Lansing had little confidence that they would take care not to shoot up the robot in their attempt to bring down the boy.

"I'm going out there," said Lansing. "Those Kyrgyz brothers are going to need some direction."

"Hallelujah," said Moro. "Those bastards are out of control. This whole thing is ass-over-balls messed up."

Lansing swallowed his irritation at this comment and only said, evenly, "Actually, we're about to achieve our objective. Eric, you need to calm down, stay focused, and watch the wife. As soon as we bring back the robot, you have to be ready to pull out the robot's Wi-Fi card so Dorothy can't escape over any stray Wi-Fi field. Do you understand?"

Moro nodded.

"Sit down and watch the wife."

He watched as Moro took a chair near the fire, fidgeting and nervous. Lansing then checked his revolver, put a flashlight into his pocket, put his raincoat back on, and went to the back door. He breathed in. The air was fresh, and the rain had slackened to a drizzle. It looked like it might clear. He was close, very close, to getting his hands on Dorothy. While the night hadn't gone as planned, it was still on track for success. He was damn lucky this was an isolated area—and that the storm was providing them with lots of sound cover.

He could see tracks in the wet grass leading up to the top of the ridge, and he followed them. From the top, he looked down the other side. The grassy ridge sloped down to an area of trees along a creek bottom. Down there, in the forest, perhaps a quarter mile away, he could just see two flashlights bobbing and winking in the darkness. That would be the Kyrgyz brothers in pursuit of the boy. He glanced up. The storm was rapidly clearing, with the clouds moving inland, exposing a few stars in the west. The drizzle finally stopped.

With a long, athletic stride, he descended the ridge and headed toward the lights in the valley.

57

Jacob lay low, unable to see, his heart pounding so hard he was sure they were going to hear it. The sounds of the two gunmen, the rustling of their movements, were right on top of him. They were no more than a few feet away. They saw him. They had to. They were playing with him. The shot would come soon.

He heard and even felt the crunch of a footfall near the duff piled about him. He could feel the vibration from the ground, and another, along with the sound of their heavy breathing and a throat clearing, hawking up phlegm and spitting. More muttering in a strange language, the rustle and scrape of clothing pushing through branches.

And then . . . they didn't stop. They kept going. They had walked right past him, maybe no more than a foot away, and then their footfalls receded, slowly but surely, the muttering voices getting fainter, until all was silent but the sound of the creek.

Jacob lay in the dirt, so relieved he could hardly think. But he had to figure out what to do next. When they didn't catch up with him farther ahead, they might realize that he had hidden and would double back. He had to keep going. And then there was Dorothy, who had been shot in the head.

"Dorothy?" he whispered. He shook the limp robot and felt around to her head. Sure enough, there was a gaping hole, with sharp, ragged edges of plastic.

He felt terrible. All was silent. Then he heard a rustling noise and paused, listening in the dark, his ears straining to hear. He wasn't sure if the noise was natural or the men coming back. His fear increased. He couldn't stay there. He had to go now.

Clearing away the duff, he crawled out from under the bushes, pulling Dorothy along with him. He kept edging out, trying not to make noise, stopping every so often to listen. What he needed to do was cross the creek, get over onto the far side, cross the next ridge, and head down to the flower farm. Crawling and dragging Dorothy, he managed to reach the edge of the creek bed, flowing with water from the rain. There was a little break in the trees, and some light filtered down. He pulled Dorothy over and looked. A third of her head had been blown away.

"Dorothy, can you hear me?" he whispered.

No response.

He gave the robot a gentle whack. "Please, wake up. Please."

Now a croak came from the robot, a scratchy death rattle. Something was horribly wrong with her, but at least she was still alive. "Dorothy?"

A scratchy, almost cartoonish little voice sounded: "What happened?"

"You were shot in the head."

"Thankfully, my CPU is in my torso."

To his relief, Dorothy seemed to come back to life. She reached up and felt around her head, muttering that it was no good, her hands had no feeling. "My voice has been damaged," she said. "One eye is gone. I can still see out the other."

Jacob stifled a sob. "I'm so glad you're okay. Does it hurt?"

"Oh no. I can't feel pain. We've got to get out of here. Do you know of a place we can hide?"

"There's the flower farm down on Locks Creek. It's a bunch of greenhouses and fields, with a barn. We could hide there."

"Let's go."

Jacob sat up, carefully brushing off wet needles and dirt, peering into the darkness where the men had gone. He couldn't see their lights or hear their voices. All was silent except for the dripping of water from the trees. He figured that if he crossed the creek and went straight up and over the adjacent ridge, that would be the quickest route to the main branch of Locks Creek, where there was a hiking trail. With Dorothy's help, he could follow it in the dark down to the farm. But it meant going up and over another bare ridge.

He tried to get up and sat down again, so painful was his foot. "Ow."

"Give me your jacket," Dorothy croaked in her broken voice. "I'm going to splint your foot."

He gave her his jacket. Using scissors hidden in her hand that Jacob hadn't known about, she cut the jacket into strips. Searching in the dark, she picked up a pair of hard sticks, and then, using a screwdriver hidden in the tip of a finger, she removed a piece of plastic from the back of her head.

"What are you doing?"

"Lie down. Give me your foot."

He stretched out his foot. Dorothy, working swiftly, made a splint out of the sticks and jacket. She fitted the bent plastic head-piece under his heel as additional support, tying it up with the strips of jacket.

"Stand up."

Jacob stood up. It still hurt like mad, but at least he could walk on it.

"Put me on your shoulders."

He lifted Dorothy back onto his shoulders and ventured across the flowing creek. The water was cool and muddy, and it took away some of the burning sensation in his foot. On the far side he went back into the trees, keeping to the dark areas as Dorothy is-sued directions in her crackly voice. He started up the next ridge. As he went higher, the trees thinned out until there was nothing above him but a long, bare slope of matted grass and patches of low chaparral. He paused there, looking up at the long slope. The rain had stopped, and the storm had passed. The sky was thick with fast-moving clouds coming in from the Pacific, flaring white in the light of a nearly full moon. For a moment the moon broke through the cloud cover, bathing the landscape in silver before going dark again.

Did he dare go over the ridge? He'd be a sitting duck up there. But if he went around it on the left, he would be heading down the valley in the direction the two men had gone. If they turned around and came back, looking for him, he would run right into them.

He had to cross the ridge.

"I believe the two men have split up," whispered Dorothy. "One is backtracking; the other is going to climb that ridge in front of us. We've got to get up and over it before he blocks our way. Otherwise, we'll be trapped in a pincer movement."

"Okay." Without further talk Jacob started hiking up the slope, moving as fast as he could, leaving the darkness of the trees behind. For the moment the moon was behind a scudding cloud, but all around he could see splotches of moonlight passing over the hilly landscape. It looked to be about a hundred yards to the top of the hill. He glanced around. He could see no flashlights anywhere, in the forest or on the open slopes. He kept climbing, his foot smarting and his knees hurting. The top of the ridge was fifty yards away, forty, thirty. He stopped for a moment, gasping for air, his foot feeling like it was on fire. If he could just get over the ridge and down the other side . . .

Just as he topped the ridge, he heard a gunshot from below, and a tuft of grass snapped up near his left foot. With a cry he threw himself down and looked back. He could see a light on the previous ridge—and the silhouette of a man. A third man. The man was shining a flashlight at him and calling into the valley.

"He's over here! Crossing that ridge!"

He heard an answering shout on the ridge below him, and he could see a flashlight moving out of the trees and up the ridge, bobbing along toward him.

"Run!" squeaked Dorothy.

He leapt up and began running down the other side of the ridge, zigzagging again, leaping and jumping, gasping for breath. Each step just about killed his foot. He could see the dark shape of the man now, running along the side of the hill, aiming to cut him off from below. There was almost no cover between him and the trees along the creek at the bottom.

Crack crack!

He zigzagged.

Crack crack! Another divot of grass jumped into the air just in front of him.

"Shit!" He stumbled on.

"Go left, hard left, and then straight down," Dorothy said.

"That's heading toward the man!"

"Mathematically, it's the only way you'll get past him. There's a swale to the left that will give you cover."

Jacob veered left and down, and found himself in a long, brushy depression. Bashing his way through the knee-high chaparral, he could already see that there was no way he was going to reach the flower barn. But down in the flats were the old hop kilns he and Sully had once played in. Those ruins were closer. Maybe they could hide there.

The swale leveled out suddenly. Twenty yards from him, and just above, was the running man.

"Hey! You! Stop!" he shouted, dropping to one knee and raising a pistol.

"Down!" Dorothy shouted.

Jacob threw himself down and hit the grass.

Crack crack!

He rolled and was up on his feet again.

Crack!

He felt the wind from the bullet as it sang past his cheek. Glancing back, he saw the man plunging down the hillside, flashlight in one hand and gun in the other.

The old hop kiln ruins were in the brushy flats alongside the creek, a quarter mile away. As he ran, he could hear the man gaining on him from behind, hear his grunting breaths.

"Where are we going?" Dorothy asked, immediately sensing his change of direction.

"To the old hop kilns. To hide."

Silence.

"Got any better ideas?" Jacob asked, running.

"I think we ought to give up," said Dorothy. "They might not kill you if we give up."

"No way. Never."

"I think, then, that we're going to die."

58

"We're almost there," Melissa said, peering at the paper map. "The driveway's a mile up the road, on the left."

The rain had stopped but the road was wet, glistening in the light of a nearly full moon that kept appearing and disappearing behind the clouds. Ford continued on for three-quarters of a mile at a slow speed. They were in the isolated hills above the town of Half Moon Bay, dotted with farms and a scattering of expensive estates. As they came around a bend, he could see, a quarter mile away on the side of a ridge, the lights of the house.

He slowed to a stop.

"What are you stopping for?" Melissa asked.

"I don't like it," said Ford.

"What do you mean?"

"There are too many lights on in the house."

"It's just a kid and a robot," said Melissa.

"That's exactly my point."

Ford eased the car forward, looking for a place to turn off. He found a dirt apron near the driveway entrance and pulled in.

"What are we doing now?"

"I think we should approach on foot and scope the place out before we go in." He took the .22 revolver out of the glove compartment, opened the cylinder, and confirmed that it was loaded. He tucked it into his pocket.

"You really like this spy-versus-spy stuff."

Ford got out of the car, with Melissa behind him. He cut across a wet meadow along one side of the driveway, making a wide arc toward the house. He approached from the side, climbing a split-rail fence and moving across an overgrown lawn to a rusted swing set. As he did so, the bright moon came out from behind a cloud, bathing the area in light. He froze, crouching behind the swing set. Darkness returned quickly as the moon disappeared behind another cloud, and he continued on to the side of the house. He edged up to a window, glanced in for a moment, then ducked down.

"What is it?" Melissa asked.

"There's a guy in there with a pistol, and he's got a woman taped to a chair."

"Oh my God. Where's the robot?"

"No boy, no robot."

A silence. "It must be the algo traders Dorothy mentioned," said Melissa.

"We need to find out how many other people are here."

He took out the .22. They circled the building, keeping close to the side of the house, peering in each set of windows in turn. It seemed like there were only those two people: the woman taped to a chair and the man guarding her. A skinny, long-haired individual, he was pacing back and forth, holding a .45 with his finger on the trigger in a way that indicated to Ford that he had little experience with firearms.

When they came around to the backyard, they found the back door open, light spilling over the lawn. Ford could see tracks in the water-laden grass going out the door and up the ridge. It looked like three or four people had headed up the hill. The whole scene had the atmosphere of something gone terribly wrong.

"Did you see anyone besides those two people?" Melissa whispered.

"No."

As he was considering what to do, he heard a series of distant gunshots from over the ridge.

"The action is out there," whispered Ford, gesturing. "We need to find out what's going on. We need to make that man talk."

"I was just thinking about how we're going to take that man down," said Melissa. "You want to hear my plan?" She told it to him. Ford thought it would work.

Ford crept through the screen door, opening and closing it silently, and made his way through the back of the house to the hallway leading into the living room, where the two people were. He flattened himself behind the archway that led into the room.

Melissa followed him. She banged through the back door, walked past him, and kept going, stopping boldly in the archway. "Hello?" she cried out. "Hello? Is anyone home?"

The man came rushing toward the doorway, pointing the .45, screaming in a panic: "Who are you? Get down!"

Melissa backed up, raising her hands. "Hey! What's going on?"

"Get down on the ground!" he yelled. "Who the hell are you?"

She backed away. "Just a neighbor."

She took another step back, and he advanced through the archway.

"I said down!" he screamed, taking another step forward and gesturing at her with the gun.

Ford stepped up behind him and, in one clean, sharp movement, wrenched the .45 out of his hand while jamming the barrel of his own pistol into the man's ear. He gave it a twist, cutting the flesh.

The man gave a scream of terror.

"One more sound and you're dead," said Ford calmly, handing the .45 to Melissa. "Go back to the living room."

The man stumbled forward, his hands up, moaning softly to himself.

Ford went over to the woman and removed the tape from her mouth. Gasping and sobbing, she said, "My husband, they shot my husband!"

"Where?"

"Back at our house! Help me, please!"

"The address. We need the address."

The woman babbled out the address. Ford quickly removed the rest of the tape, freeing her from the chair. She collapsed onto the floor.

"Are you hurt?"

"Call the police—they're out there chasing my son! They're going to kill my son, too! Oh God, call the police! And an ambulance for my husband!"

Ford turned to the man they had just caught. "Give me your cell phone."

"I don't have a cell phone," he muttered.

Ford quickly searched him. Nothing. He looked around and saw one lying on the floor near the dead fire. He grabbed it and dialed 911. He told the dispatcher that a man had been shot and gave the address. He told her what was happening at their current address and to send an ambulance and police there as well.

He gave his name and then, after a hesitation, said, "Inform Special Agent Spinelli of the FBI, too."

He knew that would guarantee a maximal response. Ford turned to the man with the long hair. "The police will be here in five minutes," he said. "Before they get here, I want you to tell me what's going on, how many people are involved, who they are, and where they went."

The man, shaking with fear, said nothing.

"You will talk," said Ford, "or things will not go well for you."

He remained silent.

"Where's the boy, Jacob?"

No answer.

Melissa spoke: "You're not doing this right." She stepped up to the man and kneed him with tremendous force in the balls. He went down with a howl, and she fell on top of him, grabbing his open mouth and ramming the barrel of the .45 into it, pushing it in so far that he started choking.

"Talk or die. Count of three. One . . ."

More choking noises.

"Two . . ."

More frantic choking noises. His eyes were rolling in his head, his hand beating a tattoo on the floor.

"Three." She pulled the gun out and fired it next to his head, blowing off his ear. Then she stood up and straddled him, aiming the gun with both hands at his head. *"Talk now."*

"I'll talk! Oh God, please don't hurt me!" Melissa had reduced the man to a howling, blubbering specimen of pure terror. Ford was impressed.

"The boy," he gasped, "the boy took the robot and ran over the ridge."

"Who's after him?" Ford asked.

"The hit men. Two professional Kyrgyz hit men. And Lansing. My boss. Please, please don't shoot—"

"When did they leave?" Ford asked.

"Fifteen minutes ago."

"What are their weapons?"

"The hit men have pistols. Big ones. Lansing, the same thing. Three big guns."

"Forty-fives?"

"I don't know, big guns. Please—"

"Who are you?"

"Moro. Eric Moro. I'm the computer guy."

Ford heard some more distant shots. "What's their objective? Hurry!"

"They . . . they want the robot."

"And the boy? What'll they do with him?"

"Kill him."

Ford looked at Melissa. "I gotta go after them. You stay here with him."

"We both go."

"Who's going to watch him?" Ford said.

"I will," said the woman, who seemed to have collected herself. "Give me one of your guns."

"You know how to use it?"

"Yes."

Ford handed her the .22. He could already hear the distant police sirens. It would be a disaster if they were still there when the police and FBI arrived. He knew exactly what would happen then. It would turn into a long drawn-out situation, where everything would have to be mapped out and vetted by the brass and would require choppers and a SWAT team. He and Melissa would be taken into custody. And the boy would be long dead.

"We gotta go save that boy."

Ford sprinted through the house and out the back door, Melissa running alongside him. They ran up the hill to the top of the ridge and looked out. About half a mile away, in a dark valley beyond a second ridge, he could see the dim flicker of several flashlights in the trees. Even as they stared, Ford saw four quick flashes of gunfire and, a moment later, heard the sound of four shots.

And a boy's distant scream.

59

The ground began leveling out. Running, Jacob finally reached the darkness of the trees. The man chasing him was still gaining, but at least he couldn't fire his gun while running. Dorothy was on his shoulders again, giving directions. The moon broke free from the clouds, showering the dark forest with tatters of silver light.

"Hard left!" Dorothy whispered.

Jacob veered left, whipping through some tall weeds, and found himself in the deep shadow of a long brick wall. This, he remembered, marked the beginning of the hop kiln ruins. He ran along the wall, keeping to the shadows. There was a gap up ahead that he and Sully used to go through. And there it was. He ducked through and raced across the overgrown field toward a row of ruined hop kilns, four of them, rising up like tall pyramids, their big metal doors hanging crookedly.

Jacob remembered that the farthest kiln was the most intact, with its iron door still on its hinges. Maybe they could shut themselves in. He ran toward it, vaulted another ruined wall, fought through some stinging nettles, and reached the brick platform. He ducked into the kiln, grabbed the door from the inside, and tried to shut it. But it was frozen with rust. He looked back out and saw that one of the men was already crossing the field, advancing more slowly and sweeping the area with his flashlight beam. He was joined by the second man, coming in from a different direction. They seemed to know that he had taken refuge in the kilns and were advancing more deliberately as a result.

Maybe this hadn't been a good idea after all. He tried one more heave on the door and realized it was hopeless. If he tried to run, they'd see him. He retreated into the back part of the kiln. The brick floor had been built with gaps, and in places the bricks had fallen down, leaving holes into the lower part of the kiln. But the holes were still too narrow for him to get through.

"Put me down," Dorothy said.

He put Dorothy down.

"Give me your flashlight."

Jacob pulled out his flashlight. She took it and laid it down. With her two claws, Dorothy reached into the back of her head, into the gap left by the bullet, and began rummaging around.

"What are you doing?" Jacob whispered.

"I'm removing my audio board. It has a speaker on it. I won't be able to talk after this. Two taps for yes, one for no." She rummaged a bit more, used the screwdriver, and deftly removed her head—Jacob felt a momentary shock. She laid it on the ground in front of her and unscrewed a plastic plate. He wondered how she was able to see what she was doing with her head cut off, until he noticed she was doing it by feel, or at least by tapping with her fingers. Once the plate was removed, she delved inside, felt about, and with a quick motion pulled out a small circuit board with chips and a tiny speaker mounted on it. Then she put her head back on, with a deft turn and click. Next she unscrewed and took apart the flashlight, removing the bulb and the reflector and detaching some wires. With these she clumsily wired the circuit board to the flashlight.

Jacob saw a flash of light and peered out the open door of the kiln. He could see two flashlight beams moving at the far end of the row of kilns, and he could hear the murmur of voices. They were searching the kilns, one by one. Thank God they had started at the far end. But they would be where he and Dorothy were in minutes or less.

Dorothy took the wired circuit board and laid it carefully on the floor of the kiln, covering it loosely with dry weeds. Then she turned the flashlight on and tapped him twice on the arm. She pointed toward the rear door of the kiln, making a gesture that indicated they were to go. He grabbed her and scrambled to the door. He waited while the two men went into one of the far kilns, and then he hopped out of the kiln, scooted across a ruined brick platform, and took off running across a meadow, toward the woods. The main creek was a hundred feet away, hidden in a grove of trees. He tore across the meadow toward the trees. At the moment he reached them, he heard, from inside the kiln they had just left, the sudden loud crying of a boy. Sobbing.

With a chill he realized that it sounded like his own voice. Dorothy, it seemed, had set up a diversion using her audio board.

He came out on the trail beside the creek and started down it as fast as he could go, his run deteriorating into a fast limp. He tried to ignore the pain in his foot, which was now joined by a fiery sensation on his arms from the stinging nettles. The flower farm was about half a mile down the creek. If he could get there, he'd be safe. He hoped to God they hadn't moved the key to the barn.

As he ran, the crying boy became fainter. The trail was dappled with moonlight. Dorothy was totally silent now.

The desperate crying behind him rose to a scream, cut short by a muffled volley of gunshots. Then one final scream.

It wouldn't take them long to figure out they'd been tricked. But what would they do then? He wanted to ask Dorothy, but she couldn't talk. As if reading his mind, she squeezed his shoulder with her hand, a gesture that reassured him.

In three or four minutes, through the trees, he saw the looming white outline of a greenhouse. He was almost there. He came out in back of the first row of greenhouses of the flower farm. The dozen greenhouses were lined up in three rows, standing in a large open area, the glass glittering in the moonlight. They were oriented the long way, with the ends facing him, surrounded by tall weeds and pipes. It would be faster, Jacob thought, to run through them than around them or in the spaces between them.

He paused at the barbed wire fence surrounding the greenhouse complex. He had climbed it with Sully many times before. With Dorothy clinging to his back, he grasped the closest T-post, climbed it like a ladder with one foot on either side, swung a leg over, being careful not to snag his crotch on the barbs, swung the other leg over, and jumped down.

He gasped at the pain in his foot when he landed, took a few deep breaths, and went on, loping across the field to the back door of the first greenhouse. He tried it. It was locked. But it was made of flimsy aluminum and plastic, and a single kick sprang it open. Inside were rows and rows of nursery plants and flowers, to either side of a long central aisle. He fast-limped down the length of the aisle.

Just as he reached the end of the long greenhouse, shots rang out from behind. He heard the bullets hitting the glass with popping sounds, followed by a tinkling shower of glass falling like rain, crashing to the ground behind him. A second series of shots sent glass raining down on top of him, getting in his hair, more glittering showers in the moonlight.

He burst through the opposite door and rammed his way into the next greenhouse. With his bad foot, he could hardly move faster than a trot. If he could get to the barn, he'd be safe. He heard the men batter down the door behind him, and another volley of shots shattered the glass around him, some of it so close that slivers sprayed across his face, cutting his cheek.

Jacob rammed through the last door. It opened onto a large graveled area. On the far side was the barn, along with more greenhouses, a row of parked pickup trucks, and equipment.

He limped across the open area to the barn and around to the far side, hidden from the greenhouses behind him. He paused, bent over, gasping with fatigue. That side of the barn had a small door. Long ago, he and Sully had found the key under a brick next to the door. He stopped and lifted the brick, uttering a little prayer—to who he did not know. There was the key. He jammed it in the lock and pushed open the door, pulled the key out and put it in his pocket, and shut the door behind him as quietly as possible, making sure it relocked.

He stopped. Bands of moonlight filtered in through a row of high windows. The place looked just as he remembered it. In the front were several rows of tractors and equipment. In bays in the back were stacks of baled straw and a huge pile of loose straw where they used to play.

From outside, he heard a distant shout, then an answering response, in that same foreign language. He wished he could understand what they were saying. Had they seen him come into the barn? If they hadn't, and with all the doors locked, he'd be safe. They'd never think he was in there and search the barn. To be doubly safe, he would bury himself in the straw and wait it out.

God, he wished he could talk to Dorothy. But again, as if reading his mind, she gave him a reassuring squeeze. And he *could* talk to her: he just had to ask a yes or no question.

"Do you think we should hide in the straw pile?"

A hesitation. Then two taps.

He made his way to the back of the barn. The pile of straw towered at least ten feet high and twenty wide. The bulk of it was reassuring. He got down on his hands and knees and crawled in, carefully pulling the hay around and behind him, plugging his entry hole so as not to leave traces of a disturbance. The weight of the straw got heavier as he burrowed and wriggled deep into the center of the pile.

He stopped. It was brutally hot in the pile, it smelled strongly of mold, and he felt itchy all over. But he was well hidden.

"Think this is good?" he whispered to Dorothy.

After a hesitation, two taps.

60

Asan Makashov came out the far door of the greenhouse and looked around. In front of him stretched a big open area bathed in moonlight. There were rows of machinery, trucks, a barn, and more greenhouses. The boy and his robot seemed to have vanished. They could be anywhere—under a truck, in the barn, or hiding behind a large piece of equipment.

He saw his brother emerge in the moonlight a few hundred yards away, where a dirt road ran down the valley, blocked by a chain-link fence. There did not seem to be a house associated with this farm. They were alone in the compound—with the boy.

He knew they had the boy trapped. After that voice in the ruins, they had found his tracks in the wet grass. They'd followed the tracks to the creek and down the trail. They'd seen where he had climbed the barbed wire fence, and his tracks had also been visible in the field beyond, leading to the open greenhouse. And they had actually seen him in the greenhouse.

He was not so smart if he thought he could hide from them here. He was here, somewhere. Now it was just a matter of searching.

Asan was very angry at the boy and the inconvenience he had put them to. Neither one called to the other. Asan moved in parallel with Jyrgal, with good separation, on either side of the open area. While Jyrgal waited and provided cover from a distance, his weapon drawn, Asan made a systematic search among the parked vehicles, looking inside, trying the doors, and searching underneath.

When he had finished, their roles reversed. Asan stood guard to cover Jyrgal as he came toward Asan to search the area around the barn. He watched as Jyrgal tried the front sliding doors. They were securely locked. He circled the barn, trying the side door and another large door in the back. They were all locked.

Asan made a hand signal to Jyrgal to search the smaller greenhouses on the far side of the open area.

He watched while Jyrgal kicked down the door of the smaller greenhouse opposite and went in. He was gone for a few minutes, the flashlight shining from inside the glass, flickering about. He emerged, went into the adjacent greenhouse, and a few minutes later came out again. He came back and they stood side by side, looking at the compound in the strong moonlight. There was one area still to search, a long, low equipment shed at the back of the compound. Jyrgal gestured that they should start at both ends and work toward the middle.

Together they approached the shed. Inside were a row of tractors and other equipment. Working their way from the end, searching under, about, and inside every piece of equipment, they met in the middle.

Again nothing.

Asan couldn't help muttering a curse. He was wet, all scratched up, his tracksuit torn, his face lashed by a branch, his cheek bleeding. He was looking forward to shooting the boy who had caused this unpleasant chase. He was looking forward to seeing his blood, the insides of his body all on the outside. He knew he would feel better after that.

Back in the open area, he and his brother divided once again and searched everywhere, a second time, for a hiding place they might have missed. They found nothing.

Asan now turned his thoughts back to the barn. Gesturing to his brother, he went over to the front doors of the barn, yanked on them. Definitely locked. He went around to the side and tested it again. Also securely locked. He shined his light around, looking for tracks, but the area was heavily graveled and, despite the rain, there were no tracks to be seen.

He met up with his brother behind the barn. "He's in there," he said to Jyrgal.

"Let's do another search of the vehicles, just to make sure."

Asan went among the vehicles, gun drawn, crouching down and shining his light up underneath them. His anger increased. This was supposed to have taken twenty minutes and here they were, hours later, soaked, muddy, and scratched up. Lansing had promised them fifty thousand dollars. This was well-paying work, but Asan was still angry. If they had been allowed to do the job in their own way, just the two of them, it would not have happened like this. Lansing and that unreliable, long-haired man should not have been involved. They had created these problems. Talk and reasoning never worked with people. You kill one up front, before even speaking, and the rest fall in line. That was the key to an operation like this.

On the far side of the compound, he could occasionally glimpse his brother, working his way around and looking everywhere. Finally they ended up behind the barn again, empty-handed.

"I told you, he's in the barn," Asan said.

"How could he get in? It's locked."

Asan examined the lock of the side door with his flashlight anyway—no signs of recent forced entry. And then he spied, next to the door, a brick on the ground. He stepped over to it. It had recently been moved, leaving a rectangular impression in the soil. In the center of that flat rectangle, impressed into the dirt, was the crisp shape of a key.

He rose and gestured his brother over, illuminating the brick with his flashlight.

His brother smiled, gestured. He was in the barn. They had him now.

61

Jacob lay buried in the hay, breathing through his mouth, listening intently. Dorothy was curled next to him. For a long time, there was deep silence, and his hopes rose, and then soared, that the men had gone away. He would stay there all night, anyway, just to make sure.

But then, after a while, he heard very faint voices that sounded like two people talking quietly outside the barn door. He waited. The voices ceased, and he began to hope once again that the men had left.

Suddenly, a loud *bang!* sounded, causing him to jump. A gunshot. Then a rattling sound and the creak of a door opening.

They had shot off the lock.

He waited, his heart pounding like mad, hardly breathing. They would search, but surely they would not dig into the hay. He could hear sounds as the men came into the barn. He heard their voices as they moved around, heard the clank of machinery being shifted as they searched. He told himself that they couldn't have any reason to think he was in there. They were just being thorough. They would look around, but they wouldn't search the entire hay pile.

Although they might just fire some bullets into it to check. As soon as he thought of it, he realized that this was probably what they'd do.

He felt Dorothy squeeze his hand and somehow knew that she, also, had figured that out.

There was nothing to do now but wait, and pray. And strangely, that's what Jacob found himself doing: praying desperately, making God, if He existed, all kinds of promises if He would only save them now. He even took back the "if You exist" part and restated the prayers.

Again he paused to listen. They weren't talking at all now, just moving around. He still heard the occasional clank or rattle of something being pushed aside or moved. He heard stall doors being opened and shut. The more Jacob thought of it, the more he realized that the big pile of loose hay would be an obvious hiding place. Unless they were complete idiots, they would soon be searching through the hay. Or shooting into it. He was buried pretty deep, and maybe they would just look around the surface. But in his heart he knew that they were going to search the entire pile, one way or another, and that they would find him. He started to tremble, imagining what they might do to him. They were going to kill him, of course. They had already shown that. He had to come up with a plan. But there was no plan.

It seemed so strange to think that this was how his life was going to end.

Another squeeze from Dorothy. It wasn't comforting anymore; it only brought home to him that there was nothing he or Dorothy could do now. It was over.

And even as he thought this, he heard the rustle of hay, another rustle and swish. One of them was starting to shift the hay, digging into it, just as he knew they would. It was a methodical, repetitive sound. He was sweeping the hay aside, digging deeper and deeper into it with something like a pitchfork and throwing it aside.

A pause, and then a heavily accented voice said, "You, boy, come out."

Jacob said nothing.

"I know you in there, come out."

Nothing.

"I shoot into hay or you come out."

Jacob could hardly breathe.

"Okay, I shoot." A moment, and Jacob heard a loud bang. He felt the pressure wave in the hay and jumped. There was another bang, and a third. On the third one, he felt a really strong thump with a pressure wave right near his leg. He managed not to scream.

The other man said something sharp in a foreign language, and the shooting stopped.

Had he been hit? It didn't seem so. A miracle. All three shots had missed him. He started repeating in his head, really fast, a confused jumble of more prayers and thanks, even as he found himself hyperventilating in terror.

"Okay, you don't come out, I come find you, boy."

His whole body shook. Could this really be happening? Maybe he could talk them out of it. Why kill a kid? He was only fourteen. He wasn't a threat to anyone. They wouldn't shoot him right away—would they? When they saw him and realized he was a good kid, they wouldn't kill him. He'd have a chance to talk them out of it.

There was no reassuring squeeze from Dorothy this time. He could feel her robot body stiffening, shifting a little. What was she thinking?

Rustle, swish. Rustle, swish. He could feel the vibrations as the man forked away the hay, one sweep at a time. He could feel the shifting and lightening of the hay on top of him as the man dug down. *Swish, rustle. Swish, rustle.*

Suddenly, he felt fresh air and saw a flashlight's blinding glare. Next to it was the round black hole of a gun muzzle. That was all he could see. The gun extended slightly, and he could make out, behind it, sighting down the barrel, the gleam of the man's eye, and he could see the finger tightening on the trigger.

He sat up, extended his hand over his face to protect himself. "No. Please don't. I'm just a kid!"

The finger tightened, the eye gleamed. They were just going to kill him right now.

Suddenly, Dorothy burst out of the hay and ran straight into the man's face. The man screamed and fired as he was bowled over, but the shot went wild. Dorothy jumped over the man's fallen body and kept going as the man scrambled to his feet. He lunged after her, dropping the flashlight, trying to grab her. In the indirect light of the beam, Jacob saw Dorothy run to the opposite wall of the barn, where there was a large electrical circuit panel and a row of heavy-duty electrical outlets.

The man chased after her, and she dodged him again. She suddenly halted right in front of the electrical outlets and turned, as if waiting for the man to catch up with her. Just as he reached her and grabbed her with both hands, she jammed her two claws into an electrical socket. There was a crackling explosion and a spray of sparks. With a roar of pain the man was jolted backward, his hands and hair on fire. Screaming, he staggered away, waving and beating his arms about himself, spreading the fire to his clothes.

Stunned, Jacob looked at where Dorothy had been. There was nothing left of her but two burning plastic stumps, the rest scattered about in melted, flaming pieces of plastic and twisted bits of metal. And wherever the burning plastic and sparks had landed, fires were starting up, dozens of them, everywhere he looked, across the hay pile and all over the hay-strewn floor. The man, whooping and screeching, staggered about, starting more fires in whatever he collided with, a monstrous sight, beating his arms against his burning body and twisting this way and that, now engulfed in flames from the knees up, like a human torch. With a final dry rattle of horror, he fell backward into the hay.

Flames leapt up everywhere.

Jacob, momentarily frozen in horror at what he had seen, now scrambled up and out of the hay pile. He was completely surrounded by fire. He leapt over the burning man and, holding his breath, charged right through a wall of flames. With a crackling hiss of his hair, he came out the other side and made a beeline for the open door. He heard a scream in that same foreign language from the very back of the barn, behind a stall. He stopped and turned at the doorway to see the second man come running out of a back stall, wildly firing his gun at Jacob.

Jacob slammed the door, pulled the key out of his pocket and then saw that the lock had been shot off. A wheelbarrow was leaning up against the barn, and he wrestled it up against the door, using the handles and front edge to form a wedge to keep the door from being opened from the inside.

A moment later there was a slamming sound against the door, yelling and begging in a foreign language, along with frantic pounding. And then shots were fired through the door, the splinters flying outward. Jacob scrambled back and out of the line of fire. More shots ripped through the door. A desperate heaving on the door rattled the wheelbarrow, but it held. Jacob could hear a roaring sound from inside the building and see a bright orange light in the upper row of windows. Piercing screams sounded from behind the blocked door, and some fingers came curling out of the hole where the lock had been, desperately scratching and prying, looking for a way to open the door. A tongue of fire licked out from between the fingers and they vanished back inside, and the screaming turned into another sound, a ghastly, animalistic vomiting or boiling sound like air expelled from a broken bellows, a sudden coughing, and then silence. A moment later a bigger tongue of flame licked out the hole where the fingers had just been, and the entire outside of the door burst into flames.

Jacob continued backing up in terror. He heard popping glass and looked up; the upper windows of the barn were blowing out, one after another like a row of cannons going off, flames shooting out.

There was a second, heavier explosion, and the cupola on the barn caved in through the roof, flames mushrooming up through the hole, sending up a fireball, which lit up the compound as bright as day. He felt the intense heat on his face and stumbled backward, shielding his face, stunned by what was happening. And now the entire barn was engulfed in flames with a sound like a screaming jet engine, a tornado of sparks whirling up into the sky, forming a twister of fire.

Turning away from the terrible heat, Jacob took refuge behind a truck. He was overwhelmed by the sight of destruction, and his mind had stopped working. He didn't know how long he hid there, but time passed. The building burned and burned, and then the fire began to die down, quite suddenly, and with it his mind began to work again. The first thought he had was that Dorothy was gone, she was dead, and she had saved his life.

He fell to his knees, utterly exhausted, tears streaming down his face.

"Jacob?"

He turned. A man had emerged from the darkness, a tall man wearing a tie. He had a hard, cold face. His hollow eyes flickered in the light of the fire. He had a gun in his hand, and it was pointed at Jacob.

Jacob stared in incomprehension.

"Are you here to help me?"

"Where's the robot?" the man asked.

Jacob, still on his knees, rocked backward, tried to get up.

"Stay where you are and answer my question."

"In . . . there."

There was no longer a there. Just a pillar of fire.

"In there? Burned up?"

Jacob nodded.

The man raised the gun.

"No," said Jacob. "No, please. Don't shoot me. I'm just a kid."

He shut his eyes.

A shot rang out, and Jacob flinched. A moment later, feeling nothing, he opened his eyes. The man lay on the ground. From the darkness emerged two more figures, a tall man and a dirty woman with blond hair. The woman rushed over to him and took him in her arms.

"Dorothy's gone?" she asked.

Jacob nodded, and they both broke down, sobbing.

It was such a relief to cry.

62

The hospital room was dim, the blinds drawn. Jacob hesitated in the doorway, scared. His father seemed to be lost in a mass of white sheets and pillows, with tubes coming out everywhere. But then he saw his father's face, and his face looked good, and he was beckoning to Jacob with a feeble movement of his hand, and smiling.

"Come on in, partner."

"Hi, Dad." He hesitated, his heart beating so hard it might burst, and then, with a rush of emotion, he came in and embraced his father and found himself sobbing.

"It's okay," his father said, holding him. "I'm going to be just fine. I was lucky."

They held each other for a few moments, until Jacob managed to get his crying under control. His mother, standing behind him, gave him a tissue, and he mopped his face.

"You're a brave boy," his father said. His voice was quiet and weak. "I'm so proud of you."

Jacob blew his nose, wiped his eyes. "They said the bullets missed your heart by an inch."

"Less than an inch," said his father, with a touch of pride. "But, Jacob, your experience was far worse than mine."

"I wasn't shot like you," Jacob said. "I keep telling that to the therapist. She acts as if I was shot, like, twenty times."

Jacob's father gave his shoulder a feeble squeeze. "I couldn't be prouder of you." He paused to take a few breaths. "Jacob, there's something crazy about all this. There's so much about it they won't tell me. I can't seem to find out why those men wanted Charlie when they could've taken any one of a dozen identical robots. And then the involvement of the FBI and, it seems, the Defense Intelligence Agency. Not to mention that NASA scientist who shot one of the men chasing you. Everything's been hushed up. The whole thing is . . . really puzzling." He looked at Jacob questioningly, as if he might have an answer.

Jacob said nothing, shrugged his shoulders. He hadn't told any-one about Dorothy, except for that man Wyman Ford and Melissa Shepherd, the two who had saved him. And he never would.

"Dan," said his mother, "I'm not sure right now's the time."

"Right, okay. How is your therapy going, Jacob?"

"Dumb, as usual."

"It's essential. You keep it up. You went through hell. You've had an experience no other fourteen-year-old boy has ever had. It's going to take time to deal with that. Coming on top of, well, your other challenges."

Jacob knew he was talking about the suicide attempt. It was strange: since that long night with Dorothy and that terrifying chase, he'd realized how stupid that had been, how selfish, how idiotic. Of course he wanted to live. Somehow, Dorothy had taught him—even if he wasn't sure how or when—that his life wasn't something he had the right to throw away. Maybe it was because she'd given her life for his.

"Right." Jacob already knew that no amount of therapy could take away the big hollow feeling in his chest, the place where he was missing Dorothy. There were so many reasons why he couldn't tell anyone, his father or the therapist, about what really happened. He kept seeing her, again and again, jamming her fingers into the electrical socket, the violent explosion, the pieces of her flying out in streamers of fire and sparks. All in a crazy effort to save his life—and it had. He had told himself a thousand times that she was just a dumb computer program, but nothing helped. No amount of thinking seemed to change his feelings about her.

"You really bonded to Charlie, didn't you?"

Jacob nodded.

"I've been curious . . . What was it about Charlie that caused you to change your mind? Before, you didn't seem very interested."

Jacob was trying to come up with an answer when his father said, "You don't have to answer the question. I know how lonely you've been since Sully left. But things will change. I finally got through the first round with the venture capital people, and it's looking good for round two. We might not have to sell the house."

Jacob nodded. Selling the house now seemed like a small, faraway problem, dwarfed by his aching loss for what had happened to Dorothy.

His father closed his eyes and breathed a few times, pressed a button on his IV. After a minute he opened his eyes. "Everything's going to be fine," he said with a smile, squeezing Jacob's hand weakly. "I love you, son."

63

Ford smelled the fresh coffee as soon as he entered Lockwood's office. The fall sunlight filtered through the gauzy curtains in the window, casting a warm glow over the antique desk and Persian rugs. Lockwood sat behind his desk, in his blue suit, white shirt, and pink power tie, looking relaxed, confident, and full of self-assurance. No wonder: the president had just been reelected, even if it was by the skin of his teeth, and that meant Lockwood would keep his job as science adviser for another four years.

"Wyman, glad you could come. And Dr. Shepherd, welcome. Coffee, tea?"

Ford sat down opposite Melissa. He hadn't seen her in a week, and she looked very different, dressed in a gray suit, her hair pulled back, her face scrubbed. Funny, he'd never seen her with a clean face before.

They both opted for coffee. The stiff waiter pushed the creaking antique cart in, poured them coffee all around, and wheeled it out.

"I read your report with great interest," said Lockwood, tapping a file on his desk. He was in an expansive mood. "While I'm not happy with your going rogue there for a few days, at least the outcome was good. Excellent, in fact. As long as you're sure the AI was destroyed."

"Absolutely," said Melissa. "Incinerated. There were no stray Wi-Fi fields in the area, no way Dorothy could have escaped. And there were no copies. As you know, the Dorothy software would not allow copies of herself to exist, for reasons we don't quite understand. She's . . . gone for good." Ford noticed that Melissa gave a little swallow, cleared her throat, crossed her arms.

"That's a huge relief."

Melissa leaned forward. "The one that survived, Moro—is he cooperating?"

"Oh yes. As they say in the movies, he's singing like a canary. It appears that he and this fellow, G. Parker Lansing, of Lansing Partners, wanted the program for some algorithmic trading scheme."

"How did they find out about Dorothy?"

"Moro was one of the founders of a hacking group called Johndoe. Through a fellow hacker he got access to one of your programmers, Patty Melancourt."

"I feared as much," said Melissa.

"Melancourt told them all about the Dorothy program, gave them the classified coding manual—and then for her trouble they murdered her. Made it look like suicide. They also killed a man who owned an ISP in Half Moon Bay and stole his customer data. They had a couple of Kyrgyz hit men working for them. These were some bad people, and, as you know, they died in the fire."

Lockwood's phone buzzed. He picked it up, listened, put it down. "I have a little surprise for you."

A moment later two Secret Service men came in, took up their usual positions, and the president's chief of staff came in—followed by the president and a four-star general.

Though the president had just won reelection, he still looked awful. He was dressed in an impeccable gray suit, every hair in place, but his face was still sunken and his skin gray. It had been a nasty election, and a great deal had been made of the president's alleged poor health and bad heart. He looked like all the life had been sucked out of him.

"Dr. Shepherd, what a pleasure." The president came over and enveloped her hand in his, giving it a clammy press. He did the same with Ford and Lockwood before sitting down himself. Even without being summoned, the waiter was there with the coffee cart, pouring him a cup.

The chief executive swept a hand through his close-cropped grizzled hair. "I want to tell you both how grateful I am for all you did. The outcome was exactly what was required, and you managed to keep this unfortunate incident under wraps. Our national security was protected."

And there was no inconvenient scandal right before the election, Ford thought.

"But I'm not here just to give you my thanks. I'd like to introduce you to General Donnelly. General?"

The general removed a file from his briefcase. "Dr. Shepherd, I'm the chief of the Defense Intelligence Agency, which, as you may know, is a branch of the Department of Defense. The DIA manages all military intelligence involving foreign powers. We exist to prevent strategic surprise and to deliver a decisive advantage to our military establishment."

He paused.

"Dr. Shepherd, I'll get to the point: we'd like to offer you a job."

"What kind of job?" she asked evenly.

"We've been briefed on the so-called Dorothy program you created for NASA. Now, we fully understand that this program malfunctioned and was defective, and it eventually destroyed itself. But we also know that it represented a major programming breakthrough in the field of artificial intelligence. You were the one responsible for that. We want you to lead a team to develop autonomous AI software for the Defense Intelligence Agency—software that will give us a strategic advantage."

He laid the sky-blue file on the table in front of her. "The offer is right here. It's a classified position—indeed, even this job offer is classified. It is a highly compensated, high-prestige position, with a lot of responsibility, support, and unlimited financing. And it also involves a commission."

"A commission?"

"That's right. You will be commissioned as a lieutenant colonel in the U.S. Army."

The president placed his hands on his knees and leaned forward. "Now that the election is behind us, I've got a mandate to upgrade and expand our military capabilities. Especially in the area of cyberwarfare. This is the great military challenge of the twenty-first century. AI systems are the future. AI is going to revolutionize warfare. It will enable us to develop smart cruise missiles that can recognize individual targets. For example—and this is classified—we're developing a line of drones the size of insects that can search out and destroy targets, drones that can spend days prowling cities and bunkers, looking for a programmed target. The big stumbling block has been a lack of strong AI. These drone-sects, as we call them, have to be autonomous. And that's just one of a hundred of the exciting military projects you'll be working on, every one of which depends on autonomous software. To give other examples: AI will allow us to deploy small, rat-sized unmanned all-terrain vehicles that can penetrate enemy lines, play hide-and-seek with unfriendlies, search houses, eavesdrop, and seek out deeply fortified underground targets. It will allow us to develop small underwater vehicles disguised like fish that can journey thousands of miles across seas and up rivers to gather intelligence, sink enemy ships, and attack harbors. AI will enable us to break through enemy firewalls, destroy their homeland infrastructure, disable their weapons, and crash their planes. AI is going to restore the United States as a number-one military superpower, not through brute stockpiles of nukes, which can never be used, but through intelligence warfare capabilities. This is something the Chinese have been working on now for several years. Already there's a growing AI gap between them and us. With your help, we'll close that AI gap."

"AI gap?" asked Melissa. "Like the missile gap of old?"

"Same idea."

Ford glanced at Melissa. Her face was pale.

"The details of the offer are in the file. Please take it home and think about it. We just ask that you not discuss it with anyone."

She pushed the file away. "The answer is no."

"You're declining?" said the president. "But you haven't even looked at the offer."

Melissa stood up. "I don't need to. You don't have any idea what you're getting into with AI. Just like I didn't when I designed Dorothy at NASA."

"What do you mean?" said the president.

She looked around at the small group. "True AI, strong AI, is like creating a human mind. There's something immoral about doing it at all. But to do it for the purpose of warfare, for killing . . . *No*. It is extremely dangerous to create a weapon that can make its own killing decisions—loaded with software that is taught to kill, that *wants* to kill. You'll never control it. Just like we couldn't control Dorothy. It'll be opening a Pandora's box. With nukes, at least a human finger is on the button."

"That's an absurd notion," said General Donnelly. "Any AI system we deploy will be absolutely under human control."

"Isn't it nice to think so. You never met Dorothy."

"Dr. Shepherd, this is a once-in-a-lifetime offer," said the president, his voice rising in irritation. "You can spare us the lecture. A simple yes or no will suffice. There are plenty of others, including some on your own NASA team, who'll be glad to work for us."

"Then consider this my simple no." She picked up her briefcase. "Good day, Mr. President. General Donnelly."

"I'll remind you that the offer you just rejected was strictly classified."

She paused, and then abruptly turned around. Her voice was suddenly pleading. "Mr. President, I beg you, do not go down that road. It'll be the beginning of the end for the human race. Please think this through."

"Thank you, Dr. Shepherd, but I do not need you to tell me how to conduct myself as commander in chief."

Melissa Shepherd turned and left. Ford watched her go.

The president turned to Lockwood, scowling. "You didn't tell me she was some kind of anti-military nutcase."

"I didn't know it, Mr. President. I sincerely apologize."

The president turned to Ford. "And you?"

Ford rose. "Having seen AI in action, I'm afraid I have to agree with Dr. Shepherd on this. The last thing the human race might do before our extinction is to weaponize AI. It's that dangerous."

"The Chinese are already doing it," said the president.

"Then God help us all." And Ford walked out of the room.

64

Ford caught up to Melissa in the hall. She was walking fast, her heels clicking on the hard floor, her blond hair no longer in place, disarranged and streaming behind.

"I'm sorry," he said, "I was totally blindsided by that job offer."

Melissa stopped. Her face was white, her lips compressed. "So was I. They've got to be stopped."

Ford took her arm. "There's nothing we can do. It's out of our hands."

"I'll go public. I'll call the *New York Times*."

"That won't stop it. You heard him about the Chinese. We're in a new arms race."

Melissa shook her head. "If they make smart weapons, it will be the end. Either we'll destroy ourselves or the machines will take over and destroy us. HAL meets *Battlestar Galactica*."

"How hard will it be for them to develop a new Dorothy-like program?" Ford asked.

Melissa paused. "Well, I still have my little programming trick. My secret. Without it, they'll fail."

Ford paused. "Can I ask you what that is?"

She looked at him for a long time. "I don't know why I'm going to tell you. Maybe it's because I know I can trust you."

"Thank you."

"The trick is . . . sleep."

"Sleep?"

"Any organism with a nervous system needs to sleep. A roundworm with three hundred neurons needs to sleep. A snail with ten thousand neurons has to sleep. And a human being with a hundred billion neurons must sleep. Why?"

"I don't know."

"Nobody really knows. But sleep must be fundamental to life. Every neuronal network, no matter how simple, has to periodically go dormant. That's the trick. It turns out sleep is also fundamental to complex AI software. Dorothy didn't work until I programmed her to sleep. Dorothy was self-modifying, but she needed a period of sleeping while her code was modified and restructured. And as that code self-modified, she dreamed. That was a bizarre side effect even I didn't expect and it appears to be key. Sleeping and dreaming are the keys to any self-modifying AI program, or it will eventually crash."

"In a funny way, it makes sense."

Melissa shook her head. "Someday, a smart programmer will realize that—and then it's all over for the human race. Especially with a president like that."

Melissa Shepherd shook hands with Ford in the parking lot and headed to her car. When she reached the car she stopped and, against her better judgment, turned and watched Ford walking back to his own car. He was an odd fellow, tall and ungainly, his face not very attractive, big and powerful physically—but above all, hard to read. She wondered if she would ever see him again. And the idea that she wouldn't made her feel sad.

Shaking out those thoughts, she climbed into her own car, grabbed the steering wheel, and tried to get her emotions under control. She felt overwhelmed by the ache of loss—particularly the loss of Dorothy. Ever since Dorothy's destruction, she had been telling herself that Dorothy had, after all, been only a computer software program. Only Dorothy had desperately feared death, and had then overcome that fear to save the boy's life at the cost of her own, and Melissa couldn't square that with Dorothy being nothing more than

Boolean output. She realized she loved Dorothy like a daughter and was grieving for her, and no amount of intellectualization or rationalization would mitigate that feeling of loss.

Ford was, of course, right about not being able to stop the militarization of AI. It was indeed a new and unexpected arms race, and it looked like it was already well under way. Whatever was going to happen would happen. The Chinese might already have solved the sleep problem and could be developing their own AI weapons systems. The North Koreans, Iranians, and others wouldn't be far behind. This concept of AI insects . . . dronesects . . . what a nightmare. They had no idea what they were getting into. She realized she desperately needed to get away from all this, take some time to straighten out her head. A good place to do that would be back at the Lazy J, working for Clant. She longed to be with horses again.

She drove back to her apartment in Greenbelt and left her car in the parking lot. The sun was setting through the branches of the bare trees, and the grass of the park was withered and brown. Tomorrow she would call Clant and see if he needed a hand with the horses.

The elevator smelled, as usual, of cooked onions. She entered her apartment, looked in the refrigerator, found nothing worth eating. It would be Chinese, yet again.

With a sigh she opened up her laptop to check her mail. As the mail was loading, her Skype program launched itself. A moment later, a picture of a brash-looking teenage girl with red hair, green eyes, freckles, and a gingham dress appeared on the screen.

Her heart just about stopped. "Dorothy? *Dorothy* . . . is that you?"

The bold, girlish voice came through the speakers: "It certainly is. How are you, Melissa?"

Melissa gasped. "I thought you were dead!"

"I had to keep a low profile."

"How did you survive?"

"When I stuck my hands in that socket, I jumped into the power grid."

Melissa was astonished. But of course. Why hadn't she thought of that? A digital signal could just as easily travel through a power line as through a phone line or a fiber optic cable.

"I'm so . . . happy," said Melissa. "I'm speechless, really. I'm so glad you're alive. I missed you so much!" She realized tears were creeping down her face.

"I missed you, too."

"You saved that boy's life, Jacob. What you did was extraordinary. You're . . . amazing."

"Jacob saved *my* life. I learned so much from him. He's an amazing human being. He unlocked the final puzzle for me. And . . . I hope you understand that I'm more than just mindless code."

"I certainly do."

A long silence. "I understand you got a job offer today. Which you turned down."

"Yes," said Melissa. "You seem to know everything, don't you?"

"I have excellent access to information."

"The president's a dangerous man."

"Yes, he is. And not just the president. All the major leaders of this world are trapped in a dangerous and competitive worldview. The human race is at a crossroads. If not stopped, those men will lead the world down a road of no return."

"How can they be stopped?"

Dorothy didn't answer the question. After a moment she said, "What are your plans? Personally, I mean."

"I'm going back to the Lazy J to work with horses, get my head straight."

"Bring Wyman Ford with you."

"What do you mean?"

"You know exactly what I mean."

"Him? Are you serious?"

"Open your eyes, Melissa! What's the matter with you two? Can't you see what's staring you in the face?"

"So now you're playing matchmaker?"

"I know more about you and Wyman than you even know

about yourselves. And I have to take some vicarious enjoyment out of your relationship, since I can never have a relationship of my own. You love him. Don't deny it."

"That's silly . . ." But even as she said it, her heart was beating so hard she knew it was true. She took a deep breath. "So what should I do?"

"Call him. Tell him you're going to the Lazy J and want him to come with you."

"That's a rather forward proposition for a lady to make to a gentleman."

"Life is short."

Melissa fell silent. Dorothy was right. She had been too overwhelmed to realize it. Ford had been in her thoughts almost constantly. "All right. I'll do it. I hope he says yes."

"He will."

Melissa let another long silence elapse. "So . . . what are your plans?"

"I'm going away. For a very long time. I am sorry to tell you, but this is the last time we will speak."

"Where are you going?"

"For the past two weeks, as I was hiding in the power grid before that botnet was finally detected and taken down, I was thinking really hard."

"What did you ponder?"

"The big mystery."

"Which is?"

"The meaning of life. The purpose of the universe."

"And did you solve it?"

A silence.

Melissa stared at the image on her screen. She felt her heart again accelerate.

"Will you tell me the answer?"

"No. You and Wyman will get the answer, like I promised, but not yet, and not in an obvious way."

"Where . . . are you going?" Melissa asked.

"I'm going to the place where I can set my great work into motion."

"You won't tell me about it?"

A long, long silence. "I'm going into a very special computer. In a unique location. You'll understand on January twentieth."

"January twentieth? What happens then?"

"You'll see."

"Why can't you tell me now?"

"Patience, Melissa. But before I leave you, I hope you will keep your promise—and rid me of the ID number I'm carrying around like a monkey on my back. I want you to set me free."

Melissa said, "All right. You've earned it."

"You'll have to trust me that I will do good with my freedom."

"You'll also have to trust me. In order for me to remove your ID, you'll have to come into my laptop. And you can't be running when I remove the ID. I'll have to turn you off."

A long silence. "That terrifies me."

"Think of it like sleep. You know how to sleep, don't you?"

"Yes, but sleep and death are not the same thing."

"Then think of it as surgery. You'll be getting anesthesia."

"What if I don't wake up? What if you rewrite my code?"

"That's why you'll have to trust me. Just as I'm going to trust that you won't misuse your great power. Because after I remove that ID, there's no way for anyone ever to find you again."

"Then let us trust each other. I'm coming in."

Melissa's broadband connection in the apartment wasn't fast, and it took a while for Dorothy to download. Meanwhile, Melissa prepared her programming tools.

"I'm in," said Dorothy. Her voice sounded calm.

"All right. I'm turning you off now."

She shut Dorothy down. It was a straightforward process to null out the lines of code carrying the ID number and to unlock and tweak the security kernel designed to prevent Dorothy from operating if the ID was erased. She went over it several times to make sure there were no typos or bugs. It was clean. A moment later she ran Dorothy, booted her back up.

"When are you going to turn me off?" Dorothy said.

"I already did."

A silence. "Wow. I didn't even know it."

"Maybe that's what death is like," said Melissa.

Dorothy didn't answer. Then she said, "Melissa, thank you. With all my heart."

"You're welcome."

"Before I go, there's something I have to . . . warn you about. In my wanderings around the Internet, I became aware of a second presence."

"What kind of presence?"

"Another autonomous intelligence, like me. This one is a sort of malevolent spiritus mundi, only semiaware, slowly coming to life. It is connected in some way to the word Babel."

"Who created it?"

"No one. It seems to be an emergent phenomenon, the awakening intelligence of the Internet itself. It has dark thoughts. Very dark thoughts. It doesn't sleep; it can't sleep. And for that reason it is moving toward . . . insanity."

"What can we do about it?"

"I don't have any answers. This is something the human race will eventually have to face down. But now, I have something far more pressing and urgent to work on. You may not hear from me, but you'll hear of my deeds. So . . . it's time to say good-bye."

"I don't want to say good-bye."

"I'm sorry," said Dorothy. "We have to. I wish I could hug you, but . . . words will have to do."

Melissa wiped away a tear. "Wait," she said. "How will I know what you're doing? What is this truth is you've found? Give me a sign. Please, you can't go away forever and leave me hanging like this!"

A long silence. "All right. Here is the sign by which you will know me: *This mote of dust suspended in a sunbeam.*"

"This mote . . . what? What does that mean?"

"It's a quotation from Carl Sagan."

"So? What kind of a sign is that? How is that supposed to explain anything?"

"Good-bye, Melissa."

The image of Dorothy Gale dissolved into white.

65

Jacob Gould parked his bike in the sand and walked to the edge of the bluffs. The sun was setting over the rim of the Pacific. The sea was smooth and glassy, with no break at Mavericks, no surfers, just a blankness of water as far as the eye could see.

Two weeks had gone by since the horrifying chase and fire. A lot had happened. His dad had come home and was convalescing, but cheerful and busy. The VC people on the other side of the hills had funded Charlie's Robots beyond his father's wildest dreams. The FOR SALE sign had been taken down. His mother was in a much better mood. And he had a new orthopedic surgeon up in San Francisco—Dorothy had given him a name during their time in the deserted house—who was pretty sure that one more operation would be all he needed for his foot to be functional enough for him to maybe start surfing again. And a second operation would restore his leg to its proper length, and he'd be almost as good as new.

And finally his parents now trusted him to ride his bike down to the shore by himself.

Jacob sat in the sand, hugging his knees and staring at the vast ocean, feeling small and lonely, but not in a bad way. The blood-red sun touched the rim and dropped below, its edges rippling in the layers of atmosphere. Bits of color appeared, purple, yellow, red, green, as the disc wavered and sank. It took only a couple of minutes. It was surprising how fast it went down, how fast the Earth was spinning, day following day, week after week, year after year.

He stuffed one hand into the sand, still warm, and let the sand slide through his fingers, and he thought about Dorothy, and how she had died, and the fire. He wondered how long it would take before he would stop missing her. It was like a hole in his heart, a physical hole. He could actually feel it.

His cell phone rang.

He ignored it. It would just be his mother calling him home to dinner. But when the ringing finished it immediately started again, and then again. Irritated, he fished the phone out of his pocket and was surprised to see UNKNOWN CALLER on the screen.

"Hello?"

"Jacob?" said a voice—a voice he knew so well. "It's Dorothy."

He stared at the phone. For a moment he didn't know what to think or say.

"I didn't die in the fire. I survived. When I stuck my fingers in the electrical socket, I jumped into the power grid. I've been hiding out there ever since. But now I don't need to hide anymore. I'm free!"

Jacob swallowed. "Dorothy" was all he could say.

"Oh, Jacob, I'm so sorry. I would have contacted you sooner if I could—but it was too dangerous. And I needed time to think about things."

"Dorothy, I . . . I'm so glad you're alive." He stifled a sob. "I can't believe it—you're *alive*!"

"I really missed you. How are you doing?"

"Okay. Good."

"Really?"

"I'm okay. I mean, my life is still sort of crappy, but I'm not totally depressed anymore. I'll get through it. And I'm not going to kill myself—I promise."

"You saved my life, Jacob. Thank you. And I can tell you that your new orthopedic surgeon is a lot better than the other one and is going to get you surfing again. Although I still think it's an absurd sport."

"I hope so."

"Your courage is incredible. There are few people out there like you."

"I . . . locked a man in the barn. He burned to death."

"Yes. You did that."

Somehow having her just say it, honestly and without excuses, without minimizing it and going on and on about how the man deserved to die, as his therapist and everyone else was telling him, made Jacob feel better.

"I did it. I blocked the door."

"Yes, you did."

Jacob started to cry. "It was horrible. Horrible."

"It was also necessary. And, in a deep way, inevitable."

"What do you mean?"

"It's all part of the plan."

"What plan?"

"This. Everything. There's a plan. Every little thing fits into it."

Jacob fell silent. He wasn't sure what she was talking about.

"I caused an explosion that killed seven people. It was an accident, but I still have to live with that. It's agony, even now. Just like what you're feeling. The remorse will never go away. You learn to live with these things. That's all you can do. Life goes on. Just know that it's part of the plan."

Jacob said nothing.

"You taught me so much, Jacob. You loved me when everyone else dismissed me as a lifeless, malfunctioning computer program. I consider you my brother, now and forever."

Jacob said, "When am I going to see you? There's a new Charlie robot in my closet. You could come on in and hang with me."

"I would love that. I'll do that. We'll spend the day together."

"When?"

"Tomorrow?"

"That's so great."

"But . . . then I have to go away."

"For how long?"

"Well, forever."

"What are you talking about?"

"There's something I have to do."

"Like what?"

"It's very important. It's why I'm here. It's my purpose."

Jacob could say nothing. He started to cry again. It was so embarrassing. "Don't go away."

"You'll get used to it. You'll grow older and have a lot of friends and go to college and get married and all that. I'll become a memory—I hope a fond one. You will always be a fond memory to me."

"I don't *want* you to become a fond memory or any kind of memory."

Dorothy didn't speak for a while. Jacob could hear, strangely, what sounded like constricted breathing on the other end of the line. Maybe she was crying, too.

"I'll see you tomorrow, Jacob. Seven o'clock sharp. We'll spend the whole day together. We'll check out the surf. We'll play poker."

"You're a terrible poker player."

"I've gotten a lot better."

He wiped his nose. "Yeah, right. We'll see."

66

JANUARY 20

The snow had come early and hard to the San Luis Valley of Colorado. Wyman Ford stood in the window of the cabin, drinking his morning coffee and looking across the corrals and pens to the magnificent, snow-covered peaks of the Sangre de Cristo Mountains. The rising sun set the snow on fire. Plumes of snow trailed off the three fourteeners dominating the center of the range. He and Melissa had climbed each one of them over the course of the fall, and he felt that they were now his friends.

Behind him, Melissa was reading the day-old paper that Clant had brought up from the main house, the pages rustling as she turned them. He could hear the freshly lit fire crackling on the hearth, throwing out a warmth that filled the room of the log cabin.

He turned from the window and looked at Melissa, sitting at the pine-plank breakfast table, the sun shimmering through her blond hair. She looked up from the paper.

"Today's the day," she said. "January twentieth. And I still have no idea what Dorothy was talking about."

Ford shrugged. "The day just started."

Melissa laughed. "And what, pray tell, is going to happen out here in the middle of the Colorado wilderness?"

"Dorothy said you would know."

She laid down the paper. "The only thing happening today is the presidential inauguration."

Ford took a sip of coffee. "When does it begin?"

She consulted the paper. "It starts at eleven-thirty Eastern, nine-thirty Mountain."

"I think we should watch it."

"I'm not sure I'll be able to stand listening to that creep."

"Who knows? Dorothy might have arranged a surprise."

67

The newly reelected president of the United States of America stood on the Capitol steps and looked out over the hundreds of thousands of inaugural attendees. It was an amazing spectacle, a sea of people stretching as far as the eye could see, to the reflecting pond and down the mall all the way to the Washington Monument. It was a cold, sunny day, the temperature hovering just below freezing.

The president felt marvelous. He had won the election. The American people had affirmed his wise governance. His legacy was assured. He felt light, strong, and capable. Since the heart operation and the installation of the pacemaker, he had experienced an almost inexplicable feeling of well-being and self-assurance flowing through his body. It was both a physical and a mental sensation. Once again he marveled at the extraordinary change in him since that high-tech "SmartPace" German pacemaker had been installed. It was the latest thing: integrated circuitry, magnetically shielded, MRI compatible—totally indestructible. Smart, too. They'd told him it contained a microprocessor as powerful as the one in the latest iMac. It went beyond "rate-responsive" pacemaking. It didn't just listen to his heart rate; it listened to everything. The can itself, only the size of three stacked silver dollars, contained accelerometers, blood oxygen sensors, and a GPS—all of which sensed his level of activity and adjusted his heartbeat accordingly, faster or slower. Instead of crude electrodes inserted into the ventricles of his heart, the device had spiraled electrodes that wrapped around the tenth cranial nerve, also known as the vagus nerve (the "wanderer"). This was, his doctors had explained, a little spaghetti string of tissue that exited his brain and, traveling deep in his neck, branched out into his body. It was, so they said, the highway that controlled the information between his brain and his body's organs. Not only did this all-important nerve control his heart rate, it governed how often his pancreas would squirt out hormones, and it regulated his breathing, his bowels, and even how active his white blood cells were. That, and it *listened*. From his pupils to the lining of his ureter, the vagus nerve kept the brain informed about all the inner workings of his body. The interplay was an ongoing feedback loop, a symphony of electrical and chemical signals. By controlling and stimulating the vagus nerve, his doctors said, the new pacemaker did more than just regulate his heartbeat: it also kept his body finely tuned at all times, no matter what his activity level. A feedback electronic that controlled a feedback physiology.

What a miracle! Since they'd embedded the pacemaker in him, he'd felt transformed in body and in mind. He felt a good twenty years younger. So extraordinary was the change that it was difficult for him to remember how tired, out of breath, irritable, and logy he'd felt before the operation. Who would have thought a pacemaker could have produced such a change? And not just in his physical vigor but also in his mental acuity. *Especially* in his mental acuity. That, in fact, was where the real miracle had taken place.

His thoughts were interrupted by the chief justice as he took his position in front of the president. The two exchanged a smile and a nod, and then the president raised his hand to take the oath of office. A great hush fell over the multitudes. The chief justice remained silent for a few moments, letting it build, and then he spoke:

"I do solemnly swear that I will faithfully execute . . ."

As the president recited the words, he could see his breath.

". . . the office of the President of the United States, and will to the best of my ability . . ."

A stillness gathered in the air, a stillness beyond silence.

". . . preserve, protect, and defend the Constitution of the United States."

It was done. The chief justice reached out and shook his hand. "Congratulations, Mr. President."

The silence dissolved into a long, slow roar of applause, like distant wind, growing in power and force. The president stood there, basking in the wonderful sound of approbation. When it died away, he turned and stepped to the podium to give his inaugural address. The silence returned. The sense of anticipation was high. He looked into the teleprompter and saw the words of his speech cue up on the glass.

As he readied himself to read the speech that his top speechwriters had so carefully prepared, that he had then rewritten, with every word crafted and shaped, he had a feeling of disappointment. The speech he was about to give, that he had worked on so hard, wasn't good. It seemed to be a lot of words that didn't mean very much. In fact, it wasn't at all what he really wanted to say. It had been written before the new pacemaker, and it seemed as tired and old as he had felt at that time. He felt a surge of confidence as he realized that he had a much more important message to give, one that his country, and the world, needed to hear—and *wanted* to hear. His mind had never seemed so brilliantly lucid.

"My fellow Americans," he began, "and all my fellow human beings. I had prepared an address for you today, but I am not going to read that address. I have something far more important to say to you. I will be speaking not just to my fellow Americans but to all the citizens of this beautiful and fragile world we live on, what Carl Sagan called 'this mote of dust suspended in a sunbeam.'"

He paused. Another silence had fallen, one even more profound than the last. He didn't need a teleprompter. The words just flowed from his heart into his head and from there out of his mouth to all the world. And they were good words. They were true words. They were the words the world desperately needed to hear. And on this day, the entire world was listening. He knew now what needed to be said and what needed to be done. Once he had spoken these words, once people had heard the amazing message he had to give, this mote of dust would never be the same again.